ACCLAIM FOR

Love IN MID AIR

"An intense, thoughtful novel."   —*Booklist*

"Fresh . . . achingly honest . . . Wright gets the details exactly right."   —*BookPage*

"Sharply written and emotionally accessible . . . a modern take on adultery."   —*Kirkus Reviews*

"Fascinating . . . fabulously well-written . . . Wright offers a nice array of flawed, struggling human characters."

—*RT Book Reviews*

"From the first line I was drawn into Wright's marvelous novel. This is a spare, intense, honest, and sexy book, simmering with love, powered by the will of one woman who, despite the odds, demands that she choose her destiny."

—Alison Smith,
author of *Name All the Animals*

"An insightful study of a marriage in decline and no mere chick-lit romp . . . Wright makes clear-eyed observations of suburban life, women's friendships, and how couples interact in small communities, and rigorously investigates the reasons to stay in a marriage and the reasons to go."   —*Sunday Telegraph* (Australia)

"Funny, sexy, heartbreaking, wise . . . the kind of novel you will stay up late for. I read the first page and was hooked, I couldn't put it down."

—Dawn Clifton Tripp, author of *Game of Secrets*

"LOVE IN MID AIR has great ingredients—unforgettable characters, a good story, and that 'what if' concept that one might think about now and then." —BestsellersWorld.com

"Kim Wright's brilliant first novel is not only funny and wise, but also illuminating in surprising and fresh ways . . . This is a wonderful read, from first page to last, for anyone who has ever been married or has ever contemplated it."

—Fred Leebron,
author of *In the Middle of All This*

"This novel moves in a straight flight into our hearts . . . an amazing novel, never subtle, always brilliant . . . Kim Wright ascends to the ground with truths that are universal to all women."

—TheReviewBroads.com

"An honest, intense, sometimes funny look at a modern-day marriage struggling to survive . . . a very powerful read and a hit debut for Kim Wright." —BookLoons.com

"A breath of fresh air for readers . . . It's a candid, often painfully funny look at modern love and friendship, with some surprising twists and turns along the way. A book to savor—and then share with your best friend."

—Susan Wiggs,
author of *The Summer Hideaway*

Love IN MID AIR

A NOVEL

KIM WRIGHT

GRAND CENTRAL
PUBLISHING

NEW YORK ~ BOSTON

Copyright © 2010 by Kim Wright Wiley
Reading Group Guide copyright © 2011 by Hachette Book Group, Inc.

Grand Central Publishing
Hachette Book Group
237 Park Avenue
New York, NY 10017

www.HachetteBookGroup.com

Printed in the United States of America

Originally published in hardcover by Grand Central Publishing.

First Trade Edition: July 2011
10 9 8 7 6 5 4 3 2 1

Grand Central Publishing is a division of Hachette Book Group, Inc.
The Grand Central Publishing name and logo is a trademark of Hachette Book Group, Inc.

The Library of Congress has cataloged the hardcover edition as follows:

Wiley, Kim Wright.
   Love in mid air / Kim Wright. — 1st ed.
     p. cm.
   ISBN 978-0-446-54044-5
   1. Self-realization in women—Fiction.   I. Title.
   PS3623.I54326L68 2010
   813'.6—dc22   2009007024

   ISBN 978-0-446-54043-8 (pbk.)

Acknowledgments

My deepest love and thanks go out to my friends and fellow writers: Alison Smith, Dawn Clifton Tripp, Laura Gschwandter, Mike Iskandar, Jason Van Nest, and Jennifer Lloret. Special appreciation goes to my most important teacher, Fred Leebron.

Thanks to my agent, David McCormick; my editor, Karen Kosztolnyik; my publicist, Elly Weisenberg; and the entire team at Grand Central and the Hachette Book Group, especially the foreign rights department.

And I am particularly indebted to the MacDowell Colony.

Fall

Chapter One

I wasn't meant to sit beside him. It was a fluke.

It's the last Sunday in August and I'm in Phoenix for a pottery show. I won a prize for my glazing and sold seventeen pieces, so I'm feeling good. On the morning I'm due to fly out, I go for an early hike in a canyon behind my hotel. Arizona's deceptive. It's cool in the morning so you climb all the way to the top of the trail, but an hour later, when the sun is fully up and you're winding your way back down, you can feel a pulse in the dome of your head and you remember that this is the West, not the East, and out here people can die from the heat. By the time I get to the bottom I'm so dizzy that I bend my head over a drinking fountain in the hotel lobby and let the water run over the back of my neck until my vision returns to normal.

I drive to the airport, turn in my rental car, go through security, call home, eat a burrito, and drag my carry-on to the plane. There's a man beside me in 18A, a man with a strong accent who immediately begins explaining to me that his son is stuck in 29D and he doesn't have much English and would I mind switching seats with him? Twenty-nine D is a hell seat, near the back and in the middle of a row. I don't want to switch. There's burrito juice all over my shirt and my hair has dried funny from being washed in a water fountain. I'm hot and tired and all I want to do is get home. But when Tory was little I was always asking strangers to help me in airplanes and most of them were nice about it. So I say sure, shove my magazine into my bag, and go trudging to the back of the plane.

The kid in question turns out to be about thirty years old. I try to explain that we're switching seats by showing him my boarding pass and pointing to his and saying, "Papa, Papa," but his dad wasn't lying. He doesn't speak a word of English. Everyone in the vicinity of the twenty-ninth row of the aircraft gets into the act and for some bizarre reason the flight attendant begins speaking French. We're almost ready to pull back from the gate when he finally stands up and heads toward Papa in the front of the plane. I crawl over the guy in 29C and drop into my seat, thinking this is one of those times that you regret trying to do the right thing, only I'm wrong. This is one of those times that karma turns around faster than a boomerang.

The man sitting beside me in 29E says, "That was a nice thing to do."

He's tall, so tall that he is turned slightly in his seat, his knees just on the edge of my space. I ask him why he was in Arizona and he says he was on a climb. He's an investment banker, he climbs mountains on weekends. He doesn't like to fly.

He turns slightly more toward me in the seat and I turn slightly more toward him. I tell him it seems strange that a person who can climb mountains is afraid to fly, and he shakes his head. It's a matter of control, he says, and he tells me about the scariest thing that's ever happened to him on a climb. Years ago, when he'd just begun the sport, he'd found himself linked to a guy who didn't fix the clips right and something broke loose and both of them slid. There's nothing worse, he says, than to be halfway up the face of the mountain, past the turnback point, and all of a sudden to realize you can't count on the other person. I ask him what the turnback point is and he says there's a place you get to in every climb where it's as dangerous to retreat as it is to advance. I nod. It seems I should have known this.

He asks me if I'm married and I say yes, nine years. "Nine," he says slowly, as if the number in itself has a kind of power. "Nine is sort of in the middle." I don't feel like I'm in the middle of my marriage—but I don't feel like I'm at the beginning or the end of it either. I find marriage immeasurable, oceanic. The man in 29C has put on headphones. We have our vodka and pretzels by now.

"It's such a funny sport," he says. It takes me a minute to realize what he's talking about. "Each time I summit I think the same thing, that we shouldn't have come here, that human beings have no business being in the sky. Every time I think, 'This will be my last climb,' but then I get home and in a couple of weeks I want to do it again."

"I guess once you start, it's hard to stop," I say. I've never met anyone who used the word "summit" as a verb. But he has shut his eyes and leaned back in his seat, as if just telling the story has exhausted him.

I pull the *Redbook* magazine from my bag and the cover says "48 Things to Do to a Man in Bed." I bought the magazine just for this article. Defying all logic, there is still a part of me that thinks I can save my marriage through sex. Gerry—his name is Gerry—opens his eyes and begins to read over my shoulder. His minute-long nap seems to have revitalized him because he suggests that we go through the list and each write down three things we'd like to try. Wouldn't it be something if they were the same three things?

I strongly suspect they will be the same three things. He's married too, of course, married to someone he met in the drop-add line his freshman year at UMass. At one point they'd been together so long that they just looked at each other and said, "Why not?" Two boys and then a girl, and the daughter especially, she's the love of his life, he says—but his wife, that's a whole other issue. He has pressed his thigh against mine, opened his legs as if I am a weight he must push away in order to make himself stronger.

"Marriage is difficult," I tell him. "It's the only thing in my whole life I've ever failed at."

I've never said this to anyone, never used the word "failed," but it rolls off my tongue like a fact. Maybe this is the way you should always confess things—just like this, in mid air, and to a total stranger. I wait for him to convince me that it isn't true. God knows if I tried to say this back home, a hundred people would rush in to correct me before the words were even out of my mouth. They would say it's just the vodka talking, or the altitude. Or maybe my desire to intrigue this man by saying something dramatic, anything that will keep him turned toward me in his seat. Any marriage can be salvaged, my friends would tell me— especially a clean, well-ordered little one like mine. No, of course I haven't failed. We're just going through a rough spot.

But this man doesn't correct me. He is smiling as he screws the top off his second bottle of vodka. His hands are very beautiful. I need for a man to have beautiful hands, hands you can imagine slipping down you at once, hands that can make you feel a little breathless even as they go through the most mundane of tasks, even as they rip open a package of pretzels or reach up to redirect the flow of air.

"The list?" he says, pointing toward the magazine.

"Do you have paper?"

He digs something out of his pocket. "You can type it into my BlackBerry."

"I'm supposed to type three things I want to do in bed into your BlackBerry? Are you going to delete it?"

He smiles. "Eventually."

The flight goes fast. When the pilot comes on to say we are beginning our descent into Dallas it startles me so much that it's like I'd forgotten we were even on a plane. "Can I hold your hand?" Gerry asks me. This is the part he hates, the landing. This is the part where you are statistically most likely to crash, and he explains that this is true for climbers too, that most are killed on the way down. He smiles again as he tells me this, flashing strong white teeth. I have visions of them ripping flesh from bone. Good hands and good teeth. He's a type, of course. He's a player. He's the kind of man who meets women at 30,000 feet and persuades them to type sexual fantasies into his BlackBerry, but for some reason I don't care. He asks me how long I'll be laid over in Dallas.

Almost two hours. He thinks maybe we should have a drink. There's definitely time for a drink. At least a drink. He says he's a little lightheaded too, the result of the climb. It's been so strange, such an intense day. He changed planes at the last minute, and maybe he needs something to press him back into himself. This is probably all quite meaningless. He's probably the sort of man who does this all the time. People meet in planes and do it all the time, huddled under thin airline blankets or in those cheap hotels that offer shuttle service from the terminals. An in-flight flirtation, nothing special, and I shouldn't even be talking to him. I have not had sex with any man other than my husband in nine years.

"I suppose we could have a drink," I say.

"Here comes the dangerous part," he says, and he reaches out to hold my hand.

We land without dying. He helps me retrieve my bag from the bin above row 18. We walk down the tunnel and find a departure board. The time at the bottom flashes 5:22.

"That can't be right," says Gerry.

We were supposed to land at 3:45. We were supposed to have a two-hour layover in Dallas. I look at my watch but I'm still on Phoenix time and when I find Charlotte on the departure board I see that my flight is scheduled to leave in fourteen minutes. "What time is it?" Gerry asks the guy standing beside us, who got off our flight and presumably is privy to no more information than we are. He looks at us with a kind of pity and says, "Five twenty-three," and then adds, "We circled fucking forever."

I am leaving out of Gate 42 and this is Gate 7. Gerry lives in

Boston. He is leaving out of Gate 37 in twenty minutes. "Come on," he says. "We're going to have to hurry." It seems easier to follow him than to think, so I do. Follow him, that is, away from the departure board and down the long corridor that leads to the higher numbers. We put our bags over our shoulders and begin to run, run full out until we get to the moving sidewalk and hop aboard. My chest hurts and I feel sick.

"We're being cheated," Gerry says. "We could just forget our flights and find a hotel. This is Dallas. Nobody knows us. We could say we missed our connection." We are walking fast on the sidewalk, cutting right and left around couples and old people, blowing past them like they were obstacles on a video screen, until we come up behind a woman with a baby stroller and we have to stop.

He glances at me. "I've offended you."

"No," I say. "I'm thinking." We might run like this and miss our planes anyway. If we stopped running right now it would be one of those lies that isn't much of a lie, and they're my favorite kind. He's quite right, this is Dallas. Nobody here knows us. He is sliding his hand up and down my spine and I lean into him a little, feel the sharp angle of his hipbone cutting into my waist. The moving sidewalk carries us past Gate 16 and the clock there says 5:27. There's a very good chance we won't make it.

"I just have to be back for a meeting on Monday," he says.

"Monday's tomorrow."

He frowns, like maybe I'm wrong.

The moving sidewalk ends, spilling us in front of Gate 22. I see a cart that sells bottled water, but there isn't time. I put my bag over my right shoulder, he puts his over his left, and we join hands and start running again. The airport is interminable, it's like a dream, and he looks over to me at some point and says, "It'll be all right." What? What will be all right? I catch a glimpse of myself in a mirrored wall as we pass. My shirt is stained with burrito juice and my hair has dried really strangely and I start to tell him that usually I don't look this bad. Which isn't exactly the truth. I often look this bad but I guess what I want to tell him is that I am capable of looking much better. I am watching him for a sign that he does this all the time, for surely he is the sort of man who does this all the time. He's strong and tall, with the kind of teeth that are designed to rip flesh from bone, and just then—the clock says 5:32—he pulls me to the side and I go with him, unquestioning, into the Traveler's Chapel where he drops his bag, puts his hands on my shoulders, and kisses me.

It's one of those kisses that gives you the feeling that you're falling, that the elevator floor has dropped out from under you, and when I finally break away I see a mural of Jesus, a sort of Hispanic Jesus looking all flat and distorted, with long thin hands reaching out to hold a 747. His eyes are sorrowful but sympathetic. Here, in the Traveler's Chapel of the Dallas airport, apparently he has seen it all.

"I need your card," Gerry says. "Your business card."

"Okay," I say. The blood has rushed to my face and my ears are ringing. Gerry and I are practically screaming at each other, as if we are climbers high on a mountain, as if we have to yell to be heard over the sound of the whipping wind. "But you can't call me. I'm married."

"I know," he says. "I'm rich."

"You're rich?"

"I make a lot of money, that's all I mean. I don't know why I make a lot of money, I don't really understand why they pay me what they pay me, but it could make things easier." He glances over at Jesus.

What does he mean, it could make things easier? For the first time I am wary. He's like an actor suddenly gone off script and I don't know what to say. He has been so smooth up to this point, so smooth that I could imagine he would slide right off me when we parted, never leaving a mark. I have already been practicing the story I will tell Kelly on the phone tomorrow, imagining how she will laugh at the cliché of it all. Elyse drinking two vodka doubles and getting herself picked up on a plane. ("That's a vodka quadruple," Kelly will say. "Exactly what did you think was going to happen?") Elyse making out in an airport chapel. ("With some Tex-Mex Jesus watching you the whole time.") Elyse walking toward her plane while the man walks away in another direction, toward another plane that will carry him to a different town and a different life. ("It's just one of those things," she will tell me, as I sit on my kitchen countertop with the phone pressed to my ear and my legs swinging. "Nothing really happened so there's no point in feeling guilty.") Kelly is the only one who knew me when we were both young and pretty, when we were impulsive and the world seemed full of men, and we would find ourselves sometimes transported by sex, picked up and carried into situations that, in the muddle of memory, seem a bit like movie scenes. She is the only one who would understand that I am relieved to find a sliver of this girl still inside me. Relieved to find that, although older and more suspicious and heavy with marriage, under the right circumstances I can still be picked up and carried. That I remember how to kiss a man who doesn't seem to have a last name.

But now, suddenly, this man standing before me isn't acting like a player. He's awkward and embarrassed and real. He is determined to make me understand something, something that I suspect will not fit well into the story I've planned to tell Kelly. I raise my fingers to his mouth to stop the words, but it has been a long time since I have been in a situation like this and perhaps the lines have changed. If a mistake is being made here, it is undoubtedly mine.

He pushes my hand aside, squeezing it for a moment to soften the rebuff. "No," he says. "I need you to hear this. My first car was a fucking AMC Pacer, do you even remember those? They blew up if somebody ran into you. I spent a whole summer sleeping in a tent on my friend's grandmother's back porch because a bunch of us were going to move to New Orleans and start a blues band but we couldn't half play and we were stoned all the time and you know how it is with the blues . . . I used to eat those ramen noodles, do you know what I'm talking about, those kind that were like four packages for a dollar? I didn't think I was going to turn out to be some rich asshole banker flying all over the place. Today was probably the first time I've sat in coach in five years, can you believe that? I fucked up and missed my earlier flight, I wasn't even supposed to be on that plane. Do you understand what I'm telling you? I wasn't even supposed to be on that plane and the money isn't who I am. It's just, you know, energy, a kind of raw energy, and it could make things easier. That's all I'm trying to tell you, that it could make things easier." He exhales sharply. "Are you mad at me?"

I shake my head. He kisses me again. This time he breaks away first and I am left hanging and abandoned in the space between his chin and his shoulder, my eyes still closed and my mouth still open. "A card," he says into my hair. "I need your card."

I am trying very hard not to faint. I flatten my back against the stucco wall and open my eyes. Gerry is adjusting his pants, looking away from me as he arranges things, his face as flushed as a teenage boy's. I am digging in my purse and my hand is finding ink pens, breath mints, Tampax, everything but the business card that could propel this madness into the future tense.

"I'm shaking," I tell him as he presses something into my hand, and then we are running again, out the chapel door and through the airport to Gate 37. People are lined up waiting to enter the tunnel.

"I'll go with you to your gate," he says. "If you've missed your flight, I'll miss mine." I look at the monitor behind the desk. My flight was supposed to have left two minutes ago. There is nothing I can do about the situation one way or another and this thought thrills me. We are walking now. Five numbers down to my gate and the sign says CHARLOTTE and there are no people except for one woman in a US Airways uniform. "Are you still boarding?" I ask her and I am amazed at the neutrality of my voice. She asks me my name and I realize this is the first time that Gerry has heard it. She looks down at the monitor and says, "They haven't pulled back. I can get you on."

Somewhere in the high thin air between Phoenix and Dallas we took turns reading the *Redbook* article about what a woman can do to a man in bed and Gerry picked three things from the list. The only one that I can remember now is that he said he likes for women to show that they want it. Jump the guy. Take charge of the situation. All men like that. I know he wants me to be the alpha female, the un-wife, the person you meet in strange cities who is cool and aggressive and uncomplicated and self-assured, and so, right on cue, I burst into tears. Gerry kisses me again, only I am so weak that I can hardly move my mouth. I slide off his tongue like a climber with bad equipment.

I break away and follow the US Airways lady down the tunnel. I don't look back. As we walk I sniffle and she pats my arm and says, "Airport goodbyes can be very hard." I have never been the last person on a plane before. Everyone looks at me as I bump my way down the aisle to the only empty seat. A nice-looking older lady is beside me and I want to tell her everything but the overhead is full and it takes my last ounce of strength to shove my carry-on under the seat in front of me. Gerry's crumpled business card is in my hand. I never found a card so he can't call me. I can only call him and this is no good. If I call him first he will always know that I walked in free and clear, that I'm willing to have an affair, that I don't care that he's married and I'm married, that I chose it, that I wanted it, that I knew what I was getting into before I picked up that phone and made that call.

As we pull away from the gate I am calm, or rather I am in that strange state where you're so upset that you behave as if you were calm. I close my eyes and try to picture a flat thin Jesus holding up my plane. Gerry doesn't like landings, but I don't like takeoff. I don't like the feeling of being pushed back in my seat. This is the point where I pray things like, "Into your hands I commit my spirit," or maybe it's "Into your hands I commend my spirit." Neither one makes a lot of sense but I'll say anything on a runway.

I'd speak Hebrew or Arabic or Swahili if I knew them, anything to hedge my bets. But today I am too exhausted to bargain with God. Hell, we all have to go sometime.

I open my eyes and look around. The nice lady beside me has bent her head forward and her lips are moving. Good. Let her pray for all of us. The odds are if God chooses to spare her, I'll live too, through sheer proximity. I look down at the card in my hand and practice saying his name aloud. I'm not sure what has just happened to me. I don't know what it means. I press my palms against my trembling thighs and listen to the engines beneath me gain strength. Strength enough to thrust us into the sky where we have no business being, but where we go sometimes, nonetheless.

Chapter Two

In the morning Phil's alarm goes off first. I lie in the bruise-gray darkness and wait for the sound of his shower, his zipper, the jingle of his car keys, the opening of the garage door. At 7:05 the coffee begins to drip. Tory's ride comes in thirty-five minutes. She does not want to wear her new twenty-two-dollar rugby shirt from Gap Kids. She is not destined to spell the word "scientist" correctly in this lifetime. Her vocabulary list hangs on the refrigerator with a magnet. It's only Tuesday, so I have to keep checking the list, but by Friday I will know the words by heart. I call them out to her while I refold the Gap shirt and get out the old Target one that she loves. I bring her cinnamon toast to the recliner where she is curled up watching TV. The Coyote is still chasing the Road Runner after all these pointless years.

One cat wants out, the other wants in. They rub themselves across the French doors, their tails flicking the glass. There's a station break, which means we should be farther along. I call to Tory to brush her teeth as I close the lunchbox, zip the backpack. She dumps her crusts into the part of the sink that doesn't have a disposal. I kiss her head and send her out to the end of the driveway to wait for the mother who has this week's carpool.

The cats' morning kill lies on the deck, a small unblinking mouse. It's the ultimate perversity—they're so well fed and yet they stalk. The mouse has already gone stiff and I sweep him to the edge of the deck where he freefalls into the bushes, into a mass grave for all the animals that the cats have killed on previous nights. The plot of ground below the deck is dark and rich with small curved skeletons and it gives up flowers in waves. Through the glass of the French doors the TV flickers. The Coyote's Acme rocket has failed him once again and he is falling into the canyon. He holds up a sign that says HELP.

I make it a point not to think about how the mouse died. He and the birds and squirrels and openmouthed moles I've found on other mornings or the baby bunny that I wrapped in a dishcloth and buried in the soft ground behind the swing set. I put down the broom and scoop Friskies into the green bowl. The cats are brother and sister, Pascal and Garcia. They fall upon the food as if they've never eaten, their heads nudging my hand away from the dish.

I go into the kitchen, pour another cup of coffee, and stand at the sink eating the crusts of Tory's toast. The house is silent. This is the part of the day I like, the only part I can truly control, and my thoughts run, swift as water, to the place where they've been collecting for the last forty-eight hours. I deposited the checks from my Phoenix trip in the bank yesterday. Paid the bills that Phil had left stacked neatly on the kitchen counter. Unpacked my suitcase, threw the little lotions and soaps that I always swipe from hotel rooms into the wicker basket under my sink, rinsed out my green silk blouse. All evidence of the trip has been wiped away and there is nothing but a single business card to prove that the man was real. Thinking about him is addictive, I know that from yesterday when I became so drunk with memory that I took to my bed like some old-time Hollywood starlet. I look at the clock. I give myself five minutes, exactly five, to think about how much and how little my life has changed. Five minutes to indulge this ridiculous and intoxicating notion that there is a man somewhere up in Boston who wants me. Five minutes, and then I will start work.

★   ★   ★

When we moved in here seven years ago, I turned the garage into a studio. Well, not exactly. At first only half of the garage was a studio, leaving Phil a space for all his gardening supplies and room to park his car, but these things have a way of expanding. There is my wheel, of course. There is the bin lined in plastic where I store the clay. There are bags of grout, and three sets of shelves and my kneading table. And then there is the little storage closet where, as Phil says, normal people would keep their lawn mower. This is my damp room, where I take the pots just after I throw them. It has a hospital-strength humidifier. You want the pots to dry slowly, I try to explain to Phil, so they need to dry in a damp room. But he tells me that this makes no sense. He seems to think I have expanded my studio just to displace him, that I have moved out his tools and taken over his storage closet to prove some sort of housewife-feminist point.

On this particular morning I find—not for the first time—a note. A Post-it stuck to a pot I have left on the kneading table, and it bears a single word: "Mine." It is, like so many of my husband's messages, nearly impossible to interpret. Does he mean he likes the pot and wants it, perhaps to take to his office and put on his desk? Highly unlikely. That the kneading table is intruding into what is officially his half of the garage? A more plausible theory, but the table has been inching its way into his territory for weeks, ever since I added an extension and turned it so that I could avoid working in the afternoon sun. Hard to say why either the pot or the table would irritate him at this particular moment in time or, for that matter, why he wouldn't have told me about it last night over dinner. I have often lobbied for direct conversation, but Phil seems more comfortable with Post-it notes and it doesn't bother him that I'm never quite sure what he's trying to convey. The notes are sometimes a single word: "Good," "Why?" and "8:15" have all been previous messages. At other times they're longer and a little more clear: "Please take" left on a pile of clothes meant for the dry cleaners, or "Not now" on a brochure for a nearby bed-

and-breakfast. I save them, this never-ending stream of Post-its, and sometimes I arrange them across the refrigerator in sentences: Not now good. Why please take?

But this morning I'm not in the mood to play detective. I pull the "Mine" off the pot and stick it to the front of my T-shirt. Yesterday a gallery owner in Charleston called and said she'd take three sample pots in anticipation—my anticipation, possibly not hers—of buying more. I've got four good hours until I meet the other women at the elementary school track.

There are a lot of steps to making a pot. I open the bin that is lined in plastic, push aside the damp towels, and remove the clay. I carry it to the table, sprinkle a little grout on top, and begin to knead. Mindless work. Actually rather hard work. I am proud of my arms. People are always asking me if I have a personal trainer. After kneading I cut the clay, over and over, to remove the air bubbles, and then it goes onto a small round platform called a bat. The bat goes on the wheel and from there I shape the pot. Ironically, this is the easiest part of the process, although other people seem to think that shaping is where the art comes in. And then I carry the bat into the damp room, where the pot will dry over the course of several days. It's greenware at this point, still embryonic, and still, I suppose, monstrous in that way that un-finished things sometimes are. I plug in the humidifier and wait until it rumbles into action, leaning back against the doorframe as I inhale the raw, wet smell of the clay. When the gallery owner phoned yesterday I didn't recognize her number on my caller ID and my heart had jumped. I should have known that 843 is South Carolina, not Massachusetts, but still, just for a moment . . .

At any point something can go wrong. You can get through all the steps just fine and still break the pot. Getting it off the bat is tricky. I've even lost a couple while flipping them over to trim the bottom. The pots can shatter in the kiln if you weren't careful to get out all the bubbles during the knead, and they can shatter in the kiln even if you were. Sometimes you get all the way to the glazing and just suddenly stop and think, "This wasn't how I pictured it in my mind." Possibly one piece in three is salable and in my line of work that's a pretty good average. Potters have to get comfortable with the act of throwing things away. My studio is full of abandoned projects, literal misfires. Sometimes I recycle the clay, sometimes I just toss the pots into the trash, but sometimes, if I leave them sitting around long enough, they begin to look almost beautiful to me. Beautiful in an ugly sort of way.

It's one o'clock before I look up. I'll be a little late for the daily walk, but one of us is often late and the others all know that things can happen, that no one's schedule is entirely within her control. We have agreed that whoever arrives first will just start and let the others join in or drop out on their own pace. It's one of the advantages of walking in a circle.

Yeah, Kelly and Nancy and Belinda are all there when I arrive. I park the car and wave at them, but they don't see me, and I stand there on the hill above the elementary school track and watch them. Kelly is leading slightly as she often does, glancing back at the others as she talks. She could walk much faster if she wanted. In fact she could run. But what would be the point of that?

Because it isn't really about walking, it's about talking. Out here, in the suburbs, we live and die by our friends. There may have been a time when it would've surprised me to realize that nearly every woman I know is someone I met through my church, that the highlight of my day is meeting them at one o'clock to walk for an hour before we pick up our kids. But I'm over that by now. I can't afford to think about it. I need these women too much. I begin picking my way down the damp overgrown grass. Over the years we've shared secrets and toys, passing down car seats and strollers and cribs as the kids grew older, taking turns keeping them so that we can occasionally get a free afternoon. Once, in a dreadful pinch, I even nursed Belinda's sobbing daughter when I couldn't find a bottle, although it makes me feel strange to say that, as if even our bodies are interchangeable. We have a running joke that some Sunday we should all go home from church with the wrong husbands. We debate how long it would take them to notice, but the truth is I'm not sure we would notice either. We're too busy, the details of our lives wrap around us like cotton, and we meet almost every afternoon at the track, trying to walk off the weight from the baby, trying to walk off the weight from the baby who's now in second grade, trying to get down to 130 or 140 or something decent. We're always moving, more like nomads than housewives, circling the drop-off for preschool, pulling around to load the groceries, hitting the drive-thru and passing back chicken nuggets one at a time at stoplights, running the middle one to soccer and the oldest one to the orthodontist, putting in sheets and taking out towels, spinning in the cyclic world of women.

By 2:30 I've picked up Tory and we're back to the house. It's early in the school year and she's tired from having to get up so early. She isn't used to it yet and probably needs an afternoon nap, but she seems to have caught my restless mood. She tosses her brand-new backpack on the table and throws her arms around my waist.

"Can I help you make coffee?" she asks.

I start to tell her I don't drink coffee before dinner, but seeing the eagerness on her face, I relent. Phil gave me a cappuccino machine for my birthday last week but I have taken my time in getting it set up. The machine has many little cups and dishes, like a chemistry set, and Tory is obsessed with it. She sits on the floor, carefully unwrapping each element. There's jazz on the radio. I think it's Miles Davis, but then I think everything is Miles Davis. I wish I could play the trumpet, or maybe the saxophone, that there was something cool and sexy and indifferent about me. I throw my arms over my head, arch my back.

"Look," Tory says. She has pulled all the cups from their cardboard tunnel. "Are there enough for a tea party?"

"Plenty," I say. "You did a great job." It would be easy to let her just sit there all afternoon stacking cups, but I have seen her homework sheet. I know she has to do a timeline of her life by Thursday and I won't be home to help her tomorrow night. We get out the big roll of yellow paper and a box of fireplace matches so that I can burn the edges and make it look like a historical document. We did this same trick last year in second grade when she had a report on Thomas Jefferson and the teacher liked it so much she hung it in the auditorium lobby. So now Tory thinks this is the secret to academic success, to burn things around the edges. She holds the paper steady while I run the match back and forth along the bottom, a wet sponge in my other hand in case things flare up. We've finished three sides of it when Phil comes in. He looks at the timeline and asks me how I learned to do this. He seems surprised when I tell him my mother taught me. Phil thinks my mother is crazy and he's always reluctant to accept evidence that she can contribute anything practical to daily life.

"Now you won't have to go out for a good cup of coffee," he says.

It takes me a second to realize he is talking about the cappuccino machine. "I love it," I say. "I tried to use it yesterday but I'm doing something wrong. The steam came out but the milk wouldn't bubble." Phil is flipping through the mail. He looks a little blurry to me. I take out my contacts when I'm in the studio because of all the dust and I can't seem to find my glasses. I may have left them in Phoenix. Or maybe on the plane. "You know I've got book club tomorrow night. You remember I told you that."

Phil rips open a bill, looks at it idly. "You're using too much milk."

"What?"

"The frothing device isn't working because you're using too much milk."

"Did you hear me about book club?"

Tory and I have finished with the last side of her timeline and it looks great. She blows around the edges. Her hair is pulled back in a low ponytail and her face is as serious as a pilgrim's. I wonder how much she notices between me and Phil or if she thinks this is the way all married people talk.

Maybe it *is* the way all married people talk.

I've been cutting things out of the paper, descriptions of apartments, tips for how to establish your own credit, starting times for computer programming classes. I don't know what any of this means, but I told Kelly that I'm looking for a sign. She says the only sign I'm looking for is EXIT. Part of me wishes something final would happen, like a car crash. Not the kind that kills you, just the kind that shakes you up and makes you do something drastic. Maybe Phil will hit me or be arrested for fraud or run off with his dental hygienist, but I doubt he'll make it that easy. I married a nice man and this is what will defeat me in the end.

"Look, Daddy," Tory says, waving a picture in his face. She went through the photo albums all last night and she's especially transfixed by this one shot of me and Phil, taken two days before she was born. I am huge, wearing his red velour bathrobe, and it is still gapped open, but I'm smiling and the focus is clear enough that you can see the title of the book beside me, a grisly murder mystery, the only kind of reading that kept me calm in the last ponderous month of pregnancy. Phil is smiling too and he looks young and confident as he reaches around me to put his hands on my belly as if it were a basketball he's getting ready to bounce-pass directly into the camera. "Be careful with that one," I tell Tory. "Tape it, don't glue it, and don't let it get lost or bent." It's my favorite picture of us.

"Who took it?"

"I set it on a timer," Phil says. "Then ran around to be beside your mom before it snapped. I wanted to take the picture because I knew something wonderful was just about to happen." Tory ducks her head like she's embarrassed, but she's really pleased.

"You're a good daddy," I say to Phil. Quietly, as if this is some kind of secret we have to keep from Tory.

"Nice to hear I can do something right," he says.

It's almost six. I stand before the sink letting water run over the mushrooms and tomatoes. I blow air into my imaginary trombone. Tory is climbing Phil's back, putting her feet into the pockets of his pants as if they were steps. He cups his hands to make her a better push-off point and she struggles her way to the top of his shoulders. She shifts her weight back and forth, gripping his beard with her small fingers, knocking his glasses unsteady as she stretches up and slaps the ceiling with her palms. There aren't too many more years he will be able to lift her like this. I stand at the sink and watch them, my daughter and this thoroughly decent man whom I cannot seem to love.

Chapter Three

Kelly is hosting book club this month, which means she gets to choose the book. Kelly isn't much of a reader so what we're reading isn't much of a book.

Kelly is the rich one in the group, although it would make her mad to hear me describe her like that. Her house is in the kind of community where you have to call down and give the gatekeeper somebody's name before they'll let them in—just dropping by to visit in this neighborhood is completely out of the question. But I come over so often that Kelly finally took a picture down to the guardhouse—a snapshot of me at her wedding that she copied at Kinko's and printed beneath it: LET THIS PERSON IN NO MATTER WHAT. Now all the guards know my Mini Coop by sight and this one looks up from his newspaper and waves me through. I am not a dangerous woman. Anyone can see that at a glance.

Mark's car isn't there when I pull into the driveway, which I assume means he's having dinner at the clubhouse. Most of the husbands have found a way to avoid being home on book club night. Kelly is fanning out brownies on a platter when I walk into the kitchen.

"Look at these," she says. "Just like a fucking magazine, huh?"

"You amaze me," I say, and it's true. Kelly is liquid—her personality takes on the shape of any container you pour her into.

She only started cooking when she married Mark, and now she's probably the best hostess of the group. She's the kind who will see a certain dish on the Food Channel and spend the whole morning tracking down obscure ingredients at the organic market. Kelly throws her heart into things. Kelly knows how to fill a day.

"How was Phoenix? You haven't said much about the trip."

"I cut it really tight on my connection in Dallas. I wasn't sure my bag would even make it."

She turns to me, spatula in hand. "You've told me that part twice already. Why do I have the feeling there's more to the story?"

"I'll tell you, but not with everybody else on the way."

She nods, gives me a quick distracted hug, and runs upstairs to put on a clean shirt. I sit in her designer kitchen with its speckled marble countertops and shiny potted herbs and catch myself smiling at the sight of an avocado perched on top of a wooden bowl. Kelly hates the way avocados taste but likes the way they look. "The texture's fantastic, isn't it?" she asks, sometimes rubbing one against my cheek for emphasis. "They're so slick and bumpy." So she buys an avocado every week for her fruit arrangement and at the end of the week she throws it out to the birds, a fact that infuriates her husband. Once Phil and I were over here for a cookout and Mark took the avocado out of the bowl and shook it in my face and said, "Do you know how much these goddamn things cost?"

"Yeah," I said. I know how much everything in this house costs. I probably know a lot more about it than he does. "They're a dollar eighty-nine."

"Did you know she throws them out in the goddamn yard?"

"Women do weird things," Phil piped up helpfully. He tends to agree with everything that other men say, one of the personality traits I didn't notice until after we were married. Plus, I think he's a little intimidated by Mark. We all are. He always seems to be on the verge of losing his temper and he makes so much money.

"Humph," Mark said, smacking the avocado back into the bowl. "She acts like they grow on trees."

For the record, I did not meet Kelly at the church. Kelly and I go all the way back to high school and she's my best friend, even though I am too old to call anyone a best friend and we're careful not to flaunt our closeness in front of the others. At least we try not to flaunt it, but I know they can tell. It's always like there are two conversations going, the one that everyone hears and then there's the one between me and Kelly, the one that is just beneath the surface. It's this unspoken conversation that makes other people nervous. They think we're laughing at them, and sometimes we are, but mostly we're just trying to figure something out. It's like Kelly and I share a secret that neither one of us can quite remember.

And there's one other thing. Kelly is beautiful, so beautiful that people stop in their tracks just to watch her walk by. Sometimes, even after knowing her so long, I forget this and then I see her coming toward me and I am like those strangers on the street. Shocked by her blondness, dazzled by her height. Amazed by the ease with which she navigates the world, and I remember how I've spent twenty-five years wondering why someone so tall and thin and perfect would ever have wanted to be my friend. Because me, me at fourteen, I wasn't that cool.

I never even would have made cheerleading if it hadn't been for her.

That's where we met, at tryouts in the summer before ninth grade. I'd cheered for two years in middle school, but you don't have to be that good to cheer in middle school. It's not like you need gymnastic skills or anything, you just have to be cute and loud. So when I showed up for the high school tryouts it was obvious at once that these girls were on a whole different level. Especially Kelly. I noticed her the very first day. Lots of the girls were good, but she was the only one who was casual about it, lithe and nonchalant as she went through her fallbacks and kicks.

On the third day they taught us a pyramid formation and I was placed, along with the other girls who were sure to be cut, in the bottom row. Kelly was top tier and she put her foot on my thigh as she climbed me, then her other foot on my shoulder, and then there was this strange moment where the length of her body dragged across my face. And then, with the arches of her feet trembling against my shoulders, she slowly stood. I held her ankles, but once she got herself righted, which took her only a few seconds, she was completely still.

She didn't speak to me until it was time to drop out, always the most perilous part of any formation. She called down, "You're going to catch me, right?" and I said, "Absolutely," and I did, even though the force of her falling weight jolted me and for a moment I lost my breath. One of the coaches stood in front to spot us, but it wasn't necessary. I caught her perfectly and the other girls, the returning cheerleaders for whom tryouts were just a formality, clapped.

"You're good," Kelly said. "I'd even let you catch me in a flip."

On the first full day of school I was at the end of the cafeteria line, ready to pick up my tray and go sit with the girls I'd known from middle school, and I heard her call out, "Elyse?" We'd worn nametags at tryouts but I was still surprised she would remember my name or know how to pronounce it. Most people don't. Half the time in middle school I'd answered to Elsie. Kelly was sitting at the table with the other cheerleaders, the most popular girls in the whole school, and she said, "Come eat with us." The room blurred. She was a star—of course they'd wanted her, and apparently she had somehow managed to convince them to bring me on too. I looked down at my tray, ignoring the faces of my former friends who had already cleared a place for me to sit, and took a deep breath. That's it, one casual invitation, and I knew in that moment that my whole life was going to be different.

Our periods were synchronized within a month. We used to—I can't for the life of me remember why—slip into the bathroom between classes and switch shirts, and then I would smell her baby powder scent all day. Kelly would sit in class drawing medieval-looking pentagrams on the backs of her spiral notebooks and then coloring them in purple and magenta. I learned to draw these patterns from her and for years they encircled my pottery. Her mother, in fact, was the one who first taught me how to throw pots, and Kelly slept over at my house so much that my father, who used to call me Baby, started calling her Baby Two. We got the same haircut—a long curly shag that was known as a "Gypsy" and required twenty minutes in hot rollers every morning. We lined our eyes in kohl and our mouths in a light shimmery lipstick by Yardley called Berryfrost. We bought matching pairs of black platform boots and wore them with long V-neck sweaters and short pleated plaid skirts, a juxtaposition that struck us as sophisticated and ironic, as if we were prep school girls hooking on the side. Looking back at pictures from that time, it amazes me how much we willed ourselves to look alike.

At one point we even dated twins, shy studious boys that I doubt we ever would have noticed if there hadn't been two of them. Fridays were for ball games but on Saturday nights we would go to the drive-in with the twins, whom Kelly insisted on calling the Brothers Pressley. Frank and I were always in the back, Kevin and Kelly in the front, and we knew each other so well that there was no pretense about watching the movie. Even as the previews were rolling, we were shifting into position, and almost the minute Kelly would lie down, with Kevin poised above her, her foot would begin to tap out a nervous rhythm against the seat.

Now I hear that it's all about blow job parties, that it's all about what the girl can do for the boy, but I grew up in a time when girls weren't expected to do anything, when you could render a boy speechless with rapture just by leaning back and letting your legs fall apart. Every Saturday night for most of our junior year and into the summer that followed I would lie there passively while Frank bent over me, his face gone sweet and serious with concentration. He studied me as if I were a lock.

I was as mysterious to myself as I was to him. Frank would unzip my jeans and turn his hand . . . I can still feel it. The hand slowly sliding, the middle finger grazing the full length of my opening, the palm cupped around the mound, the grip, the slight shake. Once I finally got him going on the right spot, once I finally managed to persuade him that—despite what logic dictated—it wasn't down there but actually up somewhere higher, once I finally got him to stop rubbing me in that hard, systematic way that he undoubtedly used on himself and got him instead to do this small delicate flutter . . . then something would begin to build and my foot would shake too, answering Kelly's taps in the same nervous rhythmic pattern. Such bad girls we were, so bad, so conspiratorial, and it was always worse when we were together. She tapped. I tapped back. We may as well have been convicts passing news of a jailbreak.

Frank was intent on his mission, but somewhat confused by my constant navigational redirection. Once he whispered to me, "Are you sure this is right?" I was sure, suddenly so sure that I put both of my hands on Frank's wrist. "Yes," I said, and I think I said it out loud. I gripped his wrist with both of my hands and guided him up and down and in small circles, just there, holding him back to where he had no choice but to touch me lightly. Over and over again we traced a pattern of curves and circles, my hands clamped around his, almost as if I were teaching him to write. "Are you sure?" he said again, and now I realize that he probably could hear me just fine, but that my muttered "Yes, yes, yes . . ." must have excited him, that it must have pleased him to think he'd made me so lost in the moment that I didn't even care if Kelly and Kevin heard me cry out.

Years later Kelly and I were drinking wine and the conversation fell to the twins. Older and kinkier then and slightly drunk, I said, "You know, at some point or another, we should have swapped them."

And Kelly said, "What makes you think we didn't? They were totally into the twin thing, remember? Always switching off to fool teachers, so why wouldn't they have tried it with us?"

I was shocked even at the suggestion, but she's right, it isn't hard to picture. The two of them plotting at the snack bar, walking back and simply sliding into different seats. It isn't hard to imagine them sharing notes later in their bedroom about the ways she and I were different, or alike. I imagined them smelling their hands, as boys do, as men do, and breathing in the combined scent of her and me. But I hid my unease and said, "Well, that would explain why I had to keep teaching him the same things over and over," and Kelly laughed, still willing to accept, as she has always been willing to accept, the myth that I am the more sexual of the two of us, that I am the risk-taker and trailblazer, although her tapping from the front seat all those years ago should have told us that this was never so.

When the Brothers Pressley would go to the snack bar to get my popcorn and her Twizzlers, I would climb into the front seat, loose-limbed and giggly, and Kelly and I would watch the movie until they returned. The owner of the drive-in showed a lot of oldies; I guess he figured the kids weren't paying attention at all and it was a good way to save money. But Kelly and I watched, and we loved Katharine and Bette and Lana and Ingrid. We watched them storming in and out of elegant rooms, crying and throwing martini glasses, taking the stand to testify, going beautifully mad, sobering up, checking their lipstick, and setting sail for Europe. We watched their flawless faces fading into the shadows of sex while their eyelids fluttered closed and the music swelled. The drive-in was where we first got our passion for Elizabeth Taylor, an obsession we share to this day.

"Frank's better-looking," Kelly would say, poking me, and this always made us laugh harder.

"He is not," I'd say, "Kevin is the prince and Frank is the frog."

But Kelly would only shake her head, sighing in that mock-tragic way of hers. "Face it, baby. You got the better-looking twin."

What'd you think of the book?" Kelly asks, coming back into the kitchen. She hasn't just changed her shirt but her pants as well, and she's used a flatiron on her hair. She makes me look like shit.

"Next month, I want to do *David Copperfield*," I say. "We need to get back to the classics. He's got this great line, he says, 'There is only one question, whether or not a man is to be the hero of his own life.' Isn't that great?"

"Huh," says Kelly. "Is it in paperback?"

"Yeah, it's old, it's Dickens. Charles Dickens. Of course it's in paperback. You don't think that's a great line?"

"It's a great line."

"Because that's what I want. I want to be the hero of my own life."

"Just exactly what happened in Phoenix?"

At that moment there's the pop of an opening door and Nancy and Belinda come in, Belinda already apologizing because she hasn't read the whole book. "Good God, you look terrible, what happened to you?" says Kelly, who frequently greets Belinda this way, never seeming to notice how tactless she sounds. Belinda does give the impression of someone who has just rolled out of bed, no matter what time of day you see her, and she launches into a long story about how her youngest busted a tooth out on the coffee table just as she was leaving the house and Michael didn't want to be left with a hurt and whimpering kid and she felt bad about it herself, but this was her one night out and she had read most of the book, or at least about a hundred pages.

Nancy rolls her eyes at me and Kelly. Belinda is the youngest of us by nearly ten years and we're all accustomed to the way she lurches from crisis to crisis.

Belinda says all the time that she's getting fat, and she pulls up her shirt as she says this, in case somebody doesn't believe her. She says that she's stupid, although she doesn't bother showing any concrete proof of this, and—perhaps most telling of all—she refuses to do anything by herself. Her list of phobias is long and bizarre, ranging from cake batter to suspension bridges. She's afraid to drive at night, which is one reason Nancy always picks her up and takes her places. And Belinda constantly points out, especially when she's inside the guarded gates of Kelly's neighborhood, that she doesn't really fit in here.

Which is true enough, but what Belinda doesn't understand is that nobody fits in here. We're all transplants in a way—come from up north or out west—and even me and Kelly, who grew up just a few miles from these very wrought-iron gates, are perhaps the most aware that this isn't the world we came from. These suburbs didn't exist twenty years ago but now the farmland where we used to ride our bikes seems to grow red brick. There are no longer open fields, just streets lined with enormous Georgian houses. "They spring out of the ground," my mother says darkly, and it's true that if you go six months without driving a particular country road, the odds are that the next time you take that route you won't recognize it. My mother exists in a permanent state of disorientation, something I believe is common in southerners of her generation. She often calls me crying on her cell phone, reporting that she was just trying to take a shortcut and all of a sudden nothing looks familiar. "I'm lost in my own hometown," she will say, and I will assure her that she's not, even though the truth is, I get lost sometimes too.

This would surprise Belinda, who is convinced that all of her self-esteem issues spring from the fact that she was born in Alabama. She came up poor and Michael had been poor too when she met him at the university. Poor but brilliant, one of those lanky stooped-over idiot savant country boys—and who could have foreseen he'd write some sort of computer program when he was still a sophomore, that he'd sell it to the Bank of America before he even graduated? Not her, that's for sure. Everybody said she really knew how to pick them, but she hated it when people talked like that. It made her sound so calculating, and the truth is, girls never know what boys are going to become. It's just that once, early in the morning, when they were walking to class, Michael told her she was pretty. She'd met some guy at a kegger the night before, a guy who'd spent six blessed hours humping her and then left without saying goodbye. Belinda had been walking to class hungover with her pajama top on and Michael—sweet, shy Michael—had fallen into step with her and told her she was pretty.

They got married, she got pregnant, or maybe it happened the other way around, and they lived for two years in that awful student housing, and then, bingo-bango, he signs with the bank for six figures. Six figures and five babies in five years and now her mother keeps a picture of Belinda's house on her refrigerator, held with a magnet. "She doesn't have a picture of my kids anywhere in her whole trailer," Belinda has told me, several times, her voice rising in indignation. "But Mama sure is proud of my house."

So it's hardly surprising she feels a bit like an imposter, but the truth of the matter is, she belongs here as much as anyone—just one more fact to go into that bulging file labeled Things Belinda Has Not Yet Realized. She's always trying to catch up. She goes to those expensive old-lady stores and buys sweaters with pictures on them. Not just for holidays. She wears them all the time. Sailboats and dogwoods and animals. Most of the sweaters are stretched in the front from being worn throughout Belinda's poorly spaced pregnancies and it makes the pictures a little surrealistic. Tonight she is wearing a dog whose legs look much too long. The sweaters, along with ankle-length jean skirts and bright-colored suede flats, are what Belinda imagines the sophisticated suburbanite should wear and she refuses to be deterred from this vision, even though God knows none of the rest of us dress like that. I've wondered why Nancy hasn't tried to set her straight, about the sweaters and other things too. Belinda does everything Nancy tells her to do.

But Nancy, I guess, is uneasy in her own way. She moved

down three years ago from New Jersey and she still seems over-whelmed by the sheer size of her house. A lot of people moving in from the Northeast are like that—they had a $400,000 ranch house in some commuter town and then they come down here and it boggles their minds what $400,000 will buy. It's the way of the world. The Realtor punches some buttons and tells you what you can afford, and it's more than you think you can afford. But if she says you can qualify, who are you to argue? You move in and then one morning you wake up and wander around and ask yourself how the hell you ended up in this mausoleum of granite and marble. This obscene square footage, it makes us all nervous in a way—me because I retain a little bit of the bohemian art-ist thing, Kelly because she misses her single-girl condo, Belinda because she's afraid we can still smell her trailer-park past, and Nancy because she's not from the South.

Nancy has red hair and very white skin and it's a great source of pride to her that, despite her vulnerable coloring, she does not freckle. She has a nearly pathological fear of the sun. She dresses as if she's in the middle of some never-ending safari and she keeps a tube of sunscreen in the compartment between the front seats of her car. Every time she hits a stoplight she dabs some on herself and her kids. The whole family smells like tropical fruit. Nancy keeps the Weather Channel on all day long and surrounds herself with thermometers. At any given time she can tell you what the temperature is. "It's 94," she will say, "and it isn't even noon. Can you believe it? No, wait, wait, look at that. It's 95."

She tries, I mean she really tries, but I remember the first time we had book club at Nancy's house. We came in, we sat down, and then she just started talking about the book. Back then there were seven of us in book club and we all kept glancing around, not quite sure what to do. I was uncomfortable, but then I was a little uncomfortable with how uncomfortable I was, because exactly what did it say about me that I'd let something like that make me so upset? And Nancy just kept talking about the sym-bolism and the point of view until finally Lynn said, "Excuse me," as if she was going to the bathroom. But she went into the kitchen and emerged a few minutes later with glasses of iced tea on a tray.

"I think you forgot to set these out," Lynn said softly, and Nancy stared at the glasses as if she'd never seen them before in her life. She probably hadn't seen them in years. They looked like her good crystal. God knows how Lynn had managed to find them and drag them out and dust them so fast.

"Oh," said Nancy, still confused but trying to rise to the occasion as best she could. "Does anybody want anything to drink?"

I think of the Yankee woman in the barbecue scene in *Gone With the Wind* and how she referred to the southerners as "puzzling, stiff-necked strangers." I suspect that is how Nancy sees us, as puzzling and stiff-necked, as people who splash around a kind of surface friendliness but who are easily offended when she breaks rules she didn't know existed. Perhaps she views her time in North Carolina as some sort of extended anthropological study. She does look a bit like Margaret Mead, peering out from her oversized hats and gauzy scarves, taking mental notes about the incomprehensible rituals of the aboriginal people. Because there are a lot of rules and even though Kelly and I may not always follow them, it's a bit shocking to come up against someone who doesn't even seem to know what they are. You don't put dark meat in your chicken salad. You write a thank-you note and send it through the U.S. Postal Service instead of relying on an Ecard. You don't correct anyone's pronunciation of anything. You call anyone over seventy "ma'am" and you call your friends "ma'am" if you're mad at them. You don't brag about how cheap you got something, or, even worse, how much you paid for it. Especially not real estate. Now, on the flip side, it's perfectly okay to drink like a fish, or curse, or flirt with someone else's husband. In fact it's a little insulting if you don't. To refuse to flirt with her husband implies your friend chose badly, and if you and she both damn well know she chose badly, you need to flirt a little bit more just to help her cover up the fact.

And when people come to your house, you immediately offer them something to drink. I mean, Jesus, girl, don't you know it's 95 degrees out there?

So Jeff took the job down here and Nancy followed—I think that may have been one of the worst days of her life, but she'd never say that. She does what's expected of her. She joins every club and she chairs every committee. And she has tried to make her house, uncomfortably large and scantily furnished as it is, into a home. Kelly and I have always laughed at her, just a little bit, with all her crafts and rehabbing and cheap-chic decorating. The fact that she's painted her master bedroom with some sort of technique that she calls Bellagio faux glazing so that it looks like her bed is floating in a mottled pastel cloud. How she drives around with the back of her old Volvo station wagon full of fabric books and half-filled paint cans and some broken endtable she's rescued from a yard sale. They greet her by name at the Home Depot. But it makes me sad too. All the hours she sinks into that house, I know she's just trying to put her mark on something. She's trying to make it hers, the same way a dog pees on a tree, and it's not her fault she doesn't quite get it.

"Elyse didn't like the book," Kelly says.

"Ah," says Nancy. "And exactly what should we be reading, Elyse? Why don't you just make up the list for the rest of the year? It would save everybody else so much time."

"I think we should get back to the classics," I say.

"Well of course you do," says Nancy.

"It wouldn't kill us to read something serious once in a while. I was thinking *David Copper*—"

"Where's Lynn?" Belinda suddenly asks, and Kelly shrugs. Lynn hasn't been to book club in months. The official story is that she is too busy with her new job, but we all know something else is afoot.

Maybe it's not true that none of us was really born to this place. When I first moved into my neighborhood, Lynn was the one I wanted to be like, the one I most admired. She's the one who started book club and I always tried to be her partner when we had whist night at church. She had—still has—that blue-blooded quality certain women have where they give their children last names as first names and a natural, easy athleticism that reminds me of Kelly. Lynn did a half-marathon and then a marathon and then a triathalon and finally when she dislocated her knee—stepping off a curb, ironically—she switched to walking. Within a couple of months, she had the rest of us walking with her. Yeah, come to think of it, Lynn has always fit in better than anyone, which is what makes it so mind-numbingly ironic that she's the one who seems to be pulling away. Lynn is subtle, and gracious, and feminine, and kind. The sort of woman who can serve iced tea out of someone else's kitchen and make it seem okay.

But Lynn is also the only divorced woman among us.

She keeps her chin up—she unloaded her dishwasher and got the kids to school on time the very morning that her husband left her. Rumor has it—at least according to Nancy—that he fucked her one last time for the road and then, while she was pulling her panties and gown back on to go fix the kids' breakfast, he cheerfully informed her that he had fallen in love with his secretary. Lynn did everything you're supposed to do—she fought for the house, she got full custody of her boys, she lightened her hair, she went back to school. But she doesn't come to book club anymore.

At first everyone thought it was because of the money. We used to eat in restaurants. We would get a table in the back and order wine and talk a little bit about the book, but then Nancy pulled us aside one night and said, "You know, not everyone in the group has thirty dollars to throw around on ahi tuna." Referring of course to Lynn, and we all were quick to say yes, that it would be better if we met in homes, and that was when the competitive brownie making began. Nobody really likes meeting in homes. Everybody liked eating out and drinking wine a lot better. It's a little funny that we changed because of Lynn and now Lynn no longer shows up and yet no one has suggested that we go back to restaurants. Maybe that would make her absence seem too permanent. That would be admitting that she's so far outside of the circle that she's never coming back.

I lean against the counter and watch the others. Nancy and Kelly are talking about how Lynn might be losing her insurance now that the divorce is finally final, Belinda is gazing at the brownies and smoothing back her hair, which is in one of those sloppy French braids you can only get away with if you're very young. I feel a little nervous being around them, as if they can see—what could they see? I feel as if there is a small high vibration under my skin, running throughout my body, but no one is treating me any differently, not even Kelly, who would be the one most likely to hear the hum. She knows something happened in Phoenix, but she thinks I spent too much on clothes or drank too much in a hotel bar. The thought that I might have kissed a stranger wouldn't even cross her mind. We are all so thoroughly married. Our idea of being bad is eating cheesecake.

"I would have bet Elyse liked this book," says Belinda. "It had sex."

Okay, so maybe I'm wrong.

"Stupid sex," Nancy mutters. "I almost gagged when I got to the part where he was moving over her like a tiger. Who says that? What woman says, 'He moved over me like a tiger'?"

"I just about gagged through the whole thing," I say. "She didn't have to just stay there all those years and be long-suffering and pitiful. She could have done something."

"Like what?" asks Belinda. I don't know like what.

"And it's an old book," I say, more to Kelly than anyone else. "Why the hell are we doing such an old book?"

"You wanted to do *David Copperfield*," Nancy points out, in that way that makes it hard to know if she's teasing or really being dumb. "It's what, two hundred years old? Three hundred?"

"That's a totally different thing and you know it."

"Y'all want to move into the den?" says Kelly. "There's no point in just standing around in the kitchen."

"What'd you mean she could have done something?" Belinda asks. "Because I was reading along thinking that if some perfect man just showed up at my door one day . . ."

"She shouldn't have had the affair in the first place," Nancy says. "If she wasn't happy with her lot afterwards she only had herself to blame."

"She wasn't happy with her lot before she had the affair," I say.

"I really don't know what I'd do," Belinda keeps going, "if all of a sudden I heard a knock and I looked out and saw a truck in the yard so I opened the door and boom, he was there."

"Really," I say. "It's not like she took some fantastic marriage and ruined it."

"She was content," Nancy says.

"Oh wow," I say. "Content."

"It's not such a dirty word," says Nancy.

"We could sit down," Kelly says.

"Come on," I say, "you can't unexperience something."

"So what do you think she should have done, Elyse? Please tell us, considering how you're about a thousand times smarter than everyone else."

"Of course, when you think about it," Belinda says, "what are the chances of a perfect man's truck breaking down in your front yard?"

"Let's move to the den," Kelly says. "Everybody's standing here in the kitchen like they think I don't even have chairs."

"Oh, I agree with you, Nancy, I agree with you completely. She never should have had an affair and risked losing all that contentment. While her family was gone to the state fair she should have used the free time to faux glaze her walls . . ."

The minute it's out of my mouth I regret it. Nancy and I banter, we banter every month and the other women expect it. It's probably why they leave their children at home with bleeding gums and travel out at night to discuss books they haven't read. But I've never been mean to her before. Nancy goes white, her lips thin and motionless. I glance at Kelly but she doesn't meet my eyes. I've gone too far this time. And then, quickly and calmly, Nancy unzips her purse, pulls out her keys, and walks out of the kitchen. A few seconds later we hear the crank of her engine.

"Wait a minute," says Belinda. "I rode with her."

I'm shocked, even though I'm not totally sure why. We have been meeting for seven years and no one has ever walked out of book club.

"She doesn't like me," I say.

"Why'd you have to say that?" Kelly asks. "That house is her work of art."

"She's never liked me."

"And you make a big deal about having a job."

"So what, I throw pots. I make like two cents a year."

"I'm not talking about money. You can be real snotty about things, Elyse. You act like you're the big intellectual of the group and you're going slumming by just hanging around with the rest of us . . ."

"That isn't it," Belinda says. Belinda puts her words together slowly when she talks, as if she's remembering a dream. "I mean, you're right, Nancy doesn't like Elyse, but it doesn't have anything to do with making pots or what we read for book club. Nancy's mad because Jeff said he wants to climb her."

A complete silence falls on the kitchen. The word "climb" hangs in the air like a curse. When Kelly slams the pot back into the coffeemaker we all jump.

"You're telling us," Kelly says to Belinda, "that Nancy actually told you that Jeff actually told her he wants to climb Elyse."

"Yeah, but I'm wondering if Nancy thinks he's really saying something worse. Like saying climb her means, you know, something else."

"Belinda honey, you've got to back up," says Kelly. "You're not telling this story in a way that makes any sense."

Belinda stops, sighs, looks out into space for a moment. "About a month ago we're all at the pool and it's getting late, it's getting a little bit chilly but I can't get the kids out and dressed, because everybody's having too much fun. I'm dried off and sitting on a lounge chair shivering and Nancy comes up to me and says, 'Don't you even have a coverup?' and I say, 'No,' because you know how it is, you get all the stuff for the kids and load it in the car and forget to bring anything for yourself. So I say no, and she takes off her shirt and wraps it around me. She's like Jesus, you know, she's so sweet that way, she's patient with me even when I can be kind of ditzy, and that night it was cold and she literally gave me the shirt off her back. It's something I'll always remember."

"Right," says Kelly. "Right. She's great about stuff like that."

"She's great about a lot of things," Belinda says. "I don't think either one of you know how much she volunteers. It's not just the Friendship Trays. She does Habitat and Hospice . . ."

"She's a saint," says Kelly. "What does this have to do with Jeff wanting to climb Elyse?"

"Elyse was there, we all were, everybody was there, and Nancy and I were sitting on the lounge chair with her shirt kind of half over both of our shoulders and we're looking across the pool area and we see them talking, Elyse and Jeff on a lounge chair too. I mean, nothing was wrong with it, everybody was there and they were just talking, or maybe it was more like they were fighting. It looked like they were having an argument."

I remember that night.

"And Nancy just sits there looking across the pool and she says that Jeff likes to fight with Elyse. He follows her around at every party or whatever and gets her in a fight because he likes it, and then Nancy's voice got kind of funny and she said, 'He told me he wants to climb her,' which is a weird thing to say, and later I started thinking that must be why Nancy doesn't like Elyse. Although that thing about the faux glazing was pretty mean too."

Kelly looks at me. "Did you know any of this?"

He does follow me around. I've noticed that much. He wants to talk politics, he wants to talk religion, he wants to talk books.

I shake my head. "That's ridiculous."

"Why?" says Kelly. "He's a minister, he's not dead."

"Among about a million other reasons, Jeff is Phil's best friend."

"So what? I'm not suggesting he'd ever really hit on you. We're talking about what people think about doing, not what people actually do."

I shake my head again. "That's not what he meant by climbing. You know how Jeff is—he just blurts stuff out and he doesn't stop to think how it sounds. All he meant is he likes talking to me. Jeff's really kind of innocent, you know? He acts tough and he wears that silly zip-up jacket . . ."

"Oh yeah, he's the regular James Dean of the pulpit," Kelly says, sliding the plate of brownies toward us and refilling our coffee. "You're saying that's fake?"

"The night Belinda was talking about, we were arguing about *The Canterbury Tales* . . ."

"Come off it, Elyse, nobody goes to the swimming pool and argues about *The Canterbury Tales*."

"It's just that Jeff used to be a history major all those years ago and he likes debating obscure stuff. It juices him, and let's face it, nobody else around here will argue with him. You all stand back from him like, 'Whoa, he's the minister so his opinion has to matter more,' and sure, there's a part of him that gets off on that, but there's another part of him . . ."

"A part that wants to climb you," Kelly says, and her mouth twitches a little.

"A part that wants me to tell him when he's full of shit."

Belinda looks up from her brownie. "Oh, I see what you're saying. He thinks you're smarter than Nancy."

The door pops open and Nancy walks back in. We'd been so preoccupied I didn't even hear the car drive back up. "Sorry," she says. "Sorry."

"No," I say. "I was completely out of line." We smile at each other.

"It sucks," she says. "I was halfway down the block and so pissed off that my mouth had gone dry when I started thinking that the kids are bathed and they've done their homework and Jeff got home early to keep them so, come hell or high water, I'm out for the night." She throws her car keys on the counter, drops her purse on the kitchen chair. "Okay, Elyse, tell the truth. What did you think about the book?" Everybody laughs.

"All right," says Kelly, "whatever. I'm just glad you're all staying. I thought I was going to have to drive Belinda home and eat a plate of cream cheese brownies all by myself. I don't care what we read, I just want everybody to get along. Next month we'll do *David Copperhead*."

"*Copperfield*." I can't seem to help myself.

"Is it sad?" Belinda asks. "Because even though I didn't get to the end of this one, I could tell it was going to be sad."

"You can't expect everything to be some old-fashioned romance," says Kelly, picking up the plate of brownies and walking into the den. "It's supposed to be a realistic treatment of an affair."

"What do you mean?" Belinda asks, following her. "That things have to be sad to be realistic?"

"What she means," Nancy says patiently, as patient as a saint, "is that in novels women run off with their lovers. In real life, women stay."

Chapter Four

———··◦∞◦··———

In my dream, he seems to have the power of flight. Or at least of hovering. He is above me, like a hummingbird. He moves from one part of my body to another and I can feel the rapid flap of wings against my skin. He lowers his head, over and over, as if to drink.

I can't seem to move. I don't want to move. A phone is in my hand. He drops his head to my breast and I see the wings growing out from his shoulder blades and the strong taut tendons running from his back into the rippling white feathers and then I am up, off the ground and trembling beneath him, seemingly held by nothing but his mouth.

The phone rings.

No, it's the alarm. I hear the sound of Phil's hand slapping the clock, I hear the bed creak as he rises. I wait until he is in the bathroom and has the shower going before I get up too. Wrap his robe around me and shuffle into the kitchen.

"He moved over me like a hummingbird," I tell Pascal, who is sitting on the counter. He raises a leg and languidly begins to clean himself.

Phil emerges from the bedroom a few minutes later. He seems surprised that I am making omelets. Swiss cheese and spinach and a crumpled piece of deli ham. I found a counselor, I tell him. A woman. He does remember, doesn't he? He remembers that he promised? Of course he remembers, he says, and the omelets are a nice surprise. It's a shame he doesn't have more time. He eats standing up at the counter.

In real life, women stay. Women stay better than they do anything else.

It's Track and Field Day at the elementary school. Kelly, Nancy, and I are sitting on folding chairs at the edge of the playground, watching the kids go through the events. Kelly has brought a gift bag for Tory, with a purple-and-orange rugby shirt inside.

"She'll love it," I say, and she will. It's very much like the Gap Kids shirt that I bought her, but this one is a gift from Kelly so Tory will happily wear it, just as she happily wears everything that Kelly brings her. She may even insist on sleeping in it.

"Very cute," Nancy says. She's wanted to ask Kelly for years why she doesn't have kids and she never believes me when I say that I don't know either. It's obvious Kelly wanted them. Is Mark too old? He has adult children from a previous marriage so there isn't anything wrong with him physically. Is she the one with the problem or did they just make some sort of deal before marriage that he wouldn't have to go through that again?

Sometimes I think that Nancy looks like the heroine of a Victorian novel, and never more so than on a day like this when she has swathed herself in a thin, long-sleeved white blouse and a loose cream-colored muslin skirt. She has a floppy straw hat on her head and she takes great care to tuck her feet under her skirt. She is telling us about her mother's best friend's daughter. I don't know why she is telling us this story, since neither Kelly nor I know the woman in question, but Nancy is full of stories.

Anyway, this particular woman had an uncommunicative husband. Her marriage was in trouble. I guess she's secretly talking about me, or maybe even Belinda. I glance at Kelly. Mark never speaks. Hell, it could be any one of us.

"He was a little like Phil," Nancy finally says. Okay, great, we're talking about me. She tells us how this girl followed her husband from room to room, trying to get him to have a conversation. When he would shut the bathroom door she would lie down and put her cheek on the carpet and talk to him beneath the crack. I wince with recognition. In the middle of the night this woman would sit up in bed and cut on the lights and shake her husband's shoulder and say, "Wake up, we have to talk."

"She made him talk to her," says Nancy, "and they've been together twenty years." She says this last line with triumph, as if it were the last line of a joke. Apparently this is what it takes to stay together for twenty years. You have to want a marriage so badly that you're willing to wrestle it out of a man while he sleeps.

"Some people find a way to make anything work," Kelly says, in that sanguine sort of voice that I never can quite read. She's either being very agreeable or very sarcastic. Her ball cap is pulled down low over her face. "You're always hearing about people who don't start with much but somehow they make it work."

"Look at Megan," Nancy says, referring to the choir director at church. "Her husband was so jealous he'd follow her to work and sit in the handicapped space until he was sure she'd gotten into the building."

"Yeah, I wouldn't have given you two cents for Megan's chances when she first married that whack job," says Kelly. "But they're still together, aren't they?"

"They're knocking out the whole back of their den and adding on a sunroom," Nancy says, her voice rising with enthusiasm. She picks up a stick and begins drawing the new floor plan of Megan's house in the dust. "It's going to double the size of the first floor."

"Amazing," says Kelly. "Double the size."

"She hung in there," Nancy says. "Time helps everything.

You've got to be willing to fight it out, talk it out, pretty much build your marriage brick by brick."

I don't seem to have anything particular to contribute to this conversation.

"Have you considered counseling?" Nancy asks, abruptly turning toward me. "Because Jeff might be the perfect person for you to talk to. I know he likes you, Elyse. He's always trying to get you into some discussion about politics or religion. Have you noticed that, Kelly?"

"He corners her at every party," Kelly says, pulling out binoculars and turning them toward Tory. "What was it y'all were talking about at that swim club cookout? The two of you sat over there by yourselves on a lounge chair for an hour."

"I recited him the prologue to *The Canterbury Tales*," I say. "In Middle English."

"That's exactly what I figured you were doing," says Kelly.

"Jeff was a history major back a hundred years ago before divinity school," Nancy says.

"Yeah," I say. "He told me."

"He likes you," Nancy says, her voice a little flat. "He says he's intrigued by the intricacies of your mind."

Kelly makes a sound, somewhere between a cough and a snort.

"We're seeing someone at ten on Monday," I say. "A woman. We thought about Jeff, of course, but then we decided it would be easier to talk to someone we didn't know." This is a small lie. It had taken a lot of pushing to get Phil to agree to meet with anyone at all and we'd never discussed seeing Jeff. Even I can't imagine us talking to a man who is (a) Phil's best friend, (b) Nancy's husband, (c) our minister, and (d) intrigued by the intricacies of my mind.

"I guess I can see that," says Nancy, so slowly that it's clear she can't. "The important thing is that you're working on the marriage."

There's a sudden scream from the field and we all sit up straight.

It isn't one of our kids but Nancy still stands and walks toward the fence.

"I've got ice if you need it," she calls, and the teacher bending over the wailing child waves and nods. Nancy always brings ice in a cooler and ziplock bags to any even vaguely athletic event, whether it's our daily walks at the track or the volleyball games at church. We tease her about it, but she says that if life has taught her anything, it's that sooner or later somebody's going to get hurt.

The teacher pulls the little girl to her feet and gives us a thumbs-up. We settle back into our chairs. It's a beautiful day, the sort of Indian summer Carolina is known for, and we sit for a moment in companionable silence. The field is crowded with kids and the school has rented one of those big inflatable castles for them to jump in. There's a machine that makes funnel cakes and a clown twisting balloons into shapes. Kelly is humming, a sound so low that it almost sounds as if she's purring. I stretch my legs out, half close my eyes.

One of the fathers comes by, a guy I recognize from the athletic association. He tells me he's starting a girls' coach-pitch team and he sure would like to see Tory at the conditioning camp. She's fast, he says. He just watched her run the 440 and thought to himself, "That little Bearden girl is fast."

I must have slept funny last night because when I look up it feels like my whole head is getting ready to snap off. I shift in my seat and tell him I'm confused. Isn't softball in the spring? But he says if the girls want to be competitive they need to start getting ready now, and then he says something about Tory's "athletic career," which makes me want to laugh. She's too young for coach-pitch at all, but it seems pointless to argue. This is the sort of thing that appeals to Phil's ego. If he gets wind of the fact that a coach is trying to recruit his daughter, he'll drop anything to get her to those practices, even if it means canceling every appointment in his books.

"Okay," I say, "I'll tell her daddy." The coach makes a little tipping motion with his sun visor and walks away.

"Did you hear that?" I say, when he's out of earshot. "He's talking about a seven-year-old having an athletic career. These people are crazy."

"She really is fast," Kelly says. "Sometimes I wonder if you even see it."

"Just remember, Jeff wants to help," Nancy says. "He blames himself for what happened between Lynn and Andy."

"No one could have seen that coming," Kelly says.

"That's what I tell him," Nancy says, sighing. "But now he feels like he has to . . ." She doesn't need to finish the thought. We all know that Jeff hired Lynn because she needed a job where she could get health benefits and still be able to meet the bus when her kids get home from school. There wasn't even a staff position called Director of Grounds and Maintenance until he proposed it, and I doubt that anyone, including Jeff and Lynn, could tell you exactly what her duties are. But the session agreed to fund the job and hired her on the spot. Feeling sorry for Lynn has been our collective smugness since the day her husband walked out. I suspect that in the bag where Kelly has the rugby shirt for Tory there are two more shirts for Lynn's boys, whom she hardly knows. Their mother can't come to Track and Field Day, so Kelly will bring them a gift.

"I'm sure Jeff's a great counselor," I say. "I just don't want to talk to someone we know socially."

"Yeah," said Kelly. "In case the trouble turns out to be in the bedroom." I'm glad I can't see her eyes beneath the ball cap. It's all I can do to keep from bursting out laughing.

"Have you considered making it more . . . interesting?" Nancy scoots her chair a couple of inches closer to mine. "Because sometimes you have to do that."

"Phil doesn't like it when things are interesting. Phil's perfectly content with the way things are right now, you know that as well as I do. The problem is me."

"You could have an affair," Kelly says.

My body jerks. I pretend to brush away a bug. Gerry's business card has been in my purse for three weeks, in the side pocket where I keep my keys, so that I see it and touch it several times a day. Sometimes I take it out and stare at it, run my finger over the raised lettering. I've memorized the number, even though this is a number I'll never call. I'm Working on My Marriage. My husband I have an appointment with a counselor this Monday. Women who are Working on Their Marriages have no business daydreaming about strangers they meet on airplanes.

"Why do you think people add on sunrooms whenever somebody's having an affair?" Kelly asks.

Nancy twists around to look at her. "You think Megan's husband is having an affair?"

"No."

"Well, Megan certainly isn't."

"You're probably right. It's just, why do you think people who have been sitting in the dark all these years suddenly get this urge to knock out a wall?"

Nancy finally figures out that Kelly's just jerking her chain and she sits back, relaxing. "If remodeling means you're having an affair then I must be the whore of Babylon."

"No, I'm just thinking maybe Elyse should have an affair."

"Oh God," I say. "With who? The only men I know are your husbands, and your husbands are worse than mine." Kelly and Nancy both laugh.

I've gotten as far as dialing nine of the ten digits in his phone number before hanging up.

"Well, the coach-pitch coach certainly seems interested," Kelly says.

"Men like Elyse," Nancy says idly. "I've always wondered why that is." She squints at me. "I didn't mean that the way it sounded."

"Are you kidding?" says Kelly. "It's because she's a sprayer. Always has been, always will be. Men can smell it a mile away. I've spent my whole life groping my way through this mist of sex she sprays everywhere going, 'Elyse? Elyse? You in there anywhere, baby?'"

"Please. Maybe I was once, but not now. Not for a long time."

Nancy is frowning, as if trying to reconcile the theory that I'm a sprayer with the theory that my husband and I are having trouble in the bedroom. "I just don't see it," she finally says.

"That's because it isn't there," I say, pulling the binoculars from Kelly's hand.

"Women never see it," Kelly says. "Men do." She drops her voice, does a good imitation of the coach's low-country drawl. "I said to myself, 'That little Bearden girl is fast . . .'"

We laugh again. Tory has just finished the long jump and she is lining up for the hurdles. She waves and we all turn in unison, like gazelles at a watering hole.

"I don't know why," I say, "being a mother would come so easily to me when being a wife seems so hard . . ."

"On Monday things could look totally different," says Nancy. "It's bad luck to even be talking this way. Do you want to end up like Lynn?"

". . . or why Tory, my greatest success, would come out of my greatest failure."

"Don't say failure."

"My marriage is a failure."

"You don't have to use that word."

No, you don't have to, but ever since I said it to Gerry on the plane, I can't seem to stop.

"It's the right word," I tell Nancy.

She grimaces. "There are lots of words."

I didn't start calling my marriage a failure all at once.

At first I tried. I tried for years. I made all those little efforts, silly gestures like buying a CD called *It's Not Too Late to Have a Great Marriage*. I ordered it from QVC because it had such a needy-sounding title that I was embarrassed to buy it from the local bookstore. With my luck someone would see me holding it in line and report back to all my friends. There's just the tiniest bit of hypocrisy around the whole issue—everyone agrees you should Work on Your Marriage, but if you're ever caught actually Working on Your Marriage, you look ridiculous.

And the only thing worse than being unhappily married is being ridiculous.

So the CD series arrived UPS. There was a woman on the front of the box who was pulling her husband by the tie—pulling him playfully toward a kiss. The back of the box explained that this man wouldn't talk. This man was detached. This woman was weepy and frustrated. She was demanding things he couldn't seem to give her. (Maybe she was demanding too much.) From the husband's expression it wasn't clear how he felt about being dragged against his will into this passionate new marriage.

There were six discs. I was supposed to listen to them for six weeks in a row and I did, squirreling the box away underneath my side of the bed. If I listened to one in the car I made sure to pop it out after each session. It wasn't just to hide it from my friends—I was hiding it from myself. It's embarrassing to try this hard. I felt like a political candidate standing by the side of the road on election day, waving at every car that passes. I felt like a dog in a pet shop cage, an ugly girl at a dance. This painful eagerness, this hope that wore down every day but grew back at night while I slept. In time I came to understand that this hope was what I must squash, if I wanted to survive. And then one Sunday I sat there in a pew beside my husband and I looked up at Christ, dangling above me like he couldn't decide what to do either, and I prayed, "Okay, if you won't make him love me, at least make me stop caring." (This is the one prayer that would eventually be answered, although I didn't know it at the time.)

At the end of the series, on the very last track of the sixth CD, the woman therapist answers twenty commonly asked questions about how to revitalize a marriage. What do you do when he won't talk? When he works too many hours or you suspect there's another woman? When you disagree about the kids? When he brings you gifts that aren't your taste? When you feel so fat and unattractive that you're sure you can't draw his attention? When you feel so fat and unattractive that you don't want to? Did we mention he's not talking? Do only women live in the land of feelings? What do you do when you've tried everything and it still hasn't worked? What if it's just not the way you thought it would be? How did you think it was going to be? Can you even remember? The woman on the tape answers every question except one: Why do women stay?

Chapter Five

---◆◇◆---

When I wake up Monday morning, Phil has left me a note on the counter. He wants me to have a complete physical. He has begun to suspect that my problems might be chemical, or even hormonal. Maybe my blood sugar is low. There's always the chance of early menopause. He has taken the liberty of calling the therapist we were supposed to see today and postponing the appointment. It just seems prudent to rule out any medical causes first. He believes that we can fix this. Everything is fixable.

It is the longest note he has ever written me.

I call Dr. Bennett because he's the only doctor I know, even though he's a family practitioner and we don't see him much unless Tory needs a booster. Usually it takes a couple of months to get in—unless you're sobbing like hell when you call, I guess. If you're sobbing like hell when you call they put you on hold and come back and say they can see you that afternoon.

Dr. Bennett is a very kind man who speaks barely above a whisper. His nurse takes my blood and urine and weighs me and asks a bunch of questions about what I'm eating and how I'm sleeping. I'm overdue for a pelvic and he gives me one, only I can't seem to stop sniveling and at one point, after the Pap smear and before the anal, he looks up at me between the vee in my legs and says, very softly, "It looks like you've hit your limit."

"What?"

"Everybody has a personal limit and it looks like you've hit yours."

This strikes me as being so true and so kind that I start crying again and I say, "Would you please tell that to my husband?"

Dr. Bennett tells me to get dressed and meet him in his office, which has cheerful pumpkin-colored walls and is full of photographs of children on a sailboat. I tell him Phil's work number. This is a little awkward for him, I realize, for while Phil is a dentist and not a doctor there is still some sort of professional-courtesy issue. He says, "This is Dr. Bennett and I have just finished examining your wife." He pauses and then says, "No, her blood sugar is normal." He pauses another minute and says, "She doesn't appear to be anywhere close to menopause. We did check her levels." Pause. "Dr. Bearden, your wife is in good health but she's depressed." Pause. "No, it's not a diagnosis, it's an observation. Have you noticed that she cries a lot?" And then finally, after the longest pause of all, he says, "Yes, I suppose pastoral counseling might be a good place to start."

I'm fucked.

There was a part of me that knew we'd never actually see that woman therapist. When I called to make the appointment and the receptionist had given me directions, I hadn't bothered to write them down. Going to see a therapist seems like a big step to a man like Phil, a public admission that something has gone publicly wrong. Phil doesn't like big problems. Phil likes problems he can solve.

By the time he gets home that evening I'm calmed down and chopping vegetables for a salad. He stops at the counter and puts down the mail. "I guess you're pissed," he says.

I shrug. "I thought we could eat on the patio."

"I guess you're pissed," he says again, and without waiting for me to respond, he rushes on. "I know you might have preferred a female counselor, but I don't think that would have been fair to me. A woman would automatically side with you."

What Phil doesn't know about women is a lot.

I look up at him and shrug again, more elaborately this time, so that he will be forced to notice my cosmic indifference to the situation. "She might not have been able to help us anyway."

My acquiescence makes him even more nervous, like a gambler who's won an early hand. "The part you might not agree with," he says, "is that I'd like for us to talk to Jeff. In fact, he called me today and for some reason counseling just came up out of nowhere. He's agreed to see us the day after tomorrow." Apparently I've been elevated to emergency status all over town. "And that doesn't seem quite as drastic, you know, just driving over every now and then to talk to Jeff."

"Drastic?"

"There's no need to treat it like that, is there? Like we're in the middle of some kind of crisis? I'll be honest, I wouldn't know we even had a problem if you didn't keep telling me we did."

"You may as well start the grill."

"He'll be fair," Phil tells me. "No matter what you might think about Jeff, he's fair."

"I guess so."

"You don't think Jeff will be fair?"

"I think Jeff will be fair."

"And he could give us a Christian perspective."

"Yippee."

"Don't be sarcastic. We don't know what's going to happen."

Of course we know what's going to happen. I'm getting ready to get hit upside the head with a Bible. But I've been thinking about this all afternoon; I knew where Phil was heading before even he did, and besides, there are advantages to seeing Jeff. It might be good for down the road when I'm gone, and I think like this sometimes, I actually let myself use the phrase "when I'm gone." Phil will need someone to talk to, so maybe it's smart to draw Jeff into the situation, to maneuver him toward the hole I'm getting ready to rip in the middle of this family.

But Phil is still troubled by my calmness. He had evidently psyched himself up for a conversation with a hysteric and I'm denying him the chance to use all his best lines. "I thought you liked Jeff," he says.

"I do, but what does that have to do with anything?"

"He said the two of you had always had a certain rapport."

"And all this just came up out of nowhere? Come off it, Phil, I was sitting in Dr. Bennett's office when he called you."

"Jeff was thinking we could meet with him together one week and you could meet with him alone the next. That way I'd only—"

"Have to come in every other week? That would make more sense, wouldn't it? Since you're a dentist and important and I have all this free time."

"Jeff thinks—"

"No, it's fine," I say. "Just have one of your office girls set it up and cc me on the schedule. I'm waiting for you with the steaks, you know."

Still frowning, he heads outside to fire up the grill. The phone rings. Kelly.

"Turn on Channel 27," she says. Kelly often begins conversations like this, without preamble, and sometimes she hangs up without telling you as well. There have been plenty of times I've been left talking to empty air before I realized she was gone.

I hit the remote. An old movie is on. Elizabeth Taylor looking gorgeous and cracking up, Montgomery Clift trying to save her, Katharine Hepburn riding up and down the elevator in that creepy veiled hat with her creepy voice.

"Yeah," I say. "I love this one."

"Turn up the volume," says Kelly. "They're fixing to lobotomize that poor girl."

Elizabeth Taylor is in the asylum and it's all a horrible mistake. Montgomery is going to figure this out, of course, and save her, but he hasn't figured it out quite yet. Elizabeth has gotten out of her room and ended up in the section with the true lunatics. She's walking on a bridge over a pit of people who look crazy, or handicapped, or maybe just unbathed. Can't they see she isn't one of them? She's Elizabeth Taylor, for God's sake. Her makeup is perfect and her waist is so small. The inmates are shrieking at her, leaping up to grab at her ankles, and I can't seem to stop watching. There's no telling what Phil has told Jeff.

"Phil and I talked about it and decided to cancel the woman therapist," I tell Kelly. "We're going to see Jeff instead. We have our first session on Wednesday."

"Oh really?" says Kelly, "Wait a minute—here comes my favorite part." I turn the volume up a little higher and walk toward the screen. Montgomery is telling another doctor that he's done a professional diagnosis and concluded that Elizabeth is an erotomaniac.

"I love that," says Kelly. "Erotomaniac. This is a great damn movie."

"I know."

"Do you want to talk about the thing with Jeff?"

"Not now. We're grilling out."

"Oh, okay. What are you having?"

"Phil thinks that Jeff will be fair."

"Well, yeah, absolutely. I mean, after all, Jeff is Phil's best friend and everybody knows he's just crazy about you."

"He wants me to see Jeff alone one week and then we see Jeff as a couple the next week."

"When does Phil see Jeff?"

"You keep forgetting," I say. "Phil doesn't need counseling. There's nothing wrong with him."

"I don't like any of this. You should have your own therapist, Elyse."

"It's too bad Montgomery Clift is dead. I think he was the only man in America who could truly save me."

"Do you want me to come over?"

"No," I say. "We're cooking out. And I don't really care, Kelly, who I talk to or what we talk about. It's not like any of this is going to make any difference."

Phil comes in to get the tray of meat. He points at the phone and I mouth the word "Kelly," even though she's already hung up.

"I've got a question," I say.

He continues to sprinkle salt and pepper on the steaks.

"I've got a question."

"Oh." He looks up, pushes his glasses back with his index finger. "I thought you were on the phone."

"You know how you're always asking me why I'm unhappy? I've got a question for you. Why aren't you unhappy?"

"Do we have to do this now?"

"Seriously."

"Look around you. We've got a good life. We've got—"

"Yeah, I know. We've got Tory and the house and our friends and our health."

"And we've got each other."

"We don't talk."

"It seems to me like we talk all the time."

"We don't have fun."

"Well, there you've got me. But I don't think you're unhappy because we don't have fun. I think we don't have fun because you're unhappy. This could be fun. Right now. This. With the patio and the corn on the cob and the steaks."

He has a point. I stare at the TV screen. Montgomery Clift puts his arm around Elizabeth Taylor's shoulders.

"You get so overdramatic," Phil says. "You want too much."

"I don't understand why you don't want more."

"I do want more. I want peace."

Peace. He goes back out onto the deck. He has forgotten the tray of meat and I hang up the dead phone and carry it to him. He takes it from me and we both pause for a second, wordless, watching Tory beyond us in the yard. She is digging something.

He bought her a junior gardener set a few weeks ago so that she could help him with the landscaping and now she is furiously focused, striking the open ground around the hydrangea bushes over and over again with her pink plastic spade. Phil makes a half-gesture toward her but then drops his arm. Our eyes don't meet. I go back into the house, begin to unload the dishwasher. And then something strange happens.

I always load the knives pointy side down. Phil may think I'm overdramatic, but the truth is I am a creature of habit, cautious and ritualized. I always arrange the knives the same way, but tonight, as I reach into the basket of utensils, there is a single paring knife pointing up. Put there by someone else? No, I'm the only one who ever loads the dishwasher. A single paring knife, left, against habit, pointy side up, and as I reach down to remove it, I stab myself. The blade of the knife pushes right into my palm.

For a second it doesn't hurt, doesn't even bleed, but then the slash is obliterated by the blood rising and it pools in my hand and runs down my wrist. I have cut myself, possibly badly.

I could scream. I could call for help. I could go out on the deck and extend my palm toward my husband. I could show him my stigmata and I know that Phil would clean it up, and bind it, and tell me that nothing is ever as bad as it looks. He is good in these circumstances. Kind, calm, methodical. A man so kind that he still gives a day every month to the free clinic, a man who comes to Tory's school and talks about oral hygiene, who passes out toothbrushes and dental floss and teaches the kids some sort of rap song he made up about plaque. I feel lightheaded, shaky on my feet. My hand seems to have a pulse of its own and little gray paramecia are swimming across the surface of my vision. I twist a washtowel around my palm and shut my eyes. Breathe in and out slowly, press down the bubble of panic that is rising in my throat.

Seconds pass. It does not appear that I am going to faint. When I open my eyes, I go to my purse on the kitchen desk, where I always leave it, because I am a wife and a mother and a creature of habit who always leaves her purse in exactly the same place. Standing here, looking out the kitchen window, I can see my husband and my daughter. She has brought something to show him—a caterpillar maybe, since they're her favorites, or perhaps a pretty leaf or stone.

It's the familiar sting I always have when I observe Phil with Tory. He closes the hood on the grill and turns to her fully, crouching to her eye level. They bend their heads together, staring down into her flat palm, and it strikes me how much they look alike. They have the same profile. She is her father's daughter, but, perhaps even more to the point, he is my daughter's father. And of course I'm glad he gives himself up to the role, that she lives in the warm glow of his constant approval. Of course I'm glad she never has to work for his attention, and yet, watching them now through the window, there it is, the familiar sting. Because as he bends over her hand I can see that he is capable of caring. That his indifference to me is optional, a choice. Sometimes I tell myself that he is just wounded. This is what women say about men. That they can't show their feelings, that they can't speak their truth. That they're wired differently from us, almost as if they're a separate species, and that we shouldn't take their silence personally. But then I see Phil like this, lowering his knee down to the deck, taking Tory's hand in his, and I know that he's not as wounded as I have told myself. He could love me. He just doesn't.

The bleeding has almost stopped. I drop the damp washtowel to the desk and take the phone out of my purse.

I dial quickly. All ten numbers this time. "Gerry," I say, "it's Elyse."

Chapter Six

------◦⟨∞⟩◦------

Once a week the Women of the Church send food to shut-ins and new mothers and people who have had deaths in the family. It's mostly the old ladies who do this, except for Nancy, who not only heads up the Wednesday Friendship Tray project at our church but goes to another church to drive their Friday route as well. She's guilt-tripped Belinda into helping her, mostly because she's always telling everybody about how the trays are so heavy that the old ladies can't lift them into the van. If Belinda isn't there, Nancy has to carry thirty-five trays all by herself.

I have to walk past the church kitchen to get to Jeff's office. For a minute I think about going all the way around the building and coming in the back, but no, that would make it seem like I'm ashamed or something, and I have nothing to be ashamed of. Besides, the back door has an alarm that's easy to set off and that's all I need. I walk by the kitchen fast, but Belinda still sees me and says, "Elyse?" There's nothing to do but go in. She's alone, thank God, and she doesn't ask me why I'm there so early on a Wednesday morning. Nancy probably told her Phil and I were going to start counseling with Jeff. Nothing is private, at least not in a church as small as this one.

"I want you to look at something," Belinda says. "This is going to amaze you."

She walks me back to the double-door freezers and pulls them open. There, wrapped in tinfoil and stacked as neatly as bricks, are about a hundred casseroles.

"What are they for?"

"Emergencies," says Belinda.

"They must be expecting a lot of emergencies," I say, struggling to unstick a brick from the one beneath it. Each casserole has a three-by-five index card taped to the top with instructions and I squint down at the spidery handwriting. " 'Chicken-noodle mushroom casserole. Heat for an hour at 350.' My grandmother used to make this stuff."

"Mine too," says Belinda. "I don't think she ever made anything that didn't call for a can of Campbell's cream of mushroom soup. Look at this, look at these down at the bottom, they've got names on them. There's a whole bunch from Miss Bessie Morgan and she's been dead for years."

"How'd you even know they were in here?"

"Nancy got out three of them this morning. She's taking them by David Fontana's house." Belinda's voice drops, even though we are alone. "His wife left him."

It takes me a minute to think who she's talking about. "He doesn't even come to church here, his wife and kids do, and they only come at Christmas. Why is he getting three frigging casseroles?"

"I guess he's having an emergency."

"How many are they taking to his wife?"

Belinda seems confused by the question. "She left him, Elyse. She just up and walked out."

Phil is already in Jeff's office when I arrive and he's taken the time to change out of his dentist whites and into jeans. "You look good," I say. "Did you take the jeans to work?"

"Obviously."

Okay. So it's going to be that kind of day.

Jeff walks in, says hi, asks what we think of this weather. He seems prepared to make small talk, to ease us into what might be an awkward situation, but Phil evidently has a surgical scheduled for the afternoon.

"She's not happy," he says.

If Jeff is startled, he recovers fast. "Is that true, Elyse?"

"I'm not happy in the marriage, that much is true. But sometimes I'm happy. I'm happy when I'm with Tory or when I'm throwing pots or when I'm out on my own . . ."

Jeff waves his hand in the air as if he's trying to erase my words. "I don't get what you're saying."

I frown. "I don't get what you're saying."

"You have an odd way of talking about marriage. You say 'in the marriage' or 'out on my own' like it's some sort of door you go in and out of."

"Maybe it is."

"Are you kidding? You're always married. You're married every day, every second, whether Phil happens to be standing beside you or not."

"Okay, then, I'll be more blunt. You remember that sermon you gave a few months ago about gratitude? You said we should make a list of all the recent times we've felt joy in our lives, and I actually did. I went home and listed the last ten times I was really happy, and you were right, just seeing them on paper made me feel good. I thought, 'Well, I bitch a lot but when it comes down to it, I have a pretty great life.'"

"It's gratifying to know there's actually somebody out there listening."

"Yeah, well, the trouble is there's actually somebody out there thinking. Because when I looked at the list I noticed there was a common denominator to all ten of my happy times. Phil wasn't there."

I look over at Phil as I say this. I don't want to hurt him, and if he ever said anything like that, it would hurt me. But he doesn't look sad, just exasperated.

Jeff pushes back in his chair, fingers knit, peering over the tops of his heavy black glasses. They must have taught him this pose in counseling school. "What do you think that means?"

"It means I can be happy. I'm capable of it. I have the capacity for joy . . ."

"Just as long as I'm not there," Phil says.

Jeff turns to him. "Do you feel the same way, Phil, like your capacity for happiness is affected by whether or not Elyse is present?"

Phil smiles smugly. "I feel exactly the same whether she's there or not."

Jesus. Even I know that's the wrong answer.

Jeff decides to let it lie. He swivels his chair back toward me.

"Okay, so Elyse has the capacity for joy. Let's look at that more closely. Tell me about the last time you were happy."

I decide to tell him about the next-to-last time I was happy.

It wasn't that long ago, really. Two days before I met Gerry, back at the Phoenix art show. Several of the exhibitors were going out to dinner and they invited me to come, but I didn't feel like it. I'd been talking so much to customers and potential customers that my voice had gone hoarse. I considered room service but at the last minute I decided that no, I'd go somewhere great. I went back to the hotel room and showered and put on a nice dress and wore the scarf I got in Florence years ago. It drapes really beautifully and I went to a restaurant the concierge recommended.

"You went by yourself?"

"Yeah."

"That's interesting. Some women don't feel comfortable going to a restaurant alone."

"There's nothing wrong with a woman eating by herself," I say. This is going just great. He's probably going to stand up in the pulpit Sunday and announce to everybody that I'm an eroto-maniac.

"No, I think it's a good thing," he says. "Tell me about it."

It had been a wonderful night. It was one of those restaurants where the walls are all lined in mirrors. I sat down at the bar and I ordered foie gras and an arugula salad and a wine with this really beautiful name—something like Covenant of the Moon, but maybe I'm remembering that part wrong. And I sat there all alone and watched myself eat. I had slicked back my hair and I was wearing my pewter earrings, and the scarf of course, and when I looked at myself in the restaurant mirrors I decided I was pretty. Okay, not pretty exactly, but significant. I decided that I looked like a significant person. I didn't pull out a book like I usually do when I am alone in a restaurant. I just ate very slowly, and I looked at my reflection, and then at some point I began to look at the flowers. There were three blooms on each table—white, yellow, and orange—and the vases undulated in such a way that the flowers all fell in different directions. The brass bar fittings had been recently polished and I further noticed that above me someone had painted tiny gold stars across the deep purple ceiling. But mostly it was the mirrors, so many that when I headed toward what I thought was the exit, I'd only walked smack into another image of myself.

"So what made you happy?" Phil asks. "The fact that you looked good?" Poor Phil. It has to bug him, the way I slop around the house in cargo pants and dress up when I go out of town.

"No," says Jeff, who surprises me sometimes. "You were happy because you just gave yourself a moment and sat there and were open to everything."

"Yeah, I was open. And I was seen. I want to be seen."

"I see you," says Phil, and I swear he's trying to sneak a peek at his watch.

"I mean really seen. I'm happy whenever I'm noticed, even if it's just me noticing myself."

"You don't have to be in a restaurant in Phoenix to have that feeling," Jeff says. "There are ways to make you feel like that in your day-to-day life."

"Oh yeah, that's a great idea," says Phil. "We'll go home and cover all the walls in mirrors so she can watch herself coming and going just like Louis at Versailles or something. Will that make her happy?"

Jeff blinks, turns away as if he is embarrassed. He's not used to this side of Phil.

"I want you to see me," I say, even though I'm pretty sure that this is no longer true.

That night, during a station break, Phil asks, "What time were you thinking about going to bed?" It's his signal he wants to have sex and the weird thing is I want to have sex too. Gerry hasn't called me back. I know it's only been two days but the anticipation is running neck and neck with the disappointment and it's all worn me out. The phone rang about four, and when I picked it up there was no one on the other end. For a minute I almost said, "Gerry?" but of course that would be stupid and maybe it's best if he doesn't call me back because I am too stupid to have an affair. Stupid, stupid, stupid.

"Ten," I tell him, and saying that I'm going to bed early is my signal that yeah, tonight is okay. He grins and I remember, just for a second, how charmed I once had been by his boyishness and shagginess and his Amish-collared blue denim shirt. But that was eight years ago. Now we usually have sex in the shape of an X, with our heads facing in different directions, our bodies touching only where mine overlaps his at the pelvis. I believe I first saw this position in an old issue of *Cosmo* and at the time I thought it would be fun, something different, the sort of thing you try every once in a while. I brought the magazine to bed that night and Phil glanced at it and said, "Can do." I'm not sure exactly when it became our default position, but now we move into it without consultation. You can't kiss in the X. You don't look into each other's eyes. But the advantage is that one person doesn't crush the other person's chest and neither of you has to hold your weight in that kind of unnatural push-up. I'm not sure at what point Phil and I first realized how heavy we are.

Twenty minutes later, after brushing teeth and putting the cats out and checking the locks on the doors and setting the alarm, we get into bed. We move toward the middle.

I lie back, close my eyes. Once you're in the X it's easy to forget where you are. It's easy to imagine you're with someone else—in fact, it's easy to imagine that you are someone else. Two thousand dollars and some bank stock won't go far. I need to take every commission I can, even the crappy ones, and I need to stay at least another year. That means fifty-two more times in the X position, fifty-six if we go away on vacation. Phil makes a halfhearted effort to pull me on top of him but I roll back and when we connect at the hips and he starts his familiar rocking rhythm I think that it's not bad, really, it's kind of calming and sweet. Gerry has not called and I am being ridiculous. What if I break a marriage and a family only to arrive at the same place? What if this thing that seems to be a doorway turns out to be just another mirror? Maybe I'm doomed to spend eternity walking into reflections of myself and saying, "Damn, I guess it was my fault, after all." Maybe Jeff is right, that there are ways to feel like a significant person in my day-to-day life. The last track on the fourth CD of the marriage series suggested new lingerie. I suppose I could do that. Sure, it's a cliché, but clichés sometimes work. Phil mumbles something, slips a hand underneath my hip to turn me a little more toward him and get the angle better. It's not so bad, I tell myself, it's really sort of pleasant, but then I wonder how I would have felt this afternoon if it had been Gerry's voice on the line and I know, in my secret tiny heart, that I would do anything to be back in that Traveler's Chapel in Dallas. I'm beginning to think I'm like Elizabeth Taylor in an old movie, that there is something fundamentally wrong with my mind, that I can't seem to see anything the way a normal woman would.

I made a mistake when I married Phil and I know I'm going to have to pay for that mistake—the only question is, how long am I going to have to keep paying? It seems like I have already been paying for a very long time. And Gerry, Gerry is a player, definitely a player. Definitely unavailable, definitely too polished of a kisser, definitely married, definitely the wrong choice. Not to mention the fact that he hasn't called back. Phil was a mistake and Gerry probably is too—but sometimes it seems like the only way to erase one mistake is to make another. "I need to . . ." Phil says, and I tell him it's okay, I'm not close. He pounds for a few seconds, shudders, and rolls off of me, his hand brushing my hair in what I can only assume is a gesture of affection. "Sorry," he whispers, and I tell him that I'm fine.

Chapter Seven

The coach-pitch coach calls and, as I predicted, Phil is thrilled. I take Tory to the first day of conditioning, where she is the youngest by six months and a full head shorter than the next shortest kid.

But I think the coach likes Tory. He keeps coming over to the fence to make little comments about her, looking down at me in his reflector shades as if he were a cop. T-ball is one thing, he tells me, but she's ready to start hitting a moving target. And that's what separates the men from the boys. Most people see something coming right at them and they freeze. Do I know what he means? I know what he means.

Then he moseys his way back to the infield, walking not quite all the way to the mound, because he doesn't want to have to throw too hard. Tory looks so small at the plate and when she puts on the helmet her head is as huge and wobbly as an alien's. The coach throws and she swings way too late. The ball smacks the chain-link fence behind her and the assistant coach retrieves it and throws it back. "You got yourself a good look at it," says the coach, who throws again, a slow, high-arced pitch that gives her plenty of time to think. Apparently too much time. Tory stands there as the ball floats past her. My phone rings and I dig in my purse for it, my eyes still on Tory. "Now you're ready," says the coach.

A man's voice asks, "Is this the right number?"

"What?"

"Is this your cell phone? You're a hard person to find."

I jump up so fast that the folding chair collapses under me. I walk to the end of the fence out of earshot of the other mothers. "This is Elyse," I tell him.

"Yeah, I know who you are," he says. "I just called you, remember?" Then he goes on to tell me that he had Googled me, but he was spelling my name wrong. He thought I'd said Burden, not Bearden, but he kept trying different combinations and finally Google asked him, "Do you mean Elyse Bearden?" And from there he got the name of a gallery in Charleston that carried my pots and called the manager and lied and said he collected me and that he wanted to commission something specific and she'd given him my number. Only that was my home number, and when he called a child had answered and he'd panicked and hung up. Then he checked his cell and got the message from me.

I am laughing. I don't know why. Everything he says to me is funny.

"Have you always been this hard to find?"

"I don't know. I can't remember the last time anybody looked for me."

"Where are you? Can you talk?"

"I'm at the ball field. My daughter is only seven but they want her in coach-pitch. It's the first practice." The coach releases the ball, and Tory looks up at it, the helmet shifting, dropping, nearly covering her eyes.

"That's great," says Gerry. "Coach-pitch already?"

"Tell me again," I say. "Tell me how hard it was to find me," and he does the whole story all over again, including the Charleston gallery owner's accent, how she's always saying "oot" instead of "out" like she's British royalty or some damn thing. How he normally checks his cell every day but he'd lost the charger, left it in Arizona maybe, and then when he finally bought a new one and got the phone back up he'd had twenty-seven messages, including the one from me. His voice sounds different than I remember and there is something unreal about the situation, something magical and electric. I have never thought before about the science of a ringing phone, but now I am entranced with the miracle of our connection—the idea of satellites above us in the dark of space, releasing signals, wavelengths of impulses bouncing from one solid thing to another, so that the sounds leave his mouth and travel immeasurable distances before they reverberate within my ear. The coach releases the ball and Tory swings, the effort nearly pulling her off her feet.

"She said you were talented," he tells me. "She said I'd be smart to get as much of you as I could."

"She's right," I say. I am standing very straight, gripping the chain-link fence. My posture perfect, as if he can see me.

"Do you like being a potter?"

"It gives me freedom."

The coach steps a few feet closer and tries again.

"Freedom in the sense that it would be easy for you to get away for a couple of days?"

"Oh my God. My daughter just hit her first softball." The ball falls between second and third and the kids, some of whom have become so bored that they're actually lying down in the infield, push up to their knees and watch it roll past. Tory's coach turns toward me and grins.

"She hit it?"

I tell him that she not only hit it, she hit it solid. He says that sometimes he hates the bank. Sometimes he thinks there's a whole other life out there. Teaching, or running a bike repair shop in Key West. Something real. Something simple. Something with heart. Do I ever think about it, that we might all have another life out there? A pop, louder than the first, and this time Tory's ball is high in the air, dropping somewhere in the empty green field behind third.

It's been so long since I've felt desire that at first I mistake it for the flu.

There has to be some explanation for why I wake up queasy the next morning, why I have to place a hand on each side of the bathroom sink until I can steady myself. When I look up at the mirror, my face is pale and foreign.

It's a bit like pregnancy, but I'm not pregnant. I take a small blue pill every morning, and I am happy that Phil didn't have the vasectomy we considered several years ago, that we opted to keep, as he says, this door open. For it gives me an excuse to take the pills and perhaps . . . I haven't asked Gerry this. He has three children so there's a very good chance he's been, as Phil would say, clipped. I don't know how to ask the question so it's good I don't have to. I push the pill through the tinfoil and swallow it.

All day I am languid and fitful. I can't seem to concentrate on the wheel and I wander back into the den and surf channels until I find a Bette Davis movie. Maybe I'm sick, I think, as I lie on the couch. I blow off walking with the girls and nothing sounds good for lunch. When I go for carpool at two I mistakenly turn into the driveway for the school buses and have to do an awkward three-point turn while the mothers in the other cars sit and watch. I drop off the first kid and when Tory whines to get out at her friend Taylor's house I walk with the girls to the kitchen door and ask Taylor's mother if it would be okay. She says of course, it's fine, and that I do look a little tired. It might be the flu, I tell her, and she says yeah, she hears something's going around.

All day I've kept my cell phone in my bra. I turned it off for carpool and when I get home I check for messages. But of course he hasn't called. It's only been one day. He won't call every day. I go out to the garage and sit at the wheel. I walk out in the yard and pull some weeds. I lie down on the bed and get back up. I put a load of laundry in the washer but do not turn it on.

At 4:16 my breast vibrates.

"I think I'm getting sick," I tell him.

He says he doesn't feel that great himself.

Chapter Eight

I'm standing in front of a circular table in Frederica's Lingerie, my hands sunk into a stack of eggplant and cinnamon camisoles. I've read that in order to sell things to women you should name colors after foods. Artichoke and eggshell and mango and cabernet. It sounds logical. Women are always hungry.

The mall is nice in the morning, before the teenagers come, when they play classical music and the sun from the skylights falls across the slate tiles. Through the open doors of the shop I can see the courtyard fountains throbbing in their irregular rhythms, shooting arteries of water high into the air. It's the kind of fountain you want to wade into, climbing the marble steps in stiletto boots, standing over the jets until the pattern changes course and a cannonball of water rises up between your legs.

"Ready?" The saleswoman, who has announced her name to be Tara, holds out her hands and I release the clothes to her and follow her to the dressing room. It is small but pretty, with a padded chair and framed oval mirror, and I stand back while Tara struggles to fit the hangers on pegs. There's too much stuff here. Too many choices. The sign of a woman who doesn't know what she wants or what she wants to be.

I strip down to my high-waisted cotton underwear and begin to go through my options. Loose, drapey pajamas that remind me of Katharine Hepburn movies. She always thinks she can jerk

Spencer Tracy around, but he's way too much man for her. I button the pajamas and stand tall in front of the mirrors. Tara calls through the slats in the door that she has hot tea brewing and I say that's nice, I'd love a cup. I move on to the kimonos. They're my favorites anyway, the way they hide everything and yet can fall to the floor at any moment. One swift pull of the silk tie at your hips, and it's done. Tara brings in the tea while I wrap a yellow and tangerine sarong beneath my armpits. This is good—light and campy. Dorothy Lamour joking around on the beach with Bob and Bing and my shoulders look strong above the knotted cloth. I ask Tara about those hose with the elastic tops, the kind that are supposed to stay up by themselves. Do they really work and would she bring me a pair in black, medium opaque?

Frederica's is full of ghosts. The last time I was here I was lingerie shopping with Kelly just before she married Mark. When they heard that Kelly was shopping for her honeymoon, they put us in the dressing room on the end, a room so large it had a pedestal for her to stand on and a full sofa for me. The salesgirl kept calling Kelly "the bride" in hushed tones, as if she were referring to the recently deceased, and irritation had flashed across Kelly's face, so fast that only someone who knows her as well as I do would have even noticed. It's like when people are all the time saying she's pretty. Kelly hates being reduced. But the salesgirl had insisted on bringing these big flowing peignoir sets, formless filmy clouds of pink and white.

"They look like something Eva Gabor would wear to make flapjacks," Kelly said, handing them back.

The girl was too young to get the reference to Eva Gabor and flapjacks but she did seem to understand that we would be requiring something sexier. She returned with a black bustier with long flapping garters, and Kelly had nodded and begun pulling off her jeans. Her body still looked great, her waist as tapered as always. I flopped down on the sofa and watched her struggle to pull on the bustier, writhing like a snake trying to get back into its skin. It was a punishing sort of garment, thrusting her breasts out the top and cupping her hips into an exaggerated curve. I asked her how you took it off when it was time to have sex.

"You don't, silly, that's the whole point," she said, and she'd twirled in the mirror, the garters slapping her thighs like small whips. The salesgirl had brought us champagne—another perk, I suppose, if you're in the big dressing room at the end that is evidently the Frederica's equivalent of a bridal suite. It was clear that she wanted us to be happier than we were. She produced the champagne flutes with such a flourish that I think she expected us to squeal, maybe applaud or propose a toast. When Kelly just said, very calmly, "That's fine, put them down on the table," the girl's face had fallen in momentary disappointment. But she pushed it aside with a professional smile and finally left me and Kelly alone. Kelly insisted that I try on something too and—even though I was a little self-conscious about how my post-baby body looked in comparison to hers—I stood up and yanked off my jeans and grabbed the first hanger on the peg. It was a red satin teddy that kept sliding down my shoulders as I popped the champagne cork.

For the next hour Kelly and I gulped the cheap champagne, and we swapped the camisoles and slips and teddies back and forth in a wild, pointless effort to mute our grief. Even though we were speculating about which of these garments might best seduce her fiancé or my husband, the truth is we were really deep in mourning for men who weren't there. The man who had left her, the man who had not yet come for me. When Kelly had climbed up onto the pedestal, holding the empty champagne bottle with her cheeks bright pink and her hair disheveled, I had almost asked her what she would do if Daniel came back. I had never told her that he called me that time, never told her that his cell phone number was scribbled on the last page of my phone book under the single letter D. "Leave her alone," I had told him. "You broke her heart once and I'll kill you if you show up here and break it again." It sounded good at the time I said it but when I saw her there in that dressing room, so flushed, so beautiful, and so in despair, I wondered if I was really trying to protect her. Maybe I just knew that if Daniel returned and swept her away that I would be left, for the first time, utterly alone.

This is not a happy story. Why am I remembering it now? I exhale sharply and pull a plum camisole over my head. It looks good against my skin. Tara pushes open the door. She has the black hose and an armful of bras as well. She wants me to try them. She says they're the most comfortable bras on the market, and once women try them on they get one in every color. You know how it is. Ladies will do anything to find a really comfortable bra, and I realize this is how I look to her, like a woman who buys in bulk.

"Bring me some of those black satin heels," I say. "The ones in the window." I sit down on the little chair and pull the stockings on carefully. I love the sound the nylon makes when one leg rubs against the other and I imagine the rough tug of Gerry's hands pushing my knees apart, Gerry's head sliding up between my thighs. Tara knocks at the door, hands the shoes in without a word. They're too small but I jam my feet into them anyway and stand up in front of the mirror. This is all quite nasty and lovely, the way the shoes lift your legs up to the eye level of the consumer, and isn't that what they do with candy at the checkout counter, after all? It's the way of the world. What you see is what you want, and I would like to be candy at the checkout counter, at least once in a while. I would like to be the guilty pleasure, that thing you know isn't good for you but you grab it anyway. You grab it hastily, guiltily, looking over your shoulder to make sure that your gluttony is unobserved. I stand shakily in the high-heeled shoes, turning my hips one way and then the other in front of the mirror and murmuring, "Would you like some of this, sir?"

"You're sure you don't need the bras?" Tara asks, but within five minutes I am out and walking through the mall, with the shoes, the plum-colored silk slip, a silvery camisole, and the elastic hose nestled inside a swirl of hot pink tissue paper. I am humming as I swing the bag back and forth in my palm, headed toward the bistro where I will meet Nancy for lunch. Headed toward Gap Kids where I will buy a parka for Tory, toward Home + Garden where I will stir the tails of each wind chime hanging in a row, my eyes closed, swaying in a small and private dance. Headed toward Nordstrom where I will spray a different perfume on each wrist, headed toward Barnes & Noble where there are so many stories of so many people who have loved and lost in so many ways, headed past the courtyard fountains and through the puddles of light that spill across the pretty slate floor. Headed wherever it is that women like me go.

Chapter Nine

———•◦∞◦•———

What do you want?" Jeff asks me.

"That's just it, I'm not entirely sure. I know, I know, you're thinking that it's unfair to make Phil try to guess what I want when I don't even know myself."

Jeff shakes his head. "You sound human. But you've gotta know something—Phil is very sure about what he wants. He wants to keep this family together at any cost."

"At any cost?"

"Those were his exact words."

"I guess it's easy to say 'at any cost' when you know the bill is going to be delivered to somebody else."

Jeff sits back in his chair and folds his hands very carefully in front of him.

"Didn't you think it was weird," I ask him, "that Phil was the one who called to schedule our counseling?"

It was damn weird and he knows it. "Couples have all sorts of arrangements," he says. "I thought maybe at your house Phil was the one who scheduled the family appointments."

"Please. He wouldn't know the name of Tory's teacher or her pediatrician if you held a gun to his head. He just wanted to make sure we ended up here. He wanted to make sure that this whole thing would be argued in a court that was sympathetic to him."

"I take it you don't think the church is as responsive to the needs of women as it is to the needs of men."

"Bingo."

"Well, you're right. Of course you're right. But you're not talking to the church, Elyse, you're talking to me." Jeff rubs his eyes. "Does it make you uncomfortable—that we're all friends?"

"I thought about putting up a fight for my own therapist. It doesn't seem like too much to ask, that I'd just go out and hire somebody like a normal person, but then I thought that it's not that big a deal and I should just give Phil what he wants. Keep it within the family."

"The church family."

I laugh. I'm not sure why. "Yeah, the church family."

"You sound like you've thrown in the towel and we haven't even started."

What can I say? He's right. "Don't take this the wrong way," I say, "but it doesn't matter who we talk to. It's too late."

"Phil said one other thing. He doesn't think you've fully considered what all this could mean for Tory."

He starts talking about those studies that show, even now, that children from broken homes don't do as well in school. They have sex earlier, their own marriages fail. I've read the same studies. Then there are the biographies. Go to the library, pick one up. The famous person came from a broken home and from there the dominoes begin to fall. There's something different about these people, these children of divorce. They walk with their legs farther apart than the rest of us, like they grew up on a boat. These are the people who've learned to expect changes at any minute. They may grow up to be famous, but they're not happy.

Jeff pulls off his glasses and I wonder, not for the first time, if they're real. They have thick, heavy black frames like the kind Michael Caine used to wear and I've never seen Jeff use them anywhere outside this office. "Of course I know what happens to the kids," I tell him. "That's all that's keeping me here." Which is a small lie but one I figured would shut Jeff up. I wouldn't put it past him to wear fake glasses. Jeff has a lot of props.

"I don't know, Elyse, you just seem so . . ." Jeff stops, fumbles for a word.

"Angry? Stubborn?"

"Well, yeah, of course you're angry and stubborn, but there's something else going on."

"You think I'm scared? You think like Phil does, that I make these wild statements but when push comes to shove I'm too scared to go out there and live on my own. You think I'm just some dentist's wife living in a four-hundred-thousand-dollar house with twenty bucks in her purse who talks this big game but doesn't have the balls to see it through."

Jeff fidgets a minute, straightens the Bible on his desk. I wonder if it's an unconscious gesture or a bit of a threat. Phil has made it here first, practically painted the walls with his interpretation of events. It's very hard to prove you're not crazy. Hard to prove you're not selfish. Almost impossible to prove you're not paranoid. No matter what I say, Jeff—well, all of them, really, the whole chorus—will try to call me back. My reasons will never be good enough. My explanations will always fall flat. The only way I'd be allowed to leave this marriage is by stretcher.

"What happened to your hand?"

"What?"

"Your hand. Why is it bandaged?"

"Phil accused me of being overdramatic so I stabbed myself in the palm."

Jeff has a strange look on his face and we sit there for a long time before he finally speaks. "Marriage is funny, isn't it?"

"Hilarious." I stare at the cross behind his head and bite my lip. For some reason, he's the last person I want to see me cry.

As I walk down the hall from Jeff's office I see Lynn standing in the atrium, talking to a man with a clipboard. Evidently the church has decided to go ahead with the renovations and she has taken charge of getting the estimates. She is wearing a pale pink suit, a Chanel-style knockoff, and she seems absurdly overdressed for the occasion. Her hair is blown into a neat little cap and she looks good in the suit, slender and tastefully accessorized. The fact that she's stopped walking with us doesn't seem to have affected her weight. Lynn is disciplined and always has been. When we used to go out to eat for book club she would order an appetizer and swear she was full.

I start to wave at her, but that feels wrong. She's trying to be professional. She's trying to figure out what her new job is. The last thing she needs is me hanging around.

Gerry says give him a minute and he'll call me back. When he says "a minute" my heart sinks. It was a mistake to call. He calls me. I don't call him. Maybe he thinks I'm being pushy. Maybe he's already starting to feel trapped. But I drive to the mall anyway and pull into the far side of the parking lot, the section that only fills up around Christmas. I've only been there a few seconds when the phone rings.

"Sorry," he says. "I had to find an empty conference room."

"I just left a counseling session," I say. "This time it was only me and Jeff."

"Did he talk mean to you?"

"No. That's the bad part. He was nice."

"I've got to tell you something," Gerry says. "Don't laugh at me."

I am giggling already. "What?"

"I get hard dialing your number."

"No you don't," I say, although the thought makes me absurdly happy. I am smiling at the steering wheel.

"I swear. I'm like Pavlov's dog. I hit that 704 and go hard as a rock. Where are you?"

"The mall parking lot. The far corner, where they put tires on your car at Sears."

"Very romantic. Where's your hand?"

I look down at my bandaged palm. "You're always worried about where my hand is."

"Can you talk?"

"I have to be at the school—"

"Not until 2:05." He knows my schedule. "I'm not asking you to fly to Europe, I just need five minutes."

"I've never done phone sex."

"We're not having phone sex. God, that sounds awful. We're talking, that's all. Nobody gets in trouble for talking." An outrageous lie, but I find myself laughing anyway. The clock on my dashboard says 1:15.

Five minutes later my underwear is stretched down around my knees and my head is flung back against the car seat. He asks if that will hold me for a little while.

"I think so," I tell him.

I call him back that afternoon.

Chapter Ten

On Saturday mornings the kids come with us to the track and they play on the swings and climbing forts of the elementary school playground while we walk. Kelly and I are moving fast today, fast enough that we break away from Belinda and Nancy. A group of cheerleaders is practicing in the middle of the loop, building pyramids and collapsing, taking long flipping runs down the field and rounding off.

"Look at those girls," I say. "They're so young and pretty."

Kelly sighs. "It's a long life."

Tory has decided she wants to walk with us. She is trotting to stay with our pace but evidently it's worth it for the chance to be let in on adult conversation. She looks at the girls too, then back at us. "When you and Mommy were cheerleaders did you throw each other in the air?"

"Not anything like what they're doing," Kelly says. "We weren't gymnasts back then. We didn't go away to camps and learn fancy stuff. But we did have this one lift . . ."

"You lifted Mom?"

"She lifted me."

"Kelly was what we called a flyer," I say. "I was a catcher so I stayed down below."

"Why did they put you on the bottom?"

"Because your mom was strong enough to pick me up."

"Oh, tell her the truth," I say. "I was always on the bottom because I never had the guts to jump."

"You never trusted me to catch you."

"It's true," I admit. I put two fingers up to my throat to feel for my pulse. "I've never trusted anybody to catch me."

"You kept making a big deal about that time I dropped Tracy McLeod."

"Who's Tracy McCrowd?" Tory asks, reaching out to hold Kelly's hand.

"Some whiny little nobody who completely doesn't matter. But one time I kind of dropped her and your mom never got over it. I think it was the way Tracy kept limping around school telling everybody that her ankle was broken."

"Her ankle *was* broken."

"Tory, do you remember that story you made up when you were little?" Kelly asks, clearly ready to change the subject. We have been walking at this pace for twenty minutes and she is getting a little breathless. "You climbed on my lap and I wrote it down and then your mom put it in your baby book. It was about being a cheerleader."

"You wrote it down?"

"Well, yeah, but I remember it by heart." We come to a stop as Kelly clears her throat and recites:

> *Once upon a time there was born a baby girl.*
> *She was a ballerina.*
> *She was a cheerleader.*
> *Then she was a wiff.*
> *Then she died.*

Tory frowns. "What's a wiff?"

"You were probably trying to say 'wife,'" I tell Tory, smiling at the memory. "But it was kind of strange that you knew 'ballerina' and 'cheerleader' but you didn't know the word for 'wife.'"

"You were so funny," said Kelly. "I would have written down everything you ever said if I could."

Tory nods, as if that would have indeed been a sensible response to her brilliant youth. We begin to walk again and she gazes at the cheerleaders. "Were you and Mommy pretty?"

"Oh God, we were gorgeous."

"And your aunt Kelly could fly."

"It wasn't really flying. It was more like falling."

Tory looks up at Kelly. "Will you teach me how to fall?"

"There's nothing to teach. You just let go."

Tory squints into the little frown she gets when she's thinking hard. She wants to believe Kelly, but some part of her is unconvinced.

"It's not like you're really learning anything," Kelly says, staring out at the field, out at the young girls climbing on top of each other. "It's more like forgetting something. But I'll lift you up and drop you if you want . . ."

"Okay," Tory says, but her voice is soft.

". . . and your mom can catch you because your mom is the strongest woman in the world. Just ask her."

"It's two different kinds of strength, that's all."

Tory is still not sure. "How high would you fly?"

"She could do a full inverted pike," I say. "She was the best."

"Do you have a picture of it?"

I laugh. Typical Tory. She wants proof.

"I think I can dig one up," says Kelly, laughing too. "You've got to give us a break, Tory. We weren't always wiffs."

Chapter Eleven

Kelly was in love once.

The man was married. She told me this defiantly one morning when we were sitting in front of our favorite coffeehouse, the one with an Asian-looking patio and Frank Lloyd Wright–style light fixtures. I don't remember how I felt or what I said. I'd only been married about a year or so myself. I probably told her marriage was a door people walk in and out of, something ridiculous like that. But I must have said enough that she knew I wasn't going to judge her, that I wasn't going to frown and ask her just exactly where she thought all this was heading.

In those days Kelly always seemed to be slightly drunk. Perhaps that's because I was pregnant with Tory and not drinking myself, so I was in a position to better observe her increasing giddiness. She was telling me about all the men she'd dated during the time we'd fallen out of touch, how sometimes she would give them blow jobs just because she was uncomfortable, and dropping to your knees seemed like a good thing to do when you weren't sure what to do next. "Isn't that awful?" she said. "Isn't that sad?"

I shook my head because there isn't a woman alive who at some point hasn't looked at an erect penis and thought, "Oh Christ, what's the fastest way I can deal with this?"

"Yeah, it's awful," I said. "It's awful and it's sad and it happens all the time."

But sex with this new man—it was furtive, ecstatic. It was, she said, dropping her voice to a whisper, sort of a religion. All of a sudden, here at the age of thirty she had met this man and—she flapped her hands around, at a loss to explain it. They were doing everything, they were trying it all. He wanted her to blindfold him. He wanted her to tie him up with some sort of rubber tubing left over from when he'd hurt his back and had physical therapy. They did it in swivel chairs, in cars, on the picnic tables of a park near her house. Once, in a gas station restroom, they ripped the sink completely loose from the wall. "That BP station at the corner of Providence and Rama," she said. "You know the one?"

I nodded, so deeply shocked and sick with jealousy that I could hardly hold myself upright in my chair.

"It's amazing," she said. "It's like it never ends."

To prove the point, her phone rang. Kelly was the first person I knew who had a cell phone, and she had one back when they were big and heavy and only worked if you were outdoors and standing on a hill. I always wondered why she would own such a thing, but now it made sense. She fished the phone out of her purse, answered it, and turned toward me as if to include me in the conversation. "No," she said, "no, I'm with Elyse. She's right here. It's okay. She's my best friend and she totally gets it." A longer pause. She looked at me. "You want to talk to him?"

I almost shook my head. She might think that I totally got it, but to me it seemed like we were growing farther apart than we'd ever been. Here I was pregnant and driving a minivan that still had that new-car smell and sticker marks on the windows and she's ripping the sinks out of BP stations. "Do you want me to?" I asked, and she nodded.

"Talk dirty. You used to be good at that."

I guess talking dirty is like riding a bicycle. I sat there and spun out this whole story about him being under the table while she and I were having coffee. I said things I'd never say if I knew him, things I'd never say if I thought he could see me, but it was strangely intoxicating, this disembodied voice of an unknown man coming out of the phone saying, somewhat frantically, "And then what, and then what?"

Kelly was bent double in a fit of giggles and later she said my story was perfect, that this was his fantasy, two women, and that he was always submissive, always held captive and forced to serve them in some way. We were barely thirty. We were too young to realize that's what they all want. We believed we'd stumbled on some sort of miracle, how easy it was to taunt this man, how desperate he seemed for every syllable of every promise.

But then I got nervous. I don't remember why. Perhaps someone else came out on the patio. Perhaps I caught a glimpse of myself in the coffee shop window and remembered that I was pregnant. I was not one of those pregnant women who glowed. I was perpetually sweaty and queasy with a splotchy face and Phil and I hadn't had sex for three months, not since the night where I had suddenly, right in the middle of things, turned and thrown up on the bed. Kelly was smiling, leaning across the table and nodding to encourage me on, but when I saw my reflection in the window I stopped talking. The man on the phone was silent. Finally I said, "I hope I haven't made a bad first impression," and he said, "Quite the contrary, I don't ever remember anyone ever making such a good first impression." I handed her back the phone and said, "He's adorable."

She raised it to her ear, listened a minute, and then smirked at me. "No," she said. "I told you. Elyse and I are going to the movies. I won't be back until five." Then she paused again and said, "No, I don't think she'd be game and don't use words like that. It makes it sound like you're planning to shoot her."

In the months that followed, I was the only witness to their affair. Kelly would call, giggly and talking fast, and I would assure her that I wasn't asleep anyway. I rarely was. And through the restless nights of late pregnancy and the long sessions of breastfeeding that followed I would bend my head to hold the phone in the crook of my neck and I would listen as the words flooded out of her, stories that she told all out of sequence, stories that seemed to have no logical beginning or end. Stories that opened with a mumble of, "My God, I don't know how to tell you . . ."

She would pause sometimes, even in the middle of her wildly careening life, and say, "How was your day?" But, my God, I didn't know how to tell her. For starters, I often didn't know what day it was. And while life gives us words for what she was going through, there didn't seem to be any words for what was happening to me. How can you describe hours where you stare at a baby's hand or whole days in which you seem to be neither asleep nor awake? Everything around her was risky and sharp, but I was moving into a world without edges. Padding around beds, pillows stacked against fireplaces, locks on cabinets, plastic discs covering the holes in electrical outlets, vaporizers that muffled every sound into a soft dull purr. How could I explain a world in which it was impossible to get hurt? "My day was fine," I would say. "Tell me more."

Of course she couldn't understand my pillowed life, of course she couldn't slow down to look around. Of course she had tunnel vision; she was in a tunnel. There is a time to draw back and see the big picture, a time to consider another point of view, but not then. "Do I talk about him too much?" she would ask, and then immediately add, "I know, I know, I talk about him too much." But these brief moments of lucidity were not enough to slow the process she was being pulled into. Something primordial was happening to her and to ask her to stop and look around would have been like asking a woman in labor if she'd like to discuss politics. She would tell you, quite rightly, that at the moment she had other things on her mind.

Although I never said this out loud, I couldn't conceive of any way that Kelly and Daniel would end up together. Marriage is not designed for that kind of passion. It would be like pouring boiling water into a glass pitcher. I imagined Kelly breaking, flying into shards and bouncing in a thousand pieces across my kitchen floor.

Part of me wanted to rouse ~~myself from my~~ stupor and tell her to be careful, but another part of me knew that what I called protectiveness was really just envy. Romantic lightning finally hits, after all these years of waiting, and it doesn't strike me, it strikes the person standing right beside me. Even if Daniel was a cad and an infidel, they were creating some phenomenal stories. And we needed those stories. She needed to tell them, and as I sat in the dark, rocking, with my daughter fussing in my arms, I needed to hear them.

She was my best friend. It happened to one of us, and so, in a way, it happened to both of us.

Their plan was actually pretty simple. Daniel would ask for a transfer to St. Louis based on his theory that it would be easier for him and Kelly to start fresh in a new town. When the transfer came through he would tell his wife he wanted a divorce. Clean and quick, just like that. He'd go and his wife would stay here. He'd let her have the house, of course, that seemed only fair. ("There's always a guilt tax," he once told me. "But when the time comes you're more than willing to pay it.") Kelly would join him a few months later. His wife would never know he'd been having an affair. His kids would never think of Kelly as the evil stepmother who broke up their somewhat happy home.

He went to St. Louis. He never sent for her. After a week of frantic speculation she finally called him, only to find that his cell number had been disconnected. His company said that he was no longer in their employ. No, he hadn't left any sort of forwarding address. When we drove past his old house there was a SOLD sign in the yard.

"The only thing on earth that could possibly make this moment more pathetic," Kelly said grimly as we sat in the end of the cul-de-sac staring at the empty house, "is if I turned to you right now and told you I was pregnant."

I was the one who took her to have the abortion. Tory was

five months old by then and I may be the only woman who has ever shown up at an abortion clinic with a baby in her arms. I felt funny sitting there nursing her in the waiting room, so once they called Kelly back I carried Tory outside and walked her back and forth. When the women coming up the sidewalk would see me, they probably thought I was there to stage some sort of protest. The only thing worse than me greeting them with pictures of mangled fetuses was me greeting them with an actual infant. They were mostly girls, really, not women, mostly very young and terrified-looking. For some reason Kelly had insisted on going to the public clinic where the chairs were plastic and there were pamphlets about STDs and domestic violence and AIDS everywhere. Okay, I'd figured, if she's hell-bent on punishing herself by paying eighty-nine dollars for a cut-rate abortion, the least I can do is sit and wait for her. She'd looked over at one point on the drive there and asked, "How'd you even know how to get here? This is hardly your part of town."

"This is where I met Phil," I reminded her.

"You met Phil at an abortion clinic?"

"Of course not."

I said it too quickly, my voice too sharp with denial. I took a deep breath, glanced at Tory sleeping in the backseat, then at Kelly's profile. "He was volunteering at the free dental clinic and my mother asked me to take this kid—"

"Oh right, I remember," she said, her voice vague as if she were slipping down the side of something. "The free clinic. That's where you met Saint Phil."

I walked and paced and bounced Tory for over an hour, until I finally saw Kelly emerge from the door, pale and clutching a bottle of orange juice. "I don't want to talk about it," she said and I strapped Tory in the car seat and drove us all home. We didn't know that was the only time she would ever be pregnant.

She suffered for exactly one year.

She suffered so hard that she scared me. I would call her every morning and I saw her almost every day. She kept Tory when

Phil and I went out and each time she came to visit she brought her a gift, wildly impractical dresses and books more suitable for a ten-year-old. And then—a year to the day after I took her to the clinic—she called me and said, "Enough."

"Okay," I said. "Enough."

"It's a long life, Elyse."

"I know," I said. "A very long life. And we have a lot of it left."

"Do you know what day this is?"

"Yeah."

"That's why I figured it's time to say enough."

She was true to her word. We very rarely spoke of Daniel and after a while it almost came to seem like she and I had experienced some sort of collective hallucination. When I happened to go into the bathroom at the BP at the corner of Providence and Rama, the sink looked like any other bathroom sink. Kelly got a better job and then an even better one. She began to date other men—handsome men, men with good jobs, men who took her on exotic vacations. I could not count how many now if I tried, largely because in most cases I never knew their names. She and I had a rule that until she had dated a man for a month, I didn't have to bother to learn his name but rather had permission to call him merely "the boy." Even now when she and I speak of that time we call it the Year of Many Boys.

And then one day she said that she was going to marry Mark. She had come to my house to tell me and she had brought something with her, a packet bound with a rubber band. All the letters Daniel had written her during their affair.

"Burn them," she said.

Flipping through, I could see that there were ten, maybe twelve of them and they were in chronological order, which surprised me. Kelly isn't usually that organized.

"It doesn't look like much, does it?" she said. "But then, when I stop and think about it, I didn't know him for very long."

Holding the letters made me feel a little sick. "Are you sure you want me to do this?"

"You have to. I can't do it myself."

That night, after Tory was down and Phil was asleep I got up and built a fire. Let me be very clear about this. I never intended to burn the letters. It was more to set a mood. I poured myself a glass of wine and stretched out on the couch and began to read.

I had seen Kelly and Daniel together several times and I had witnessed the desperate way his eyes followed her every movement. God knows I had heard every detail of their sex, but I was still stunned by the raw passion in Daniel's writing. The humor, the openness, the sense of a shared history, the way he seemed to notice everything about her and remember everything she said. Daniel had done to Kelly everything a man can do to a woman—he had pursued her and screwed her, worshipped her and betrayed her, but somehow it had never occurred to me that he'd loved her.

Of course, that didn't explain why he fled to St. Louis, or wherever it was that he actually went. It didn't explain how she ended up in that tawdry public clinic, or why she was now marrying a man who I could only think of as Plan B. But the more I read the less I seemed to care how their story ended. Of course I couldn't burn the letters. She had known that all along. She had entrusted them, in fact, to the one person who she knew would protect them with her life. I carefully put Daniel's letters back in chronological order, bound them up, and hid them in a bag in the back of my closet.

Occasionally, even now, I take them out and read them. When it's late and I'm lonely or sad. Daniel had followed the rules of infidelity beautifully—the letters contain no names and no dates, which makes them perfect for my purposes. Over time it has become easier and easier to pretend that these are my letters. Over time it has become easier and easier to pretend that someone had written them to me.

★   ★   ★

I heard from Daniel one final time. We'd been born on the same day, and that had always given us a funny sort of connective tissue. A sense of shared destiny, he once told me, when we'd met at Kelly's apartment to blow out the sixty-eight candles she'd stuck on a cake—thirty-one for me, thirty-seven for him. So I suppose I shouldn't have been completely surprised when he called me, a couple of years after his disappearance, to wish me a happy birthday. Talking to him was so bizarre that it took a while for the reality to sink in and me to become really angry. We chatted as if we had seen each other just the week before, and finally he came to the point.

"Is she all right?"

"She's getting married."

I will never forget the sound he made next, a sort of raw animal sound, almost a wail. I was hit with a wave of anger. I started to tell him she'd been pregnant when he left, did he even know that? And how she had wasted away in the weeks and months that followed and if he cared so damn much how could he have just walked out?

But then he got himself together and asked, "Does she love him?"

"He'll take care of her."

"That's not what I asked."

"It seems to me you've forfeited the right to ask anybody anything."

"She's really going to do this?"

"We're going lingerie shopping tomorrow. For her honeymoon. He's taking her to Paris." Actually he was taking her to Vegas, but I figured Paris would sting more.

"Should I come back?"

"Why? Has anything changed?"

"Are you even going to tell her that I called?"

On the day of the wedding, Tory was Kelly's only attendant. She walked carefully down the makeshift aisle of the hotel ballroom in her blue organza dress, dropping white rose petals one by one. I couldn't stop looking at the door. Maybe this was the day that all the romantic hysteria was finally leading up to. Maybe Daniel was going to burst in like that scene in *The Graduate*, scoop Kelly up, and carry her away.

He didn't, of course, and at the reception Kelly came up to me and said, "So now I'm married."

"Yeah, you're one of us."

"It doesn't seem real," she said. "How long does it take before you actually start feeling like you're somebody's wife?"

"I'll let you know."

I think I was right not to tell her about Daniel's call, although my decision is one I still wonder about, even after all these years. Kelly looked happy, borderline radiant. "White's your color," I said, and we were laughing as we linked arms and turned to gaze at our husbands. It was a pleasant little scene. Mark was quite handsome in his tux, very stately with his cigar. He waved it expansively as he talked to Phil, who was leaned back against the silk-covered wall, holding Tory. She had been wound up with excitement for days and she'd fallen asleep nearly the minute the ceremony was over. She lay sprawled in her father's arms, her head thrown back, her mouth open, still clutching the basket of rose petals. Kelly sighed.

"Do you think it will work out for me this time?"

"I hope so."

"I'd never do anything to hurt Mark."

"I know that."

"It's different, but it's good in its own way. He's there for me and that's worth something."

"It's worth a lot."

"You burned the letters, right?"

"Of course I burned the letters."

She leaned over and kissed me on the forehead. She knew I was lying.

Chapter Twelve

O ctober comes and goes. He continues to call.

Not every day. But often enough that we develop a sense of continuity, a strangely detailed knowledge of each other's lives. He listens to me talk about the sort of things that are either so big or so small that you ordinarily don't discuss them. The pot that came out more blue than green, the expensive shoes that Kelly gave me because they pinch her feet, the dream where my mother turned into a bear. This strange white patch of hair that has shown up in my eyebrow, seemingly overnight. It means I'm getting old. It means I'm going to die. I tell him I'm afraid to die. I tell him I've lost my favorite ink pen.

"I've never done this before," he says. "Whatever this is we're doing."

The phone lies on the kitchen counter, a constant temptation, like a cake on a plate. Just a nibble here, a smear of icing on my tongue. This, of course, is the most enormous kind of cheating there is, the fact that I have made this man my confidant, the fact that I have become his. The fact that he reads me road signs as he drives by them, the fact that I open the refrigerator and tell him I forgot to get cream. The fact that I know his best friend's sister tried to kill herself or that he helps me solve the Sunday crossword when they have a word in Latin. He knows when I start my period. I know it took eleven hundred dollars to fix that dent in his car. I tell him that the red and yellow peppers in my frying pan smell like summer, smell like the last of summer, like the end of something, and he tells me he's in line at the drive-thru but he wishes he was there in the kitchen with me. He wishes he could walk in the door, come up behind me, and put his arms around my waist. I close my eyes and hear the surprisingly clear voice of some teenage girl in Boston asking him if he wants any sauce with that. "My life sucks," he says and I unclench my fist, releasing the pine nuts into the pan. There's not a word for what Gerry is to me, although Kelly, when I finally broke down and told her the whole story, arched her brow and called him "the distraction."

I phone him each time I leave counseling. Jeff always ends our sessions by reminding me I should do something for myself. A little something for myself every day, and I'm pretty sure he doesn't mean calling Gerry, but that's the only thing that soothes me after the impossibility of a therapy session. Fifty minutes of trying to describe what I wanted at the beginning of my marriage and trying to describe why it's no longer what I want. Fifty minutes of realizing that I'm no longer sure exactly what I want but that I'm pretty sure Phil will never be able to give it to me. Fifty minutes of admitting that I'm using the wrong language and that really, of course, of course, it's my job to give things to myself. Fifty minutes of Phil looking at me in exasperation, Jeff nodding eagerly and telling me to go on. Because, after all, the more confused and inarticulate I am now, the greater the adulation he will receive when he saves me. I am the lost sheep whose return will bring about more rejoicing than the others who are now safely munching arugula in their pastures.

Behind Jeff's head are rows of marriage manuals crammed from every direction and angle into an overstressed bookcase. Jeff has a hundred guides, each with a hundred theories on how marriage should work, and he won't rest until we have explored them all. "Each marriage is its own country," he said at our last session. "The married couple are the king and queen of that country and they can decree whatever rules they want." I felt a momentary flash of pride when Phil said, very calmly, "That's got to be the dumbest thing I've ever heard in my life." Even Jeff had to laugh. Never mind. If we don't like that analogy, he's got plenty more. I wonder how many people leave therapy because they've really figured something out and how many leave because they're so worn down with the steady drip of words that, in the end, they'll agree to anything just to get out the door.

So each time in the car, on the way home from Jeff's office, I hit number 3 on my speed dial. This is not the time for talking about small things. This is time for a conversation that propels me to the mall or the airport or the track where I sit alone in a remote section of the parking lot and listen to this man explain how he will run his tongue down the furrow of my spine and press the arches of my feet to his forehead. Gerry never asks me what I want.

It can't happen," I tell him.

"So why do we keep talking about it?"

"Because we like to torture each other."

"Okay, torture me now."

"You know I bought some lingerie."

"Great, great, wait a minute. Service stinks in this area. I don't want to lose you."

"I can't talk long. The ladies and I are getting ready to walk."

"Tell me about the lingerie."

"I didn't get it for you. I got it for my husband. He's going to take one look at this new underwear and everything is going to be totally different. He's going to say, 'Hallelujah, I see you as both a wife and a mistress and this marriage is absolutely forever one hundred percent saved.'"

"What did he say? Give me a second. I'm on a bridge . . ."

"He didn't say anything. I haven't worn it yet."

"Why not?"

"I'm afraid. He has this way of being sarcastic, I think he's trying to be funny . . ."

"Poor baby."

"I know. I keep taking it out of the bag and spreading it across the bed and looking at everything."

"Tell me about it. Describe every piece."

"Well, there's a camisole, do you know what that is?"

"Yeah, that's great."

"And on the bottom are these black hose with elastic tops that are supposed to stay up by themselves, and high heels."

"That's really great."

"When I tried them on in the dressing room, I imagined my legs sliding around your neck with the hose on. I imagined that sort of swooshing noise the hose would make against your skin if I . . ."

"Wait a minute, damn, trucks everywhere. I'm going to take one of the exit ramps and find a place where we can really talk. Wait a minute. Hold that thought. Are you trying to kill me?"

"I'm trying to kill something." I've just pulled into the elementary school parking lot and my car is the first one there. I tell Gerry not to find an exit ramp, that the other women are bound to show up any minute and I'll have to hang up. He says he wants us to meet. He has told me this before. I haven't said yes but I haven't said no. This is dangerous, he tells me. It's stupid, I tell him. He says he just wants to make sure we're clear about everything. On the plane I told him that marriage was a door people walk in and out of and I need to understand he's not going out that door.

"So all we would be is sex," I say.

"Friendship and sex," he says. "Can you handle that?"

I tell him I can handle that.

He figures maybe it would be best if we meet somewhere neutral, at least the first time. Somewhere other than his town or mine.

"New York," I say immediately. I have a friend there. Nobody would think anything if I went up to see her. It's good for him too—there are a million reasons for a person to be in New York. He says there are ways to set up a business file in my name so I'll look like a client and he can pay for my ticket. The client thing seems a little double-edged. Maybe he's done this before, and that's not good. But if he's going to the trouble of setting up a file on me, he must be planning for us to meet more than once, and that is good. My system is flooded with something—adrenaline, endorphins, some liquid that I imagine to look just like vodka, running clear and straight to my brain.

"Can you hear me?" Gerry asks. "There's so many fucking bridges here." He's breaking up.

"I heard you. This is never actually going to happen."

"So what will you be wearing in New York?"

"You've already forgotten what I look like?"

"I know what you look like. I'm trying to talk dirty."

"I'm going to wear the lingerie tonight."

"Yeah, I guess you might as well give it a stab. Call me to-morrow and let me know how it went." Nancy's van has pulled into the parking lot and she is driving toward me. Gerry's voice is nearly lost in an ocean of static. "If it goes well I'll never hear from you again, will I?"

"You'll have the consolation of knowing you saved a marriage," I say, watching Nancy get out of the van and tighten the ties on her walking shoes. "You can tell all your friends that meeting you was what turned me into the greatest sex kitten of Charlotte, North Carolina."

"You're right. That will be an enormous consolation."

"Besides, cheer up. The odds are it won't go well."

"If it goes badly will I see you in New York?"

I say goodbye and hop out of the car, slamming the door and walking toward Nancy. She is strapping her heart rate monitor around her chest and she looks up, squinting in the sun as I approach.

"I can see right through you," she says.

"What?"

"That top is a little thin."

"It's that new breathable fabric. I have a sports bra underneath."

"Oh yeah, well, I didn't mean anything bad. As long as you have a sports bra. It looks comfortable. Want to start?"

"Sure," I say, and we head down the steps toward the track.

"Is it okay if I run something by you? It's kind of big."

"Sure," I say again. "We tell each other everything." I'm still a bit unnerved by the seeing-right-through-me line, but the lie comes to me easily. Nancy's big news is that she's thinking about putting down hardwood floors in her kitchen, and I murmur, acknowledging the enormity of the decision. It's not entirely rational. We work so hard to create a façade and then we blame each other, just a little, for not being able to see past it.

She tells me the exact dimensions of the space and how much the laminate costs per square foot versus how much the real wood costs and she tells me what Jeff said and how, if they go with the real wood, the price could cut into their vacation plans and she tells me, in detail, the three places they're talking about going for fall break. Kelly's car pulls into the lot with Belinda's right behind it. I help Nancy do the math in her head. Three hundred and twenty square feet of laminate equals a whole week in Cancun and is this or is this not greater than 320 feet of hardwood and four days at Hilton Head? Telling someone everything is just another way of telling them nothing.

That night after Tory has gone to sleep I go into the bathroom and put on the camisole, stockings, and heels. Phil usually comes into the bedroom just before the ten o'clock news begins and, right on schedule, he walks through the door and sees me there, draped across the bed.

"What are you doing?" he asks, smiling faintly.

I feel foolish at once, lying on the bed with high-heeled shoes on. I struggle to pull the camisole down over my belly.

"What exactly are you trying to be?" Ah, the question that has no answer. "Really," he says, "where'd you get this stuff? Did you borrow it from Kelly?" I bolt from the bed and teeter my way into the closet, my face burning with shame.

"Don't be mad," he calls after me. "Just let me watch the weather and then you can come back in here and be that little thing." But I have already pulled the camisole over my head and the stockings down around my ankles, I am already beginning to cram the evidence of my stupidity back into the pink Frederica's bag. "You're not taking it off, are you?" he calls again. "Because really, it's kind of cute." I pull on my loose gray sleepshirt with the big UNC on the front and pad back into the bedroom.

"I guess you're pissed," he says.

"At least now you can't say I never try."

"Okay," he says, making an imaginary notation in an imaginary notebook. "Let the record show that on October 27 at 9:56 p.m., Elyse tried."

Two days from now, when we tell Jeff this story, Phil and I will remember it differently. I will tell Jeff that Phil had smirked at me and asked me what I was trying to be. Phil will say that he didn't smirk, he only smiled because he was surprised. "I've never seen her wearing anything like that," he will say to Jeff, but Jeff will not be looking at us. When we get to the part in the story where Phil describes my outfit, Jeff will swivel his chair away from the desk and shut his eyes.

"Okay, so maybe you surprised him a little too much," Jeff will say. "The important thing is that you not read so much into this one reaction . . ."

"She spent the night on the couch."

"He made fun of me."

"The important thing is that you realize this was just one little hiccup," Jeff will say, his voice muffled because he's facing the wall. "A tiny misunderstanding. The important thing is that you remain open to the sexual possibilities between you."

"You don't know her," Phil will say. "Elyse is the kind of woman who's capable of making a very big deal out of something like this."

Chapter Thirteen

They think I'm going to New York to see a friend named Debbie. Debbie is my escape chute—every married woman has one. The friend from your single days who stayed single, the friend in another city, the friend whose life you can periodically disappear into without raising alarm. My mother agrees to stay at our house. She'll get Tory after school and make sure she has her homework done, and I suspect that she'll also have her fed and bathed by the time Phil gets home. It's only three days, she tells me, don't worry about it. I sound like I could use a break.

Phil is not concerned either. "Have fun," he says. "Tell Debbie hello for me." Debbie doesn't like him. He doesn't like Debbie. But I'm surprised that getting away is this easy. I've already begun to wonder how long I should wait before I try it again. But no, I'm getting ahead of myself. A couple of kisses and a few giddy phone calls don't mean that Gerry and I will hit it off in the real world. Not that a hotel room in New York necessarily qualifies as the real world.

I'm going up on Tuesday afternoon. I will spend the night in a room he has reserved and paid for, in a hotel that he says is very nice. He will be there early Wednesday morning. This is best, we decide, since his plane lands at 8:15 and otherwise we would have to wait until three to get into the hotel room. We can't afford to kill most of the day walking around and having lunch. Time is too important, we have too little of it, so I will come up a day early and check into the room.

On Tuesday I wake up at five. I feed the cats twice. When Phil kisses me goodbye he misses my mouth and the kiss stays, a damp smear on my cheek, until I wipe it off. I drive Tory to school and hug her too hard as I say goodbye. "Have a good vacation," she says. "Break a leg." She is taking drama for the first time this year and she loves that phrase, loves the idea that it's bad luck to wish for good luck and you should always say the opposite of what you mean.

I have allowed a full two hours to get to the airport. At the last minute, as I am backing out of the driveway, I look down at my wedding rings, then cut off the car and run back inside to take them off. I start to put them by the bathroom sink, but that seems risky, like I'm practically begging somebody to knock them down the drain. That's the curse of the women of my family. Over and over again, through the generations, we keep managing to knock our wedding rings down the drain. My mother did it multiple times, my grandmother too, and both of my aunts. My earliest memories are of plumbers frantically summoned in the middle of the day to fish rings out of sink drains before the husbands got home. We can't let the men know how stupid we've been. How careless. It's almost as if we want to get caught. If you didn't know us better, you'd think we're the kind of women who enjoy trouble. Oops, there they go again.

Besides, if I leave my rings by the bathroom sink, that would be too dramatic a gesture to be ignored, even by Phil. I move them to the top drawer of my bedside table and leave a note for my mother on the kitchen counter, telling her all the things she already knows about Tory's schedule, the phone numbers of doctors, the location of insurance papers, and what the cats eat. It's pure compulsion, or maybe superstition. If this were a fairy tale then something horrible would happen while I was gone fecklessly fucking this stranger. A fire, an earthquake, a carelessly slung baseball bat, a monster crawling out from beneath the village bridge.

I want to make sure that I'm gone before she gets here so I

scribble the note fast. My mother's no fool. She would ask too many questions about what I was doing in New York, she would demand the name of a hotel, the exact times of my flights. She would notice immediately that I was not wearing my wedding rings. My mother has a natural talent for guilt and a keen eye for detail. When the plumber would pull her rings out of the curve in the pipe, she would always collapse into fits of weeping. "Another close call," she would say to me. "That was another close call."

It takes a long time to get my bags and find the shuttle, and when I arrive at the hotel and unpack, my suit is wrinkled and I realize I've left my makeup bag at home. I took it out at the last minute to get mascara and it must still be there, beside the sink.

It's a sign, clearly, a sign I need to simplify. I wash my face and walk out into the street. I want a red lipstick. One single elegant tube.

It turns out that this is not easy to find, not even in New York where you can find anything if you're willing to walk long enough. There's one called Plainly Red at Macy's but the adverb offends me and I keep searching. Finally I see it in a Chinese herb shop in Chelsea. Red. Seventeen dollars. I want to pay more.

The shop owner holds a small mirror while I very carefully paint my lips and then I am back out on the windy streets of Manhattan. Maybe this is enough, I think, maybe I have had my big adventure simply by coming this far. I like this new face—plain, pale, with a single slash of color. I stop on a corner and dig into my purse until I find an elastic band and then I pull my hair away from my face and that's even better. Maybe I need bigger earrings and to have my brows professionally arched, but it's growing dark and these are things for another day. For now, my mouth will have to carry me through.

Back at the hotel I order three vodka tonics and a spinach salad from room service. I take a shower, wrap the complimentary basketweave bathrobe around my wet body, tip the girl ten dollars, and settle down with the food on the bed. The robe is soft and has a hood and the minute the cloth curls around me I think, "This is what it feels like to be a mistress." God knows what this suite is costing Gerry but it pleases me that the hotel is so elegant, so discreet and obviously expensive. It pleases me that he has arranged for flowers to be waiting in the room. Tory has given me a flower too. When we stopped for gas this morning on the way to school she asked me for two dollars and I gave them to her, thinking she wanted a candy bar but too distracted to object that this was not a good snack for 7:45 in the morning. She came back with one of those roses they keep wrapped by the convenience store register, the kind that never open and never die, the kind that just eventually go soft and begin to droop while still in the shape of a bud. I carried the rose on the plane. I carried it in my hand in the cab. Now it is slumped in the hotel ice bucket, its head barely visible above the broad chrome rim.

But the suite is nice. It tells me that he likes me and that my eagerness has not yet devalued me in his eyes. I down the first drink and suck the small lime. I rub the almond-scented lotion from the bathroom into my feet. I read all the guest copy magazines on the bedside table and study what is showing this week in the museums because my mother will ask me how I spent my two days in New York and she will expect to hear something sensible. When I call home to let her know I got here okay, I dial the first four digits from the room phone and stop. It would not do to have the number of a Mandarin Oriental show up on our caller ID. So I use my cell phone, that savior of infidels, that invention that makes it so easy to claim that you are where you are not. I dial my own number— funny how hard it is to remember it—and leave a vague message. Then I pick up the second drink and walk to the window.

Across the street from my hotel there is an office building. Many of the windows are still lit, although the clock beside the bed says that it's almost nine. A man is sitting at a desk. I can see him quite clearly, even the can of diet Coke beside his computer screen, and I think about the telescope we had when I was a kid. My father developed a great thirst for astronomy during the Kennedy administration. He subscribed to *Omni* magazine and watched *The Outer Limits* and told me that by the time I had children, it would be a routine matter for anyone, even civilians, to fly to the moon. In the meantime he used the telescope to look through the neighbors' kitchen windows. He would play with the focus, nudging it this way and that with his stubby fingers, until he could see every item on their countertops, and then he could lean back and say with great satisfaction, "Nabisco."

I suppose spying is in my blood, this sort of mindless, pointless need to observe the minutiae of other people's lives, and I press myself against the glass of the long, narrow hotel window, willing the man to look over. Perhaps he will notice me across this great divide, and I think that if he does I will flash him, drop my robe, or maybe use my fingers to signal my room number, something wild. There are so few days when I am alone. For a minute I wonder what would happen if Gerry didn't show. I haven't talked to him today. It's possible he could be the one with a last-minute attack of panic, or conscience, or sanity. The man remains bent over his desk as if he were praying. It is only when I give up and push away from the glass that my focus wanders and I see another man, three floors higher. He is standing at his window too, gazing down at me and smiling, and I jump back as if I've been shocked.

Gerry will be at the hotel by 10 a.m. tomorrow. My best suit, my only Armani, is all wrong for this weather but it hangs on the showerhead, unwrinkling, in case we go somewhere nice for dinner. There are men everywhere here, all over the city, looking down from office windows or even higher, suspended in mid air, circling in planes, heading to the beds of women like me. Women who take off their wedding rings, women with bright red mouths who wait alone in darkening rooms, drinking Tanqueray. I lie down and pull the nubby gray comforter over me. I am drunk and alone in a rented bed. Nobody here knows me and nobody at home knows exactly where I am, and I think, somewhat illogically, that this is the happiest night of my life.

Chapter Fourteen

W hen he knocks on the door the next morning, I jump. Even though I am expecting the knock, even though he has arrived, in fact, within fifteen minutes of the time we predicted he would arrive, even though he has called me from the cab to tell me that he's landed and to get the room number, even so, when I hear the knock, I jump. I push off the bed and walk to the door. I have been up for two hours. Plenty of time to order breakfast, shave my legs, and blow out my hair. I painted on the red lipstick and then blotted it, blotted it again, and finally rubbed it off, leaving behind only a faint stain of red, a color that could possibly be the color of a real woman's lips. I don't want him to think I've put on makeup. I don't want him to think that I'm trying too hard.

I stand on tiptoe. This is the moment I become an adultress. My hand is on the knob, my eye is at the spyhole. He is looking to the side, which is good because this is the angle I know him best. This was how he looked to me on the flight from Tucson to Dallas, a profile, a man on a coin. What's he watching? Is housekeeping coming down the hall with their carts of toilet paper and towels or is he just nervous, afraid of being caught? But this is New York, the most anonymous place in the world. He looks first one direction, then the other, as if he is getting ready to cross a street.

And I say to myself—out loud, like a crazy person—"This is the moment."

But it isn't, of course. Our actual affair began sometime back. Yesterday morning when I boarded the plane, or perhaps last Tuesday, when he e-mailed me the ticket information, or maybe it was even earlier, when I agreed to come to New York, when we set a date to meet. Or maybe the turnback point was the very first day he called me, when I was watching Tory on the ball field, or when I kissed him, in the chapel in Dallas. The idea that you can change your fate is illusory and I do not indulge it for long. This decision was made years ago. Before I ever met Gerry Kincaid.

He knocks again.

I open the door.

I'd like be able to tell you that the sex is not a big deal.

It's a revelation.

Not just that there is sex like this somewhere in the world. I already knew that. There was a part of me that always knew there were people out there somewhere having sex like this. The surprise is that it's happening to me.

He kisses me until I am weak with it and I roll my head back and forth on the pillow and mumble, "I want love." I am immediately shamed. This was not our deal and why am I such a blurter? But he just as immediately takes my hand and says, "Okay, let's go find some." He may as well be wearing a pith helmet. He may as well have picked up a walking stick and a canteen or strapped a knapsack to his back. He never releases my hand and I have the sensation that I am moving across space, of closing my eyes in one location and opening them to find myself somewhere else. There are so many emotions that it takes a while to realize that chief among them is the feeling of relief. All these thoughts that have been inside of me for so long, that have circled around and doubled back upon themselves, that have almost convinced me I'm sick and strange and unfit for love—suddenly all these thoughts have somewhere to go. He catches me looking at the clock at one point and I'm trying, I'll confess, to calculate how long we have been doing this, how many years I have lived upon this bed. But he doesn't want me to know what time it is. He reaches toward the table. His shoulders and back are glazed with sweat. I expect him to turn the clock to the wall but instead he lifts it with a jerk, a movement so abrupt that for a second I think he is going to bring it down on my head like a stone. But instead the plug releases from the outlet with a pop and the red numbers sink immediately into a sea of darkness.

"You killed it," I say, or perhaps I just think it. He flings the clock across the bed, its black electrical cord slapping back against his arm. This is the point where most men would smile, a quick grin to blunt the violence of the movement, to acknowledge the irony of the situation, but, as I am to learn through the course of this long, hourless day, Gerry is not a man who smiles during sex. In fact, he looks like he's dying.

It's big of you to go slumming like this," I say. "Flying up to fuck me when I'm not even a Yankee or a banker or anything."

"Trust me, the fact that you're not a Yankee or a banker is working entirely in your favor." I pick up Gerry's gray jacket and slip it on. The silk lining is cool against my skin. "The smartest people I ever knew were southerners," he says. "Like Custis."

"Who's Custis? Can I lie down in this jacket?"

He inches over and I crawl in beside him, putting my head on his shoulder.

"This broken-down old guy who lived on the farm where I worked summers. The farm belonged to my mother's uncle— she'd found the pot under my bed and decided I needed to know what real work felt like. That's what she said—real work, man's work, although God knows where she got that idea. My dad was a lawyer. It was hot as hell, no shade anywhere, but Custis, I swear he must have been a hundred and he had this kind of folk wisdom."

"It doesn't get hot in Boston."

"This wasn't Boston. It was in Virginia."

"So Custis taught you . . ."

"He taught me about life. I don't know exactly what my parents were trying to prove sending me down there to bust my ass for two sixty-five an hour, but Custis showed me how to do all kinds of things."

"Like what?"

"It was Custis who taught me how to fuck a watermelon."

"You're kidding."

"A watermelon was my first."

"I can't believe you lost your virginity to a gourd. That's not just going out of your species, that's a whole new phylum or genus or something."

"No, they're good . . . really they are. Because they're pulpy, pretty much like a woman, and when they're just off the vine they're still warm inside. Body temperature."

"And they don't talk."

"A melon's never going to tell you what you're doing wrong."

"So you split them open . . . how does it work?"

He shakes his head. "No splitting. You take your pocket-knife and cut a hole. Small enough to give you some kicks, but big enough to impress the other boys, and then you go behind a bush . . ."

I'm laughing, and he is too, flattening himself on top of me, opening his jacket and rubbing the tender arc beneath my breast as we roll back and forth. "This feels good," he whispers, and I stop rolling. We're face-to-face but not looking at each other.

He feels heavy all of a sudden and I shift my weight a little. "Watermelon fucking doesn't sound like something that takes a lot of skill," I say. "Where did Custis come in?"

"He taught me how to choose a good one."

"You thump it?"

"There's more to it than that. You get your eye on a particular melon out in the field and you watch and wait until it's the right size. Every day you pick it up and bounce it a little in your hands." He illustrates, using my breast. "Once I had one in mind I'd go out several times a day and check on it. Because you don't want to pull it off the vine until you're sure it's ready. You want it heavy in proportion to its size, so it's juicy."

"You're so funny. Not that you'd do it, because you were what, fourteen or fifteen? But you had this whole relationship with it, you were practically dating it."

"Sometimes I named them." Now we are giggling again, rocking again. His mouth is close to my ear. "I'm getting hungry," he says. "What time is it?"

"I don't know," I say. "This fancy hotel room you booked us into doesn't seem to have a clock." The bed is gray with afternoon shadows. It's been hours since he knocked on the door, but I don't know how many.

Gerry gets up and roots around in his pants for his watch. It's a climber's model and it glows in the dark. "No wonder we're hungry. It's almost seven."

Exactly twelve hours until he's leaving. I inhale and exhale slowly, trying not to make the sound of a sigh. "Wear my panties," I say.

"What?"

"Wear my panties and I'll wear your boxers."

"That won't work."

I pull the twisted wad of his navy silk boxers from the bottom of the bed with my foot. I wonder if he wears stuff like this every day to the office or if he bought them special. The shorts pull easily over my hips. "I regret to inform you that they are a perfect fit."

"You know, for the record, it does get hot in Boston. You ever been there?"

I shake my head.

Gerry moves closer. "We could get room service," he says.

"No, I want to be with you in public. I want to put on clothes and sit up straight and look across a table at you with other people there."

"Can you do it again before we go?"

"Girls can always do it." I'm going to be sore tomorrow.

"Yeah," he says softly, leaning across the bed to thump me with his thumb and index finger, traveling from my collarbone down to my navel, and stopping just short of the elastic waist of his boxer shorts. "Yeah, I'd say you're just about ready."

At the restaurant they tell us it will be fifty minutes before they have a table. Many men would be dismayed and demand that we go somewhere else, but this is something I've noticed about Gerry, that he is always willing to wait. We put in our name and take the buzzer and walk across the street to kill time in a Restoration Hardware. I like Restoration Hardware. The music is soothing and the salespeople are nice. They have coiled hoses and brass kickplates, heavy lovely dishes and leather chairs. They sell marriage.

Gerry is standing across the store from me, looking at books. He is frowning, his face intense. When I walk up to him he shows me a recipe for coq au vin cooked over a campfire. He also has a basketful of some old-fashioned bay rum soap and he tells me that just seeing the wrapper reminded him of his grandfather. "This is what a man is supposed to smell like," he says, holding out a bar for me to sniff. "This is a smell you can trust."

He pays in cash. We link arms as we leave the shop. I like the fact that he is so much taller than me, and when I put my arm through his he almost pulls me behind him. I stumble a couple of times because he takes long strides. His wife must be closer to his height, I think, or else they do not often walk arm in arm. We pass our reflection in the window. We are a handsome couple.

The next morning he will leave very early. His flight is hours before mine and I tell him to wake me. He doesn't want to. There is no reason for me to get up before dawn to see him off, he says, and he would rather leave with the image of me sleeping in the plush white bed. I suspect he doesn't have the stomach for good-byes or questions about when I will see him again. "I promise I won't make a scene," I tell him. "Please get me up." And yet the next morning I will awaken alone to muffled noises from the maids in the hall. He will have left me the breakfast menu on his pillow, along with a bar of the bay rum soap.

But I don't know any of this as we go in to dinner. I can't see the future and this is my great gift. I only see us happy, hand-some, our arms linked as we walk, our outlines reflected in the windows of expensive stores. I see him jumping, laughing as the buzzer in his pocket goes off, us escorted to a booth, us bending over our menus, deciding to begin with a plate of mussels. I tell him stories about me and Kelly at the drive-in and he quotes me lyrics of a song he wrote back in the seventies for the first girl he ever loved.

"She broke my heart," he says.

"She's probably dead by now," I tell him. "Or she should be." He smiles and for a minute there in the restaurant we expand and the air around us shimmers with possibility. He pushes the last mussel toward me, just like Tramp gave Lady the last meatball. That was my favorite movie when I was a little girl.

Chapter Fifteen

ex can save you. You're not supposed to say this, but it's true. After I get back from New York, I am high for three solid days. I send him an e-mail, the entire text of which reads, "I am happy."

I know this isn't the way it's supposed to happen. You're supposed to go into therapy and work on your issues. You're supposed to journal and do yoga and breathe deeply. You're supposed to go somewhere very blank and plain—a beach house perhaps, in a town where you don't know anybody and the walls of the house are all white without a single picture. Or instead you go to Ireland with a group of women, and everyone wears homespun shifts and eats nourishing root vegetables and the sky is perpetually on the verge of rain. Or maybe India. Probably India. That or Nepal. The point is you must journey somewhere far away and stay gone for a very long time. Happiness is tough. It requires silence and solitude and contemplation. And then maybe, somewhere in year seven or year fifteen or twenty-two, happiness comes to you. Maybe not. I know that's how it's supposed to be. I know you're not supposed to use men like shortcuts and off-ramps, I know that, and yet if I had to count the times that sex dragged me back to life versus therapy or religion or meditation or the love of good friends, it wouldn't even be close.

*   *   *

I'm not sure how men know when they're better, but when women recover from something they cut their hair. On the third day after New York I wake up, walk into the bathroom, look into the mirror and think, "It's time to cut my hair."

8 a.m.: I call the most expensive salon in town and they say that Antonio has an unexpected opening. They assure me that I'm very lucky—apparently, this rarely happens. When I arrive they bring me Italian *Vogue* and bottled water and drape a long aromatherapy pillow around my neck. When Antonio asks me to describe my vision, I tell him I want a haircut that makes me look good when I'm lying flat on my back. He makes that European sound, something between a snort of derision and an exhalation of cigarette smoke, but he's very careful with my hair, snipping my bangs three times to get the layers just right. Later he tells me he's from Tennessee.

10:40: With my hair swishing around my chin, I go to buy wrapping paper for Belinda's birthday present. This takes longer than expected, because I am transfixed by the beauty of the Hallmark store. Everything seems as strange and exotic as if I were back in the Chinese shop in Chelsea wandering among the dusty jade statues and bins of dark aromatic teas. I walk up and down the aisles and finally, after much consideration, I buy ballerina-blue tissue paper and thin, serrated ribbons that you can curl with the edge of a scissor. That will do for Belinda, but I also take a ball of rough twine, two red silk boxes filled with confetti, a velvet bag tied with a gold cord, a shiny silver cylinder, and olive green paisley paper. All bought with no plan for how or when I will use them. I run my hands along the displays and touch the points of the satin bows as if they were sea anemones, capable of recoiling at my touch. I had forgotten that life had this much texture.

11:20: I buy thirty pounds of potting soil from Wal-Mart, take it home, drag it into the backyard, and plunge a steak knife into the belly of the bag. I collect all the pots that aren't quite right to sell and then I take my houseplants outside. There, one by one, I pull each from its container, exposing the tangled white roots to the air. I'm hit with a sudden, nearly blinding wave of guilt. The roots on some of the plants are interwoven so deeply that it's clear they've needed larger pots for a long time. After the rooted ones I move on to the bulbs, yanking at the base of each stem until there is this soft little sigh and the soil releases the flower into my dirty hands.

The bulbs are my favorite anyway. They have always seemed to me like small miracles, the way they have the power to regenerate themselves, to push up time and again through the soil. They have slept so patiently all summer and fall in my garage, their pots covered in cobwebs. I hold each one in my hand and imagine I can feel its small beating heart and I bury them back into much larger pots, cover them with fresh soil and a sprinkle of water, leave them with a small prayer of apology for the neglect they have suffered. At one point I become quite emotional about the whole thing. I have to stop and lie down in the hammock and cry. I figure that if Phil asks me that night why I'm not wearing my wedding rings I can say, "I spent the afternoon repotting plants," but as it turns out he doesn't ask.

12:40: Afterwards I'm smeared with potting soil so I go into the house to take a bath. At the last minute I squirt a dollop of bath gel into the water. This bottle of Vitabath has been in the bathroom cabinet for years but I can't remember who gave it to me or what I was saving it for. It falls from the bottle with a big gelatinous thud and makes the bottom of the tub so slick that when I step in I slide straight down and make a splash. The sound of my laughter surprises me and I look up, thinking maybe somebody else has come into the room.

1:30: For lunch I stop by a sports bar near the mall and order a draft beer and chicken wings. The beer is so cold that with the first swallow I feel an icepick stab in the back of my brain. I've brought a big heavy book with me, one of those classics you always mean to read but never do. I keep a pen in my hand so that I can underline anything that strikes me as particularly interesting or well written—it's a quirk left over from my days in graduate school. I used to be smart. I used to be able to remember things. Now I am just a woman who has cats with clever names. But today everything strikes me as significant and I am underlining nearly every sentence. It's like I'm wearing 3-D glasses and the page is no longer flat—some words seem to be moving toward me and others are receding.

The bartender asks me if I have everything I need. People are always asking me these sorts of questions: How you doing today, ma'am? What are you looking for? Ready for a refill? Would you like to see those in another color? Did we save room for dessert? When you have this much, people can't seem to stop themselves from asking if you need a little more.

"I'm fine," I tell the bartender, but the truth is I am starving—greedy, ravenous, greasy and vulgar with appetite. The wings are great, charred and spicy, and I go through three cups of the blue cheese dressing. It's like the first time I've tasted food in months. It's like food is a secret that only I have discovered. Enough, enough, enough, who can say what is enough? I have a daughter and a home and a husband and a lover and my pots and my books and my cats and one true friend and this should be enough, but if I knew how to count to enough I wouldn't be in this situation in the first place.

I close my eyes and wonder how long this manic joy can continue. I've been a wild woman for days, screaming out the letters on *Wheel of Fortune*, pouring the pancake batter in the shapes of ships and bunnies, just like my dad used to do. Pancakes were vehicles of vision for him, sort of like a Rorschach test, and he believed you could read a person based on what they saw in the swirls of batter and syrup. My father would make pancakes for me every Saturday morning, and I suddenly miss him so much that I put my hands over my face and feel tears rising for the second time that day.

"What are you reading?" asks the bartender.

"*Ulysses*."

"Uh-huh," he says. "How about some key lime pie?"

Tory has noticed the change in me but she is still young enough to notice things and not wonder at the reasons behind them. Besides, she likes this new mommy who takes her on walks to waterfalls and lets her get the whole front of her shirt wet. This mommy who sings Motown in the car, who screams "Olé!" every time the light turns green, who says we can skip the vocabulary words just this once. This happy mommy who slaps misshapen pancakes onto her breakfast plate and asks, "Now just what does that look like to you?"

Okay, I get it, you've been high as a kite for a week," Kelly says. "What happens after this?"

"I don't know. Maybe nothing. Maybe everything."

"I don't want to see you get hurt." We're sitting on the patio outside our favorite coffeehouse, the one with the Frank Lloyd Wright light fixtures. All the tables were taken so we have dragged three chairs to the only shady spot and now we sit facing each other with our feet propped on the seat between us.

"You're the one who told me I should have an affair."

"I didn't mean it."

"But you were right."

"When are you going to see him again?"

"It's one of those Zen things. It happens when it happens."

"Oh shit, you're getting ready to fall in love, I can hear it in your voice."

Gerry is not my life, I tell her. We plan to see each other once a month, in different cities, a pace that we have agreed shows continuity but not obsession. Tory will never know he exists. Phil doesn't know anything, doesn't have to know. It's just once a month. Gerry is not my life, I tell her. I hold my hands apart to show her what a small part of my life he is. He is about the size of a fish.

"You're dreaming," she says. Kelly has this way of half sitting, half lying in chairs with her knees flexed and her legs slightly open so that she always looks as if she's just made love. As if her lover has just risen up and walked away from her. "I can't even figure out what you did that was worth a six-hundred-dollar hotel room."

"I think it was a matter of how many times I did it."

"Think he'll ever be available?"

"Available?"

"Unmarried."

I shake my head. "There was Paxil in his duffle bag. I saw it when he got out this special shampoo he brought." I look away from her, suddenly shy. "He washed my hair."

"He washed your hair."

"Yeah."

"He brought a special shampoo to wash your hair."

"Why is that so hard to believe? It can't be you every time, Kelly."

"What's Paxil?"

"It's what they give you when you've been on Zoloft so long that the Zoloft's stopped working. Look, he's depressed, and he has been for years. He's where I'd be if I let the first doctor who ever wanted to put me on drugs actually put me on drugs." And I know it's true. As long as he's taking those pills, Gerry is never going to get up a big enough head of steam to actually break out of this life. He's not contented enough to stay, he's not miserable enough to leave. He's in that gray band between the two, vibrating in some frequency that only the unhappily married can hear.

"Do you think he washed your hair because he saw it in a movie?"

"Probably," I say, remembering the warm trail of suds running from my shoulder blades down my spine, Gerry's careful, climb-callused hands cupped above my brow to shield my eyes as he rinsed. When a man puts Paxil and sandalwood shampoo into a duffle bag and spends six hundred dollars for a hotel room just so he can wash a woman's hair it only means one thing. That he's a thoroughly married man.

Kelly lifts her feet off the shared chair, balances her coffee mug on one of the light fixtures, and bends forward. I follow suit until our foreheads are nearly touching. Despite everything we've been through and all the years we've been friends, Kelly and I frequently don't understand what the other one is talking about. It's not like we think alike. We never have. We are friends of the body. If I asked her to go with me to the bathroom and change shirts, she'd do it, no questions asked. If she took off running toward me right now, her arms outstretched and her feet in a stutter step, I'd drop my cup of coffee and catch her in mid air, without hesitation. Because the body, it remembers everything.

"How does he call you?"

"On the cell."

"What's the code to retrieve your messages?"

"1-2-3."

She frowns. "You might want to think about changing that."

I take her hands between mine and squeeze them. It's a game we used to play where she'd press her palms together and chop the air up and down between my hands and I would try to trap her. She was too quick for me back in high school but today she is preoccupied and I catch her easily. We sit for a moment like this, hands meshed.

"It would probably be smart to slow it down," she says.

"Yeah."

"Maybe like talking once a week instead of every day."

"Right."

"It would be easy to let things accelerate, but that's dangerous."

"I know."

"Because when you're in these situations, like, you know, getting in planes and going places and somebody washing somebody's hair . . . you've got to be careful because sometimes people start feeling things."

"I know, baby," I say.

Winter

Chapter Sixteen

Kelly and I went to different colleges and spent our single-girl years in different cities. When she talks about this time in our lives, the years between eighteen and twenty-seven, she always says that our paths were diverging. She likes the word "diverging." She likes to say it out loud, extending every syllable, but the truth of the matter is I don't know that our paths ever diverged. Wouldn't that imply that she was out of sight? She was never out of sight.

I was living in Baltimore, teaching art and sleeping with an artist when, out of nowhere, I was swept away in a tide of baby fever. This sort of thing happens to women in their late twenties, everyone knows it, but I didn't expect it to happen to me. I'd never played with dolls as a child or babysat as a teenager but suddenly I found myself in supermarkets staring at other people's children. "Excuse me," I would say, "but how old is that baby? Is it a boy or a girl?" It was like remembering a past life, one I'd spent in a hut by the sea with a wooden bowl for grinding corn and long strips of bright cloth tied around my hair, a life where I had babies one after the other, always pregnant or nursing. It was all I could go toward. It was like I was possessed, caught in some sort of lunar pull.

And then, sometime in the spring of the year I turned twenty-eight, my mother broke her foot. I was teaching at one of those post-hippie-quasi-Montessori-rich-kid schools and spring break was coming up. They didn't talk about Easter up there—they called it the Equinox Festival. Either way I had a week off and it seemed unkind not to use the time to drive down and check on Mom, so I did. What was bothering her most was that she'd been forbidden to drive, which meant she couldn't do all her volunteer work. Funny, but it's lately hit me how much my mother is like Nancy, how completely she throws herself into all her good causes. She stays so busy that no one can ever criticize her, or say they really know her.

After three days I was screamingly bored with being in my childhood home, and I wondered why I'd never noticed that my parents kept the TV too loud and the heat too high. It was easy for Mom to talk me into driving a little boy named Keon to the free dental clinic. I borrowed her Volvo, picked Keon up at his preschool, and followed her carefully detailed instructions to a medical complex that was in the middle of a block of public housing.

Keon was a silent child. He had no idea who I was, but went with me willingly enough. Even at the age of four he seemed to be accustomed to taking the hands of strange white ladies and climbing into station wagons. When we got to the clinic there was a chalkboard in the waiting room with the doctors who were volunteering that day listed on it, as if they were specials at a restaurant. Phillip Bearden was the dentist du jour and I remember thinking it was a pleasant name. A pleasant name for a pleasant man, for who else but a pleasant man would volunteer at the free clinic?

When they finally called us back, Keon, who had been playing with blocks in the waiting room, panicked. I don't think he'd realized where he was or what was getting ready to happen until the moment he saw the big hydraulic chair. He dug in his small heels with surprising ferocity and Dr. Bearden, a broad shaggy man with an unkempt beard and a gentle voice, was only able to persuade him into the chair by promising I would climb up too and Keon could sit on my lap.

That's how I met Phil. He was one year out of dental school. I did the math. That made him at least a year younger than I was, maybe two. "The kids call me Dr. Phil," he said, and it was before the TV show, so I didn't laugh. Keon clutched my wrists with his small hands, pressing in as if he were trying to take my pulse, and Dr. Phil rubbed his cheeks until he was finally able to coax his mouth open. "This little guy was hurting," he said, more to himself than to me. "Two of them need to go."

You could tell he was used to children, good with them, so careful to cup his large palm around the novocaine needle that Keon never really saw it coming. He gave one little twitch as it slipped into his gum, and when Phil pulled his hand back, Keon spoke for the first time. He said, "Sing."

"That's right," I said. "It stings a little bit but it's over now."

Phil shook his head. "He wants you to sing."

"What am I supposed to sing?"

"Sing," Keon said again.

"Apparently," Phil said, and his eyes crinkled so that I thought he might have been smiling under his mask, "there's someone who sings to him when he's scared."

"I don't sing. I never sing."

"Sing," Keon said more forcefully, twisting his body so hard that he almost pulled loose the cotton bib.

"It looks to me like you're going to have to sing," said Phil.

So I started singing. I sang "Happy Birthday," which was the first thing that came to my mind. I have a bad voice. My bad voice, in fact, is legendary among my friends, but I realized that Phil was right and that somewhere, sometime, somebody had sung to this child to keep him calm. Almost immediately his body slumped against me and when Phil told him to open his mouth, he did. So I sang "Happy Birthday" and then I sang "Camptown Races" and "Free Bird" and "Jingle Bells" and "Girls Just Want to Have Fun." Every time I stopped Keon would say, "Sing," and I'd start up with another song, something always different but always inappropriate, and I could tell Phil was trying not to laugh.

But he got the one tooth out and then the other, and as I was sitting there, holding this boy in my arms and singing and looking at Phil's large hands, I began to wonder exactly where I was going with my life and why I was still teaching when it didn't pay worth shit and didn't give me time to do my own pots. The idea after art school had been that I would teach part-time and spend my afternoons in the studio, but none of this seemed to be working out. The kids didn't want to learn about weaving or watercolors. The kids were all stoned on better stuff than I could afford and it was the kind of school where I was expected to say everything they did was wonderful. They got certificates of completion just for showing up and their art was exhibited in the lobbies of buildings that their fathers owned, even if I sometimes suspected this work was done by the family domestics. I could only afford to rent six hours a week in the studio and I didn't have health insurance. I started thinking that after Dr. Phil finished with Keon I should ask him to clean my teeth too. God knows how long it had been.

I thought about the guy I was sleeping with at the time, and for a second, just a second, but still—I couldn't seem to remember his name. And I thought about how it had been snowing when I left Maryland but here the trees were already beginning to bud and I was ready for spring, damn it, my parents were right, there was no reason to live in the cold and why was I still being so pointlessly rebellious, here when I was closing in on thirty? I wanted to come home. I wanted a house. I wanted to be pregnant. Phil was singing too, softly and on-key, singing some song about a horsey and a frog. Some song that was a logical thing to sing to a child, because he was the sort of man who knew how to sing to children, he was the sort of man who knew lyrics about a horsey and a frog.

Maybe he wasn't my type—he was too conventional, too big, and too nice—but who's to say that your type can't change? Who's to say you can't put your childish ways aside and find a deeper joy with the gentle and the gainfully employed? Maybe I was done with Baltimore. Maybe I was done with boys. I thought about my job and my apartment and the guy I was dating and the guy I dated before him and none of it seemed to matter much, not compared to being here with this child in my lap and this man before me, kind and smiling, with a smear of blood across his shirt.

Afterwards as I was carrying Keon, who was half asleep and clutching a balloon, out to my mother's car, I heard footsteps coming up behind me fast, crunching in the gravel. I whirled around—it wasn't my part of town, as Kelly would later point out—and saw Phil running toward me, carrying a jacket.

"You forgot your coat."

"That's not my coat."

"I know," he said.

And then he asked me if I liked Indian food.

Marriage didn't seem that hard back then.

Witness the first holiday that Phil and I spent together as husband and wife. Thanksgiving is the major gathering time for his family, which is lucky, because it's Christmas for mine. It seemed to bode well that we were able to negotiate this so easily; we agreed to drive north in November and south in December. We literally shook on it.

And so on the Tuesday before Thanksgiving we were on I-81, going toward his uncle Simon's farm in Pennsylvania. We were running ahead of schedule and had decided to venture off the main road and weave our way through Amish country. It was beautiful, placid, a little misty. Like a picture on the front of a jigsaw-puzzle box. We stopped in a town with the ludicrous name of Intercourse and there, in a general store, we bought three things. The first was a quilt, which seemed a sweet and appropriate purchase for newlyweds. I think it even had what they called a wedding ring pattern, but no, that's too sickeningly perfect, so I may have that part wrong.

We also bought pumpkin ice cream. I'm sure about that. It

seemed odd to me even then, a bright adobe color, more red than orange, but Phil was uncharacteristically insistent that we try it. He said that pumpkin was the fruit of fall, and, looking around the yard outside this country store in rural Pennsylvania, I saw his point. Pumpkins were everywhere—lining the porch, heaped in piles near the parking lot, perched on fences out by the road. But I wasn't sure about the ice cream. Later, two days after we got home from the trip, I learned that I was pregnant with Tory, but things had already begun to taste funny to me. I took one lick of the pumpkin ice cream and threw the rest away.

The third thing we bought was an Amish shirt for Phil. It was collarless, pale and stonewashed, made from a soft thin denim that crushed in my hand. The shirt cost forty-eight dollars, more than we paid for clothes back then, but I loved it.

I loved it so much that I insisted he wear it for the rest of the trip, and he did, stripping off his red plaid flannel shirt right there in the parking lot and putting on the denim. Phil's neck is thick like that of a football player, with very little indentation, and this embarrasses him. He says it makes him look stupid, and I doubt that a collarless shirt was the right choice to minimize this condition, but in the early days of our marriage I was hypnotized by the muscularity of my husband's neck. I used to dream about lacing my fingers behind his head, closing my eyes, lifting my feet, and just starting to swing back and forth. Back and forth with my eyes closed, hanging from this strong place.

I was drowsy all the time on that trip. On the way home I fell asleep in Fredericksburg and woke up in Durham, missing Richmond completely. But somehow I did not associate this mild nausea, this leaden tiredness, these sudden fits of petulance with pregnancy. Maybe I thought this was the way women felt when they had someone to take care of them. And I did have someone to take care of me. "Go to sleep," Phil would say. "I'll drive."

★　　★　　★

Nothing prepared me for the violence of Tory's birth. None of the books, none of the classes, none of the women who'd stopped me in the street to tell me their own horrible birth stories. The long labor, the despair, the moment when the doctor put his hands fully inside my body to turn the baby, saying, without irony, that I might feel a little pressure. I'd planned to be braver than this. The anesthesiologist showed up and introduced himself as Dr. Wineburg. He said he was sorry he was late but he'd just come from a pig-picking. I was the only one who seemed to find this disconcerting. It was like being the only sober person at a party of drunks. The nurse stretched herself over me so that I wouldn't see the needle or jerk at the moment of puncture, but the epidural only worked on one side. I went half numb and Dr. Wineburg shook his head and said it happened this way sometimes, that they could always pull the needle out and try again, but the obstetrician said no, it's coming too fast now. The side of me that could still move kept trying to crawl off the table and leave the side of me that was just lying there taking this shit.

In the end the doctor was pulling so hard that he braced one foot on the table and Dr. Wineburg stood behind him to hold him up. Dr. Wineburg's freckled arms were what I focused on during the last contractions, and if anyone had told me that it was possible for one human being to pull this hard on another I wouldn't have believed them. Phil snapped at one point, "She can't take much more," and I realized he was talking about the baby, whose presence I had long since forgotten. But Tory emerged in one piece, long and angry and blinking, and the nurse unfolded her across my stomach like a map.

The obstetrician knelt down with needle and thread, made some stupid joke about how tight did I want to be. I told him to just sew the whole damn thing shut. Phil was running from corner to corner with his camera, taking so many pictures that it looked like his face was flashing at me from every angle, and Dr.

Wineburg, smiling, said not to worry about it, that the second one would be easier.

We went to stay with my mother after the delivery, ostensibly because her house didn't have stairs, but the truth is that I needed to lie on the same saggy couch where I'd napped as a kid and have someone bring me cinnamon toast with the crusts cut off. Tory nursed every two hours and a deep exhaustion fell over me like a blanket. The memory of it scares me even now. My milk came in, wild and indiscriminate, so much that if I heard a baby crying in the supermarket or saw a commercial about starving children in Uganda, the front of my shirt would be flooded within seconds. At my insistence, Phil brought over my clay and drop cloths and set it all up in Mom's dining room, and each day, when the baby napped, I would grimly shuffle to the table. I didn't get much done, aside from making a stain on my mother's oriental rug. Tory was a bad sleeper and I never knew how long I'd have at the table before our fragile peace would shatter. "I can't work like this," I told my mother and she said that nobody expected me to. After a baby comes things are never quite the same.

But I wanted to work. In the low gray moments of my own shallow sleep I would dream about the clay, then awaken with my hands cupped in front of me. I was trying to hold on to something, even though it was beginning to occur to me that when my mother said things weren't going to be the same, what she really meant was I'd never be the same. One day when Tory was about a week old I locked myself in my childhood bathroom and held a mirror between my legs, straining to see over the mound of my still distended stomach. What was reflected back to me was such a tangle of gashes and stitches that I let the mirror drop to the floor. For a second I thought that the doctor had taken me seriously and stitched me completely closed.

The books all say that the genitalia of women are easily wounded and easily healed, something about the high concentration of blood vessels in the pubic region. Maybe so, but that image of the doctor propping his foot against the delivery table would come back to me at odd times, like when I was blowing Phil. It was pretty much the way we did things then, even after the six weeks they tell you to wait had come and gone. "As far as I'm concerned," I said, "Intercourse is just some town in Pennsylvania," and he laughed, a little uneasily because I could tell that I frightened him then, wandering around the house weeping, sleepless, dripping milk. He seemed to think that if we would just get into our bed naked together he'd somehow have his wife back, but I couldn't see going back to sex—not real sex, not the kind that led you down this road. I could hear the baby stirring in the next room, the small hiccupping sounds of her rousing coming through the Fisher-Price monitor on the bedstand as I knelt, keeping my mouth as tight as I could, keeping pressure to the point of giving myself a headache, and prayed that he would come before she cried, that I would manage to get one thing done that day.

Phil had worn his collarless denim shirt for Tory's birth. A few days after the baby and I finally moved back from Mom's house I found the shirt wadded in the closet. I was shocked by the smell. I hadn't realized how much he'd sweated during the delivery, and the shirt had been marinating for over two weeks. It was his favorite, my favorite too, and I felt compelled to save it.

I washed the shirt, using an extra scoop of Tide, and then I washed it again. It was the first time I had ever done his laundry. We'd more or less taken care of our own stuff the first year we'd been married, but now that I was going to stay home with the baby it seemed logical that I would do these little chores for him . . . Only logical, and yet I knew that I had suffered, through no fault of my own, a sudden and drastic drop in street value, like the way they say a car's worth goes down five thousand the minute you drive it off the dealer's lot.

I hung the shirt in his closet, but when Phil saw it he said that the odor was still there and we should throw it out.

I told him he was being ridiculous. The shirt didn't smell,

how could it? He didn't argue, but he never wore the Amish shirt again.

Was I happy? Hard to say, even now, and maybe that's the wrong question. I healed. Over time, I learned the art of the nap. I would catch myself sometimes singing little songs, even when the baby wasn't in the room. I developed that great gift of wives and mothers: I began to see the beauty in small things. Mothers are like Zen monks who have no choice but to live in the present moment. I'd watch green beans rising through the bubbling water of a silver pot and stand paralyzed at the sight, thinking that it was beautiful, like some type of moving art that I would never capture and never fully see again. Kelly would call to tell me she'd spent the night in the rain making love on a picnic table and then she would say, very gently, "What are you doing?"

I would stand looking down into the violently roiling water beneath me. I would say, "Nothing." And I would exhale in a kind of prayer.

One day, on an impulse, I pulled into the parking lot of a church with a sign saying they had a Mom's Morning Out. Tory was getting old enough to leave her for a few hours every week and it was thrilling even to consider the possibility of running errands alone. Grocery shopping without her carrier taking up the whole basket. Getting my hair cut without having to make the stylist cut off the dryer every few minutes so I could tell if she had started crying. And oh dear God, just the thought of meeting a friend for lunch. When I was in college I used to say that churches are cults, but this particular cult was willing to keep my daughter two mornings a week, and that was good enough for me.

I put Tory into the Mom's Morning Out and the next Sunday Phil and I went to the church. Just to check it out, I told him, to make sure it really was an okay place to leave her. It was a Presbyterian church, the denomination I'd been raised in, and when they sang I knew all the hymns by heart. Phil knew them too. He could sing through the first and second verses without looking at the hymnal and it wasn't until we got to the third and fourth that we had to lift the book and really focus on the page. This surprised me about him, and I think it surprised him about me a little too.

After services, they swarmed us. Of course they did. We were a young couple with a child. We were what they wanted. Did we play whist? Softball? Handbells? Would I be interested in joining the book club? Would he like to sign up for Habitat? Everything that starts out as comfort ultimately becomes a vise—I know that now and I knew that then. But there was a part of me that wanted a community. I craved the God of my childhood. We picked Tory up from the nursery, where a big-breasted woman told us she'd been an angel, and ran the gauntlet of well-wishers out to the car. And as we were backing out, waving at all the people who were waving at us, Phil said, "Maybe we should do it. For her. To give her a base."

"Yeah," I said. "To give her something to rebel against when she turns thirteen." I looked in the rearview mirror as we drove away, watching the church grow smaller and smaller. When I was a kid I'd gone to church and learned the hymns and the Bible verses. I'd drunk the sweet juice, and eaten the thin cookies, played with the broken dolls in the nursery, and listened to the flies drone and thump against the stained glass windows. It hadn't hurt me.

Phil was squinting into the midday sun. "There's something sweet about it."

"I know."

"Did you see they had a basketball team?"

It wasn't long before I fell into the kind of relationships you have with women whose children are the same age as yours. Belinda first. She was aggressive in her efforts to befriend me. She came up and invited me to coffee the second week I dropped

Tory off, and before long she was calling me every day, sometimes in the morning even though I repeatedly told her that was when I worked. I used the answering machine against her like a shield. In the afternoons, when Tory was fretful and all concentration was shot anyway, I'd call Belinda back. I'd walk around the house with the baby in the Snugli and the portable phone in the crook of my neck, carrying out the trash while she said that Michael had worked late every night that week, watering the plants while she whispered she was pregnant again, folding the laundry while she told me she was losing her mind. It was a relief when Nancy moved down from New Jersey and Belinda abruptly quit calling me. Nancy was so well-organized that she alphabetized her spices. Nancy was better equipped to save Belinda, anyone could see that.

So Phil and I settled in. We joined the church and bought a house on a tree-lined street in what is considered the better side of town. The women here subscribe to *Martha Stewart* and *O at Home* and we like to believe that our houses reflect our particular personalities, that each has its individual charm. I suppose that's true to some degree, but for the whole first year I lived here my mother got lost every time she came to visit. She said she couldn't help getting turned around, that every house on my street looked just alike.

I guess I was happy—or at least, to use Nancy's term, I was content. If I was losing touch with my husband, that did not bother me unduly at the time. Phil was building his practice, and I took over half the garage and announced to everyone who would listen that I was working on my art. I carried my pots around to local vendors where they sold them for fifteen dollars, or sometimes—if they stuck a plant in them—for eighteen. We passed the baby back and forth like a baton. It was all very bloodless and civilized, and even now I can't think of another way we could have done it. Before long it came to seem like it was a total waste of energy for the two of us to be in the same room at the same time. I would hear his door slam in the driveway and I would already be picking up my purse. I didn't greet him in the foyer like some sitcom wife, my stiletto heel rising behind me as I reached up to kiss his cheek. I greeted him in the driveway, in passing, saying, "My God, could you have been any later?" This was my chance to go out for an hour, and when I got back he would leave for his run, and when he came in I would make a phone call, and when I hung up he would go into the shower, and I must remember this now, that it wasn't just Phil who was cool and businesslike. It was me too.

Did he ever stop and think that this wasn't exactly how he'd planned his life, that something inside him was going dim or slipping away? I don't pretend to know what men want, what they dream about, or when their dreams stop. All I know is that when we were moving into the house I put his collarless denim shirt in a bag for Goodwill. He hadn't worn it since the day Tory was born, but when Phil found the shirt, the sleeve trailing out of a Hefty bag full of pink baby clothes, he was furious.

"I told you to throw this away," he said.

"There is absolutely nothing wrong with that shirt," I said, pulling it out and sniffing it again just to prove my point. It was two weeks before Christmas. We had built our first fire in the new house, we had put up our first tree, and I was trying to unpack in the middle of it all. I'm sure there was anger in my voice, maybe even accusation. "But since you've always been such a nutcase on the subject I'm giving it to Goodwill."

But Phil said you couldn't give clothes that stank to other people, even if they were poor. He grabbed the shirt from my hands and balled it up and threw it into the fireplace where it slowly caught flame and bits of blue cloth flew against the screen.

This is, to my knowledge, the only irrational thing that my husband has ever done.

Chapter Seventeen

———✖———

N o really," I tell him, "I want you to restrain me."

He says he can do that. Maybe we could buy hand-cuffs. You can get them on the Internet. You can get anything on the Internet. You can get blindfolds and harnesses too, and those white Catholic candles, and whips.

I don't know. Maybe. Part of this game is trying to determine how much I can take. Perhaps I can take being handcuffed, but maybe I can't take being blindfolded at the same time, or feeling hot wax dripped across my belly. I ignore what he says about the whips.

"If it gets bad," he says, "you can stop it."

He is eating lunch. I hear him crunching on the other side of the line. It sounds like an apple. He thinks I should eat more fruit. He talks about this all the time, how I don't get enough fiber. The books say to choose a safeword, a way to communicate that you've hit your personal limit, and they suggest that it be an utterly incongruent word. Not "no" or "stop," because people always say these things in bed, even when they don't mean them. For all I know, "stop" is the most frequently uttered word in the universe.

"We could make it 'apple,'" I tell him. "That's a word you wouldn't normally say during sex."

"The fruit of temptation, very appropriate. We'll try it in Miami."

I was making the bed when he called. I hardly ever talk to him on my home phone. We mostly talk on the cell and I was surprised when he called me here, on this traceable line. This number that could show up so easily on his phone bill, if anyone bothered to check. And if someone bothered to pick up my bedside phone and hit star 69, they would reach him. Or at least they would if I didn't make a habit of calling Kelly immediately after I hung up from Gerry. We take precautions. He assures me that most of them are not necessary, that his wife is no more interested in his daily activities than my husband is in mine.

"I'm not sure about Miami."

"In New York we agreed that we'd meet once a month. And by the time we're together in Miami it will be exactly one month."

"I know," I say. I flatten a pillowcase, ironing it with my palms. Normally I only pull up the duvet and let it hide the snarled sheet underneath, but today for some reason I have decided to make the bed up properly. Layer by layer. He's probably right. When we were in New York I probably did agree that yes, we'd meet once a month, but now that I'm home it's different. A month seems fast. It seems too much.

"What's wrong?" he asks. "What are you thinking?"

"That meeting you one time seems like something that could just happen. Something forgivable, you know? But meeting you every month, that's an affair."

"There's not any moral difference between doing it once and doing it a hundred times. If we're going to hell anyway, we might as well go completely to hell."

"Well, Kelly said . . . you know Kelly?"

"Of course I know Kelly. My God, Elyse. You talk about her all the time."

I flap the duvet in the air and it falls over the sheet like snow. "When I got back from New York Kelly said, 'Okay, so now you've got it out of your system. You just needed to go up there and get it out of your system.' "

"Is it out of your system?"

He knows it isn't.

"You just said," he continues, picking up steam with his argument, "that the next time you wanted me to restrain you. The next time. Implying that we'd meet again."

"I know. But maybe once a month is too much."

"When we were in New York you pushed for twice a month."

Did I? I can't seem to remember what I said when we were in New York.

"Do you want Miami or not?"

"You know I want it," I say, arranging the throw pillows on the top in the careful way I do when I expect company.

"So we're locked in?"

"I guess." I stand back. The bed is perfect.

"I'll get the tickets. Are you having any trouble explaining—"

"How I can fly around for free? I've had an airline credit card forever so Phil thinks I have a bunch of frequent flier miles." Which, come to think of it, I actually do.

"Great," Gerry says. "And don't worry. Meeting once a month is the perfect amount. Twice a month would be too much, like we're always coming and going."

"I know. It would look suspicious, like we're almost in each other's real lives."

"And we certainly can't have that."

I can't tell if he's being sarcastic or not. We e-mail every day and right now we're just wrapping up thirty minutes on the phone during which the main topic of conversation has been his wife. Not how awful she is. Not how he's going to leave her. But about how much she and I are alike, at least when we're up and dressed and walking around. Her name is Susan and he says she'd fit in great at book club, that she'd want to walk with us at the school-yard and then get coffee with me and Kelly. "You'd like her,"

Gerry says, and I have no reason to believe that I wouldn't. "It's just that she's sexually broken," he adds, and I murmur in sympathy, even though this is probably what Phil says about me.

"Miami's fine," I tell him. "Miami in two weeks."

"And I'll restrain you."

"You know what Kelly said? She said we're like kids in a candy store, grabbing everything we see with both hands."

"Kelly's right."

"Do you think it's weird that we're getting kinky already?"

"This isn't that kinky."

I'm offended. "It is to me."

"I know. I think it's kinky too, that was just my half-assed effort to reassure you. Promise you'll tell me if it gets to be too much."

"I tell you everything." I say it flippantly, but the minute it comes out of my mouth, I realize it's true.

I always glance at the church as I drive by and this afternoon I see Lynn, dragging something across the parking lot. I pull in and roll down my window to ask if she's okay.

"I'm fine," she says. "It's just tarps from Home Depot. They're bulky but they're not heavy."

"You're painting?" I ask, rather stupidly.

She lets the tarps drop and pushes her hair up with the back of her hand. "You wouldn't believe the estimate those guys came up with. Absolutely outrageous. I've decided to do some of the work myself. At least the Sunday school wing."

"I don't think anybody—"

"Expects me to really do anything?"

It feels like she's smacked me and I guess it shows because she looks down and taps the tarp with her foot. She's wearing heels. Only Lynn would wear heels to Home Depot.

"I'm sorry," she says. "It's been a long day."

"Do you need some help?"

"Aren't you on your way to carpool?"

"I mean can I help you when you're ready to paint?"

"It's not your job."

"I'd like to," I say. "We never get to talk anymore."

"I see your car here a lot."

"I'm in counseling with Jeff. You don't have to act like you don't know it."

She smiles then, for the first time. "What kind of counseling?"

"Marital."

Lynn bends down and gets a fresh grip on the tarps. "It would be nice to have some help," she says.

Chapter Eighteen

———✦———

By the beginning of December, Nancy has cut her hair like mine. She's also wearing bright red lipstick, a fact Kelly gleefully points out to me as we arrive at the track to put in our four miles.

"She's going to trade in the Volvo for a Mini Coop next, I swear," Kelly says, gripping my waist from behind and putting her mouth to my ear. "She can't help herself. She wants to be you so bad she can taste it."

I shake my head. That's not what she wants.

Today's conversational agenda is the Christmas pageant. After three straight seasons on the manger and wise men detail, I've begged off this year and Nancy has agreed to be in charge. As we walk she asks me what I did with the bales of straw and angel wings from the last pageant and she asks me exactly how I managed to rig up that movable Star of Bethlehem. It preceded the wise men down the aisle last year and it was a big hit—several people came up to me afterwards and said it was the best nativity scene the church had ever done. Nancy can't quite admit this. It galls her that I actually came up with something she never would have thought of doing. But she asks me lots of questions about the mechanics and she's wearing lipstick, even just to the track. I guess it is sort of flattering.

It's funny, these little ways we're interconnected. Belinda often uses the phrase "all in the same boat," and the rest of us exchange glances when she says this. We don't really think of ourselves as being in the same leaky rowboat as Belinda. But she does have a point. Any change in me seems to make the others feel unstable. I slide a couple of inches to the left, and suddenly the world shifts beneath their feet too. At some level I'm sure they were all sick of my whining. It's like I've had this disease for so long that by now I should either have recovered or had the decency to die. That's one level. On another, they counted on my bad marriage to make them feel better about their own. If I agree to be the angry one, then the rest of them don't have to feel it. But if I'm happy, where does that leave them?

I say, when they ask, that thanks to the counseling I'm learning how to make small gestures that I know will please Phil. I brew decaf in the morning in my new cappuccino machine because he prefers it that way. (And, for the record, he was quite right—the reason it wasn't frothing was that I was using too much milk.) I wear blue because he likes that color. I lay his robe out on the bed while he's taking a shower and I leave the paper beside his cereal bowl in the morning, already turned to the sports section. We have sex once a week. As Jeff has repeatedly pointed out, all Phil really ever wanted from me was kindness, and ever since I got back from New York, I have suddenly found that I can give it to him. The coffee . . . the paper . . . the robe . . . the sex. I can give him all those little things that add up to kindness. It turns out it's quite easy to save a marriage. All you have to do is stop caring about it.

But the fact that I'm no longer bitching has thrown the rest of the women for a total loop. Kelly has begun to admit how harsh Mark can be in his criticisms, how he's never there, and when he does come home he drinks too much. Nancy has begun to say, "Well, you all know how he can be . . ." when she talks about Jeff. But it is Belinda who surprises me most, Belinda who seems to be heir apparent for my title of the Discontented Wife.

"Phil and I are getting along," I tell the women and it's like waving a red flag at a bunch of bulls.

Immediately Belinda blurts out, "Why does Michael act like he's doing me a favor when he keeps the kids? They're his kids as much as mine, but whenever I walk out the door for five minutes he acts like he's doing me this big favor."

"At least he comes home," says Kelly.

Belinda says that maybe she should get a job, but she barely got through two years of college and the only job she'd be able to get would be a crap job. Nancy has started tutoring high school kids in math, and maybe Belinda could do something like that. Not math, of course, because Belinda stinks in math, but something like that, part-time. She doesn't want to end up like her mother. You know, bitter. Kelly says maybe we can list all the things Belinda is good at while we walk, but I suspect this will be no help at all. Women like Belinda never get jobs that have anything to do with what they're good at. Belinda is very close to that most dangerous of questions—"But what about me?"—and I dread this for her. It's the potato chip of thoughts. You're better off not opening the bag.

"It's not like I'm asking for the world," Belinda says.

"The key is to have balance," Nancy says. "Time for the kids and your husband and volunteer work and maybe a job, and you need to keep a little bit of time for yourself."

Belinda doesn't even bother responding to such a ridiculous statement. "I need to join that gym you guys go to," she says. "I'm fat. I weigh thirty pounds more than I did the day I got married and I was pregnant the day I got married."

"We've all gained weight," says Kelly, who clearly hasn't. "You're being way too hard on yourself."

But Belinda is having none of it. She starts telling us how one night she wasn't in the mood for sex but Michael was, and you know how it is. Sometimes it's easier to have sex than it is to sit up and turn on all the lights and talk about why you don't want to have sex, so she says fine, just make it fast. But in the middle of it she starts crying.

"And he didn't stop," she says. "He could tell I was crying and he didn't stop."

"Let's list all the things you're good at," says Kelly. Her voice is a little desperate. She doesn't like it when Belinda's unhappy.

Belinda wipes her face on her sleeve like a child. "Maybe Lynn had the right idea."

"At least try," Kelly says. "You're great with children and dogs. And don't you know some Spanish?"

Nancy and I have dropped a few steps behind. "This little party's turning sour," she says.

I shake my head. "She's not going anywhere." And she's not. When a woman's ready to leave she's not talking about crying during sex. She's not talking about feelings at all. Suddenly it's all about getting passports out of safety deposit boxes, buying new lamps, making sure the apartment you're looking at is located within the kids' school district. When a woman is ready to leave there's no anger in her voice, no hurt. Belinda is still rising and falling in the rhythms of a wife—she'll probably go home and make up with Michael tonight.

But there's no way to explain all this to a woman like Nancy. There's no way to make her understand that Belinda's anger means there's still hope for her marriage or that my calmness means I've completely given up on mine. If you're screaming at the man at least you still see the man. But once your voice goes flat, picks up speed, and turns matter-of-fact, then your husband, for all practical purposes, has already begun to dematerialize. He's fading out of the picture, vaporizing like raindrops on a hot highway. He's nothing but a town you've got to drive through on your way to somewhere else.

"What's a man thinking," Belinda says, "when he looks down at a woman and she's crying and he just keeps doing it?"

"They don't think," says Kelly.

"Maybe you should try counseling," Nancy says. "Look how much it's helping Elyse."

Belinda suddenly stops, stops so abruptly that Nancy runs right into the back of her. "Is it just me," she says, "or does it seem like we're always walking in circles?"

Later that afternoon Pascal comes into the studio with a live bird in his mouth. I scream and he runs. He likes to do this, to show off what a great hunter he is, and in the past I've sometimes been able to catch him and pry his mouth open with my index finger. But the release of the wounded is a gray area. It's hard to tell how badly they're hurt—sometimes the animal is able to get away, sometimes not, and if they aren't strong and fast enough he is soon back on them, more businesslike this time. I've never been able to decide if it's kinder to let Pascal finish them off in the first attack or if I should take them outside, leaving them alone in the grass to die their small deaths.

Just as Pascal enters with the bird, Garcia lunges out of nowhere, causing Pascal to snarl. The bird escapes. It makes an unsteady arc toward the ceiling and I realize one of its wings is broken. I manage to use a drop cloth to herd it out of the studio and get the cats shut into the laundry room, but it's hard to say if my decision is the right one. The bird flaps frantically around the house for more than an hour, repeatedly striking walls and leaving behind small explosions of blood and shit. I open every door and window and it finally flies out to God knows what kind of fate. When Phil comes home I'm walking around the house trying to clean the walls with a sponge and a bottle of Fantastik.

"They've gone completely wild," I say.

"That's what cats do," he says, reasonable in that way that only people who've been gone all day can be reasonable. "They kill birds. If it bothers you that much, keep them inside."

"Damn you two," I say to Pascal and Garcia, who are curled on the ottoman, as innocent as a calendar picture, looking just like the sweet kittens I adopted three years ago from the Humane Society. "I feed you all the time. Why are you always hungry?"

"It doesn't have anything to do with being hungry," Phil says. "It's just their nature."

Chapter Nineteen

Miami is hot, even in December. I am dozing out on the hotel room balcony in the afternoon sunlight with a newspaper spread over my lap. Gerry comes out and sits down beside me on the chaise lounge. He presses his hip against my thigh and I move over a little.

"It's hot," I say.

He fishes an ice cube from a clear highball glass and rubs it over my wrists, as if he is a medieval doctor trying to cool the humours in my blood. I love this. There is no greater pleasure than to be hot all over except for one small place, and he uses the ice cube as a brush, stroking coolness across my palm, painting over the heat. I stretch my hands above my head to remind him, but it's not necessary. A pair of neckties has already been threaded between the slats of my lounge chair and this startles me. I didn't see him do it—I must have actually slept. It takes only a second for him to bind my wrists and he does it very loosely. He slips down to his knees beside me, knocking the paper aside with one flat swipe of his arm, and I startle with the movement, as if he's hit me. He takes a second ice cube and places it in his mouth so that it extends between his lips like a small transparent tongue.

This is the moment I find the most unbearably erotic, the intensity with which he stares at me, the lowering of the head. He circles my navel, traverses my belly. He is slow. He knows that it's important that I feel we have all day. He slips the ice cube lower, running it along the waistband of my shorts, and I mumble something.

His mouth is strong. I noticed this the first time we kissed, that his tongue was muscular and he has no trouble forcing it beneath the elastic leg of my shorts. No trouble forcing the remains of the ice cube, thinner and more pliable now, between the folds of my skin. I make a noise to let him know that this is right, he's right, that this is what I want, this slow winding approach, this focus.

As the ice cube grows smaller his tongue grows larger. It's just as cold but the texture is different, flatter and broader with more nuance, a few bumps, the ability to curl or flutter. Even though he has not yet centered his attention, even though he is deliberately stalling the moment when the high tight climb to my orgasm begins, even though he is not doing what we both know he will eventually do, even so my fingertips begin tingling and my face is hot. The ice is gone and I am surprised by the sudden feeling of hands upon my breasts.

I sit up. Or rather I try to sit up because as I struggle to rise, my hands do not come with me. They remember that they are fastened behind my head, trussed with a pair of eighty-dollar Gucci neckties. I am in this strange position, neither sitting nor lying, but somehow suspended, with my back awkwardly arched, and I am suddenly awash with panic.

"Stop," I say. He pushes his tongue into me and begins to lick slowly, systematically, as if he is sweeping.

"No, stop," I say, "really stop. I have to sit up. My back hurts."

He can't seem to hear me. He's focused now. It's good in spite of itself, good and bad, good-bad. He is rough with my breasts. He pulls on the nipples and then twists them as they're being pulled and no one has ever done this, both the pulling and the twisting at the same time. I hear myself make a noise halfway between a moan and a scream, even though we are outside, possibly within earshot of the other balconies, even though part of me likes it.

"I lied," I say. "I lied to you, I lied, I'm lying."

I can't take this. I don't know why I told him I could. I pull on the neckties and dig my heels into the lounge, trying to push myself back to a sitting position. But he follows me, butting his forehead into my pubic bone and the orgasm and the panic are running beside each other now, like horses neck and neck, and my face is so hot that when I lick my lips my tongue feels cool.

And then suddenly I see it coming toward me and there's absolutely no doubt. He's carrying me toward the field in St. Kitts. I know this field. I've been there before. Out from Basseterre about forty minutes with a sweating Coke in your hand, the Crayola-blue ocean on one side and on the other there's yellow wheat blowing in the breeze, turning back into itself, folding into gold. A narrow road, a bumpy road, a rental car with mushy brakes. It's like being dropped into the middle of a Van Gogh painting, like being dropped into heaven, and I remembered it the first time I saw it. It's the orgasm field, the one I sometimes glimpse, just for a moment, before I come. Not every time, just sometimes. But when I see the orgasm field, I know it's inevitable and it's going to be a good one.

I say help and I say no but it's all rising, that blue water, that yellow wheat, coming toward me in a wave. You can't ride it, it's going to engulf you and I try to scream and just at that moment when it hits I say, "Apple." Apple finally comes to me, apple. The next thing I see is Gerry holding his arms out to me. I reach for him, my hands trailing neckties. I don't know when he untied me or if I was ever tied at all.

"It was too much," I tell him.

"Why didn't you say 'apple'? Earlier, I mean."

"I didn't think of it."

"I wasn't sure what to do."

"You did right," I say. "It was my fault. I didn't think of it."

"You seemed to come hard."

Well . . . yeah.

He slips the ties off my wrists. He lies down beside me on the narrow chaise lounge, pulls my head to his chest. I catch the scent of his bay rum soap. His breathing begins to regulate and mine does too, rising and falling with his pattern as if we were mated, as if we have known each other for years. I am unaccustomed to this, to being held in a man's arms after sex. For the first minute I feel confined, and then it starts to feel good, and then I almost tell him that I love him, and then his arm feels too heavy against my ribs and I feel confined again. This is a mysterious land. A mysterious shore I've crashed into, and I am like the explorers who, centuries ago, started for India and hit the Caribbean instead.

He says something. I think he calls me sweetheart, and there are birds, he says, something about birds in the distance. I don't see any birds. "They're beautiful, aren't they?" he asks, and I say yes, because they probably are.

"The game's on any minute," he says.

"I know. We need to bet something on it."

Neither of us move.

When I read about the explorers as a child I had been infuriated by their white man arrogance. How dare they call people Indians when they weren't in India? I wrote a paper titled "The Big Mistake" and my teacher pinned it to the bulletin board with a bright red A. Maybe that's where I first got the idea that being angry was the same as being smart. But I am older now and I feel some compassion for the explorers, crammed all those weeks into their airless little ships, half crazed with scurvy and thirst, so disoriented by their long journey that of course they would think they were in India. Of course they would call things whatever they wanted them to be. Gerry and I set sail intending to find Friendship with Sex, so I guess that is what we'll name this new continent, no matter what it really is.

There are trees all around us, hiding our balcony from the others, making this a safe and somewhat private place to lie naked on a warm winter afternoon. I suppose that's what he's paying for—this luxury, this spaciousness, this illusion that we are in a high room with green walls, walls that have leaves and, apparently, birds. I could sit up and reach for my glasses but I'm not sure that would help. My vision is changing and the last time I went to my eye doctor she said I should consider bifocals. When I told her absolutely not, not yet, she just laughed and said okay then, I had a decision to make: Would I rather be able to see what's close to me or what's far away?

Chapter Twenty

When I get back from Miami there's a call waiting on my machine from the gallery owner in Charleston. A couple of weeks ago, I'd sent her a picture of a pot with a new type of glazing I'd been working on and she says she liked it. The gallery owner is old, with a voice so thin that she is hard to understand on the phone. She always sounds as if she is breaking apart. But she has been my lucky angel on more occasions than one. She is the person who told Gerry how to find me.

I call her back and she says they'll be resuming their gallery crawls in the new year and she wants several pots. Maybe thirty, she says, in her quivery voice, and for a moment I think I haven't heard her correctly. It is an astounding order for someone who works out of her garage and an astounding amount of work. We decide I'll have the first ten to her by January 18. Ten more in February and the final ones in March. Once-a-month delivery seems like a good rhythm, she says, and I agree.

And then, just as we are about to hang up, she warbles to me, "Haven't you forgotten something, my dear?"

"Oh," I say, ashamed of myself. "Thank you. Thank you so much, Mrs. Chapman."

"No, dear," she says. "The price."

"I can do them for a hundred per." I don't know why I say it.

It just blurts out. I've never sold a pot for a hundred dollars in my life. She hesitates for probably no more than a few seconds and I think I've been greedy, that I'm getting ready to be scolded and reminded of what a favor she's doing me. Then she says, "I believe that will be just fine."

I spend the afternoon in a frenzy. I place the pot that I photographed on my kneading table and look at it from every angle. The shape and color are good but the one thing I'm not sure about is the texture. It's a little too rough, not rough enough to show up in a picture, but perhaps unpleasant to the touch, and we can't have that when Mrs. Chapman is paying a hundred per. She'll probably mark them in the gallery for twice that. Maybe I should cut down on the grout. I call Kelly and ask her to pick up Tory after school. I get on the phone and order more clay and then I haul what I do have—maybe twenty pounds—out of the bin and over to the table.

There is something mindless about the kneading and the cutting process and usually this is where I lose myself. Usually there is something in the swollen malleable mass that rises between my fingers that cuts off my mind and sends me back into a sort of God. But today is different. I work the clay but it does not work me. My mind is spinning with logistics. To get ten good ones I'll have to make fifteen, and it takes at least ten hours of work on each pot, and it's December, the busiest month of the year. Not to mention that I told Lynn I'd help her paint the Sunday school rooms. Maybe I should try and get out of that.

At some point the door from the kitchen opens and Phil says, mildly, "You're working late."

"You're not going to believe this. I got a commission. Mrs. Chapman in Charleston wants thirty pots." And then, God knows why, but I can't seem to stop myself from saying this next part. "She's paying me a hundred dollars apiece."

"Wow," says Phil. "That's thirty thousand dollars."

"No. No, it's three thousand dollars."

"Well, that's still good. I'm guessing we're picking up supper."

"That's a funny mistake."

"You know I've never been good with zeroes. You want Thai?"

"Thai's okay." I stand up. My back is hurting and I realize I have been in this same position, hunched over, for hours. "Can you swing by and get Tory while you're out? She's at Kelly's."

He nods and heads toward his parked car. "One green curry and one yellow?"

"Fine." I cut through the clay, looking for airholes. They're small but treacherous. This mound seems well kneaded, but you can never be sure. I cut through it from another angle, and then another. "Phil?"

He turns back. "Yeah?"

"I need you to say you're proud of me."

He hesitates, just long enough that I know he's getting ready to ask me if I'm proud of him whenever he finishes a root canal. He could point out that I don't burst into applause every time he drags home $3,000, or $30,000 for that matter. It would be a fair point to make.

But instead he just opens the car door.

"Of course I'm proud of you," he says.

I'm proud of myself. I've let something go and Phil and I have reached a state of equilibrium."

Lynn is throwing toys into a black Hefty bag. "What did you let go of?"

"I don't know. But whatever I lost, evidently it wasn't necessary. We do better when there's less of me there."

"Do you think it would work to run everything through the dishwasher?"

"Yeah. Most of them are plastic. I wonder how long it's been since anyone sterilized this stuff."

"My guess would be . . . never." Lynn pulls the drawstring on one bag and gets out another. "And you're okay with all this?"

"Jeff says that you can't expect one man to give you everything you need."

"Jeff said that?"

"Well, I mean everybody says that. It's standard marriage counseling advice. You accept a man for what he is and then you find ways to fill in the gaps. Like you used to run."

"And you saw how well that worked out." Lynn pauses, takes the headband out of her hair and shakes it. I have brought her a Christmas gift and it lies unopened on the small table that's here in the toddler room. There's a pair of stretchy gloves inside— navy and gray herringbone, a pattern that struck me as sophisti- cated and subtle, right for Lynn. "You know," she says, "when I was first voted onto the church council, Phil and I got there early one night . . . it was just us and he started talking about you. I can't remember what story he was telling, but at the end he said, 'Elyse is a pistol.' And he sounded proud."

I can't picture Phil saying that, but okay. Lynn has cleaned off the shelves and is beginning to wipe them down with disinfec- tant. She's frowning, or maybe it's just the fumes.

"Do you know what Andy told me the day he left? He said part of me was missing."

"Did he have any theory as to what part?"

"He said . . . this is so weird. He used the exact same words you just used, he said I'd let something go. And this . . . this is strange too. He said it bugged him that I didn't fight with him anymore. He said it seemed like I wasn't all there."

I think of Gerry, how feisty I can be with him, how we bet last week on the Panthers-Patriots game, the way I wrap my legs around his waist and try to flip him in bed.

Lynn mistakes my silence for skepticism and rushes on. "I do have a point, I promise. When I stopped fighting and started running and doing all those things to distract myself, it was just like you said. It seemed like a good idea at the time. Everybody was worn out from all those years of arguing and we needed the break. There was peace in the valley."

"Equilibrium."

"And I thought just like you, that whatever I'd given up on was something he didn't want anyway. But then he wakes up one day and out of a clear blue sky he tells me I'm not all there. And what I can say? All I could say was, 'Yeah, you're right, I'm not all here.'"

"I would've liked to have heard that conversation."

"You just did. That was the whole thing. He said I wasn't all there and I said yes, you're right, I'm not all here, and then he walked out the door. I mean, literally walked out and went to the end of the driveway and turned and started down the road. He didn't take the car. I still don't know exactly where he went."

I pull the sheet off the bottom of the playpen and groan out loud. We got the industrial-strength cleaning supplies from Home Depot this morning but I'm not sure they're up to these stains. Plus I'm a little worried about the amount of toxins we're spraying all over the room. There has to be a choice somewhere between chemically poisoning children or exposing them to the plague. "Maybe somebody was waiting for him. You know, like in a car at the end of the block."

Lynn shakes her head. "It doesn't matter. Ultimately he ended up with the girlfriend. I guess she still had whatever it was that I'd lost along the way. But you know, all I had to tell people was that he had a girlfriend and they were ready to stone Andy in the village square. My lawyer loved it. Good Lord, do you think we should just throw the whole thing out?"

"Let me try the bleach first. How old was that girl? Twenty-four?"

Lynn sighs. "Oh yeah, textbook case. Everybody's telling me I can take him to the cleaners. We're walking into mediation and my lawyer said we'll get him to sell his boat and give me half the money. Andy loved that boat. I didn't want half his boat. Something went click in my head and I said to my lawyer, 'You know, part of this is my fault so it's okay with me if he keeps his boat.' And do you know what my lawyer did?'"

"I have a pretty good idea."

"He clamps his hand over my mouth right there in the hall"—and here she uses her own hand to illustrate—"and he says, 'Don't you ever say that again. You just remember that there's a victim in every story, and in this story, it's you.'"

"Jesus."

"And do you know what else I wonder? Sometimes I wonder what would happen if a woman was completely herself within a marriage and said everything she wanted to say and did everything she wanted to do and just let the chips fall where they may. What kind of marriage do you think she would have? Maybe it would be bumpy in the short run but in the long run the man would say, 'She makes me mad but at least she's all here,' and he'd eventually come to respect that, what do you think?"

Bending over isn't giving me enough strength to scrub so I decide to crawl into the playpen. Lynn helps me swing my leg over the side and then hands me the sponges and spray bottles. "How's it working out with Andy and the twenty-four-year-old?"

"Fine, as far as I can tell."

"Why do you think that men sometimes leave their wives for their girlfriends and sometimes they don't?"

"I have no idea."

"The thing is, when a single girl is sleeping with a married man people always tell her not to be a fool, that the married man will never leave his wife. But if a woman isn't working on her marriage 24/7 the same people say, 'You better watch out, he's going to leave you for a girlfriend.' It's like the woman is screwed either way. But which do you think is more likely to happen—does the man stay with the wife he's used to or go with the girlfriend who excites him?"

"I guess either one can happen. If we're talking about me, then evidently the man goes with the girlfriend who excites him."

"I didn't mean to hurt your feelings."

"You didn't. My feelings don't get hurt anymore. But you didn't answer my question. What do you think would happen if a wife acted like a girlfriend?"

"The wife can never be the girlfriend."

"Never?"

"At least not to her own husband." I stand up and study the rubber bottom of the pen beneath me. "I'm not sure any of this is working."

Lynn shrugs. "I know you're not me, I know we're totally different people, but I can't stop thinking how I did what I thought would save my marriage and it ended up killing everything. You were . . . I always thought if anyone could really make her husband sit up and take notice, it would be you. When Phil said to me, 'She's a pistol,' he sounded so proud."

This is the second time she's told me that Phil said I was a pistol. I'm not sure why Lynn is stuck on the only sentence Phil ever said to her. Maybe it's just that Phil speaks so rarely that anything he says makes a big impression. I used to think that. That when he talked it had more meaning than when other people spoke.

"I always believed that about you too," I tell her. "I thought you had the best marriage in the bunch."

She laughs, shortly. "And why was that?"

"I don't know. You're smart."

"Well so are you."

"And here we are the first two out the door. Evidently a high IQ renders a woman unfit for marriage."

"You don't really believe that."

"Sure I do. Being smart hasn't done either one of us a flipping bit of good. All it means is that if this were in *The Stepford Wives* it'd take them an extra week to clone us." I stop scrubbing and turn toward Lynn. "Do you want to know a secret?"

She is spraying the doorknobs, her back to me. "I don't know."

"I'm happy."

"Well. That is news."

"Don't tell anybody."

"Your secret's safe with me." Lynn glances at her watch. "You don't have to stay all day, I swear. I'm getting ready to take a break myself."

"Want to run to Qdoba's?"

"I'm bringing my lunch now. It's in the fridge."

It's a moment. A reminder that she couldn't keep up with the utilities on the house, that she's moved out, that she's in an apartment now. That they called an emergency session meeting just last week to make sure she was covered for disability before she started climbing the scaffolding and painting the church walls. A reminder that Belinda showed up to walk one day nearly in tears because she'd driven by the church and seen Lynn out by the road with a spear picking up trash.

The silence sits there. I climb out of the playpen, drop the sponges and scouring pad into the bucket. Finally Lynn says, "What do you think Phil's going to get you for Christmas?"

"I already know. A gas grill."

"I thought he was the big grillmeister."

"He is. But the old grill finally crashed and so he got a new fancy one and put a red bow on it."

"He got you something he plans to use himself? Did that tick you off?"

"Are you kidding? You're talking to the new, improved wife. Equilibrium Girl. I just took a deep breath and said to myself, 'I'm lucky to have a husband who cooks.'"

"This equilibrium thing," Lynn says, pulling off her rubber gloves with a smack. "It can only work for a while."

I nod. I don't tell her that I only need it to work for a while.

She walks me down the hall. It's raining hard and has been all morning. I've left my umbrella in the foyer. We pause at the door and look into the December gloom. Jeff's car—a little black Solstice he drives to prove that there's more to him than meets the eye—pulls up in the minister's space close to the building.

He jumps out wearing shorts and Nikes. Evidently he's just come from a nooner workout, and he's really cute, Jeff is, with his stocky legs and the way he bounces when he walks. Lynn and I smile, almost involuntarily, as we watch him slosh through the puddles and head toward the door.

"This man you're sleeping with," she says, "he's not from around here, is he?"

I shake my head. "I'm not that stupid."

Chapter Twenty-one

I've been working hard to make it nice. I took Tory to my mother's last night and Kelly came over this morning, along with the two completely silent Honduran women who clean her house. We have the tree up, the wreath on the door, the mantel decorated, and the tables almost set. As hostess of this year's group Christmas party I am not expected to do one of the main courses, merely the salad, and I have all the components washed and stacked in the refrigerator, ready to be assembled at the last minute.

"Why aren't we using the good plates?" Phil asks. It's a little after six and I've just stepped out of the shower. He has taken one of my handcrafted plates off the table and brought it into the bedroom where he has put it down on a pillow and is looking at it suspiciously.

"Those are the good plates. I made them a few years ago, especially for Christmas, remember?" The plates are pale beige, shot with strands of crimson and forest green. It's not a technique I'd use now—in fact, it looks a little too self-consciously Christmasy. But they're still good for a holiday party.

"This is a formal dinner," Phil says. "I'd feel more comfortable if we used the wedding china."

"We're using the wedding china in the dining room," I say, struggling to keep my voice neutral and wondering why this conversation is hurting my feelings quite so badly. Equilibrium Girl seems to be taking the day off, but I don't want to have a fight with our guests due in less than an hour. "Wedding china in the dining room, where I've set for five, my plates in the living room, where I've set for four."

"We're not all sitting together?"

"We went through this last week. I can't believe you don't remember. I don't have enough of either kind of dishes to seat us all together and nine at the dining table is a stretch anyway. You're in the formal room, so don't worry about it. I'll be in the living room."

"That's a little strange. Who are we putting in the living room with the pottery plates? It seems like we're telling two of the couples they're not as important."

"I'm splitting the couples," I say with exaggerated slowness. "We had this entire conversation last week." Phil is pulling his green cashmere sweater over his head. The color looks good on him, it brings out his eyes, but for some reason he only wears this sweater at Christmas. "Besides," I say, before he can launch into further criticism, "if we don't split the group it'll look like four couples and Lynn and that's not good. I'm sure she feels uncomfortable enough as it is." I actually don't think that Lynn feels uncomfortable at all, but this argument is the one most likely to shut Phil up. He is a careful host. If he had his way, we'd entertain every week.

"Everything looks great," Kelly says as we walk into the kitchen. She'd gone home to change too and I didn't even know she was back. She's wearing a long gray silk skirt and cranberry wrap top and I automatically glance at myself in the mirror beside the phone. My hair is still wet and my face looks mottled and flat. "The other women are on the way," she adds, as Phil brushes by us and heads outside to light the luminarias. "Nancy was parking on the street when I came in."

"Great," I say. "Look at my hair."

"Go and finish. I'll handle things out here. You know they

just came over to bring the food—the guys are at least a half hour behind them. Do you want me to start a bottle of champagne?"

I nod and head back into the bathroom. My blow dryer is loud, but when I cut it off I can hear their voices in the kitchen, the clanking of glasses and plates, the muted pop of a champagne cork, and Kelly saying, "Ah . . . such a festive sound." I stare at myself in the mirror. My hair turned out fine, and the silver slipdress looks good on me. I hurry with my makeup and at one point I look down at the phone lying beside the sink. The women sound busy. Maybe I have time to call Gerry. But no, 6:30 on a Friday night is outside our boundaries, and besides, there's the chance that talking to him could make me feel even sadder.

"It's the holidays," I say to my reflection. "They always make you weird." Then I walk through the bedroom, pick up the stack of flat, identically wrapped boxes, and head into the kitchen.

"Present time," I call out, maybe a little too loudly. "You'll never guess what my theme is for the year."

"We were just admiring Lynn's new gloves," Kelly says, sliding a flute of champagne toward me.

"Sorry I'm not more creative," I say as the women begin to tug on their packages, but despite the surface uniformity of the gifts, each set of gloves was chosen with the woman's personality in mind. Kelly's are black calfskin, by far the most expensive, befitting her status as unacknowledged best friend. Nancy's are white mohair, as delicate as snowflakes, and I thought that Belinda's hot pink suede ones were a little whimsical, like her. That's what I've decided to start calling Belinda—whimsical. Naïve doesn't really suit her anymore.

I charged the gloves to my new credit card. It's in my maiden name and opening it was a bit of a reality check. As the wife of Dr. Phillip Bearden I have a fistful of gold and platinum cards, enough to collectively send me to the moon or at least all around Neiman Marcus. As Elyse Morrison, divorcee and part-time potter, I am entitled to a $2,500 credit line. But the gloves are a hit. The women are standing behind my work island, passing them

around, trying on each other's. Lynn has dug her navy herringbone ones out of her coat pocket, stopping to pour more champagne on the way.

"They're so cute," says Belinda. "Sometimes I think you know
me better than I know myself. Can we go shopping sometime?"

Nancy looks up.

"When I get these pots shipped, then the two of us will ride
down to the outlets," I say. "Big promise."

"Maybe we can all go," says Kelly.

Phil has come in from lighting the luminarias and he walks
right up behind me. He is standing so close that for a crazy moment I think he is going to bend his knees and force me to bend
too, collapsing us to the ground in that silly schoolyard game. But
instead he's come to hug me—a big waist-wrapping ostentatious
hug to show our guests how happily married we are. No problems
in this household, nosireebob. Phil has never understood how
much women talk. He should have saved his show for the men.

"Look at your hands," Belinda says suddenly. "Your hands and
Nancy's, they look just alike."

She's right. The pottery wheel has left me with working hands,
a dark blue glaze permanently embedded beneath the short nails,
and my palms always feel dry and dusty, no matter how much
lotion I rub into them. Nancy's are like this too, splattered with
paint and red and raw from all the solvents. Our hands look as if
we spend our lives clawing things out of the dirt—which I guess
in a way we do.

"Kelly has great hands," Phil says, and he too is right. Kelly's
hands are always flawlessly manicured and curled in a sort of
Mona Lisa position.

"Thank my salon," Kelly says.

"I don't know why Elyse doesn't get manicures," Phil says.
"It's the little details that make a woman sexy, but she doesn't
seem to realize that. You've got to promise me the next time you
get your nails done you'll knock her over the head and take her
with you."

"That would be quite pointless," I say, wrenching his arms from around my waist, "considering what I do for a living."

I don't do anything for a living and everyone standing there knows it, Phil more than most. I'm afraid he's going to say something else but my tone backs him down. He kisses the top of my head and lets the subject drop.

"Where is everybody sitting?" Nancy asks. "I see you have two tables."

"We don't have enough of the good china to go around," Phil says. "Just before you guys got here, Elyse and I were saying we really need to do something about that before next year."

"I like two tables," Kelly says. "It keeps the conversation lively."

"Not to mention," says Lynn, draining her flute, "it solves that sticky hostess dilemma of 'Where on earth am I supposed to seat the poor pathetic divorced woman?'"

Nancy nonchalantly picks up the champagne bottle as if to read the label and then places it on the other side of the sink, out of Lynn's reach. Kelly gives me her Botox demi-frown, as if to say we might be in for a bumpy night.

"You're sitting in the living room with me," I tell Lynn. "I put Jeff between us because I figure he talks enough for two men."

"Oh absolutely," says Nancy. "You and Lynn could split him down the middle and still have more than enough man to go around."

What I told Phil wasn't exactly accurate. I didn't divide all the couples. Kelly and Mark are both in the formal china room while I am sitting in the living room with talkative Jeff, loopy Lynn, and sweet confused Michael. That leaves Kelly to contend with both Mark and Phil, but she's undoubtedly up to it. She is the perfect surrogate hostess, capable of making even two dull men seem like fascinating conversationalists. I can hear her high tinkling laugh from the other room and for a fleeting second I wonder how on earth both of us ended up married to the bad twin. Jeff is telling a long rambling joke about some married couple in therapy. It strikes me as slightly inappropriate, but it's cracking Michael and Lynn up. I strain to hear the conversation at the china table and barely catch the very end of Kelly's last statement, something about "I saw it on the Food Channel . . ."

She is probably referring to the soup course, which the Honduran women are carrying in. It's quite elaborate, a swirl of two kinds of soup in a yin/yang pattern, a combination of Kelly's roasted squash bisque and white corn chowder. It's so lovely that everyone murmurs as it is placed before them and I sit back in my chair and begin to relax. This will be a successful party. The tables look good and the tree looks great. I may not be the über-homemaker of the group but I always do have the best tree and I know how to buy the best wines, and I am seated at the best table, even if I am clinking glasses with my marriage counselor. I laugh, more out of relief than anything else, but it's perfectly timed with the climax of Jeff's joke and he smiles at me. Smiles hugely, as if making me laugh was the best thing that happened to him all day.

"The thing is," Jeff says, obviously warmed up by his appreciative audience, "men and women cheat for different reasons. Men cheat because they want the variety. But women only cheat if something is fundamentally wrong with the marriage."

"Who told you that?" asks Lynn.

". . . and that explains why two-thirds of cheating men stay and two-thirds of cheating women end up filing for divorce . . ." Jeff is like this. He likes statistics. He's always working them into sermons and he gets so enthralled by his numbers that he never seems to realize the effect he's having on other people.

"So what you're saying," says Michael, shocking everyone by speaking at all, "is that if a man fools around his wife shouldn't take it personally. It's not that he doesn't love her, he's just looking for a little strange."

Jesus. Everyone's drunk.

"You guys have gotten awfully quiet in there," Nancy calls out. "Whatcha talking about?"

"What I wonder is how I managed to end up on the wrong side of that equation," Lynn says. "If two-thirds of cheating men stay, how come Andy walked out on me?"

"As fast as possible on the salad," I mutter to the Honduran woman who is clearing the soup bowls away.

"It depends on how you look at it," says Jeff, who seems hell-bent on making a bad situation worse. "That same stat could indicate that one-third of cheating men end up falling in love with the other woman."

"Well lucky me," drawls Lynn. "Married to one of the cheaters who actually fell in love." She has drained the glass of sauvignon blanc I'd chosen for the soup and salad courses and she's clearly enjoying the chance to make Jeff uncomfortable. She tosses her head and strikes an elaborate pose, both elbows on the table and her chin rested in the nest of her hands, as wide-eyed and rapt as Audrey Hepburn in a black-and-white still. Yes, she's definitely enjoying this—enjoying the chance to be the dinner partner, and thus the equal, of the man who signs her paychecks, the man who has done her so many public favors. Jeff and Nancy will be giving Lynn a ride home tonight. He made sure everyone knew that during the champagne hour, that he would never think of letting any woman in his employ drive these treacherous suburban streets alone.

"I like these plates," Michael says, saving the day. "How did I end up at the special table with the pretty Christmas plates?"

I beam at him.

The salad is coming around—my signature pear and blue cheese with walnuts. "It's fantastic, Elyse," Kelly calls in. "Did you find this recipe on the Food Channel?" She knows full well I didn't but her question sets off a smattering of distant laughter around the china table. Evidently they've got some sort of running joke going on about the Food Channel.

"She watches it goddamn 24/7," says Mark. "I came in the

other day and she was sitting on the toilet with her pants down around her ankles watching the bathroom TV. Some show about how to make three different kinds of clotted cream. Is there any wonder why this country's going to hell?"

"So what're y'all talking about in there?" Nancy calls out again.

"Nancy just said 'y'all,'" Jeff calls back. "That's the official signal to cut her off."

Lynn's Salmon in Parchment will be the next course, followed by a collection of cheeses that Nancy brought—since she's directing the Christmas pageant she also got off the hook for heavy cooking—and we'll wind up with Belinda's Mocha Panna Cotta. In anticipation of the salmon, Phil comes into the living room with the pinot noir. It's our splurge wine, and Jeff gives a whistle when Phil shows him the label.

"Wow," Jeff says. "You two know how to do things right."

"I thought I'd start with the expatriates," Phil says, pouring into the big-bowled glasses. Jeff makes a big show of twirling the glass and sniffing.

"You know, when I look at you two," says Lynn, "I always wonder to myself why you're friends." It's something I've thought about too but never said aloud.

"Me and Phil are like two soups in one bowl," says Jeff. "The contrast makes us each better. In fact, you should see us on the basketball court . . ." he adds, changing metaphors and really getting into it. "We have total Vulcan mind meld. The minute he goes up for the rebound, I turn and start down the court because I know exactly where he's going to—"

"Just a splash," I say quietly as Phil moves to my glass, and he nods. He knows that this is the expensive one and there's a single bottle to go around both tables. Besides, we have two more wines coming.

"You can fill me right up," says Lynn.

"It's okay," says Jeff. "She's not driving."

"The reason Jeff and I are such great friends," says Phil, ignoring them and giving Lynn the same small taste he's pouring for everyone, "is that we have all the same virtues and none of the same faults."

"Well said," says Jeff. "We're both loyal . . ."

"True blue," agrees Phil. "We're the men who would never . . ."

"Lynn, this salmon is amazing," Nancy calls from the china room. "You've outdone yourself."

"Everything's perfect, Elyse," Kelly adds, even more loudly.

"Let's hear it for our hostess," someone says, and I swear it must have been Mark. There is the clank of forks against glasses, a couple of smacks of applause. Phil is touchingly happy that the night is a success. He smiles as he uses the white cloth to wipe the top of the pinot bottle. Careful, careful, careful. There's not the slightest drip.

Chapter Twenty-two

I worked hard to make it nice."

"Why? You're not the kind of woman who gets stressed out over a dinner party."

What makes him so sure of that?

"It might be the last time I ever host a big sit-down dinner. This could be my last Christmas in this house."

"Why?"

It's the morning after the party and I am in the car going to pick up Tory from my mother's condo. For a minute I think we have a bad connection.

"I've told you I'm leaving. I've told you that a thousand times." Doesn't anybody take me seriously? Maybe I'm like that tree in the forest. Nobody hears me falling so evidently I don't make a sound. Just this morning I was still cleaning up and Phil came in carrying the ashy bags that had held the luminarias. He said that last night had been nice. Yeah, I said, nice, and then he said, "That's all I want, Elyse, for things to be nice. That's all any man wants."

There's some crackling on Gerry's end of the line. He must be in the car too. "Yeah, you say you're leaving, but you've never seemed to have a concrete plan. Where are you going?"

"Not to you, so don't worry about it."

"Elyse . . ."

"Relax. You're off the hook."

"What about Tory?"

"She'll come with me, of course."

"You're sure about that?"

Of course I am. The courts favor the mother. "I would only lose Tory if I did something really stupid, if I screwed up in some incredibly major way."

"And I take it you don't plan to do something really stupid."

"No. You're the stupidest thing I've ever done."

We laugh. We're ready to laugh. This conversation has scared us both. It's not really a fight, but it's the first shadow we have ever walked into. I am pulling into the complex where my mother lives, a planned community for active older adults, and I wave at the security guard, one of the residents trying to pick up a little cash. He's about eighty and wearing golf pants and he pushes the button to raise the electronic gate.

"If I left," Gerry says quietly, "my kids wouldn't go with me."

He's probably right. Marriage is a game with different rules for men and women. Different penalties for losing too. Gerry's wife would keep his kids and he would become the weekend dad.

"If you go," he says, his voice still quiet, "I mean if you really go, what happens to us?"

"Nothing," I say. I've cut off the car and I can hear him better. I can hear the hurt.

"Not nothing. If you're single, everything changes."

"I won't need you more, so don't worry about it."

"You might need me less."

In front of the parking lot there are some old people decorating an outdoor tree. The man on the ladder looks very shaky. He gets the star on but it's crooked. The ladies on the ground below him are pointing and talking, evidently offering advice, and I realize, with a shock, that Gerry is afraid of losing me, that I have somehow become a woman that a man could lose, a woman who could break a man's heart. It isn't just hurt in his voice, it's fear, and in some dim reptilian part of my mind I begin to see that Phil is afraid too. That's why he says, "Oh good, you made thirty thousand dollars," when he knows perfectly well I made three thousand, why he tells Kelly to take me to her manicurist, why he cuts me with so many tiny swords. I don't know why it's easy to hear the underemotions in your lover's voice and so hard to hear them in your husband's, but Gerry is helping me to understand Phil. To forgive him, even. The man on the ladder reaches up to straighten the star and makes it worse. It was leaning too far to the right and now it's leaning too far to the left but the women on the ground must have decided not to tell him this, because he is climbing down.

"The thing is," Gerry says, "you're either going to need me more or need me less. If you're single you're going to want a whole complete boyfriend, and if I can't be that for you, you'll move on to someone who can."

"What do you expect me to say?"

"Don't say anything. Just think about what you're risking. Not Tory and the money and the house, because I know you've already thought that part through. Think about the fact that you might be leaving your whole life."

"Including you?" There is hesitation on the other end of the line, just long enough to show me my whole future, to show me everything I can and cannot have. I lower my head to the steering wheel. "You want a married mistress," I finally say. "It's safer that way. You and me in a hotel room—we're the new status quo."

"Don't talk like that," he says. "I'll be here as long as you want me."

For some reason this statement doesn't seem to make either of us feel any better.

Chapter Twenty-three

N ancy intercepts me in the vestibule, her arms full of angel wings.

"You've got to help me," she says. "I'm sinking."

It is the Sunday night of the Christmas pageant. I've come to drop off Tory and walked into bedlam. Twenty kids, in various stages of biblical dress and hopped up on sugar cookies sent by some well-meaning mother, are chasing each other up and down the aisles of the sanctuary, using their shepherd crooks and wire-hanger halos as weapons. Except for a couple of fathers rigging up the Star of Bethlehem, there aren't any parents in sight. Apparently Nancy, overconfident as usual, didn't ask enough people to come early and help.

"Separate the boys from the girls," I say. "That calms everybody down."

"Belinda isn't here," Nancy says, a little wild-eyed. "Her parents are in town so I told her not to bother . . ."

"We can do it without Belinda," I say, surprised that she's the one Nancy thought of first. "Lynn will be here any minute and I'll call Kelly. Do you want the angels or the shepherds?"

"I'll take the boys," she says, handing me the armload of wings. "You start pinning these on the girls because . . ." Because girls will sit still and endure an uncomfortable costume for thirty minutes and boys will not. Everyone who has ever worked on a

Christmas pageant knows that. You dress the girls first and make them stand and wait. You let the boys play, then get them ready at the last minute.

I call out for a few of the older girls to follow me and take the costumes into the ladies' bathroom. Lynn comes in a moment later and we get a production line of wing-pinning going, fitting each girl and letting her out into the hall with instructions to send in another angel. We're almost finished when Nancy comes in to check on how we're doing. Now that things are rolling, she seems calmer.

"What do you think of our new picture?" she says, pointing toward a portrait of a red-haired woman hanging on the wall above the couch. The woman is draped in blue and looking out with a sort of eye-locking directness.

We'd been so busy I hadn't even noticed it. "Is that Mary?"

"There's some question as to which Mary," Lynn says, talking in a clinched way because she has pins in her mouth.

"Jeff doesn't think it's the Virgin," says Nancy, extracting a warped-looking halo from a plastic bag.

I finish with my angel and motion to the next. "Where'd it come from?"

"Well, Miss Bessie left the church a chunk of change when she died, I guess you knew that," says Nancy. "And a couple of months ago that mystery niece from Canada finally, I mean like after two years, got down here to sort through her stuff. It turned out Miss Bessie had stuck names on half the items in her house, things she wanted to leave to specific people. She must have known . . . or maybe she did it years earlier. Old people get like that. Nobody's sure why she left this picture to the church. We figure it's a saint of some sort, but Miss Bessie certainly wasn't Catholic so I don't know why she would have an oil painting of a saint."

"It's Mary Magdalene," Lynn says, a little more firmly. She's taking classes at divinity school two nights a week and it clearly bothers her that Nancy never seems to remember that. The pins are out of Lynn's mouth now and she's moved on to the halos.

"You can tell because she has red hair. It was tradition to paint—" She hesitates, just long enough that I know she started to say the word "whores" but stopped herself when she remembered all the angels in the room. Lynn hands Nancy a halo and a few bobby pins. "If a woman in a painting had red hair it was a sign she was a certain kind of woman."

"I've never heard that," Nancy says. She's a little flushed.

"She's right," I say. "But Mary Magdalene probably wasn't a—you know, a businesswoman. They're changing their thinking on that."

This is dangerous turf, even for a bunch of Presbyterians. When our book club read *The Da Vinci Code* Jeff had become so upset by the theory that Jesus was married that he'd devoted an entire series of sermons to debunking the book. It became such a crusade that even Phil had to admit Jeff was going too far. "It's a novel, for God's sake," he had said as we were driving home one Sunday. "What do you think is really upsetting him so much?" I had merely shrugged, but truthfully I was with Jeff on this one. I don't like to think of Jesus being married either. It's impossible to worship a husband.

I look at the picture, standing to give it my full attention. The woman looks back at me, her lips slightly parted, her eyes heavy-lidded, her long red hair caught in a gust of wind that does not seem to have affected her robe. No, definitely not the Virgin, and it is a little odd that Miss Bessie of the Many Casseroles would have such a painting in her house. It's double-matted and heavily framed. Someone spent a lot of money on this picture.

"Well, whoever she is and whatever she did, we decided to put her in the women's bathroom," Nancy says, stepping back and lifting an angel's chin to inspect her work. "She won't bother anyone here."

Ten minutes later Phil and I are sitting in our usual pew, halfway down on the left. The music starts and the lights go down.

The shepherds troop by with their staffs and the wise men follow, the youngest one being firmly pushed out of the vestibule by a feminine hand, probably Nancy's. A low ripple of laughter runs through the congregation. People love it when something fouls up at the Christmas pageant. Last year Kelly and I couldn't find the myrrh at the last minute and we sent little Jay Penney down the aisle with a Rolodex from Jeff's office.

Tory is crouched with the other angels behind the wall of candles. The fourteen-year-old girl who has played the lead six years running waits there for her cue. She obviously hates the role she's been cast into, the price she must pay for having a high, clear voice. Her face is martyred and the angel costume has long ceased to fit her. The bedsheets bind her down, flattening her breasts, and her tissue-paper wings scatter gold glitter with every gesture. Belinda turns to me from two rows up, mouths something back that I don't fully get. But I smile and nod even though my throat is tight and my eyes are filling with tears. I always cry at the Christmas pageant.

Belinda's middle child, the girl that she threatened throughout her long tortured pregnancy to name after me, the child who is so shy that she refuses to be an angel, leaves her mother's pew and runs to mine. I guess this is what Belinda was asking, if it would be okay for Courtney to come back and sit with me.

I pull the little girl up to my lap, her small pointy knees digging into my thighs as she climbs. Courtney has always loved me and I wonder if she somehow remembers the time, years ago, when Belinda left her at my house for the afternoon. We'd forgotten to get the diaper bag with her bottle out of the car but I hadn't realized this until Belinda was gone. I didn't know the name of the salon where she was going to have her hair cut. She'd barely been gone ten minutes when Courtney had begun to sob. Her shrieks awakened Tory, who was fourteen months older and soon sniveling too. I had nursed Tory exclusively and I had no formula in the cabinets and with only one car seat I could hardly take both girls to the grocery. I tried everything I could think of—pacing and singing and jumping with a baby on each hip.

I called Nancy and said, "Should I give her juice?" and Nancy said no, Belinda was funny about introducing sugar, and I said, "Do you have any formula?" and Nancy said, "Well, yeah, but you need to check with Belinda first. I think this one needs soy because she's lactose-sensitive."

I could barely hear her above the two screaming babies. "I can't call Belinda," I said. This was the days before everybody had cell phones, the days when mothers could be truly gone, at least for an hour. "I don't even know where she is."

"Maybe she'll look in the backseat and realize what she's done," said Nancy, but by then Belinda had been gone too long to hope for that. If she'd seen the diaper bag she'd already have come back.

"Then you're just going to have to let her cry it out," Nancy said, in that cool way she has. "It's not going to kill a baby to go without eating for a couple of hours." But if you've ever been with a hungry baby for a couple of hours you know what that means. Courtney frantically clawed the air with her fists and wailed in deep, heartbreaking sobs. Finally I couldn't take it anymore. I stuck Tory into her bouncy swing and took Courtney into the bathroom where I sat down on the closed toilet seat and guiltily took out my breast. Now Courtney sits high on my lap, kicking my shins with each swing of her legs. Nancy evidently went overboard on the instructions to the shepherds because when the part comes where the Angel of the Lord appears roundabout them and they are sore afraid, the boys begin to stagger around, some of them clutching their chests and dropping backward as if they've been shot. The congregation is laughing openly now. There is a great simultaneous click of cameras.

Six years ago I sat on the toilet seat and Belinda's baby took a couple of deep gulps, shuddered with relief, and then went limp. She was so worn out with her weeping that she was asleep within minutes. I heard my kitchen door opening and I eased my nipple from the baby's mouth, now slack and moist with milk, and jerked my blouse closed. Belinda was standing in the kitchen when I emerged. She said she couldn't believe she'd done that. She was an idiot. How had I managed, how had I coped? I knew how hard it could be to get away for an afternoon and now she was nearly in tears. She'd blown it. She'd realized her mistake just after the shampoo and she'd pulled off the plastic smock and walked out and now she was going to have to start all over again, lining up people to keep three kids and swapping off favors with half the women in the neighborhood. I said the baby had fretted for a minute but then dozed right off. I never told Belinda what I'd done, something worse than sleeping with her husband, and I wouldn't confess it to her now, although, to be honest, it's the only time in all the years we've known each other that I've been any real kind of friend to her at all.

The angels come forward, lifting their arms, and begin to sing a sweet shaky carol. Tory is near the middle and she glances at us to make sure that we're where we always sit and then she turns her full attention to Megan, the choir director who has saved her marriage and expanded her house. Tory's face is serious and beside me Phil shifts a little in his pew, as if his body is taking on the weight of her anxiety. "She knows the song great," I whisper, and he nods, but his eyes never leave his daughter.

The angels gaze down into the manger where the role of Baby Jesus is being played by a forty-watt lightbulb. Where is Mary Magdalene in this pageant? I think, and then I remember that no, of course she would not be here. She would be a baby herself at this time—a baby girl in the midst of Herod's reign of infanticide, unimportant and thus totally safe. It would be years before she grew up and met the man who saved her and thrust her into danger. I think of the picture in the ladies' room, the expression that I interpreted as desire but which could just as easily have been fear. Because they look alike, don't they? The same parted lips, entreating arms, slightly glazed eyes. What was she looking at? Or, more likely, who was she looking at?

Phil slides his arm along my back, drapes it over my shoulders. Tory's face is reflected in the dim light of the glowing manger and I smile at her although I know she probably can't see me. There are illusions all around us, some more persuasive than others, and despite what I say, I don't really believe that you can step out just a little. My foolish assertion that marriage is a door you walk in and out of . . . my comfortable myth that you can leave, look up and say, "Oh, it's raining," and dash back in. In my heart, I know better. Out is out. You are exiled to the bathroom. You are glimpsed picking up trash by the road. Or worse, they treat you with that soul-killing gentleness—driving you to parties, insisting that it's their turn to pay for lunch, talking to you in that bright slow voice that people save for small children or the recently diagnosed. The music fades and Courtney wiggles across my lap. I shush her as if she were my own daughter, with the casual entitlement we all share, that sense of a common ownership in each other's children, each other's homes, each other's fates. Think of all the things you're risking, Gerry told me. Think of them all. People here have loved me. Perhaps they love me still, but that doesn't mean I won't lose them. I might make the first change voluntarily, but the others will find me on their own.

When I was a teenager my grandmother used to tell me, "You marry the man, you marry the life," and it seems to me logical, perfectly ordinary karma, that the reverse is also true. If I leave this man then I must leave this life. I squint through the candlelight at the tallest angel, the one who has reluctantly come to tell the good news.

Chapter Twenty-four

The package hits my front stoop with a thud. I open the door to see the UPS truck pulling out of the driveway. I call Gerry. "Thank you," I say.

"Did I have a choice? When we were in Miami, you ripped my best tie."

"What are you talking about?"

"You opened them, didn't you?"

"Them? There was only one box."

"You didn't open it?"

"No. I assumed this was my Christmas present."

There is a silence on the other end, just long enough to make it clear he has never thought about sending me a Christmas present.

"That'll be there next week," he finally says. "In the meantime, I want you to know that I'm a man who honors his debts. The Panthers beat the Patriots, fair and square."

Now I understand. He has bought me handcuffs.

"I didn't think you'd send them."

"I said I would."

"I didn't think you'd send them here."

"What's the matter?"

What's the matter? Doesn't he see how easily, how casually, he could fuck up my whole life? I stretch the phone cord into the kitchen, look at the small square brown box on the counter. "I don't want you to call me on this line again," I say. "You know it's dangerous. Use the cell."

"Don't do this." He doesn't remind me that I called him. He doesn't want us to have two bad conversations in a row. Something like that can jettison a relationship as fragile as ours.

I know this too, but I'm still upset. "You just don't send something like that to a woman's home. You've crossed a boundary."

"Well, excuse me if I don't know exactly where the boundaries are. You were fine about getting a box at your home when you thought it was a Christmas gift."

"What if I had opened it in front of Tory or Phil? What if I thought it was something I'd ordered for Tory?"

"You wouldn't have done that. Look at the address. I sent it to your maiden name."

"Shit, that's the one thing that would draw even more attention to it. The one thing that would make Phil open it."

"According to you, he's never there. According to you, you spend every day alone."

"Are you going to be here to pick up the pieces?"

"What the hell are you talking about?"

"You take evidence that I'm having an affair and you wrap it up and ship it to my house. So I'm asking you—when I lose my child and when I lose my home are you going to be there to pick up the pieces?"

"You said you were leaving him."

"I am. On my own time frame and when I'm ready. Not forced out because some man in Boston has decided to be a total idiot."

"It was a joke, Elyse. You thought it was funny as hell when we were in Miami."

"I confide in you and I trust you and then you tell me everything's a joke."

"It's not a joke. It's just the day I was ordering them . . . I was having a bad day, that's all. I didn't think about your daughter. It made me feel good to go on the Internet and pick them out."

"I'm throwing them away."

"Fine. If you feel like that, I think you should. And, just for the record, I don't think you're ever going to walk out that door. You like talking about it. You think it makes you tough."

"I'm going to hang up the phone now. I'm going to hang up the phone without saying goodbye."

"Yeah, do that. I'm not going to say goodbye to you either."

I put the phone down and the stretched cord pulls it off the counter and across the hardwood floor, bouncing loudly back toward the bedroom. The sound is strangely satisfying. I pick up the box. It's light, mostly packing materials. He says it's a joke. He says it's not a joke. I turn the carefully wrapped brown cube over and over in my hands. Pascal, who likes boxes, jumps up on the counter to watch me. When did I tell him my maiden name? I've told him too much and there's always the question—the question of how far to let Gerry in. He knows my address. He knows my social security number. He knows the hours that my husband works, the time my daughter leaves for school, the amount of money I have in the bank, the way I like to be kissed and how many pots I have left before I've honored the Charleston order. The box is very light, almost as if nothing is in it. It's almost as if he has sent me a box of air.

Chapter Twenty-five

⸻◦⟨∞⟩◦⸻

"Look at this," I say to Phil, dangling the handcuffs in front of his face.

He is immediately intrigued. "What are those?"

"Handcuffs, silly."

"I know, but . . . are they for you or for me?"

We are in our bedroom, getting ready for Kelly's New Year's Eve party. I've been at her house all day, shucking oysters and wiping out champagne glasses.

Phil and I are alone. He has already driven Tory to Nancy's house where she and Jeff have hired a couple of teenagers from the church to keep the kids overnight. There are eleven of them in total and they are having their own party. Nancy has rented movies and ordered pizzas and moved the ping-pong table from the garage into the house. So now the adults can stay out as late as they want without worrying. The funny thing is, it's not New Year's Eve. We are so cautious that we do not like to stay out all night on this alcohol-sodden holiday. We like to spend the real eve at church, with our children beside us, lighting candles in a watchnight service. Our revelries, such as they are, take place on some random night between Christmas and New Year's. It's one thing our circle has always agreed on.

My new red dress lies across our unmade bed. I carefully push it aside and climb over the mattress to the headboard. If Gerry wants to send them to my house, then damn it, I'll use them in my house. I snap one end of the handcuffs around my right wrist, weave the short chain around the bedpost, and snap the other end on my left wrist. "Oh dear," I say. "I seem to be held captive."

Phil is smiling slightly, his hand running along the top of the towel tied around his waist. "What are you doing?"

It is, of course, a pivotal moment. Only two months ago that same question sent me to the closet in tears. I have always felt so vulnerable when I've tried to be sexy with Phil. A single word of sarcasm, a single suggestion that this isn't how he sees me, and normally it would all be over. But something has shifted between us. I no longer care what he's thinking. This, after all, is merely a rehearsal. I close my eyes, toss my head back and forth like some beautiful victim in a movie, and say, "I couldn't get away even if I tried."

It is a faux capture, of course. At any point I can rise up on my knees and simply slip my wrists over the top of the bedpost. But something in my helplessness, feigned or not, seems to excite him. He climbs onto the bed behind me, pulling off the towel.

"Am I the good guy or the bad guy?"

"What do you think?'

His voice is low, almost as if he is talking to himself. "I think I'm bad." I look over my shoulder. He's already hard.

"Punish me," I say. "You know you want to."

That's all he needs. He is on me with one move, entering me from behind so roughly that my knees slide from the bed and the upper half of my body is hanging in mid air from the bedpost. I struggle to get one foot on the floor. "Watch it," I say. "We're going to break the bed." Even though I have invited it, I'm surprised by the fierceness of his assault.

"Watch it," I say again, but he's gone deaf with his own pounding. He hits my cervix and a shudder runs through my body. I jerk my hips—no, that isn't right. I don't jerk my hips. My hips jerk of their own volition, jerk to the left and for a second I almost dislodge him. My mind is scattered all over the place. We've never been like this together, not even back in the early days, and what was it Jeff asked me last week? He asked me what I thought femininity was and I said it's a willingness to be penetrated. Phil gets us aligned and rams into me again, this time with so much authority that I can't help but bow my back and push my head up like a porn star.

A willingness to be penetrated. It's a good answer, but I'm not sure Jeff understood what I meant. I wasn't talking about being penetrated by a penis, but by the whole world. Noticing the way the flowers fall against the side of the vase, that's feminine—yes, come to think of it, maybe that was where I waded into this river, back in that restaurant in Phoenix when I only thought I was brave to eat alone and I didn't see the future, couldn't have seen how it would pick me up and wash me away. I never finished *Ulysses*. I just skipped to the end where Molly Bloom becomes lost in this stream of yes, yes, yes . . . and that's what we've all been talking about all along, isn't it, this wave of yesness, this prayer that begins with the words "fuck me," this absolute joy that comes in the moment where you let your life go? "I didn't read the whole book," I mumble, sounding just like Belinda, but Phil doesn't seem to be listening, and besides it isn't just fuck me, it's like wear me down, erase me, grind me off the page and let me start all over. I exhale and animal air comes out of my body.

And then there is the sudden sensation that someone else has entered the room. Yes. We're being watched. I twist around to look over Phil's shoulder.

"Who are you looking for?" he asks, his voice rough and breathless. I turn a little more, try to focus on the doorframe.

"We're the only ones here," says Phil, who's picked a damn funny time to start reading my mind. He grabs me under the hips and flips me onto my back. My wrists are crossed now and stretched straight over my head so that I am like a martyr on the rack and it occurs to me that in this position I really couldn't get away, even if I tried. Each time he lifts my hips toward him I am stretched a bit farther down the bed until my armpits ache and the handcuffs cut into my hands. I shut my eyes, then open them again and then close them. He presses his fist against my pubic bone to help me come, and I grind hard against his hand. Phil watches me with narrow eyes.

"Are you a slut?" he says. "Are you a whore?"

"You know I am," I say. "I betray you with other men. I bring them to the house and fuck them when you're not home."

He roars and begins to pump so hard that I am driven farther up the bed with each thrust until my face is crammed against the headboard. It would be comic . . . all these circus noises that are spilling from his throat, how he's pulled me first one way and then pulled me the other. It would be comic . . . if my head wasn't being pounded, if my wrists weren't aching, but I manage to lift myself into a better position. and just as I do, it's there. A strange, dark sort of orgasm that falls over me like a curtain drops at the end of a play. When I open my eyes I see that Phil is arching his back and pulling out of me, shooting across my stomach as if we were teenagers without protection. As if I truly were a whore.

Afterwards we're both a little stunned. We don't talk. He is gentle, careful with me. He helps me turn back over and slide my hands up the bedpost until I am free. Or mostly free. My wrists are still tethered. At some point we must have rolled onto my new red dress because there is a dark smear across the skirt. I walk to the closet and pull out another one, a loose black shift that fastens with two bone buttons on the shoulders.

"You're going to have to dress me."

"I don't know how to dress a woman."

"Figure it out."

I saw this once in a movie, a man dressing a woman after sex, rolling up her hose and buttoning her blouse, and it struck me as so sensual, so the opposite of what sex usually is, that the image has always stayed with me. Phil didn't see that particular movie, but he seems to warm to the idea nonetheless. He rouses himself and climbs off the bed. He takes the black dress and, with some instruction from me, holds it low where I can step into it and then he pulls it up and fastens it, one button at a time, on each shoulder.

I let him brush my hair, buckle my shoes, and thread the earrings through my lobes. We go into the bathroom where I am momentarily shocked by the redness of my face. "You want the works?" he says, and I shake my head. Just lipstick and mascara. He has steady hands, the hands of a dentist, and he darkens my lashes and traces the outline of my lips with a putty-colored gloss. We stand side by side, staring into the mirror. Just for a moment he catches my eye and something passes between us. Something . . . unmarital.

I sit on the bed watching silently while he dresses, and just as we start to leave, Phil gets a small silver filigreed key from the bedside table to take the handcuffs off my wrists. It doesn't fit.

"Where'd you get these handcuffs?" he asks, his voice suddenly suspicious. "They're not the ones I gave you."

I am flummoxed. When did he ever buy me handcuffs? Surely I'd remember that. For a dizzying moment I think maybe he has me confused with some other woman, some lover he meets in Miami or New York. I do remember seeing the key in the top drawer of my bedside table a while back and wondering what it went to. Phil tries it again and then he tries another key, one from the desk drawer in the kitchen, and finally the blade of his Swiss Army knife. He's shaking so badly it takes several attempts before he gets the knife anywhere near the slot.

I am not as upset as Phil. It isn't like him to speak sharply to me, and he says that if we can't find the key we'll have to take a pistol and go in the yard and shoot the handcuffs off. "Or we could call a locksmith," I say. "Jesus Christ." We were supposed to be at the party twenty minutes ago. He votes for the gun solution.

"We don't have a gun," I say, but then again I didn't know we had handcuffs. Apparently there are all sorts of things in this house that I knew nothing about. Phil is distraught, walking back and forth between the kitchen and the den with the Swiss Army knife in his hands. I stand perfectly groomed in my black silk dress and try to think of some way to calm him down.

It occurs to me the key might still be in the UPS box. "Call Kelly," I say. "Tell her we're running late."

He nods, relieved to have a task, and while he is on the phone I go out to the cardboard box in the garage, rummage clumsily through the packing peanuts, and finally find a square white envelope. The key is inside, small and filigreed, an uncanny twin to the other. I come back into the house and toss it to Phil. I hold my wrists very still until he gets the handcuffs unsnapped.

"You don't really have a gun, do you?" I ask. "You're kidding, right?"

He gives a funny little laugh. "I don't know why I said that."

"You spoke sharply to me. I didn't like it."

The cuffs spring open. "If you hadn't found the key," Phil says, "just exactly how were you planning to explain this to our friends?"

Whoa," says Jeff, holding up his palms. "That's way more than I needed to know."

"That's my wife," says Phil. "Sometimes she's absolutely crazy." But he says it proudly, just like I imagine that he told Lynn I was a pistol, and from the way Jeff flushes when he looks at me I realize that Phil has already told him this story, told it to him on the basketball court or in the sauna of the YMCA. Here in the counseling room of the church Phil has pared it down to a sanitized version, but earlier, in a different setting, I have no doubt that Jeff was given the fuller picture. Me cuffed to my own bed by my own accord, me on my knees and practically begging, me flat on my back and happy to be taking it hard, and now, magically, all our problems are solved. Everything I've ever said to Phil has been expunged from the record.

I could be angry but I should've expected as much. When you've been married as long as I have you know damn well that sex hits the reset button, and besides, maybe this works for me. I've spent so many years trying to get Phil's attention that I keep forgetting that this is a new game, with different rules. This time I win by persuading him that things are fine. An easier task. When a woman says things are fine, the man always believes her. He'd believe her if she was covered in blood. They think of us as simple creatures who are easily placated by roses and shiny new shoes. Trusting, child-like, easily duped—willing to trade them Manhattan for a handful of beads. Perhaps they're right. My husband doesn't understand me. So what? I don't understand him either, and besides, the fact that he doesn't understand me has set me free. He can't see that being sexual with one man doesn't sate me, it just makes it easier to be sexual with another. He doesn't know how deep I can go, how relentless I can be. He doesn't understand that for women there is no natural stopping point to sex.

Jeff and Phil are smiling in opposite directions and I suspect that if they were indiscreet enough to meet each other's eyes they'd actually start to giggle. Fine, let them laugh. I should be able to coast on this handcuff incident for quite a while. It's a story that seems to make everybody happy. Jeff thinks he was right about what women really want. Phil thinks he has his pistol back. And Gerry—because of course I told Gerry, of course I called him the very next day. I'd thought maybe it would make him jealous that I used his handcuffs to fuck my husband, but it didn't. He just stopped me halfway through the story and said, "Wait a minute," and then I heard a door close and he said, "Okay, tell me again. From the beginning."

Apparently I just can't get into trouble.

How does the saying go? The chains of wedlock are so heavy that it takes two to carry them, and sometimes three. After all, gossip and literature are made up of the unlucky ones, the people who aren't good at covering their tracks. "You only get caught if you want to get caught," Gerry tells me. "I bet there are millions of people out there who have secret affairs for years."

Jeff smiles at me. I smile back. If Lynn could see us, she would pull me aside and whisper, "This can't go on forever," and I would whisper back, "Of course not."

But the truth of the matter is I don't see why it can't.

Chapter Twenty-six

I get my pots fired at a kiln about twenty miles from my house, one of those places where they make commemorative coffee cups for businesses and sporting events. I found it one day in the yellow pages and a man answered the phone by saying, "Jesus saves and can I help you?" His name was Lewis and he told me he used to be an artist "in the medium of concrete" but now he pretty much spends all his time running the kiln and doing pulpit supply for the Southern Baptist Church. He said he could fire stuff for me "dirt cheap" on Saturdays—he was sure I could understand why he didn't work on Sundays—and I got the impression that what Lewis would consider "dirt cheap" I could consider practically free. The first time I drove out there I stopped three times thinking I was lost. You turn off the highway, then you turn off what Lewis called the main road, and then you turn off the dirt road and you drive the last quarter mile following tire tracks through an open field. Charlotte is like this. Make a couple of turns and you're not only out in the country, you're back in 1957.

On the Monday after New Year's, Lewis calls and says we might have a little problem. He's never said that before.

"A little problem like what?" I ask him.

"They busted."

When I get there he greets me with a rectangular cardboard

box whose resemblance to a coffin is impossible to overlook. The box is full of broken pieces of ceramic. It's hard to believe that twenty pots came down to such a small pile of rubble.

"What were you going to sell them for?"

"That's the bad part," I say. "I'd already sold them. A hundred a pot."

"They're bigger than the ones we usually do, aren't they?" asks Lewis, who is clearly trying not to cry.

"It's not the size, it's the texture," I say. "I didn't use as much grout. It's not your fault, Lewis, it's mine. I got fancy."

"You can tell they were going to be pretty," he says, sliding the box into the backseat of my car.

Yeah. I drive off down the long bumpy gravel road, a driveway I normally take at a crawl to protect my darlings. But today I drive fast, the box of green and copper shards bouncing and tinkling beside me. I am in big trouble.

Mark's car is in the driveway when I arrive at Kelly's house. An unusual occurrence and I glance at the clock. Damn. It's not even nine. But I'm here and I can't think of anywhere else to go. Besides, there are vehicles parked in front of the house—landscapers and some sort of stonemasons too, judging by the writing on the side of the truck. I walk up the back steps, the ones that lead to the kitchen, and rap on the glass.

One of the maids is wiping the counter, the taller one whose name, I think, is Rosa, and she waves at me in a way that seems to be an invitation to enter. I push open the door and am enveloped in music, the easy listening that Kelly plays constantly, that pours through speakers in every room of the house, music that makes it seem like you're in some sort of eternal waiting room. "Is she here?" I ask and Rosa points toward the ceiling.

I don't think I've ever walked through this house without Kelly, and it feels like a school in the summer or a museum at night. Hollow and empty, and I remember when Kelly told me she was engaged. She just said, "I'm marrying Mark," as if this were the most logical thing in the world, as if moving into a gated community was the sort of thing she'd planned to do all her life. No one had met him. She herself, in fact, had only been working for him for three months. "Working under him" was the phrase she used, with a sharp little laugh obviously meant to forestall any questions. There was no polite way to ask why she was doing this. She was the last person on earth who would marry for money, yet there seemed to be no other explanation. Well, maybe one other explanation.

Right after Kelly moved in, Phil and I came over for dinner. I was nervous. Back then I was still afraid that my friends would see my husband as foolish or unloving and I told many small lies. Sometimes I would pretend it was him on the phone when it was not. If someone said I was wearing a pretty sweater I would smile and tell them that Phil had picked it out. On the drive over I coached Phil on what not to say. It was especially imperative that he not mention their lawn. Phil was obsessed with lawn care and one of the happiest days of his life was the morning we'd awoken to find that the Yard of the Month sign had been hammered into our shrubbery while we slept. But Mark and Kelly had hired a landscape architect and I knew that if Phil started asking him how he got his hedges so even, Mark would say something like, "Our man does it," and Kelly and I would both have to be ashamed of our husbands, albeit for different reasons.

Phil didn't say a word about the lawn but it was still a bad night. Kelly cooked Cornish game hens, something I have never known her to eat before or since, and she led us on a tour of the house, a style Mark had referred to as Tuscany Tudor. "What the hell does that mean?" Phil muttered as we followed her up and down all three flights of stairs, watching her stiffly indicate points of interest along the way: the skylight above the whirlpool tub in the master bath, the humidity-controlled wine storage unit, the built-in shoe racks, the sensory-activated water faucets, the underlighting buried in the sod of the lawn.

"It's a frigging starter castle," Phil said on the ride home, and then, when I didn't answer, he added, "I guess you think you married a loser." I told him that I didn't want all that stuff. That I didn't understand why Kelly wanted it and that I certainly hadn't dragged him over there to rub it in his face. "Mark's a million years old," I told him. "That's the only reason they live like they do."

Now I walk through this house, hushed and perfect, with the arrangement of tulips and crocuses on the foyer table, the pillows plumped and dimpled on the neighboring chair. It's pretty, of course it is, and I understand it, of course I do, this need for a husband and a house and tulips on the table. Just minutes earlier, bumping down the rutted driveway that leads away from the pottery, I had found my hand reaching for my cell phone. It's amazing how automatic it is to call the husband when something goes wrong, amazing how fast my finger goes to the number 2 on my speed dial. It will always be this way. No matter what happens between us, a part of my brain will always cry out for Phil in times of trouble. Years from now, in a bed far from here, I will have a nightmare and awaken screaming his name.

The marble of the foyer floor is so shiny that I can see the reflection of my legs as I cross. It's disconcerting, as if I am walking on water, and I call out, "Kelly?" but there's no answer. Way too early to drop in, I think, but there are breakfast dishes and an abandoned newspaper on the kitchen table. They must be awake. I call her name again and start up the stairs.

Halfway up the curved steps I enter a zone without music, a spot between speakers, and it is there, floating in that silence between the first and second floor, that I hear the voices.

They're arguing.

No, it's just Mark's voice, but he's angry. One word comes through: "Ridiculous."

I freeze in midstep. It's one thing to hear about your best friend's fight with her husband after the fact, in a moment of calmer recollection, when she's had time to edit out the most upsetting parts and maybe think of a few witty observations on the unreasonableness of men. It's one thing to hear about it at the coffee shop after she has washed her face and put on her makeup and rewritten everything in her mind. It's quite another to walk into it while it's happening, to hear the tone in the man's voice, and to witness, for the first time, the depth of his contempt.

I could leave, go down the steps and out the door. The odds are that Rosa will never say that I was here. But just as I am doing that, putting my hand on the banister to turn, the double doors at the top of the stairs yank open and Mark is standing there in his underwear.

I don't know what had made him mad but my presence seems to confirm something to him, seems to be an illustration of everything he resents about living with a younger woman who has ridiculous hobbies and ridiculous friends who come by too early in the morning. I say I'm sorry, but he has already shut the double doors, and I turn, dash down the steps and back through the kitchen, nearly colliding with the maid. I wrench open the door and see that the stonemason's truck has pulled into the driveway and blocked me. Great. While I'm telling the guy he's going to have to back up and let me out, Kelly comes down the front steps and walks across the lawn. She is wearing Mark's bathrobe.

"I'm sorry you had to hear that," she says.

"I really didn't hear anything."

"So you ran out the door for exercise?"

"I shouldn't have come this early. I should have called."

"What's wrong?"

I glance toward the car. It seems pointless to show her the broken pottery now, but she has followed my gaze and is heading toward the driveway, rewrapping the robe as she stomps. He talks to her like this all the time, I realize. She's used to it. Otherwise she wouldn't have grabbed his robe to come outside—she would have taken the time to find her own. The only thing different about this morning is that I overheard it, and she's embarrassed, and maybe, on second thought, the best thing I can do right now is show her something that's going shitty in my own life.

I pull the box, which is surprisingly heavy, across the backseat and lift the lid. At first Kelly is confused and doesn't even realize she's looking at pots, and then she asks me if I was in a wreck and broke them—a question that makes no sense. The men have begun to unload large flat stones from the back of the truck and carry them around the side of the house. They stop for Kelly to inspect one and she nods. "Yeah," she says. "That's definitely a rock."

"What was going on up there?" I ask.

"Mark got ticked when he saw the bill for the retaining wall."

"Wasn't that his idea?"

"He wants me to bring in money, you know, to contribute something. He says he doesn't know why I'm tired all the time when I don't do anything."

"That's ridiculous," I say. An unfortunate choice of words but it's already out of my mouth.

She shrugs, raising her arms and dropping them with an elaborate, almost European nonchalance. "He pointed out that you have a job."

"I bet he said, 'Even goddamn Elyse has a job.'"

"That's exactly what he said."

There have been plenty of times when I wondered why she doesn't work, but the fact that Mark has suggested this fills me with fury. Mark, who'll tell anyone who will listen about his stock options and 401(k), Mark who has built this exhausting and time-draining empire of linen suits and forced bulbs and wine cellars and retaining walls. Mark who likes having a younger, thinner, well-buffed wife to squire around at the golf course dinners, and yet he can't see what Kelly does. Before she arrived this was a queenless empire, just a pile of sad money. Men don't understand how much energy it takes to pump life into everything, how women live in a state of eternal lactation, a sort of lactation of the soul. She doesn't do anything? She lights his fucking world.

"Well," I say, rocking from one foot to another. The ground is soft beneath our feet and it takes some effort to extricate my heel from the sod. "Goddamn Elyse isn't going to have a job for long unless she figures out what to do about these pots."

"Call the lady in Charleston and tell her you're going to need more time."

"That's not an option."

"Why not?"

I don't know why not. It just doesn't feel like an option.

I push the box back across the seat, listening to the clank of the broken pieces. "You don't have to do this," I say, pretending to fuss with the lid so that I don't meet her eyes.

"I told you I wanted it," she says. "I still do. More than anyone."

"You can come to my house."

"Why?"

"You don't think he would ever—"

She shakes her head, gives a little laugh, as if she's surprised by even the suggestion. "Oh God, no. No. He's just weird about money, that's all. Everybody's got something. Here. Stand on the driveway. You're sinking."

"Why's the ground wet?"

"We have a lot of . . . you know. What's the word?"

"Sprinklers?"

The man waiting to back up in the truck looks at me expectantly and I give Kelly a hug, still taking care not to meet her eyes. "I'll call you later," I say.

"You don't understand," Kelly says. "You can't. Phil never loses his temper."

Chapter Twenty-seven

—◦∞◦—

I'm sure our friends think, if they think about it at all, that I'm the one who dragged Kelly into the church and into the suburbs and into her stone-covered house with its sinking lawn. But the truth of the matter is she's quite right—as illogical as it seems, Kelly wanted this life more than anyone. I found that out years ago, on a December afternoon back when Tory was a toddler. That's the day that Kelly and I had our first fight.

The women of the church were having a cookie swap and I had agreed to bring twelve dozen cookies. Twelve dozen cookies that had to be baked, cooled, decorated, bagged, and tied with a festive bow.

I've never been much of a baker but I tried to get in the mood. I built a fire, plugged in the tree, and cranked up the Kenny G Christmas CD. I had been so excited to move out of our cramped little apartment that I'd gotten overambitious on the Christmas tree. It was so enormous that when Phil and I had finally managed to drag it through the front door we'd been unable to get it upright in the stand. Phil eventually resorted to lassoing the top of the tree and tying it to one of the exposed beams in the ceiling. It leaned a little, and if you knew where to look you could see the rope, two facts that bothered me, although everyone else seemed to think the tree was magnificent. I'd had to go to Target twice for more lights and ornaments.

It was four in the afternoon. The music was playing, the tree was lit, the cookies were strewn all across the countertops, Tory was teetering around underfoot, and I was exhausted to the point of tears. I had dropped a whole bag of sugar somewhere between Batch 3 and Batch 4 (why hadn't I thought to pick up extra cookie sheets when I was in Target getting the lights and balls?) and the heat in the room felt like it was topping out at 90. The spilled sugar had melted and turned my whole kitchen floor into a sticky mess and the sink was full of cookies with burned bottoms, the result of the time, somewhere between Batch 7 and Batch 8, when Tory's diaper had turned out to reveal such a major stinky that I'd had to bathe her and had returned to the kitchen to find black smoke rolling from the oven. My jaunty green bows were not jaunty—I have never had the knack for tying bows—and two of the allegedly completed bags were probably unusable. I had bagged Batches 1 and 2 prematurely, before they were completely cooled, and the cookies had permabonded into one lumpy ball, tied with a droopy little knot. I knew I should redo them but I was running out of walnuts and I couldn't see dressing myself and Tory and driving out to the grocery in the pounding rain.

I was debating whether it would be better to show up with (a) twelve bags of pretty cookies, two of them with no walnuts, (b) twelve bags of walnutty cookies, two of which looked like crap, or (c) ten bags of pretty walnutty cookies when I'd promised them twelve. Just when I'd decided the smart thing to do would be to (d) open up all the bags and take out two cookies from each, Tory came toddling proudly into the kitchen with her hands full of nametags that she had pulled off all the presents under the tree and Kelly walked through the door in her Missoni suit.

"Oy vey," she said, "such a day I've had." Kelly was dating a Jewish guy at the time and she was always doing a bad Barbra Streisand imitation.

"I can't stay long," she added, rumpling Tory's hair and picking her way across the sticky floor to rummage in my drawer for a corkscrew. "You wouldn't believe how jet-lagged I am. Todd and I didn't get back from Maui last night until eleven but I went into work anyway and we have this party tonight. I think it's at the Duke Mansion but he never tells me anything. It might be all the way up at the lake. It's not even like I know where we're going half the time, he just sends the car and I get in. My God, look at you. What are you doing?"

"Making cookies."

"For what? This looks like about a hundred cookies."

"Actually it's about 144 cookies and they're for a cookie swap." Kelly took off her jacket and draped it over the back of one of my kitchen chairs. She frowned and rubbed the back of her neck. "A cookie swap," I explained. "It's a Christmas tradition. I make a dozen dozen of one kind of cookie and so does everybody else and then we get together and—"

"Swap them?"

"Right."

"So you make 144 cookies and at the end you have 144 cookies."

"Right. Only you make 144 of the same kind of cookie and at the end you have twelve of twelve different kinds of cookies." I looked around my kitchen, a bubble of hysteria forming in my throat. "It's supposed to save you time."

Kelly was still frowning, still scratching her neck. "There's only three of you living here. I don't understand why you need 144 cookies, no matter what kind they are."

I leaned against the counter. I felt vaguely sick. "You make an excellent point. What's wrong with your neck?"

"I burned it in Maui. You wouldn't believe what a miserable day I've had. I wear this suit because it's a knit, you know, like the softest thing I have that will work in this godawful weather but it's still rubbed against my sunburn all day long. I tell you, Elyse, I've just about had it. The party starts in two hours and I don't even know if I've got the strength to go get my hair blown out."

"Jesus."

She poured the wine into first one glass and then the other. "What?"

"Nothing. Christmas just gets me a little wacky."

She glanced around the room. "It looks to me like you've got it all covered. Do you know I haven't even bought a gift yet? I'll probably just go online to Crate & Barrel or something and end up paying them a fortune to have it shipped at the last minute. Todd . . . he doesn't get Christmas. I mean, of course he doesn't, why should he? But it makes me kind of sad that he doesn't get it. I know, I know, I never even bother to put up a tree, I just come over here and get drunk and look at yours. I mean, he's trying, he really is. He took me to Hawaii and he did leave me a gift, I mean I guess he did, there's a Tiffany box on my kitchen counter and I don't know how else it would have gotten there. But you know what bugs me? It's in the same plain old blue and white wrapping they always use. They don't do anything special to make it look like a Christmas gift."

In unison, both of us looked toward my tree. There were probably twenty-five gifts wrapped under it, and I hoped I could remember what was in what box because I was going to have to replace all the nametags the minute Kelly left. It didn't help that they were every one wrapped in the same paper, an eighty-foot bolt of green and red plaid I'd gotten on sale. Shopping the last minute and having everything shipped was out of the question for me. Phil had sixty-two patients. We counted them. We knew them all by name. When Mr. Ziegler died of old age, we grieved him and we grieved the fact he'd no longer need his biannual cleaning. We worried that we had bought the house prematurely, that we should have stayed in the apartment another year. I read the want ads, periodically and halfheartedly, because I really didn't want to put Tory in day care. I was selling pots for twenty-five dollars by that time, when I sold them at all, and I'd been buying Christmas gifts slowly, one at a time, since the summer, when we had stopped at the outlet malls on our way to

Savannah. Bought them carefully, stored them in the closet, and then hauled them out just before Christmas and wrapped them in cheap Target paper.

"Well," said Kelly. "You're busy. I'm busy. I guess I need to go." She hadn't touched her wine. I'd probably knock off the whole bottle when she left.

She stood up, slipped on her Missoni jacket, and kissed the air over my head. I watched her leave, then pushed myself to my feet and headed toward the cookies. If I took a couple of them from each bag I'd have enough to finish the last two without any extra baking and I didn't really think any of the women would count the cookies and figure out I'd cheated. Of course, with Nancy you could never be sure.

The door creaked. I turned. Kelly was standing in the door-frame, her hair wet with rain.

"I just wanted to thank you," she said, in a thin reedy voice, "for making me feel like my whole world is shit."

"What are you talking about?"

"Your life, Elyse, does it have to be so fucking perfect? The tree and the cookies and the presents and the fire in the fireplace and the Christmas music . . . does your life have to have a fuck-ing soundtrack? I probably could have gritted my teeth and stood it . . . I mean, I could have stood the fact that this whole house smells like cinnamon . . . I smelled it before I was even in the door but I probably could have stood that and the fire and your gigan-tic fucking tree if you hadn't been playing fucking 'Silver Bells' in the background. Did you know that was my daddy's favorite Christmas carol? What are you trying to make me do, feel like the most alone person in the world? Like I'm some kind of hooker in the middle of a Hallmark movie? And does your baby have to be so cute? You and Phil both have dark hair . . . Why is Tory blond? Have you ever wondered about that? Where did she get that blond hair? Did you order her from the perfect-baby catalog or something?"

"What's wrong with you?"

Kelly slammed down her purse. "What's wrong with me? I've got no home, that's what's wrong with me. I've got no family. I've got no Christmas and at the rate I'm going I never will have. Last night I got in late and the condo was dark and there was nothing but . . ." She stopped, exhaled. ". . . a pile of mail on the kitchen table and the place smelled like chemicals because the maid had been there. It was Tilex, I guess, or bleach. It's all too white, you know, the whole place is white and there's no food in my cabinets and there's nothing alive because I'm gone too often to keep a fish or a plant and don't you tell me that it's all my fault, don't you dare. You don't understand how it is when you come in late at night alone and everything is white and quiet and smells like chemicals. How can you understand it, when your house is perfect and everything smells like cinnamon? Things come easy for you, Elyse. They always have."

"You must be joking," I said. I was so angry that the room was swimming. "I'm killing myself here. Is that all you noticed—that it smelled good? Come over here, take a whiff of that trash can. Tory had three stinkys today and I haven't even had a chance to carry the bag out to the Dumpster. I don't want to make 144 cookies, Kelly, nobody in her right mind would want to make 144 cookies. My tree is falling. It's tied to the ceiling and it's leaning and it's going to fall over completely one night while I'm asleep and then what am I going to do? How am I going to get it back up with all the lights and ornaments already on it? You waltz in here all dressed up and pretty and have you even noticed that I'm wearing my nightgown? It's five in the afternoon, it's almost dark, and I'm still in my nightgown and you tell me that the collar of your fucking eight-hundred-dollar suit is rubbing against your fucking Maui sunburn and you're jet-lagged and not sure if you can bear to have your hair blown out and well boo-hoo-hoo. We're broke, Kelly, this house is killing us, and you come crying to me because some Jewish guy gives you a Christmas gift in plain old Tiffany's blue and white paper and do you know what I want? Do you know what I want for Christmas? If I could go to your nice clean white empty condo where nobody cooks and nobody shits and I could lie down in your nice clean white empty bed for even one night and sleep for eight consecutive hours, I'd think I'd died and gone to heaven, Kelly, I'd think I was in fucking Maui for sure."

We stood there for a minute, staring at each other.

"Oh," Kelly finally said. "Wow. I had no idea. That makes me feel better about everything."

We burst out laughing at the same time and she came over, mindless of her sunburn, and threw her arms around me. Tory, who had been watching us wide-eyed, wedged herself between us and began to pat our thighs with her small hands. Kelly bent down and scooped her up.

"The thing is," she whispered. "I want what you have."

She didn't want what I had. She didn't know what I had, she only knew what it looked like. But it had been nearly two years since Daniel left and now her daddy had died and it was Christmas. "I know, baby," I said.

She smiled and pulled out of the hug, with Tory balanced on her hip. She must have cried a little bit, because her eyes were bright. "But in the meantime," she said bravely, "I'll settle for a cookie."

I winced. "You're not going to believe this, but I don't have enough to give you one."

She laughed her easy laugh. Back to the old Kelly. "Your cookie-swap friends," she said. "Do you think they would like me?"

"They'd fall down on their knees and worship you. But I'm not sure you'd like them. They're a little bit younger than us, you know, they married straight out of college. It's a different world, Kelly. Life out here is a little bit plain."

"Do they drink and curse, these cookie-swap women?"

"Not like we do."

"Then I'll stop. I want them to like me."

"Oh, they'll like you. They'll like you a whole lot better than they like me."

She shook her head and Tory imitated her, violently tossing her little wispy blond curls from side to side. "No, I mean it," Kelly said, hugging my daughter to her chest. "I want to meet these women. I want to join the church and come to book club and Pilates. I'm going to buy the whole set of Le Creuset, all of them, even the big deep baking dishes that nobody ever uses. I mean, I could live out here, why not? I want what you have."

Chapter Twenty-eight

———◦∞◦———

S he breaks things," Phil says.

My mind has been wandering so I don't know exactly what Jeff was saying. Probably something about not wanting to break up a family.

And Phil jumps in with that scary way he has of taking things too literally and says, "Oh no, she likes to break things. She likes to throw them away. You've seen our house—you know it isn't decorated like the other women's houses. When I bring something in the door she throws it right out."

"I can't breathe when the house is too full," I say. "It closes in on me," and Jeff winces, evidently thinking of the dozens of Lladro figurines parading across the cabinets of his living room. Nancy already has eight of the apostles. She's gunning for the full set.

"When people come over they think we've just moved in," Phil says.

"No they don't."

"Sometimes they think we're moving out."

"I like open spaces," I tell Jeff, who for some reason writes that down in his notebook.

"It started on our honeymoon," Phil continues. "She dropped my camera off the side of the ship."

"What does that have to do with anything?" Thank God I didn't tell him about the pots. Why did I even consider it?

"On the last day. In Martinique."

"Come off it. That was a disposable camera, the kind you buy in Wal-Mart, and it was an accident. I was leaning over the rail . . ."

"It had our pictures from the whole trip," Phil tells Jeff, twisting in his chair. "And she just casually tosses it overboard."

"Good God," I say. "Haven't you ever dropped anything?" I try to think of something Phil has dropped, but I can't.

"The whole week went in the water," Phil is saying, so curled up in his seat that he almost has his back to me. "I knew right then what it was going to be like to be married to her."

"We had the pictures that the ship photographer took," I say, in my most reasonable and cheerful voice, the one I used when I was toilet training Tory. "You've got one of us climbing the Dunn's River Falls framed all nice on your desk."

"See what I mean? See what I'm saying? Even after all these years she still has no idea what she did."

When I get home from counseling I spread newspapers all over the studio floor and begin to pick the larger pieces out of the box. I sit like a yogi, sifting through the rubble, a motion that kicks up dust and makes my eyes water. I could go in and take out my contacts but it feels good to weep for a while and I sit on the cold concrete floor and run my hands through the wrecked pots. Maybe I want to be cut. Maybe a woman who breaks so many things deserves to be cut.

But Lewis is right, the pieces are beautiful. And perhaps salvageable. After a while I wipe my face, stand up, wander into the damp room. I pull a plain ceramic vase down from the shelves and try to visualize what it would look like if I glued the shards directly to it. The patterns, now that I stop and study them, are really quite remarkable, more interesting broken that they ever were whole. I am humming as I begin to arrange the pieces around the neck of the vase. It's not what I showed Mrs. Chapman, but who knows, she might like it. Hard to say yet if I like it. I am so absorbed that I don't hear the carpool van pull up in the driveway and I am startled when Tory hits the button to open the big garage door and walks in. She drops her backpack beside me.

"I have diphtheria," she says.

"That sucks," I say. She's been playing the Oregon Trail game at school. The kids only have a certain amount of time and money to get their wagon train from St. Louis to San Francisco and all sorts of unexpected things can happen along the way. Now, through no fault of her own, my daughter has drawn a bad card and she's dying on the prairie. I like this game, and not only because it teaches her math, and history, and geography. I think for a game to be a good one, skill and chance should be equal factors, just as they are in life.

"Sucks, sucks, sucks," she says, pleased that I have tacitly given her permission to use a word that her father forbids. "Because now I can't play for two days and I have to write a paper on diphtheria." She says the word carefully, adding a couple of unnecessary syllables. Dip-a-the-ree-ree-ah.

"This is a bad day for the Bearden girls," I say. "Look what happened to Mommy's pots. Watch it," I add, as she extends a finger. "The edges are rough."

"Why do things have edges?"

"What?"

"Edges hurt people."

"Not always."

"You get to the edge and you either cut yourself or fall off."

I can't think of anything to say to that. "You can use that medical book of your daddy's," I tell her, "to look up diphtheria." She looks at me as if I'm nuts.

"I'll just Google it," she says.

"Oh. Right."

"Do people get diphtheria anymore?"

"No, it's one of the things in the DPT shots they give babies."

"What do people die from now?"

Cancer, I tell her. Heart attacks. Things that little girls hardly ever get.

The phone rings. She runs to get it and, since my hands are sticky, wedges it under my chin and then disappears into the kitchen. It's Belinda.

"I was thinking maybe we could go out and get ice cream."

"Just us?"

"Us and the kids."

"I don't know. We're having a shitty day over here. Tory got diphtheria on the Oregon Trail and a thousand dollars' worth of my pots busted."

"All the more reason you need ice cream. We'll come by and get you."

There was a time when Belinda would never think to initiate an outing, even one as simple as this. And there was a time, maybe only months ago, when she ran every decision by Nancy, even one as simple as this. But Tory will be thrilled to have a reason to abandon her homework and I don't really want to think about the pots. "Okay," I tell her. "Ice cream is a good idea."

While the kids take their cones to the little playground behind the Ben & Jerry's, Belinda and I sit on a bench and drink our hot chocolate. We are talking about how Meredith's math teacher is really too hard on the kids when suddenly Belinda grips my arm.

"Look," she says.

It takes me a second to recognize her. Lynn is coming out of the Starbucks across the courtyard. She's got on the same pink Chanel-style jacket she was wearing the day I saw her with the contractors, but this time she has it on with jeans and boots. It looks better this way. There is a man with her, and his arm is around her waist. He is bald but it is the kind of deliberate shaved baldness of the very young and he pulls her over by the fountain and removes something—maybe a scone—from a flat brown bag. Lynn is laughing. She looks careless, casual, her hair is a little mussed. She looks just-fucked.

"Oh my God," says Belinda. "Do you think they're . . . dating?"

"It sure seems that way," I say, dropping my head. Watching her like this makes me uneasy, as if I'm catching her naked.

"Did you know she was seeing somebody?" Belinda has none of my embarrassment. She is staring at Lynn as if she's the coming attraction on a movie screen.

I shake my head. "No, but why shouldn't she? It's not like she's doing anything wrong. We need to get out of here. She'd be mortified if she saw us gawking at her."

"How old do you think he is, anyway? Late twenties?"

"He's older than that."

"Early thirties?"

"I don't know. We need to get out of here. And we don't have to tell Nancy about this."

"Why not?" Belinda asks, reasonably enough. "You said it yourself, it's not like she's doing anything wrong, even though I'd say he's closer to twenty-five than thirty. I mean, if you want to say thirty, we'll go with thirty, but I really think he's . . . Oh my God, he's feeding her."

"Men do that. Men feed women."

She shoots me a strange look out of the corner of her eye and I know that she's thinking that no, women feed men, that's the way it really works, and my mind clicks back to New York, to Gerry lifting a mussel to my mouth, tilting the shell so that butter and salt and white wine poured down my throat.

"Sometimes men feed women," I repeat, speaking slowly, as if this is something important for Belinda to understand. "When you really stop to think about it, if you go all the way back to

Darwin or something, men feeding women is the way things are supposed to be."

"But his fingers were on her tongue. It's so . . ."

"I know. We need to get out of here."

Belinda shudders, as if literally shaking herself out of a stupor. "Did you know she was dating anybody?"

"Why would I know?"

"You're helping her paint."

"We don't talk about anything personal. I had no idea she was even dating, I swear. Much less . . . eating scones."

When Belinda drops us off, I ask her to come in and look at something. "For a minute," she says. She seems surprised at the invitation. The kids climb out of the van and scatter across the lawn like birds. Tory always says she doesn't like playing with Belinda's daughters but I've noticed that when they're actually together she's sweet to them, with a kind of distracted compassion. It amazes me how much my relationship with Belinda is being extended into the next generation.

"Don't go far," Belinda yells to the kids. "We're only staying a minute."

I take Belinda into the studio and show her the ceramic pot with the shards glued to the top.

"What do you think?"

"You want the truth?"

"I guess."

"It looks like something Nancy would do at Home Depot."

Shit. That's bad. I lean back against the clay bin and shut my eyes.

"You couldn't glue the pieces back together?"

"I wouldn't even know where to begin. There are shards from twenty different pots in that box. It would be trying to put together twenty jigsaw puzzles at once."

"Could you jam the pieces into clay and make a, you know, a . . ."

"Mosaic?"

"Yeah. I mean you could sort of stick them into those raw clay pots and—"

"That won't work either," I say. My voice is sharp and that's too bad. She's honestly trying to help. "The shards have already been fired and I can't embed them into greenware and fire the whole thing again. It just doesn't work that way. It's chemical."

"You could make twenty more and hope those don't break."

"Oh yeah, that's always an option. Keep doing what didn't work the first time and maybe someday it'll come out different."

Belinda ruffles her hair. "I'm sorry, Elyse."

"No, I'm the one who should be sorry. I'm being a bitch because I don't know what went wrong and I don't know how to make sure it doesn't happen again. I think they broke because I didn't use enough grout or maybe I didn't work out all the air bubbles. It's weird because I've lost pots before, but I've never lost a whole batch at once, and I keep thinking maybe they broke because I cared about them too much, you know? Like maybe they broke specifically because they're the ones I really couldn't afford to have break and I put that fear out into the universe and it turned around and bit me on the ass, and besides, you know the really weird part? The weird part is that I like the broken pieces better than I ever liked the whole pots. Look, look at this . . ."

I pull the original pot, the one on which Mrs. Chapman based her order, off the shelf and put it down on the table. Beside it I put the Nancy Home Depot pot. "See what I mean? I like the solid shape of the first one. It's not all glued on and sharp pieces and crafty crappy and all. But I like the way the pattern on the second one looks when the pieces are broken and reassembled. See what I mean?"

"Actually, yeah."

"This was my chance, Belinda. This was my chance to get my stuff out there and make some real money and have it be a real job, a real career, and not something I just do in my garage because I'm a dentist's wife who's trying to be an artist . . ." I look at her. She doesn't appear to be listening. Her mind seems a thousand miles away. Thinking of what she's going to fix for supper, maybe, or how she's going to herd the kids back into the van. "Belinda," I say, and even I can hear the desperation in my voice. "Do you know what the word 'dilettante' means?"

But Belinda is staring at the pots. "You know," she says slowly, "there's one other thing you could do."

Chapter Twenty-nine

He has a conference in San Francisco and all I have to do is entertain myself during the day. I've never seen him in full work mode and I lie on the bed naked while he sits in the chair near the window and pores over his BlackBerry. I like him with his glasses on. Later he does a conference on speaker. There seem to be several different people on the line and I hear how they defer to him. They all talk over each other, but when he begins to speak, no one interrupts him.

"You're so important," I say when he hangs up.

"Right," he says, already back on the BlackBerry.

He wears his good suit when we go out to dinner and something spills on his pants. Trouble. He needs this suit for the final day of the conference, when he'll be introducing the main speaker. So when we get back to the hotel I call down to the concierge to see if we can have the pants cleaned overnight.

The concierge answers the phone by asking, "What can I do for you, Mrs. Kincaid?" I am not totally surprised. This is the sort of hotel where the room knows when you're there and not there and when you phone down for assistance they always greet you by name. Someone asked me that very same question earlier in the afternoon when I called to make the reservations for the restaurant.

But now it stings. Maybe just because it's late or because

we finished a bottle of some unpronounceable French wine at dinner—expense-account wine, Gerry had called it—or maybe it was upsetting this time because I actually had to pretend to be Mrs. Kincaid. "My husband has spilled something on his suit," I tell the concierge. "We need to have it cleaned by 2 p.m. tomorrow." But my husband hasn't spilled anything on his suit. My husband is three thousand miles away, in a different time zone, asleep.

"What's wrong?" Gerry asks me as he comes out of the bathroom. "Couldn't they do it?"

"They're sending somebody up for it now. But he called me Mrs. Kincaid."

His face crumples, just for a second. "Oh honey, I'm sorry."

"And I answered to it. I told them my husband had spilled something on his pants."

The crease between his eyebrows is always there. It's his job to be constantly worried and I have seen that crease all afternoon as he has talked about hedge funds and buyouts and short sales gone wrong. Now it deepens. "What do you want me to do?" he asks, and without waiting for my answer, he kisses me. It's an old-movie kind of kiss. He pushes me against a wall and he likes this, the World War II romance of a man pressing a woman against a wall, but it never lasts long. Almost immediately, my knees bend. I begin to slide. I yearn for the floor, for that solid hardness beneath me, and I am thankful yet again that I am not a man, that no one really expects me to support my own weight, much less the weight of another person.

Sometimes we sink all the way like this, until we are on the floor in a heap. We have been on the floor in New York and Miami but tonight he stops me before I buckle completely and he conveys me, part carrying me and mostly dragging me, to the bed. He captures my lower lip between his teeth and pulls me in. It is not always pleasant, the way he seems to pierce my flesh at just the thinnest and most vulnerable part.

The kiss hurts. I make a noise. He lets go. And then we open our lips, the tips of our tongues barely touching. We lie very still and I think that this would probably be a good time to die. There's a knock at the door. Gerry rolls off me.

"Give them the pants," he says. "And then come back, because the situation is hopeless and I want to kiss you all night."

Chapter Thirty

━━━◆◆━━━

I don't know why she insists on debasing herself," Nancy whispers.

"It's very odd," Kelly agrees, gazing down the hall of the Sunday school wing where Lynn has just disappeared into one of the workrooms. "I expect to show up any day and see her hosing down the Dumpster. Do you think she's like—I don't know, punishing herself for something?"

The question is directed to me and I flash on the memories of Kelly at the public abortion clinic, me cuffed to my marital bed. Women punish themselves all the time, for crimes only they can see, but I don't think that's what Lynn is doing now.

"She's just trying to do her job," I say, and the comment sounds spineless, even to me.

"She's the one who decided what that job was," Nancy points out. "The session's directive was very vague. Nobody expected her to paint the entire Sunday school wing by herself."

"Is she coming with us to lunch?" Belinda asks. "Did anybody even think to ask her?"

"Oh God," says Kelly.

"She's been turning us down for months," Nancy says.

But it's still the first time that nobody thought to ask her.

Lynn emerges from the workroom, a ladder balanced on her shoulder, and we watch in silence as she makes her way down the hall toward us. "I'm up to third grade," she calls out cheerfully. "What do you think of the colors?"

"I don't guess you want to come to lunch with us, do you?" Belinda calls back.

The moment is awkward beyond words. Lynn sets down the ladder and says, very quietly, "I'm not dressed for it today." No kidding. She's actually in baggy white overalls, splattered with colors from every room in the hall, an effect so bizarre that for a second I wonder if she's done it deliberately. If she went to Goodwill and searched out a garment that would fit her badly, straps that keep sliding off her shoulders, legs carefully rolled up with one shorter than the other. It's as if she's created some sort of costume to make herself look like the neighborly handyman on a children's program.

It's hard to say who among us is the most upset. Nancy's northern political correctness, Kelly's southern manners, Belinda's embarrassment over her badly phrased question, my strange and sudden vision of the bald man placing a piece of scone on Lynn's tongue—they have all convened to form this moment in which we stand uneasy and wordless, staring at each other like strangers. Lynn moves to relift the ladder and we all throw out our hands to help her.

"No, I've got it," she says, bending her knees.

Why, I wonder, are we so rattled by this brief exchange? What has unnerved us so badly that it will cast a shadow over our traditional Tuesday lunch? Lynn's ladder is, after all, no heavier than our children, whom we lift all day long. It's no heavier than bags of groceries or a pot on a bat or the Friendship Trays that Nancy and Belinda load into the church van once a week. It's no heavier than a man in sex and certainly not as heavy as the metal discs Kelly and I stack on the bench press at the YMCA, twenty pounds at a time, as this weight that we carefully, methodically lower over ourselves and then push away. It's no heavier than the low-slung belt of pregnancy or the square books of carpet samples in the back of Nancy's car. Women bear weight all the time, so it is hard to say why we stand so silent at the sight of Lynn bending her knees and taking the ladder to her shoulder, carrying it with an experienced fluidity away from us, down the dark hall.

Kelly glances at me and I know what she's thinking. She's thinking, "So this is what you want?" She doesn't mean the work. The work is no big deal. She's asking me if I could endure the pity of my friends.

Belinda's idea was simple. Not simple in the sense it was easy to do, but simple in concept. I make a pot and then, at the greenware stage before it is fired, I break it.

The first time I try to do this, it feels like a sacrilege. It's a misshapen pot I've dug out of the recycle heap, a failed experiment from months ago, but it's still painful to deliberately destroy it. I roll it off the kneading table but, amazingly, it remains intact. I push it down the brick steps leading from the kitchen to the garage. This chips the top but leaves the body of the pot unharmed. I toy with the idea of running over it with my car. I take one of Tory's softball bats out of the sports closet, lob the pot into the air and take a swing. I miss the pot but it falls to the floor with a definitive crash.

Getting it back together is a little trickier, but I use a slip-and-score method I haven't practiced since art school and when I bisque-fire it in the little kiln I sometimes use for testing, it holds. The glaze puddles in the cracks then disappears, sucked into the bisque as if the very flesh of the pot was thirsty. There's something savage about it.

I try not to get my hopes up. I take it to Lewis for the final firing. He offers to pray over it.

Yeah, I think, let's pray over it, and he and I stand, hands clasped in his dusty little coffee cup factory, and I listen to him exhort Jesus to lift up Sister Elyse and set her free. Amen.

I'm back at eight the next morning.

"You're gonna be happy," Lewis says. "Shut your eyes." I do, and when I open them he is holding the pot up for my inspection. I feel a strange kick in the gut, some cellular acknowledgment that this is an important moment.

"Damn," I say.

"Jesus helped you."

"He sure did."

"Between me and you," Lewis says, "after you finish out this first order you need to go right up on that price. I mean shit, girl, these are like art or something."

I have now been married for ten years.

The general consensus is that we should do something special to mark the milestone. Ten's big.

"Europe maybe," Phil says to a clump of people as we're leaving church on the Sunday before our anniversary. We have never discussed Europe. Not seriously, at least. "But of course," he goes on, as everyone murmurs how nice that will be, "we'll have to wait for summer."

"Where in Europe?" someone asks. A guy on the basketball team.

"Elyse has always wanted to go to Italy," Phil says.

I've been to Italy. I spent a semester there in college and Phil well knows that, or at least he used to know that. But everyone on the steps of the church seems to think that going to Italy is a great idea. Tuscany maybe. We can rent a car. Everyone says it's so beautiful. The food is fabulous, and the art—wouldn't I like to see all that art? Well of course, who wouldn't, I say, although the thought of driving through Italy with this man, this man who forgets everything (except, of course, the times I've screwed up) . . . the very thought of driving through Italy with this man sounds like hell.

A woman tells me I'm a lucky girl.

I smile.

In the meantime we go to an Italian restaurant. You have to do something to mark ten years, even if your marriage is caving in around you. I give him a camera. He gives me a tape series called Conversational Italian. The owner of the restaurant brings over a free tiramisu.

And then we go home and get into bed. He scoots toward me and begins. It's anniversary sex—like he's giving it a little more than usual. He wants to kiss me but I have become a master of positioning bodies in bed—not just the X shape, but also asking Phil to do it from behind. "It's deeper that way," I tell him, which he readily accepts, so there's no need to add that the true advantage of this position is that I cannot see his face. But tonight he has an agenda of his own. I let him kiss me once and then I break away and slide my head down the length of his torso. Perhaps he will think I am going to go down on him. Perhaps he will think I want to cuddle. Either way he will not stop me and I pause there, somewhere on the solid ground of his chest, and close my eyes.

Between the wine and the garlic and the faint acridity of his underarm is a smell that is both familiar and unfamiliar. I freeze. Really inhale.

I ask him if he's wearing cologne and he says no, but he found some new soap under the sink and thought it smelled good, that it smelled like something his grandfather used to use. Yeah. Yeah. He'd found the bar of bay rum soap from the Restoration Hardware in New York. I don't know how. I'd hidden it under the sink behind the big wall of toilet paper and sometimes I would take it out and smell it.

But now, lying here on Phil's chest, the bay rum makes me confused and disoriented, like you sometimes become when driving a familiar road. A road you drive day after day, but then one afternoon—and who knows why—you look up and you think, "Where am I?" And there's that moment of panic, that feeling that you're lost right here in the middle of the familiar. The scent on Phil's skin is faint, but I know what it means. I am cheating on my lover with my husband.

Because here, in this moment . . . The smell of bay rum, the feel of a nipple against my cheek, the reality of the larger form beneath me and I think, just for this moment, that all men are alike in the dark. I remember Kelly laughing at me about the twins at the drive-in, Kelly asking, "What makes you think they didn't switch us?" Teasing me for being so slow to figure out what she'd known at sixteen. Kelly laughing at me in book club, saying to the other women, "We've all got to be kind to Elyse. She's our romantic. She thinks if she was with a different man she'd be a different woman." The others had laughed too. Is that all a romantic is? I still want to believe it, that one man is different from another, that I am different with one man than I am with another, but the smell of bay rum soap has confounded me and made me unsure, for just a moment, of where I am or who I am with.

"I don't like it," I say.

"What?"

"That soap. I don't like it."

Phil lifts his head, cranes his neck to look at me. "Then why did you buy it?"

"I don't know how it got there but I don't like it. Please." I push against him. "I think I'm allergic."

"You're not allergic to anything."

"I don't like it."

"Where did it come from?"

"I don't know."

Phil drops his head back to the pillow. "Okay," he finally says. "I'll throw it out."

I've been too harsh. I drag my hand across his shoulders, a conciliatory gesture, and try to think of something that will please him. "The coach wants Tory to catch," I tell him.

"Catch? Does that mean he's thinking of starting her?"

"Evidently."

"Why didn't you tell me this? That's phenomenal news, especially considering she's the youngest on the team. Is she pleased?"

"Not really. She thinks catching is kind of a second-rate position, but I told her I'd been a catcher and—"

"You never played softball."

"I mean I was a catcher in cheerleading. I caught the other girls."

"That's ironic."

"Don't start."

"I'm not trying to start." He pushes off the bed. "I'll take a shower but you need to get in with me. Come on. Get up. It's our anniversary. That has to be worth something."

Chapter Thirty-one

M ark's smoking again," Kelly says. It's the one thing she can't tolerate. At first he was doing it out on the deck, and then he moved it into the den, and last night, he did the unthinkable. He brought a cigarette into their bedroom.

"He said this was his house and he'd do what he wanted, can you imagine?"

"So what's going to happen?"

"He'll cave."

"How can you be so sure?"

"Because he says I give the best blow jobs of any woman he's ever known."

We're in her kitchen making soup. It's something we do every few months—get together and make large batches of four or five kinds of soup. Then we divvy it up, freeze it in small square Tupperware containers, and eat away at it until it's time to do it again. Making the soup is my favorite domestic ritual. Kelly puts on Miles Davis in the background, and now, after so many seasons of doing this, we have a system. I sit at the end of the counter with a small paring knife, a panorama of cutting boards, and all the vegetables and meats piled up around me. I like to chop. Kelly mans the burners, the recipes we're working on that day lined up along the countertop between us, although we've been through the soup cycle so many times that at this point recipes are a bit of a formality.

"What exactly do you do?" I ask her. Men have told me I'm good but nobody's ever told me I'm the best he's ever had.

"There's nothing to it, really. You just lie flat on the bed and let you head hang off the end. It turns your throat into a long, straight canal." Kelly demonstrates, throwing her head back like she's going to scream.

"The man stands up?"

"Yeah, the man stands up."

"Damn," I say, surprised and impressed. "I could never do that. I'd gag."

"That's the hard part. Getting your throat to relax."

"No wonder you drive a Jaguar."

She laughs. We have four different kettles of stock going. I push the first of the chopped onions and garlic toward her and she slides them from the cutting board into the kettles then turns down the burners. We have never discussed the morning of the retaining wall.

"What do you do?"

"With Gerry?"

She shrugs. "I have a feeling that's the more interesting story."

"Totally different. Gerry lies back and I get on my knees between his. I nuzzle. I lick that puckery road of skin that runs between his ass and his balls." I make a fist and run my tongue along it to illustrate and Kelly looks at me quizzically, her hand at her throat. "And when it comes to the cock—"

"It always comes to the cock," she says.

"But not right away. That's what I'm trying to tell you. It can be very slow. It can take a week or a year, and I use my hands and mouth together to simulate the canal you make with your throat. I know, I know, it's not exactly the same. It's a subtle thing. It's about texture. It's about worship."

"Worship?" she asks, smiling slightly, her head tilted to the side.

I tell her about the last time Gerry and I were together. It's not exactly compassionate, I know. I'm forcing her to be the docent of my sex life just as I was once the one who kept all the secrets for her. We haven't talked like this for years, but now she leans forward, her chin in her hand, and listens so intently that I can't tell if I'm entertaining her or breaking her heart.

We had two hours left before we had to leave for the airport. It turns out that the morning Gerry killed the clock in New York was an anomaly; that we are not, in fact, destined to live this affair in some sort of Zenlike world of the eternal moment. Quite the contrary. As the weeks and months go by I have learned the most important rule of infidelity: You must always know what time it is. How many hours have we been here, how long do we have left? Sometimes I catch him glancing at the bedside clock with a feigned casualness, the way a man glances at the form of a passing woman. I am not jealous of his wife, but I am always jealous of the clock. The clock, his other mistress. The one who has more power to move him, the one he always obeys.

"You had two hours," Kelly prompts me.

"Gerry said he was spent. He had nothing left, he was drained dry. He'd been telling me that since breakfast. There was something silly on TV—ESPN, I guess, it's what he always watches, and this show comes on about bass fishing. We're laughing like crazy because the beginning is so dramatic. All the men strapping on their gear and the music sounds like something out of a cowboy movie. The announcer said, 'There are days when you conquer the lake and there are days when the lake conquers you,' and Gerry was being totally goofy, walking around in his underwear, bowlegged like a gunfighter, and imitating that deep announcer-type voice. He does voices, have I ever told you that? He's really pretty good. I looked at the clock and I saw we had a little time left. Gerry kept saying, 'Listen to that music, it sounds like they're going to go out in the middle of Main Street and throw the bass in the air and shoot their fucking heads off.'"

"But he was spent."

"Did you turn that burner down?"

"You know I did. Get on with it, Elyse. I swear, the way you keep stopping and starting it's like . . . And I'm ready for the chicken, by the way."

"Okay, so I do everything I tell you about, only even more slowly, and he's being absolutely silent. Or maybe it was the bass fishing show muffling everything else out. The men had pulled off from shore and I could hear the lake water slurping against the side of the boat. We were fucking quieter than fishing."

"That's cool."

"And when he came it was unexpected—"

"Unexpected?"

"Well, not totally unexpected, of course, but usually he makes this little gasp and he puts his hands on my head, but this time there was none of that. It was just—this doesn't make any sense, but it was very slow. I mean we both completely stopped moving and it happened and it was different. I'm not explaining this right. You know what Milton says?"

"Of course I don't know what Milton says."

"There's this part in *Paradise Lost* when Adam asks Michael—you know the archangel Michael, I think Nancy has his figurine—but Adam asks him how angels make love and Michael says, 'Easier than air . . .'"

"Easier than air?"

"That's what this was. The sex was easier than air."

"Wow," Kelly says. "I've got to hand it to you, Elyse. That was one romantic blow job."

She is looking at me, her chin once again tilted in her hands. Sometimes I think everything in the world changes except Kelly's eyes. They're as blue as they've ever been, as blue as they were back in high school. There is still the hint of a displaced California girl about her—with her rumpled blond hair and the scattering of freckles across her cheeks. Her coloring, in fact, is very much like Tory's, so much so that when we all go out together, waitresses and sales clerks assume that Tory is Kelly's daughter. "Do you ever worry," she asks, "that it's like cocaine?"

"Cocaine?"

"That it takes a little more to get you off every time?"

"Was it that way with you and Daniel?"

She stands up straight, fiddles with the controls on the stove. "Maybe," she finally says. "I mean desire increases . . . it has to increase or else it . . ."

"Decreases?"

"I don't know. The point is, it can't stay still."

"It's the shark of emotions," I say. I try to laugh. "Maybe I shouldn't tell you these stories."

"No, I want to hear them. It's just that—"

"You worry about me."

She looks down into the soup. "I worry about both of us."

Later, after I have transported twelve containers holding four different kinds of winter soups back to my freezer, I call Gerry. I don't actually want him, I want his machine, so I call the cell instead of the office, and when his cool businesslike voice instructs me to leave a message, I spin out a long fantasy that begins with me going down on him in a hotel room. There's a knock at the door. Against his protests I answer it and my friend Kelly walks in. I explain that she and I are doing research on the best way to give a man a blow job. We're trying to decide which matters more—technique or attitude—and will he please help us decide? Of course he will. I whisper into the receiver, "You will do it in a car, you will do it on a star . . . that's just the sort of man you are."

After I hang up the phone I curl on the bed, depleted, as I often am when I talk about sex. As I lie there, half asleep, I hear the muted slap of the pet door and the soft thud of Pascal landing in the laundry room. I call his name and he pads into the bedroom and jumps up beside my pillow with a single silken leap. For all his wildness, Pascal comes when he is called.

It's been a strange day. A strange phone message, even for Gerry and me. Maybe it's just like Kelly says—cocaine sex, and it takes more every time. But Gerry and I have always told each other stories and he doesn't expect anything real to come of them. It's just how we comfort ourselves and today is no different from any other. He won't consider it a promise. At least I don't think he will. And as for telling Kelly that bit about the angels—I'm just trying to get her to talk to me again. Just giving her a yank to make sure that the bond between us still holds.

Pascal's feet are wet and his nose is cold. God knows where he's been or what he's done. "Bad boy," I say, but I'm aware that my voice is gentle, already drowsy and thick. I may as well be saying, "Good boy," and he knows that I am not really angry with him, that I never really get angry with him, despite all the blood and feathers I find on the deck each morning, despite all the things that he has hurt. "Bad boy," I say again and he presses against my stomach, as small and round as a fetus, and we both go to sleep.

Mrs. Chapman calls later that afternoon, just as Phil is walking in, to say that the pots arrived.

She says, "Well, it isn't exactly what we discussed, is it dear?" and then, before I can explain, she says, "It's better."

I am weak with relief. She and I go through the shipping dates again for the rest of the order and I apologize for not warning her that the pots would be different from the prototype, and then I begin to babble, confessing the whole story, telling her how I broke the pots with my daughter's bat and Lewis prayed over the pieces. But Mrs. Chapman says she knows how artists can be. She expects changes, and she would never tie my hands. She's just glad I got them to her on time at all.

"That was cool," I say as I hang up the phone. "She liked the new pots. She's going to pay me what we agreed."

Phil looks up from the newspaper. "Speaking of money . . ."

Oh God.

"They called me from the bank today . . ."

Oh God for real.

". . . and said you'd come in last week and opened up an account in your own name."

"I told you about that," I lie. "I told you the day I did it."

He puts down the financial section and picks up sports.

"Why'd they call you?"

He bends back the page and peers at some sort of chart. "When they ran your social security number they realized we already have accounts there and we keep a big balance. You shouldn't have to be paying for the money market. I don't know why they didn't tell you that the day you came in."

And then he is silent.

"Kelly and I made soup today," I say. "Do you want some of that corn chowder she does?" The blood is pounding in my ears but I am surprised how normal my voice sounds. I'm getting better at duplicity.

"I know why you did it."

Now I am silent.

"Shoes," he says in triumph, turning the newspaper page. "After the bank called I walked out to the front desk and asked the girls why a woman would open an account in her own name. They said it was because she doesn't want her husband to know how much she spends on shoes." He looks up with a slight frown. "Are the good ones really two hundred a pair?"

I shrug. "You caught me," I say.

It is 8:30 before Gerry calls back. Phil is watching basketball. I take the phone back to my bedroom.

"Baby, baby," he says. "I'm in a ditch. I got your message and I ran off the road."

"You liked my story?"

"Oh my God."

He's not really in a ditch, of course. He's parked on the side of a road in his own neighborhood, two blocks from his house. Cell phone reception is good on this hill, we know this from past calls, and it's important that we don't lose each other tonight, when we're both feverish. "Wait a minute," he says and I hear a long zipper sound. Too long to be his pants. He's getting something out of his gym bag. I talk to him about what Kelly does with men and what I do until he suddenly yells out and I think he's been rear-ended. I have a vision that someone has crashed into his dark car parked there on the side of a suburban street, but he says no, that he had just tried to unhook his seatbelt with one hand and it snapped loose and guillotined his cock. That's the word he uses, "guillotined." We laugh and laugh. We laugh like people who see the rescue helicopter approaching the desert island.

Later I curl up and we talk, mumbling our half-sentences to each other without purpose, as if we were really together in bed and not on the phone. He swears that he can smell me on his hands. I lift my own hands to my face, tell him Mrs. Chapman liked the pots. Then he is driving again, looking for a good place to trash his sticky gym sock. He asks me why Kelly and her husband had the fight.

"He wanted to smoke."

"Cigarettes?"

"Yeah. He's gross."

"Has he apologized?"

"Not yet, but he will. If she gives the best blow jobs he's ever had, there's no way a man is going to give up on that."

Gerry is quiet for so long that I think we've lost the connection. Then he says, "Oh, I don't know. You'd be surprised what people leave behind."

I start to ask him what he means, but he's relaxed and happy tonight, spinning out stories like fishing line. He could always come to Charlotte, he says teasingly. He wishes it were possible for him to meet all my friends. Maybe he could show up at book club. The ladies would be dressed in white lace with gloves and veiled hats—no, perhaps better that our hair is piled up on top of our heads. We sit in wicker chairs with a ceiling fan making a slow arc above and we're discussing—what would we be discussing? Ah, yes, we'd be discussing Virginia Woolf and her use of time in *Mrs. Dalloway.* Someone would serve cucumber sandwiches and champagne from a silver tray—no, maybe tea would be better, tea in very thin china cups, and then the doorbell would ring. He'd be standing out on the porch in a seersucker suit with a straw hat in his hands. I would rise, skirts rustling, and say, "But ladies, you must meet my friend Gerald . . ." and I would go to the door and let him in.

"It won't work," I tell him. "I could never get my book club to read Virginia Woolf."

Chapter Thirty-two

D o you ever think about his wife?"

Lynn and I have finished the sixth grade room, and the seventh, and are now on the last classroom in the row. We have developed a system—we both scrape and then I tape and she comes behind me, painting. We've gotten fast.

"When you were married," I respond, "did you and Andy sleep entwined?"

She shakes her head.

"Neither do Phil and I. And with this new guy . . . do you sleep entwined with him?"

The question makes her uncomfortable, but she doesn't ask how I knew she was dating. "He's never spent a single night at my apartment," she says. "I wouldn't put my boys in the middle of that."

"I know you wouldn't. But when Andy has the kids and he's at your place, do you sleep entwined?" She shakes her head again. "No," I say. "I didn't think so, because I've got this theory that you're either the kind of person who likes to sleep touching somebody or you're not. I don't think it indicates how much you like the person, or how great the sex was, or whether they're a spouse or a lover. I think you're just either an entwined sleeper or you aren't."

"You're probably right, but what does this have to do with his wife?"

I pull the ladder over to the windows and climb up with a roll of masking tape. "This is how I know that Gerry and his wife are still a couple. He's an entwined sleeper. He wants us to sleep on our sides like spoons with his top leg stretched over my hip. You know how men like to do that, throw their leg over your hip, like they're trying to climb into you, like you're some kind of canoe or something? I can't stand it. It's like he's pinning me down. I can only go to sleep if I'm lying flat on my back like a corpse."

"So how do you and Gerry sleep?"

"Badly. I tried it at first. I didn't want to push him away or make him feel rejected so the first few nights I really tried to go to sleep with him all wrapped around me. It didn't seem like too much to ask. Because that's the way it is in the movies, right? You fall asleep in each other's arms and nobody moves until morning. But it drove me nuts. I'd wait until he was asleep and then I'd ease my way out from under him and scrooch across the bed, but he's a chaser . . ."

She moves the can of paint. "Oh no."

"Yeah. He's one of those chaser people. He'd go scrooching his way after me in his sleep. I'd end up right on the edge of the bed, one cheek of my ass hanging in mid air, and I'd wait until he got settled again, and then I'd disentangle myself and get up and walk around to the other side of the bed. That would work for an hour or so and then he'd flip onto his other side and come after me again. Finally, after a couple of nights of pure torment, I tell him I just don't like to be touched when I sleep."

"And he was okay with that?"

"Basically he was. He didn't take it like some big symbol or something. So the next time we get into bed I give him this big fat goodnight kiss and roll over to my side of the bed and go right to sleep. But every time I woke up through the night he was awake. Half the time he wasn't even in the bed. He'd get up and pace."

"So what'd you do?"

"I said, 'Are you still awake?' and he said, 'Yeah,' because of course he was, he was standing up looking out the window. I asked him what he did on all the nights that he traveled for business and he finally tells me—I swear I think this almost killed him—that he would line up three pillows end to end like a fake wife and put his leg over her and go to sleep. I said, 'So, okay, we need to make a Susan,' and he said, 'Don't be ridiculous,' but I got all the spare pillows out of the closet and we made a Susan between us right down the middle of the bed. He threw his leg over her and I lay down flat on my back on the other side and we both slept straight through to morning. We do it automatically now. I even request extra pillows when we check in. Three of them. I think she's taller than me."

Lynn looks up at me. "That's a very weird story, Elyse."

"I know. But you asked me how I feel about his wife and I'm trying to answer your question. It's not like I ever forget she's there. She's literally in the bed between us, for God's sake. That's what it is when you're nearly forty and you're married and you have a lover. You do whatever it takes to make it work for everybody, for all the people in all the beds. You realize . . . you realize that nobody deserves to get hurt, not your husband or his wife or sure as hell not these four little kids who've never done anything wrong. So you find yourself doing whatever it takes."

"The day I got divorced . . ." Lynn says. "I don't know . . . Do you want to take a break?"

I nod. We go outside, across the playground and past the cabin where the youth group has their meetings, and to a bench, the only part of the churchyard that is in shade. Lynn sits down and unscrews her bottle of water.

"Okay," I say. "What happened the day you got divorced?"

"I don't know why I'm telling you this."

"'Cause you think I need to know it. And you're probably right. You're the only one who's ahead of me on this trail."

She laughs, takes the ball cap off and tries to fluff her hair. "I don't know if I'd put it that way."

"Come on. Where were you? Uptown?"

"Yeah . . . I saw Andy coming out of the courthouse and he looked awful. I sat in my car and watched him walk across the parking lot and get in his little leased Toyota. He just sat there with his head bent down over the steering wheel. I couldn't tell if he was crying or praying or just thinking. He never did much of any of those things when we were married . . ." I smile and she smiles back. "I know. But it bothered me that he was so sad and lost. Everyone said . . . you know what everyone said."

"They said you should hate him because he's the one who left." The one who leaves is always the villain. If we were to ever acknowledge, even slightly, that the one who left might have had his or her reasons, then we would become no better than animals. Pretty soon we would be chasing cars and peeing in the yard.

Lynn shoots me a look. "But I couldn't hate him. He looked so small in that car. I know it doesn't make any sense. But he sat there and I sat there and watched him and after a while he drove away and I followed him. I told myself that he was upset and I just wanted to make sure he got home okay. After all, he's still the boys' father. I didn't want him to have a wreck or do anything stupid. That's what I told myself, but I'm not really sure why I followed him. He saw me at the first stoplight. He saw me behind him and he waved . . . I don't even know why I remembered that, but you're right. It's funny the things you end up doing."

"What did you do when he waved?"

"It doesn't matter. It's just that if you leave Phil you might find yourself—"

"Fucking him in the backseat of a Toyota on the day our divorce is final?"

"That's not exactly what happened."

"Was it out of pity or because you still loved him?"

Lynn looks away. "I don't know. Probably a little of both."

"Were you already dating that guy by that point? I'm sorry, I don't know his name."

"It's better if they don't have names. Yeah, I was dating him, if that's the term you want to use. But he didn't have anything to do with how I felt about Andy. It's hard to explain."

"I understand. You don't turn it on and off like a faucet."

"Is there a part of you that still loves Phil?"

"Yeah, if that's the term you want to use. I probably would have done the same thing in the car that day. I care about him. I don't want to be married to him anymore but I don't want to see him hurt." The church doors have opened and children are running out into the playground. Soon it will be too loud to talk. So I lick my lips and ask her the question I most want to ask. "Do you ever wish you were still married?"

Lynn snaps her chin back in one quick move and looks me right in the eye. "God no. I mean, God no. Jesus and Elvis and a team of wild horses couldn't drag me back into it. I was just trying to tell you not to be surprised if you end up doing things . . . but you already know all that. In fact, I think you're farther down the trail than I am."

I lean my head back and look up at the branches above us, running through the winter sky like cracks in a pot. "Well, that's bad news. I was counting on you to tell me what's going to happen next."

"This deal about making a wife down the middle of the bed with pillows—that's a very odd story, Elyse."

"I know."

"And kind of sweet."

I link my arm through hers. This may be—other than flapping arms and air kisses—the only time that Lynn and I have ever touched. "I think your story about blowing Andy in his Toyota is kind of sweet too."

"Don't laugh at me," she says, but she's laughing too.

"No, I understand. Love makes people act weird."

"That's funny." Lynn wipes her eyes. "In all these months, that's the first time I've heard you say the word 'love.'"

I wipe my eyes too. "Exactly what did you think we've been talking about?"

Chapter Thirty-three

Two weeks later a postcard comes from Mrs. Chapman's gallery, announcing the dates for their March crawl. My pot is on the front.

When I call to thank her, she says, "But my dear, you're going to be a big hit. The cards only went out this Thursday and we've already had an order, that man from Boston."

I had debated whether I should send Gerry a pot and then decided not to. He's never seen my work and I wonder if he really liked the picture on the front of the gallery postcard or if he just wanted me to make an early sale.

"That's wonderful," I say.

"You know the one, dear," Mrs. Chapman says. "That man who likes you so much."

The gallery has already sold one of my pots," I tell him at lunchtime on the phone. "The postcard just came out on Thursday. It's a good omen."

"I'm proud of you," he says.

"Do you want me to send you one?"

"No. I mean, of course I'd love to have it. I just know you're under the gun about making them right now."

I am smiling into the receiver. "I could bring you a pot when I come up on Tuesday."

"About Boston—" He goes into a rambling, complicated explanation about my ticket, and having a driver waiting for me when I arrive because he has a meeting that could run long, and I need to bring a coat of course because it's always fifteen to twenty degrees colder in Boston than it is in Charlotte, he's tracked it on the Weather Channel, and that's pretty much the average differential, and then he says, "Do you mind that I plan all this stuff?"

"I like it."

"You don't think I'm a bully?"

"I think you're my wife."

"Because sometimes I hang up the phone and say, 'Damn, man, you were way too controlling.'"

"It's nice not to think."

"I know you're perfectly capable of handling all the details, I just don't think you should have to," he says. "You shouldn't be bothered. You're an artist."

"I love you."

"What?"

"I love it when you handle the details."

There's a pause. "I've got to go," I finally say. "I've got book club tonight."

"Bring me one of those pots," he says. "I'll put it on my desk."

"We're starting to keep secrets from each other."

"I know," he says. "This thing is getting real."

Watch *Oprah*."

"What?"

"*Oprah*. Cut it on."

I walk into the den, click on the TV. It's a program about mothers who have lost custody of their children. I check to make sure Tory is still in the playroom with the neighbor's kid and then I sit down and dutifully watch the show through to the end, even though it makes me a little sick.

Kelly is calling back before the credits even begin to roll. "You need to do it," she says. "All the things they said."

"Kelly—"

"No, I mean it, Elyse, you think just because you're the mother everything would automatically go toward you, but what if you lost Tory, have you ever really thought about that? Did you see the part about the notebook?"

"They were wrapping it up when I turned the TV on but I think—"

"Because that's what you need to do. Keep a little spiral notebook in your car and write down every time you do something for Tory. All the times you take her to the doctor, or ball practice, or go by the school—"

"Oh, come off it, I volunteer with her art teacher every week. Just yesterday I helped the second graders make bunnies out of papier-mâché."

"Write it down. Make sure you stop by the office and sign in every time too so they've got a record. You might have to prove that you're the one who does everything for her."

"Everybody knows—"

"Part of what everybody knows is that you go out of town every month."

"For two days. Are you honestly telling me that Phil being responsible for our daughter for two lousy days a month is worth more than me being on duty the other twenty-eight? What kind of math is that?"

"And watch the drinking."

"I don't drink that much."

"Because you saw the part about that guy who took a picture of their recycling bin with all the wine bottles in it . . . Does Phil have a camera?"

"I don't drink any more than you do."

"Did you not even see the show? It's not like those women were trailer trash. They're just normal people who made a few mistakes . . . We probably shouldn't even be talking on this phone. Phones are the worst."

"Phil wouldn't be that vindictive."

"You don't know what Phil might be. Picture a transcript of every conversation you've ever had all printed out word by word and stacked on some lawyer's desk. And some big blown-up pictures of your recycling bin."

That is an appalling thought.

"And you need to start documenting when you help her with her homework or do her laundry. Even cooking. Those are the things that count. And the fact that you give blood all the time and send money to that orphan in Thailand or wherever she is. That kind of stuff. Write it down."

"If I lived like that I'd lose my mind."

"You've already lost your mind, that's why I'm trying to think for you. I wake up in sweats sometimes. I had this dream that we were in a big airport and when we turned around Tory was gone—"

"Thank you."

"For what?"

"You're crazy and paranoid but at least you believe me when I say I'm going to leave him. Nobody else believes me. Phil doesn't think I'd really go and Jeff doesn't and not even Gerry . . ."

"They don't know you like I do. They don't know how strong you can be."

"Thank you."

"Or how stupid."

He loves you," Nancy says.

We're on our way to book club at Belinda's house. Nancy's driving carefully, as she always does. She goes 35 in a 45 zone.

"How would you know?"

"He's called me several times."

"You talk to Phil? On the phone?"

She glances over. "Well, not about anything important. We talk about you. He asks me stuff like what you'd like for your birthday or holidays, things like that."

"So the grill and the Italian tapes were your idea?"

She smiles. "No, even I know that Phil is the one who cooks out, and you already speak Italian. But the cappuccino machine, that was me. He said it took you a week to get it out of the box."

I don't say anything. We both stare straight ahead at the traffic light.

"He wants to please you," she says. "That's why he asks me what you want."

"Why doesn't he ask *me* what I want?"

"Men don't think like that." The light is still red. I exhale. I didn't think I did it loudly but Nancy exhales too. "Why are you going to Boston?"

"I'm taking a class."

"Oh." She doesn't pursue it. Lately I've been glad my friends take so little interest in my work.

"It's creepy that he calls you. Between counseling with Jeff and you and Phil chatting it up behind my back, you guys know way too much about us."

"It's not like that. He wanted to surprise you. We thought . . . we both thought you'd like it. The cappuccino machine, I mean."

The light turns. Finally. "Tell me something," I say. "Tell me something bad about you and Jeff."

"Why?"

"Because it's not fair. You know everything about my marriage and I know nothing about yours. Tell me something bad. Come on. Pull that marriage inside out and show me the seams."

"He didn't get me anything for my last birthday."

"Not anything?"

"So see? Has Jeff ever called you? Has he ever asked you to

give him ideas about what I'd want?" She pulls into Belinda's driveway, cuts off the ignition. "Didn't think so. Phil tries a lot more than you give him credit for, Elyse, that's all I'm saying. What do you think it does to a man when he gives a woman a gift and she won't even take it out of the box?"

Nancy opens the driver's side door but I can't seem to move.

"What would you have wanted for your birthday?"

She laughs. It comes out more like a bark.

"A cappuccino machine."

Chapter Thirty-four

There is a ceremony for the goodbye. We've spent two days in his town, where there's always a chance—slight but real—that someone will recognize him as he sits across from me at the café or as we idle at a stoplight. But specifically here at the airport, when he is dropping me off for the flight home. We have agreed in the car that we will not kiss goodbye, so, as we walk toward the broad glass doors which obediently slide open, I am surprised to feel his hand on the small of my back. It presses into me with a hint of possessiveness as we pause at the kiosk, wait for it to spit out my boarding pass. Our eyes drag past each other, and then he is gone.

I go through security. I buy snacks, a Red Sox T-shirt for Tory, and some sort of mindless magazine, the kind I'd never buy at home. I find my gate. I check my phone for messages. There are none, which is a good sign. Phil does not expect me to call when I'm away and he only phones when there's a problem. I used to resent this, the fact that just seeing his number on my caller ID would make my chest go tight with fear, but now it strikes me as a logical and considerate position for a husband to take. I sit here at the gate with my magazine in my lap and a bottled water in my hand, and gaze out at the plane that will soon take me to my—for lack of a better term—real life. Tory has a field trip tomorrow. She will need to take a bagged lunch and there probably is nothing in the refrigerator to pack. Maybe I should swing by the grocery on the way home from the airport. Or maybe it would make more sense to run by the house first and check the kitchen, because we're undoubtedly low on something else too. The third batch of pots is ready to be packed and shipped and my mother's birthday is coming up. I mailed a card before I left but I must remember to run by tomorrow with flowers, and it's a ragged shift, this transition from the horizontal world of the mistress to the vertical world of the wife. Make it too quickly and you can find yourself dizzy, so I need this time in airports, these useless hours I spend in the company of addicts and movie stars.

I flip to my favorite column, the one near the back where comedians say mean but funny things about badly dressed celebrities. What Was She Thinking? What indeed. Nobody ever knows what anybody else is thinking. I rip open a bag of potato chips. It's easier to go the other way, you know. On the mornings when I'm flying to meet him I get out my good perfume, the Issey Miyake, and my best underwear. I stand in the tub and shave all the way up. In the car I listen to Ella and Frank and in the airport bar I drink one glass of the best wine they have and I drink it very slowly. I carry Jane Austen with me and I breathe and I tell myself to open.

That's easier. Of course it is. Easier to slow down and open up, easier to move into these smooth egg-shaped days I spend with Gerry. But this, this part here, this flying away—it requires a different sort of ritual, somewhat like closing up a beach house at the end of the summer. I cram a potato chip into my mouth, look at the stars in their drooping ruffles and leopardskin prints. Yeah, that's it. Good girl. This is what you do. This is how you leave. You flip your magazine, eat your salt, inventory the contents of your refrigerator in your mind. Wash off your perfume in the chipped sink of the airport bathroom. Take care not to invade the space of the person in the seat beside you. Tomorrow the phone will ring and people will come and go and you will be all right, but for now you must open the second bag of potato chips and grieve the fact that Nicole's marriage is in crisis. Not her old one to crazy Tom but her new one, to that sweet-faced cowboy. Damn. She goes to all that trouble to switch men and uproot her kids and set up dual housekeeping in Nashville and Australia— God knows that couldn't have been easy—and now the second one is going badly too. It's almost more than you can bear to contemplate. You should have gotten three bags of potato chips.

Perhaps Nicole is sitting somewhere just as you are now, at some departure gate in some unfamiliar city, for airports are the great equalizers, aren't they? The beautiful and the strong, the disheveled and the frightened, they are all sitting with magazines and bottled water, waiting. You turn to the story of the rock star's daughter who drunkenly rode her motorcycle onto the patio of a Santa Monica restaurant. She hit a woman who later claimed to be her father's greatest fan, and finally, yes, it's starting at last, that sweet numbness that slips over you in airports, that sense of being neither here nor there. You need these pockets of time and you feel for Nicole and the woman who was hit in Santa Monica and even for the model who sources say got pregnant just to avoid doing jail time. She assaulted a photographer who snapped her in an airport. They say she kicked him, flew at him in a rage. She screamed profanities and the contents of her purse went flying. But you know how she felt. There are times when a woman doesn't want to be seen.

Chapter Thirty-five

——⟨∞⟩——

Winter turns into spring. Tory's softball team plays a few exhibition games. Her third time at bat she surprises everybody by knocking one to the fence. "That'd be a triple if we were playing," her coach shouts up at us and then he says to Tory, "Sugar, hittin' it is one thing, but now you gotta run." She takes off toward first base and he walks a couple of steps up the bleachers and says, "Your girl's gonna be a big stick by the end of the summer, just you wait and see."

When her team's not at bat, she catches. This doesn't go as well at first—in fact, whenever the other team has a runner at third the coach yells, "Back," and she obediently stands up, pulls off her caged mask, and moves to the side, so that the pitcher can run in to cover any throws to home. "Can't he tell she's blinded by that damn mask?" Phil says.

But by the end of the exhibition month, something begins to change. Tory graduates from lying in the red clay dust to kneeling, from kneeling to squatting, and she begins to catch more of the balls, even the bad throws. A couple of times she manages to reach up and snag the ball from mid air and toss it back to the pitcher without standing. "Atta girl," the coach yells. "They're gonna know what you are before this is over."

Phil never mentions the handcuffs or asks where they went. Kelly and Mark go on a cruise through the Panama Canal. Lynn and I finish the junior high rooms and move on to the teenager wing. The Friendship Tray van finally gives up the ghost and the church plans a fund-raiser to get a new one—a barbecue and yard sale over Easter weekend. I browbeat the book club into reading *Madame Bovary*.

And I work on my pots. It turns out there are many ways to break things. You can do it fast, with a single, wrenching snap, or carefully, with a hammer and chisel in hand. You can do it wildly, like a piñata, or methodically, like tapping an egg against the side of the bowl. Or—and this turns out to be the most effective way of all—you can just hold the pot over your head and drop it. Throughout the winter and into the spring I watch as the pieces fly across my concrete floor.

Spring

Chapter Thirty-six

————◦◦◦∞◦◦◦————

Wake up," Phil says. "I think the cat's dead."

I stumble behind him out to the deck, where a long smear of blood ends in the slumped shape of Pascal. He has been ripped open from his chest to his belly, a ragged uneven wound.

"Oh Jesus," I say.

Phil has a towel in his hands that he drops over the cat. "I guess he finally tangled with something bigger than him," he says. "We've got to get him off the deck before Tory wakes up."

"I'll do it." I bend over and scoop up the soft, yielding, still warm shape of the cat. He pulls away from the deck with a small sticky pop and I feel something shift in my arms. I turn him over so that he is swaddled like a baby and see that his breath is still in him, more of a shudder than an exhalation.

"He's alive."

Phil shakes his head. "The abdominal wall is ripped though. Just wrap him up and put him in the grass. He'll be dead soon."

Pascal still hasn't made a sound but I can feel him tremble. I'm lightheaded. There is blood all over the porch, as if something much bigger than a cat has been killed.

"Leave it in the corner of the yard," Phil repeats, his voice level and firm like it is when he's correcting Tory. "I'll take care of it when I get home."

I turn and carry Pascal through the kitchen and I'm reaching for my car keys, digging in my purse with one hand.

"Calm down," Phil says, reaching out to stop me, and it seems that this is all he has ever said to me over the last ten years. It is the command of our marriage, the endless echo that circles the walls of this house, even when neither one of us is here. I push past his arm and I am surprised at the effort it takes, surprised at how much he flexes his muscle against me. But I twist my hip and break loose and then I'm out in the garage and walking toward the driveway.

"What are you doing?" Phil calls from the door. "It's pointless to take him to the vet. If the abdominal wall is ripped, you're not going to save him."

I don't answer. I can't answer. I'm in the car still holding the cat in the crook of my left arm. I back up awkwardly, trying to steer with one hand, trying to hook my seatbelt. My neighborhood looks bizarre and unrecognizable to me as I roll through it and I am talking to the cat, making promises about how I'll fry eggs for him when we get back from the doctor. Fried eggs with cheese like I do sometimes on the weekend. They're his favorites. He is rumbling, making a noise that is disturbingly like a purr. The morning commute has already started and traffic is bad. I inch down Providence Road and am at a stoplight within a couple of blocks of the vet's office when Pascal's paw suddenly breaks free from the towel and makes a single straight jab into the air.

When I got Pascal and Garcia from the Humane Society they were just kittens. I put them in a deep cardboard box for the short drive home and it was Pascal who fought his way out first. It was Pascal who somehow figured out how to climb the slippery sides until his small head butted through the flaps of the cardboard. Tory had squealed with excitement, the funny and unexpected sight of the kitten, neck straining as he blinked in the unaccustomed light. At the time I had pushed him back down. "Bad boy," I'd said, and I laughed. From that moment on he was my favorite.

But this movement is not a gesture of exploration, it is a final spasm. I open the towel. The cat is still, his eyes partially closed, his mouth locked in a grimace. His gums are showing. The car behind me beeps. For a moment I feel as if my ribs are exploding in my chest one by one, but I give the car gas, jerking forward, still going toward the vet. I can't think of anywhere else to go.

The receptionist is unlocking the door as I pull up. The doctor isn't here yet but this young girl, who is sweet and country as so many veterinary assistants seem to be, sees me struggling my way out of the car cradling the bloody towel in my arms and she says, "Oh, Mrs. Bearden, this doesn't look good."

She takes Pascal from me, ascertains the situation at a glance, and pushes through the door. She heads straight back to one of the offices and she must have put him down on an examination table for she is back immediately. I raise my eyebrows in question and she nods. Gone, yes, completely gone, and then she asks if I want them to cremate him and I nod, still speechless. Even though a sign on the counter says PAYMENT DUE AT TIME OF SERVICE, she insists that they will bill me.

"I'm so sorry," she says, and she sounds like she means it, although they must deal with this kind of thing every day. "Do you want your towel back?" I can't seem to understand her question. It's as if she's speaking French. I shake my head. She says something about how maybe I should come into the back and lie down, maybe I should call someone to drive me home. I suspect that I am very pale. I feel pale. I shake my head again, and she lets me go. She even holds the door open. Of course she'd like to get me out of the lobby as soon as possible, before the regular customers start showing up in their business suits and workout gear, come to drop off Max or Ridley for their vaccinations. I am standing here at the front desk in my nightgown with my breasts and arms crusted in blood, looking like some sort of early-rising angel of death.

She keeps the towel. I go home.

Phil has evidently gotten Tory up and dressed and off to school.

An open milk carton stands on the counter. I walk in and drop my purse on the hardwood floor. I pick up the remote and cut off the TV.

I look around the house. I can see that it is a nice house. I see the mantel above the fireplace, obviously custom built, and the collection of pots clustered beneath it on the hearth. Someone has taken a lot of time with the aesthetics of their arrangement. The smallest one is artfully balanced on its side as if something were spilling out. There is a wicker basket by the TV holding video games and DVDs. A child lives here, most likely a girl, based on the preponderance of princess stories represented. There are books stacked beside a leather chair. A man who reads . . . a man who reads history . . . a man whose particular interest is the American Revolution. There are some dishes in the sink, a newspaper scattered on the counter, a pile of tennis shoes beside the back door. A little messiness, but no real dirt. Someone cleans this house on a regular basis.

I push against the walls as I walk down the hall, half expecting them to give way beneath my palms, half expecting them to collapse and drop with the pressure of my touch like walls in a movie set. But the house stands firm. I go out into the yard to call for Garcia but I don't see her anywhere and I wonder if whatever killed Pascal has gotten her too.

Finally I climb back up to the deck, unroll the hose, and begin to wash away the evidence of the monumental effort it took Pascal to die on his own doorstep. The bloody pawprints near the back gate are quite beautiful, like flowers, but they soon give way to the violent red smear that grows wider and wider, ending in front of the French doors. I let the hose run until the entire deck is dripping and then I strip off my nightgown, throw it into the trash can, and climb into the shower.

Afterwards, with my hair still wet, I go to the bank. They know me here. They know that I am not ordinarily mute. I slide a note across the counter to the teller, as if this were a stickup, informing her that I want to rent a new safety deposit box and open a new checking account. She takes me into the vault and I use the oversized keys to open first the box that Phil and I share and then the second one, which is smaller and empty. I move a few things into the second box—the savings bonds my aunts have sent Tory over the years, my passport, the gold coins from South Africa my dad gave me when I graduated college, the utility stock that's still in my maiden name.

Phil has never seen the safety deposit box. He works across town and he works all day so I'm always the one who removes and returns documents. Opening the checking account feels riskier. I transfer two thousand from our money market into the new account, and as I do this I watch the teller carefully. Is she the same helpful woman who called Phil when I opened the money market, who explained why it would be so much more logical and cost-efficient for me to never have anything of my own?

But I'm just being paranoid. The teller isn't interested in me, or what I'm doing. She and the woman beside her are discussing where they will go for lunch. That new Mexican place on the corner, they may as well try it. There's nothing strange about any of this, is there? A woman moves money from a joint account to a single account but her name is on both of them, right? It's just a little juggling of funds, some financial housekeeping. Maybe she's hiding the cost of her shoes. The teller only seems upset that I pick the plain blue checks and points out to me that for the same price I can have checks with kittens or lighthouses or my initials entwined in Old English script. It all costs the same, she tells me, whispering as if we are in some great conspiracy together, but I point at my watch to show her I've got places to be. Just the blue ones.

Next I drive to the apartments behind the coffee shop where I meet Kelly. I know that even a one-bedroom here will cost me twelve hundred a month because I have looked up these units several times in the *Apartment Finder* magazine. But this complex is in Tory's school district, on the side of town where I feel comfortable, and when I step inside the model, I can see at once that the apartments are okay. Not great, not like home, but okay. The girl behind the table tells me March is a slow month. She might be willing to waive the security deposit if I sign a twelve-month lease. She hands me a packet of floor plans and she says I can even choose my own carpet color if that's what's holding me back. She doesn't seem to notice that I don't speak.

Garcia finally makes it home about three. I pick her up and feel her small heart galloping in her chest. The carpool mom drops Tory off just a few minutes later. When Tory finds out I have a sore throat she is very grown-up about it. She does her homework without prompting and calls the number on the refrigerator magnet to order a pizza for dinner. She doesn't ask about Pascal and I wonder what, if anything, Phil has told her and how he explained where I'd been that morning. It may take her days to even notice he is gone. Pascal was a wild cat, prone to sudden leaps and fits of scratching, and I think Tory has always been a little afraid of him. I have never seen her pet him and it occurs to me that Pascal was one of those creatures who is so difficult to love that I—perhaps along with his sister—will be his only mourner. When the pizza man comes Tory pays him with the twenty I have left on the counter and sets the box on the table.

I lie on the couch in my underwear and watch *Cat on a Hot Tin Roof*. Elizabeth Taylor surprises me every time with how good she is, how her frustration comes straight out of the screen at you, how her desperation rises right through the glass. Unhappy women have always scared me. When I see a woman who is openly distraught I usually back away from her so fast that I knock over cups and stumble against the chair, and I think that perhaps that is why I came to this neighborhood and chose this church, why I elected to live in a place where the women hide their pain so well. But today something is different. Elizabeth does not disturb me, she reassures me. Today, for the first time in all the many times I have seen this movie, I am relieved that Maggie decides to stay with

Brick. The universe requires certain sacrifices, a certain kind of math. Ten women must stay for every one who leaves, something like that, and surely the sacrifice of Elizabeth Taylor counts more than that of a normal woman. She is so beautiful that she is like some sort of angel, and if anyone is qualified to take on the suffering of all womankind, it's very likely her.

I look up to see Phil standing in the kitchen. I don't know how long he has been watching me, but he looks worried.

"Why didn't you call me?" he asks.

I put my hand to my throat and shake my head to show him I can't speak. Stupid me, stupid hopeful me, stupid to the end because there is a part of me that thinks, even now, he has come home to talk about something important. Maybe he is going to tell me he's sorry for not coming to the vet with me or ask what happened to the cat.

"You should have called me," he says. "I had pizza for lunch." Then he gazes at the screen, watches Elizabeth climb up the dark stairs to her husband's bedroom, trying one more time, against all odds, to make her marriage work.

"She sure was pretty, wasn't she?" he says. "Before she got fat."

Marriage is full of so many small deaths that I'm not sure why one matters more than another. I open my mouth and tell him I want a divorce.

Chapter Thirty-seven

The cat died and now she wants a divorce," says Phil. "She thinks everything's my fault."

Jeff frowns. "You blame him for the cat dying?"

"I wanted him to go with me to the vet. I was driving through rush hour, very upset, and he should have come with me."

"You didn't have to rip out of there right that moment. The cat was already dead."

"He wasn't dead, he was dying."

Phil looks at Jeff. "It was a gut cut. He had to be gone before she was out of the neighborhood."

"He was still moving until I got all the way to Alexander."

Jeff jumps to his feet. He does this often. Like many small men, he is quick and darting, and when he first came to the church he used to scare everyone by suddenly leaping out from behind the pulpit and walking up and down the aisle during his sermon. And it startled me and Phil in therapy too, the first time Jeff bounced up and started to pace, but now we're used to it. "Okay," says Jeff, "we could sit here all day debating exactly when the cat died. I think the point is Elyse doesn't feel she was supported at a time when she needed your help."

"It was six in the morning, for God's sake. Tory was still in bed asleep and I had three surgicals scheduled before noon. What was I supposed to do, call my patients and say, 'I'm sorry you fasted last night to get ready for your procedure but I have to stay home today and drive around town with my wife and a dead cat?'"

Jeff tries not to smile.

"I've done all I can do," says Phil. "I've changed all I can change. I've always been the one who tries to fix everything and I'm sick of it. I park out in the street so she can turn the garage into a studio and all she does is sit there breaking pots with a hammer. She disappears and flies to wherever she flies and my mother comes and her mother comes and we all try to pretend like this is normal and okay because everybody knows that you do whatever it takes to keep Elyse calm. It's like we're drowning. She pulls me down and I pull her down . . ."

"I understand you're frustrated—"

"What's wrong with her? Besides the cat, I mean. What's really wrong with her? Most women would be happy if they had what she had."

"It doesn't matter how most women would react," Jeff says. "You only have one wife."

"Maybe she should leave. She's always talking about leaving, so maybe fine, she needs to just pack up and go. Move into an apartment and pay for everything by herself for a change, see how much she likes that. Elyse needs to take a big bite out of a reality sandwich."

"What does that mean?"

"He means he doesn't think I can support myself."

"Well, can you?"

Now Jeff looks mildly panicked. "I can see you're both upset about the cat . . ."

"Tory gets out of school June first," I say. "That would be a good time to separate."

Jeff is blinking rapidly, looking from me to Phil. "You're talking about a trial separation? Or a legal separation? Are you talking about divorce?"

I shrug. "We could sit here all day debating exactly when the cat died."

"Hold on," says Jeff. "Let's not be dramatic. You two were doing so much better and now you've had a little setback. It happens all the time in counseling and there's no need to make any big decisions . . ."

"It's like we're dying," Phil says. "Go ahead and say it."

"We're dying," I say.

"I can see that you're both very upset," Jeff says, "which is precisely why you shouldn't—"

"Didn't you hear her? She said we're both dead."

For a moment, for the first time in a long time, I feel a rush of sympathy for Phil. For just a moment we're connected, even if all that connects us is our despair. How do things get to this point? All those years back, when he was coming in from work and I was handing him Tory and heading out, should I have turned and stayed? Kelly said something a few weeks ago when we were at her house making soup. She said something about how you let go of somebody and then you try to find your way back to them, how sometimes you make it and sometimes you don't. That's the way Kelly's mind works. She believes that everything is in the hands of fate. It's part of what makes her kind, it's why it's so easy for her to forgive, and it is probably why she will be married forever. It's why her face is so unlined, serene almost, and mine is scrunched up with wrinkles, my brow furrowed, my eyes darting from side to side. Always looking for a way out of the inevitable. Always looking for the exit.

It surprised me when Phil said we were pulling each other under, surprised me he was just willing to spit it out like that, but he's right. We've both been drowning in this marriage, him as well as me, but now, maybe just because he is finally willing to admit it, it's like his head has popped out of the water and suddenly I see my old friend. The man I trust, the man who always does exactly what he says he will do. The man who tries so hard to be fair that when we were young and poor and first married we bought four new tires and put two on my car and two on his. "It only seems right," he told the Firestone dealer, "that we have an equal chance of blowing out." Phil is blinking back tears. He is struggling, struggling like I am, but he is still there. I am not delusional. I know that this moment will not last long. Phil cares too deeply about what other people think and there's no doubt that Jeff will come up with a plan. The books behind his head are lined up like soldiers whose sole function is to keep me in this marriage. Jeff will read about some sort of pill I should take, some couples retreat in the mountains of Colorado, some new exercise, some new study, some reason why we should hang on for another year. Jeff is momentarily befuddled, but he will rally. He has staked his whole life on the belief that any marriage can be saved, and he will not let anyone, not even his best friend and the woman he wants to climb, dissuade him from this belief. We have frightened him, I can see that, but within hours or days or weeks Jeff will have thought of a new plan and Phil will be seduced into that plan. I stare at Phil as if I am trying to memorize his face. I have to. He will be back under the water any minute.

You let go of people. Sometimes you find your way back to them and sometimes you don't. Who had Kelly been talking about? Not Mark. Possibly Daniel. She doesn't talk about him, but yet, in another way, he's all we've ever talked about. We had been making soup, we had been comparing blow jobs, and somehow we got off on this whole thing about letting people go. Was she talking about me and Phil or about me and Gerry? It's funny how I can see her standing there, ladling white bean soup into a row of plastic containers, but I can't remember exactly what prompted her little speech. Most likely she was talking about me and her, how many times we have lost and found each other. Kelly believes that she and I will end up together, living somewhere out west where the sky is wide and bright. She says we'll go there when we're old and this part with the men is over. Over? Does she mean when all the men are dead? But when I ask her that, she only shakes her head. She doesn't like that word.

They'll be finished before us. She's pretty sure of that. Men usually do, you know, they usually finish before women.

Then that's where we'll have the final chapter, in the West, in the one direction where neither of us has ever followed anyone. It's our fate. She is so sure of this that she has decided how we will arrange our furniture, the pieces I will bring from my life, the pieces she will bring from hers. She plans our house on nights when she cannot sleep. She has walked through the rooms in her mind and she knows exactly how it will be. She says I can have the bedroom with the morning light.

The three of us sit in silence for a moment. Phil has finally begun to cry. Jeff's hands are shaking as he reaches for his appointment book, thumbs through a few pages, and then puts it back down. "Nobody's dying," he says. "Nobody's dead. Whoever told you two that marriage was supposed to be easy?"

The others are seated when I arrive. It's been nice all week so a couple of days ago—before Pascal died, before I went mute—the women made plans to have our Tuesday lunch at Café Edison where we can eat out on the patio beside the fake lake. They murmur pleasantries as I sit down and apologize for being late. When the hostess hands me the menu I half expect the special of the day to be a reality sandwich.

The women are talking. I don't know about what. But it's good that they're talking because I am still rattled from the counseling session, the way Phil drove out fast from the church parking lot, how he turned onto the street without looking and how I couldn't stop myself from yelling after him to be careful. How Jeff had followed us both outside and had stood watching as Phil peeled off. I'd had trouble getting my key into the ignition. I'd had trouble remembering exactly where Café Edison was.

So it's good that they're talking, and even if they're faking this normalcy I'm still grateful for it. I sit down and look around. Spring is coming early. The air is wet and warm with the smell of bulbs regenerating. The sidewalks are bordered in yellow tulips, outlining the division between the stone and the brick so that when the well-heeled housewives back up, we do not dent our SUVs. There's a Barnes & Noble in this shopping center, and a Ben & Jerry's, a Smith & Hawken, and a Crate & Barrel. Near the fountain a group of boys from a neighborhood soccer team are spending their spring break selling candy, trying to raise money for an international camp this summer. I bet every one of those boys has a biblical name—they're all Joshuas and Gabriels and Adams and Nathans. SEND US TO PERU, their sign says. WE'LL HAVE A BALL. I listen to the recorded sounds of Mozart, the drone of the water in the fountains beyond, the still fainter sounds of car engines and children. Women driving slowly, slowly, slowly over the speed bumps and in the seat behind them there are shopping bags tied at the top with curly multicolored ribbon. The bags hold tunics made from a kind of hemp that's processed to feel just like silk, overalls for the kids, gourmet cheeses and exotic fruits, the novel that was reviewed in the paper last Sunday. This is a pretty world. This is the world the immigrants die trying to get into.

"I hear you're getting some time off," Belinda says.

"Yeah, Phil's taking Tory to see his mom over spring break."

"How'd you get out of that one?"

"Haven't you heard? I'm going crazy."

Everyone laughs.

"But they'll be back for Easter?" Nancy says. "You haven't forgotten the cookout and yard sale on Saturday, have you?"

"Of course not. I've got a million things for the sale. It's all bagged in my bedroom closet. You can come by and get it whenever you want."

"When's convenient?"

"Good grief, just come anytime, you know where the key is. I think there are like ten or twelve bags." I can't figure out what the hell Nancy is wearing. It's some sort of gauzy caftan thing with flowing sleeves and a white hood that makes her look like a bride. A bride in a burka.

"Well, good, because we've got to have a new van for the Friendship Trays. The last time I took it out—"

"I've been meaning to ask you something about the Friendship Trays," I say. "Why do you take casseroles to divorced men and not to divorced women?"

Nancy turns to me, her face inscrutable. "So maybe it's not going so well right now?" So maybe it's not going so well. I guess Jeff told her that I used the D-word and everybody ran out of therapy screaming. Or hell, for all I know Phil called her. He's probably got her on speed dial. Either way, the story beat me across town, that's the only explanation for why everyone's acting, now that I think of it, so abnormally normal, why there's been such excessively lively chatter since the moment I arrived. I've sat in Jeff's office and cried a hundred times, but now Phil has cried and that's different. The tears of women are cheap, a cheap kind of currency like yen or rupees and it takes hundreds of them, even thousands, to buy a single cup of tea. But the tears of men . . . they're worth everything. A single one can cancel out the most enormous kind of debt.

Kelly looks pained. "If he still cares enough to cry . . ."

"Exactly," Nancy says. "That's exactly my point."

"It was one tear. He cried one goddamn tear." The women all look away as if they might be struck blind in the face of such excessive feminine cruelty, as if blood might start flowing from my breasts instead of milk.

The waiter brings our salads. As he sets them down, one in front of each woman, we murmur a thank-you. All except for Nancy. For all her surface politeness, Nancy often ends up giving waiters a hard time. Something is never quite right—the wine is too warm, the fish is too cold, she requested the dressing on the side. She detects a bit of raw onion and she specifically asked the server about it before she ordered. Raw onion interferes with her sensitive palate. She claims she can taste it for hours, that a single sliver can ruin her enjoyment of dinner that night.

I watch her lift her fork and pick through this salad that she is not particularly thankful for and I think, for the thousandth time, that Nancy should work. She is smart and ambitious and she has that boundless energy and heaven knows they probably need the money. She's the kind of woman who could make a million a year selling real estate, she has that kind of blind drive. But she also has three children and a husband who's a minister, so instead of making money she redecorates constantly and chews out servers when they bring her the wrong salad dressing.

"Have you talked to a lawyer?" Belinda asks.

I shake my head. The question shocks me. It seems to come out of nowhere. Maybe it shocks everyone else too. It's hard to tell when we're all wearing sunglasses.

"Whatever you do, don't leave the house," Belinda says.

"I have to. Phil's not going anywhere."

"Nobody's saying that it's over," says Nancy.

"She still needs to talk to a lawyer," says Belinda. "If he won't get out of the house, at least make him go to the guest room."

"Come on, Belinda," I say. "It's no secret what I'm up against. Dynamite wouldn't blow Phil out of that house, so if anybody's going anywhere it's gotta be me. I'm the one who is going to be like goodbye patio, goodbye lake, goodbye ducks and BMWs and tulips and little boys with biblical names and American Express gold cards and goodbye Ben & Jerry's."

Kelly smiles faintly. "I'm pretty sure they let divorced women into the Ben & Jerry's."

"When did the word 'divorced' get thrown on the table?" Nancy snaps. "They've had a little setback, that's all."

"I'm sorry about Pascal," Kelly says.

"I just can't," I say, rubbing my eyes, "I can't seem to remember why I married him."

"Don't drive yourself crazy," says Belinda. "We all feel like that sometimes." Nancy is running her finger around the rim of her wineglass.

"I've had a bad decade."

"What you fail to understand, my dear," says Kelly, "is that we've all had the same decade."

We sit for a minute without conversation, just eating. Kelly signals to the server for another glass of wine. We all have a glass of wine when we meet somewhere nice for lunch and sometimes we have two, although this is rare, and I'm a little surprised at how fast Kelly has thrown down her first one. Belinda is near the bottom too. I haven't touched mine and I look at it, pale in the glass, and wonder exactly what kind it is. I usually go first and then the others get whatever I'm drinking, but I was late today and someone else must have looked at the list.

The wine at lunch is one of our things. We'll order four glasses but we would never think to order a bottle. Somehow drinking a bottle of wine at lunch seems completely different than drinking four glasses. There's no numeric logic to it, but this is how we do things, one of the ways we hide from ourselves and each other how much we're really drinking, that there are times—not too often, but maybe once or twice a year—when we have no business leaving these cafés and heading straight for the carpool line.

"You look pretty today," Belinda finally says to Kelly.

"Thank you," says Kelly. "We all look pretty." And it's true enough. Despite the palpable strain at the table, despite the fact that Nancy has wrapped herself like a mummy and my eyes are puffy and red, we are an attractive group of women. For all the good it does us.

"Those men sitting over there," I say, pointing with my head, "why do you think they don't look at us?"

Nancy shifts a little in her chair. "This isn't exactly a pickup joint."

"No, I know that. I know they're not going to come up and start talking to us or pay for our lunch or anything like that. But why do you think they don't even look at us?" The other women turn slightly in their seats, glancing at the men with extreme nonchalance. I've been buying stuff lately—calcium tablets and better bras and ergonomically designed bedpillows and the whole La Mer skin care line. Pointless gestures, futile attempts to hold back the inevitable. I see a horizon going narrow, hear a window slamming shut. "Time's running out," I say. "I'll be forty next year. Anything that doesn't happen to me right now, maybe it's never going to happen."

"Time isn't running out," Nancy says.

"Of course it is," I say. "It's time. What else is it supposed to do?"

"People go in and out of stages," Nancy says, her voice a little singsong, as if she's repeating something Jeff had told her. "Tory will grow up and she'll leave and you and Phil will be in a whole different stage."

"No. He'll still be the same man. I'll still be the same woman. I'm sorry to be like this, really I am, I'm sorry to ruin this lunch and all the other lunches that I've ruined through the years, but it's true, and you all know it. I married the wrong man."

"Elyse . . ." Kelly says.

"Excuse me," Nancy says abruptly. She stands up, pushing her chair back with a squeal, and heads in the direction of the bathroom. I have a bad effect on Nancy. She's always walking out.

"It's hard on her when you talk like this," Kelly says. "Jeff is so much like Phil."

He is?

"You do at least get that, don't you?" Kelly goes on. "If you leave Phil it'll be like you left Jeff. It'll be like you're saying she should leave Jeff, and she doesn't want to leave Jeff."

"I never said she needs to leave Jeff."

"You don't have to say it out loud, it's your whole philosophy of life. You think if a woman is smart that automatically means marriage is going to make her miserable."

"She becomes disenchanted with the bourgeois life," Belinda says. "Like Madame Bovary."

It may be the one sentence she could have said that would shut both me and Kelly up.

"Yes . . . like Madame Bovary . . ." Kelly says, speaking slowly as she tries to regain her momentum. "So if you're saying that the smarter a woman is, the more she's going to resent her marriage, it only makes sense that the opposite is true too. If a woman is content, then she must be stupid, at least according to the world of Elyse."

"You know the one thing I thought was funny in that book," Belinda says. "Madame Bovary didn't have any girlfriends."

I take a gulp of my wine. Pinot Gris. "We all used to sit around . . ."

"Yeah," says Kelly. "We all sat around and bitched about our husbands, we all bitched about our lives, and you bitched louder than anybody. That was sort of your job. But I didn't really think you were going to do anything about it, Elyse. Nobody did. You're scaring the shit out of people."

"I know," I say, and I really do know, and despite what everybody thinks, I'm sorry.

"Can I tempt you?" A server is pushing a three-tiered dessert cart toward us. It sways precariously on the cobblestone patio and she begins to point out items with her shiny black fingertips. "We have butterscotch crème brûlée, margarita mousse, berries in a Galliano broth topped with mascarpone and biscotti, grapefruit sorbet, chocolate pot pie with peanut butter ice cream . . ."

"Stop," I say. I feel like crying.

"It's obscene," says Kelly.

"Or, if you'd prefer, Chef can make you a strawberry milkshake." The server is young and very thin, and her hair is so blond that for a moment I have to avert my eyes. It's like looking directly into the sun.

"Just bring us a sampler platter," says Kelly.

"Great choice," she chirps and teeters away, pulling the cart behind her.

Kelly gazes after her. "Jesus, it really is all too much sometimes, isn't it? We should tell those guys at the next table to drag over their chairs and pick up a fork."

"Do you think Madame Bovary would have gotten away with it if she'd had some girlfriends?" Belinda asks.

"I think Madame Bovary would have gotten away with it if she'd had a cell phone," I say.

"Please," Kelly says. "Don't encourage her." I'm not sure which one of us she's speaking to.

"Actually, Belinda, you've got a point," I say. "I didn't even notice it, but Madame Bovary didn't have any girlfriends."

Nancy is back from the bathroom. It looks like she's washed her face. "What did I miss?"

"We ordered a dessert sampler," Kelly says. "And, oh yeah, Elyse is having some problems in her marriage."

"It was your anniversary a couple of weeks ago, wasn't it?" Belinda asks.

I nod.

"Did you have sex?"

"Yeah. In the shower."

"In the shower? You had that special shower sex where you were standing up? You gotta stop doing that, Elyse. Move him into the guest room. As long as you're giving him shower sex of course he's not gonna take you seriously."

Kelly smiles at Belinda. "You're really fired up today."

I smile too. "She should have read Madame Bovary years ago."

"We just make it way too easy on them, that's all I'm saying."

The sampler platter is upon us. Someone has squirted a grid of sauces across the white plate, caramel tic-tac-toed with chocolate, a swirl of raspberry in a corner. Four desserts, four forks, a knife in case we want to get geometric about things. Enough for everyone to have a little bit of everything. I drag my finger across the pattern of sauces on the plate and lift it to my mouth. Paint it on my lower lip, wait a second, and then lick it off.

"But I didn't kiss him when we were in the shower," I say. The bright blond girl is pushing her three-tiered cart toward the men. They look up at her, smiling and hopeful. "Why do you think that's the first thing to go?"

"Oh Lord," mutters Kelly. "Why don't you just pick up that knife and stab us all in the chests?"

"Well, I guess you win some and you lose some," Nancy says,

stuffing a bite of the chocolate pot pie into her mouth. Kelly and Belinda look down at their plates.

"What does that mean?"

"Haven't you heard?" Nancy says sweetly, pushing her sunglasses back and looking at me, straight in the eye. "Now see, that's weird. I would have sworn you'd be the first to know. Lynn and Andy left for Belize this morning. She got him back."

Chapter Thirty-eight

Not only wasn't I the first to know, but it turns out I was the last to know. Throughout the rest of the week, the story comes to me in pieces.

The thing with the secretary didn't work out, Kelly tells me on Wednesday at the gym. The girl was so damn young, what did Andy expect? Anyway, he called Lynn and he was abject. Bereft. Contrite. He'd moved into a Residence Inn, one of those pathetic places out by the airport that are full of men who've screwed up.

She's got him right where she wants him, Belinda adds, when she calls on Thursday. He told her to start looking for a new house and that money was no object. They were even thinking about moving north of the city, up toward the lake. That would mean the kids would have to change schools, but Lynn thought they needed a fresh start. Smart of her, Belinda says. She's playing it real smart, but then Lynn always did. The Belize trip is sort of a second honeymoon. They're going to swim with the dolphins.

Not exactly a second honeymoon, Nancy corrects me, when I see her in Trader Joe's later that day. Lynn and Andy aren't married anymore—their divorce has been final for almost a year. So there will have to be some sort of ceremony, maybe a whole new wedding, and wouldn't that feel a little strange, to go through it all again with the same man?

The weirdest part, Kelly whispers, during coffee hour on Sunday, was that while Lynn was packing to go to Belize, this young man shows up in the parking lot of her apartment complex and starts honking his horn. A boy, really. He'd evidently developed a crush on Lynn, because there was some sort of scene . . .

The cops came, Belinda says. Can you believe it?

Who knows what the kid got in his head, Nancy murmurs. You know Lynn. She's always been too nice for her own good. Obviously he'd misread the situation, he'd interpreted her kindness toward him as something else . . .

Situations can get out of hand so fast, Kelly says.

Can you imagine the cops showing up at Lynn's door? Belinda asks. Lynn, of all people?

No, she's not coming back to her job at the church at all, Nancy explains. Jeff was a little upset about it at first—he'd gone out on a limb to convince the council to cough up the money and hire her. But if this is what's best for Lynn and Andy and the boys then of course he understands. Because that's all that really matters. What's best for Lynn and Andy and the boys.

Twenty-three, Belinda says, raising her eyebrows. That's how old the boy in the parking lot turned out to be. Twen-ty-three.

Look, Nancy says, waving a postcard of a jungle under my nose. She says it's beautiful there. Like some sort of Eden.

Kelly got a postcard from Belize too.

So did Belinda.

Lynn had been a good wife—probably, I think, the best of us all. She was the one who had the greatest mastery of the myriad skills the job requires. Not just running the house, raising the kids, cooking, or providing her husband comfort and pleasure. That's the easy part. Lynn was also gifted at the interior tasks of marriage. She knew how to create pockets to disappear into, places to tuck her true mind away, like an extra set of car keys.

But it didn't seem to matter in the end. One morning her husband informed her, with the stickiness of his semen still on her thighs, that she had been replaced. When he walked out the door that day, walked out and turned left and started down the block, she followed him. Followed him until he was no longer in sight. "I lost him," she told me. "Literally lost him." What is this, some sort of muscle memory that all women have, some dark part of our brain that takes over and compels us, apart from all logic, to follow men? If it compelled Lynn—sensible, disciplined Lynn— then it must be a very strong impulse indeed.

But then, at some point—probably not the first year, possibly the second—she had begun to like being alone. Maybe it was that bald boy from the Starbucks, but I suspect it also had something to do with her hard solid work at the church. The smell of turpentine, the weight of the trash sack on her shoulder, the comforting heft of the hammer in her hand. Each day this week I have gone out to my mailbox and looked for my card from Belize, half believing that Lynn would write something on the back that would explain everything to me. She would tell me why it is so hard to leave and—here's the shock that has me now standing flat-footed and numb in my kitchen, a cup of coffee raised to my lips—why it is apparently so hard to stay gone. That's the part I didn't bargain for. I understand the gravitational pull of marriage. But I believed that if I ever got up enough power to break out of it . . . What am I to think now? That Jesus and Elvis and a team of wild horses must have shown up and dragged her back into this marriage that everyone honestly believed to be over?

He came after her. That's what men do, apparently. Once you're gone, really gone, finally gone, then that's the point when they decide that they want you back.

On the morning that he left her, Lynn followed Andy until he was out of sight, then she turned and walked back to her house. She got the kids up and dressed and ready for school. She made the beds and loaded the dishwasher. She strapped on her heart monitor and did her four-mile lap around the neighborhood. She opened a bank account in her maiden name. She ordered a college catalog online. She cut her hair. She got an apartment, she got a job, she got a new boyfriend. She began wearing her pink Chanel jacket with jeans and boots.

At what point did Andy notice she was no longer following him? At what point did he turn around and see that the woman who had always been there no longer was? I can imagine her picking up the phone one night, her heart a little in her throat, wondering what could be wrong that someone would call so late. His voice is on the line. He says he's sorry. It's all been a mistake. He says he still loves her. Nothing has been done that cannot be undone. And then there's the fact that her children call him Daddy.

People can change, he says.

He tells her he wants to come home.

I carry my coffee out onto the deck, superstitiously stepping over the spot where we found Pascal. Everyone thinks that Andy has learned his lesson but Kelly says no, that Lynn is really the one who's different. ("I'm basing this theory," she says archly, "on the fact that it's always the woman who changes.") Kelly is on that dark path where she believes marriages work best when women expect little. She thinks Lynn has seen how hard it is on the outside and adjusted her expectations. But I remember Lynn saying that it wasn't until Andy left her that she'd remembered how reasonable he could be. For the first time in years they had begun making joint decisions—the selling of the house, the divvying up of funds, the scheduling of their sons—and she had to wonder. Why couldn't they do that when they lived together? "It takes divorce," she said, "to show you how to be married."

Garcia ambles up. She does not jump into my lap as her brother used to do but instead curls around my feet and begins a loud purr. In his absence she has gotten sweeter. It's almost as if her personality has expanded to fill the space where Pascal once was. When I picture divorce my mind leads only to the threshold and no farther. Try as I might, I can't quite visualize that first day alone and I think, sitting here on this sunny deck, that perhaps my sanity depends on not trying to. It has taken too much effort to build up my escape velocity, it has taken me too long to put together the right combination of momentum, anger, and money, and now that I can finally, finally feel the engines beneath me I can't afford to stop and think. At least not about Lynn.

"She got him back," Nancy said, in her heartless way, and it's strange how the language of revenge echoes the language of reconciliation. Nancy considers this some sort of victory for our entire gender. Lynn gained an advantage, she leveraged her position, she won a free trip to Belize. It can only be a matter of time before she's knocking out walls and putting a sunroom on the back of her house. "I'm so proud of her," Nancy said, and I think, finishing my coffee and pulling Garcia against her will into my lap, of Belinda's mother down in that trailer park in Alabama with a picture of Belinda's big red-brick house stuck on her refrigerator door.

"She told me," Belinda said grimly, "that you've gotta learn to love the game you've won. Do you think that's really true? That none of us will ever be happy until we've learned to love the game we've won?"

That afternoon when I check the mail my postcard has finally come. A picture of Mayan ruins is on the front.

The postcard is bent and battered. It looks as if it came from Belize to North Carolina by way of Guam and I wonder if Lynn wrote it last, if she had trouble thinking of what to say to me. Perhaps she carried the card in her purse for days, debating whether it was worth sending. Or maybe she wrote them all at once, sitting at a pool bar with a fruity drink by her side, and mine was simply the message that mysteriously went astray.

I walk down the driveway with the card on top of the stack of mail, carry it in, and place it on the counter. It stays there for a couple of hours as I go back and forth between the house and the studio, as I'm taking the chicken out to defrost, as I come in to pick up my keys for the afternoon carpool. It is not until I start supper that I pick it up again.

The ruin is dark, imposing. The man standing at the top of it looks as small as a splinter, barely recognizable as human against the bright blue sky. I turn the card over and over in my hands until the writing on the back, Lynn's neat round letters in heavy black ink, turns into a blur. Whatever Lynn has seen, I will have to see it in my own way. Whatever she knows, I'll have to figure it out for myself. I throw the postcard into the trash and begin to rinse the salad in the sink.

Chapter Thirty-nine

veryone's talking about us," Phil says.

Actually, everybody's talking about Lynn. We've finally been knocked off page one, but there's no point trying to explain that to Phil. "Well, if they are, whose fault is that?"

Phil frowns. "I never tell anyone anything."

"Come off it. I know you call Nancy and basically ask her to spy on me. And then there are all these so-called counseling sessions. I'll bet we were hardly out of Jeff's office until he was on the phone. I'll bet he's called Nancy every time we've gone in and given her a blow-by-blow account of everything we said. We talk to him, he talks to her, she talks to everybody else, and I go out to lunch with my girlfriends and look like a fool. I'm sick of it. It's a sick situation."

For a moment, Phil looks guilty. It's not an expression that comes easily to his face. "You think we should get a different counselor? Someone we don't know? I could make some calls."

Perfect. I've begged him to go into counseling for three years and now all of a sudden the idea has just occurred to him. He is standing in front of me, the very embodiment of a concerned husband, eager to do everything he can. I suppose I should take comfort that I've done a good job breaking him in for his second wife. But as for us—it's too late to even bother explaining why it's too late. I shake my head. "I don't see why we're in counseling at all."

"You want to quit?"

"Phil, we already have quit."

"Because Jeff called me this afternoon and had a suggestion. I think we really upset him with all that stuff about the cat, and anyway, he said that Nancy could sit in on our sessions too, if that would make you more comfortable. You know, so you wouldn't feel like the men were ganging up on you."

"You're kidding."

"They've done couples therapy together. Back a long time ago, before their kids were born, but he said in our case he was sure she'd be happy to—"

"Jeff and Nancy have a shitty marriage."

"You think everybody has a shitty marriage."

"No, just me and you and Jeff and Nancy." I can think of a few others too, but it's not the right time to go into it. "I don't want them working with us. I don't want what's left of our privacy to go completely down the drain. Have you managed to somehow forget our entire last therapy session?"

"Nancy's your best friend."

"God help me if that's true."

"She cares about you."

"In her own little tiny way, I guess she probably does. But the fact that she's married to your best friend doesn't make her my best friend."

"Jeff wouldn't have told her if he didn't think—"

"Do you really want to be having this conversation?"

"No," Phil says, but he's uneasy. He remembers the days when I would do anything to get him to talk to me. He remembers me curled up in a fetal position, pleading with him under the bathroom door. He remembers the brochures for bed-and-breakfasts I'd leave lying around the house on the off chance he'd see them and suggest going away for the weekend. The way I'd reach for his hand in movies. Now he's got a wife who walks out of the room while he's still talking.

"Maybe you should reconsider and come to Florida with me and Tory," he says, following me out through the garage.

"No. We need the break." This is my chance to prepack a few things for the June 2 move and take them to Kelly's. I don't want to be actually lugging boxes around while Tory is in the house. I've given this a lot of thought and I believe it would be better to only tell her we're moving about a week before the actual event. But that doesn't mean I can't get a few things out while she's in Florida.

"I'll be back by Easter."

I turn to him, trash in my hands. "Is that what you're worried about? How this is going to look to the neighbors?"

"We'll actually be back by Saturday. In time for the cook-out."

"Well, I certainly hope you've made sure that Jeff and Nancy have a copy of your flight schedule."

"It's not just that," he says. Phil takes off his glasses and pretends to clean the lenses. He makes a great show of blowing on them and wiping, but his eyes are lowered. At some point he has become afraid to meet my gaze. "I thought you might get lonely."

It would be enough to make me cry if I had any cry left in me. "Don't worry about it," I say, raising the heavy gray lid of the garbage bin and dropping the bag inside. "I don't get lonely as much as I used to."

I can't believe he'd even think of coming here. This is your town."

Kelly has begun wearing her hair up and it makes her look like a schoolteacher, or maybe more like a porn star playing a school-teacher. I imagine her releasing the clip from the back of her hair and tossing her head. Pulling off her glasses and being suddenly beautiful.

"I've been to Boston."

She rolls her eyes as if she can't believe my stupidity. "That's completely different, you know it is. If some guy he worked with happened to run into the two of you together, he would've just turned away. Hell, next time he saw Gerry he'd probably high-five him. But what do you think would happen if somebody saw you here, walking with some man that nobody knows? Do you think they'd just snicker and turn away?"

"They'd probably chase me down with bows and arrows."

Kelly's eyes narrow. "This isn't funny,"

"I wasn't joking."

She pushes away her uneaten muffin. "You don't even have enough sense to be scared. You're not thinking of taking him to your house, are you?"

"I don't know. I mean, why not? Phil and Tory are leaving tomorrow."

Kelly reaches across the table and grabs my wrist. "For once just slow down and listen to me. If Phil decides he wants Tory, what will you do? You don't have any money, Elyse, you don't have anywhere to go."

I start to say, "Not even to your house?" but I don't. Her house isn't really her house. It's Mark's house, and he wouldn't want me there. Much less me and my daughter and my cat and my pots.

"Nancy's seen bruises on your arms," Kelly continues, her voice dropping a little as she leans toward me. "She was talking about them back around the holidays, months ago, and despite what you might have told yourself, Nancy's not an idiot. If you give her enough time she'll put it together. And if Nancy could see marks on you when you're fully dressed, how can you pretend that Phil isn't going to notice anything?"

I don't tell her that the bruises Nancy saw were from the night Phil handcuffed me to the bed. "It's fifty-two days until June first," I say. "That's when the apartment will be ready."

"A lot can happen in fifty-two days."

"Is it really so wrong for him to come to my house? I want him to see who I am."

"You want him to see what you're giving up. It's a dangerous game, that's all I'm telling you. That you're playing a dangerous game."

Kelly thinks I haven't got enough sense to be scared, but she's wrong. Ever since I said the D-word the whole world has begun to look like a dangerous game. I threw up twice yesterday. I slept three hours last night. All my friends are married. They might not be my friends if I'm not married. I only have four thousand in my checking account. Last night Tory went straight to Phil with her certificate for placing second in the spelling bee. She crawled on his lap. Maybe she loves him best. Maybe she would want to stay with him. I turn on the news and there's been a plane crash in Brazil, an earthquake in Taiwan, a woman from a nearby town who ran out to the grocery store and ended up locked in the trunk of her car. This woman was just like me, just somebody who was going to pick up a few things and all of a sudden they find her in the trunk of her own goddamn car. Fear swirls around me, invisible but real as air. I try not to breathe it in but I do, every day.

Kelly sighs, pushes her hair back. It falls into her face again immediately. "So when is Wonder Boy flying in?"

"Wednesday."

"Will I meet him?"

"I doubt it."

"Sometimes I wonder if he even exists."

Sometimes *I* wonder if he even exists.

"There's a chance he doesn't love you, Elyse."

"Maybe I don't love him."

"No," she says. "Listen to me. There's a chance he doesn't care about you at all. No matter what he says, no matter what you feel, this isn't real."

"He does cartoon voices," I say. "He does Pepé Le Pew."

Kelly refastens the wayward strand of hair back into her bun. "Are you talking about that skunk?"

"Yeah, the French skunk in cartoons. Pepé Le Pew."

"Pepé Le Pew was a rapist."

"Pepé Le Pew was not a rapist."

"I can't believe we've gotten to the point in our lives where you think something like that is romantic. Jesus Christ, what's happened to you? You used to be Homecoming Queen."

"No, really, he was putting my legs around his shoulders and he saw I had this bruise. He pulled my ankle toward his face and he said it all French, he said, 'She has injured herself to prove her love to me. It is strange, yes, but romantic, no?'" I wait for a moment, but Kelly doesn't react. Her face is blank, as if she's having trouble even following the story. "You don't think that's cute?"

"You don't speak French."

"He wasn't speaking French, he was speaking English with a French accent."

"Oh yeah, that's totally different."

"You're just pissed because I'm happy," I say. "You're afraid I might actually get what I want and you can't stand it. Because you've always been the golden girl. You're supposed to be the one who gets the Pepé Le Pew."

"This isn't about me."

"That's what I'm trying to tell you. You think what happened back then is going to happen again, but you've got to know this, Kelly. I'm not you."

"You don't have to sound so damn pleased about it."

"You've forgotten. You've forgotten what it feels like. Try. Just for a second. Do you remember the day we called him on the patio?"

"Do you remember the day you drove me to the clinic?"

"Gerry's not Daniel. You've never even met him."

"I don't have to. Men like him use women, they use them completely up."

"Is this what you tell yourself late at night? Is this how you justify marrying Mark and going to live in that big marble house?"

"Go to hell."

"When I get there, be sure to open the gate and let me in."

We push away from the table in one move, as if we've planned it. I pull out my car keys and, just as abruptly, she sits back down. "He's playing you," she says. "Someday you'll wake up and see this for what it is."

That night, I dig out Daniel's letters to Kelly and read them all again. I read them slowly, in sequence. I read them out loud. Somebody has to remember. I sit on the floor as I read them, squinting in the dim light until I hear Phil's car pulling into the garage. Then I run into my closet and cram them into the first bag I can find.

But it isn't Phil at the door, it's Kelly.

"Don't be mad at me," she says. "You don't know how much I hope I'm wrong."

Chapter Forty

It's no longer possible to meet someone at the airport in a romantic way. Modern security measures forbid going to the gate, much less standing on the runway with your arms full of flowers. Gerry and I have lost each other in airports all over the country and when he flies into Charlotte we manage to get really separated. The arrivals board says his plane touched down twenty minutes ago but I can't find him in baggage claim.

My phone rings.

"Where are you?" he asks.

"Upstairs, walking away from the US Airways counter."

"Okay, we're close. Oh, wait a minute, maybe we shouldn't even try to get together today, because I've just spotted this gorgeous woman. She's walking right toward me, wearing this bright red jacket . . ."

I laugh, look around, but I still don't see him. "Where are you?"

"Oh shit, forget it, she's on the phone. Maybe she's already got a boyfriend. Yeah, yeah, she's definitely looking for somebody. She's turning, doing a 360 just like a ballerina . . ."

Then I see him, leaning against a ticketing kiosk with his carry-on thrown over his shoulder and the phone pressed to his ear. His face is split open into a smile and it's like looking into the world's best mirror because I am smiling too and I feel beautiful, incredible, bright, thin, young. I walk toward him and he catches me in a kiss, the cell phones still wedged to our ears so that we are connected, through satellites high above us sending out signals through space and through our skin, through a series of nerve impulses that still snap and shudder as he presses his mouth against mine.

You've changed," says Gerry. He is looking at a picture of me and Tory, just a couple of Christmases ago.

"Not much. My hair's shorter."

"It's more than that. Why are we here?"

"I'm not sure."

He is standing in front of the refrigerator, reading Tory's softball schedule, the list of upcoming Easter activities, menus from the local Chinese and pizza places. Garcia weaves herself around his ankles and he bends down and picks her up. She settles over his shoulder like a baby waiting to be burped. In this house even the cat is unfaithful. There is a cartoon on the fridge, one I cut from the *New Yorker* months ago. A husband is sitting on a couch saying, "I really don't understand what's bothering you," while behind him the wife spray-paints on the wall NOTHING EVER HAPPENS.

I wait to see if he laughs. He doesn't.

"I have to tell you something," he says. I put my arms around his waist and listen to Garcia purr.

"I know."

"If you do this, I can't go with you."

"I never expected you to." And, like everything I've ever said to Gerry, I realize it's true while I'm saying it. Does he think I will cry? I don't feel like crying. It's not the end of anything, although it may be the end of the beginning of something. I thought that bringing him here would help him see me more clearly, but the opposite has happened. He is so overwhelmed by my pots and pictures and schedules of family activities, that he has shut his eyes. I pull him to me a little tighter and shut my eyes too. My knees are slightly bent, my legs are apart, and I realize, not totally to my surprise, that I am holding him up.

I planned to cook for us tonight. I've bought pasta and truffle oil and prosciutto and Parmesan but this sudden domesticity has been too much for him. I tell him that it's funny, considering I am such an old-movie buff, but I have never seen *Casablanca* all the way through. So I rented it for us tonight and I bought stuff to cook. But we don't have to stay here. We can go to a restaurant. We can find a hotel for the night.

He opens his eyes, lets his arms slide from my shoulders to my hips. "If that's what you want," he says, but his voice is relieved. We are not pasta and Blockbuster. We are foie gras and wake-up calls.

"Actually bringing you to my house," I say, "it was a little too much, wasn't it?"

"No," he says, "it's just that it looks like my house. We've got the same stuff stuck on our refrigerator. You've got our bathtub. I know exactly how much that bathtub costs."

"You can't believe there's a woman in America stupid enough to leave that bathtub."

"You know I'm not talking about the money. Not just the money. I'm talking about the way it feels when it's all together. You and this man—"

"Phil."

"What?"

"My husband's name is Phil."

"If you're willing to leave all this stuff that you and Phil have accumulated—do you think I'm just talking about money here?"

"Not really."

"But to leave this . . . you must have been unhappier all along than I realized."

"It'll be all right," I tell him, and I feel something shift inside of me as if my heart is resettling into a different, deeper part of my chest. He's talking into my hair. I think he says that he's sorry, but he has nothing to be sorry about. He was clear with me from the start. He's a climber. He is good at holding on to things but just for a second. He holds on long enough to catch his balance and sight the next grip. And then he lets go.

Hold and release, hold and release. This is what my time with him has taught me, this rhythm of moving from one scary place to another, this rhythm that allows you to cross great divides without falling. It's the cliché of climbing—don't look down—but he has told me, many times, that looking up is risky too. Don't think about what you've left or what's ahead, because safety comes only from focusing on the thing right in front of you. This is what my time with him has taught me, so why does he seem so surprised that I know it now? I think of the first conversation that we ever had, somewhere in that dangerous air between Phoenix and Dallas, how he told me that you never lose your grip on someone who's in trouble. But if you are the one in freefall, it's considered honorable to pull your clip, to make sure that you do not take anyone else down with you. These sorts of games, he told me, they require such a high level of trust. Not just believing that the other person will hang on, because hanging on is the easy part. The harder part is trusting that the other person will know when to let go.

"We could drive over to the hotel now."

He shakes his head. "You got the movie. Let's watch it."

"There's not a happy ending. The lovers don't end up together."

He sighs. "I can take it if you can."

We go into the den, start the DVD player. We sit on the couch and I put my feet in his lap. The Nazis threaten Paris. Ingrid walks into a bar. Things there are quite shadowy. Sam plays the piano. Gerry lifts my foot and kisses the arch. Thirty minutes into the movie the phone rings. Nancy. She asks me if I've had time to get lonely yet, and before I can tell her no, not really, she starts describing the new curtains she's putting up in the living room. She hasn't really called about the curtains. She's called to get a read on the situation, to see if I want her to sit in on the next counseling session, if indeed Phil and I are coming back to counseling at all. She's called to show she's forgiven me for causing so much trouble. She's forgiven me for being a nutcase and a malcontent. She doesn't know that I'm a slut but if she knew, she might forgive me for that too. Nancy says perhaps I'd like to ride to the outlets with her sometime next week and look at material. She values my sense of color. This is what she says to me, that she likes my sense of color and that we never seem to do anything together, just she and I. We could make a day trip out of it.

Ingrid Bergman is leaving Humphrey Bogart and I know enough about the movie to know that she's going to have to leave him at least twice, maybe more. Leaving a man is so hard that it doesn't always take the first time, not even in the movies. Gerry is absorbed by their story, and he holds my feet tenderly, one in each hand, while Nancy talks about valences and cornices and how much it's all going to cost. She says no matter how carefully you plan, it always ends up costing more than you think.

It's not necessary to answer her, never has been, just to murmur once in a while, and I love Gerry for not asking who's on the phone, for not ever asking, even later when we have to go back and replay the parts I missed. Ingrid is crying. She cries so beautifully. Perhaps almost as beautifully as Elizabeth Taylor, although it makes me feel disloyal to even think this thought. Nancy says she likes a soft green, that color between moss and sage, but maybe green is too much, maybe it will exhaust her over time, and she might be happier staying with blue, moving from periwinkle into more of a cobalt. "Jeff would think I'm crazy," she says, "replacing blue with blue. But you know how men are. You can't make them understand that there are lots of kinds of blue."

"Right," I say. "Lots of kinds of blue."

By the time she hangs up I'm not mad at her anymore.

*　　*　　*

Exactly one hour and twenty minutes later, although we mustn't measure and we mustn't count . . . Exactly one hour and twenty minutes later, after I have leaned back against Gerry in the shower and let him wash my hair . . . after I have pressed my palms against the tile wall and bent forward so that he could soap my legs, first one and then the other, saying "Change" as I shifted back and forth, the gentleness in his voice reminding me that he is a father . . . Exactly one hour and twenty minutes later, after we've found the remote under one of the couch pillows and watched the first round of *Jeopardy!* . . . after he has called his office to check messages . . . after I have shown him the two boxes I already have packed and hidden in the guest room closet . . .

Exactly one hour and twenty minutes later I pull a pair of handcuffs out of a drawer and hold them up.

"Hey Pepé," I say. "Do these look familiar?"

When I was a child I read the superhero comics, just like everyone else, and I decided—living as I was in my small country town with my sweet anxious parents—that the power I'd most like to have was invisibility. This would have to be the ultimate freedom, I thought, far greater than the ability to fly. This power that would let me walk through the world unjudged and unseen.

What I couldn't have predicted was that someday I would have that power. It's easy. It works like this. Get married, give birth, put on certain clothes and drive a certain kind of car, and then, somewhere just before the age of forty, you awaken one morning to discover that your childhood wish has been granted. You've become invisible. You can walk down the street holding hands with your lover and no one notices the handcuffs at your wrists. But then no one really ever notices anything, do they? The last nine months have taught you that if nothing else.

* * *

We decide to just pick up food. We leave my house and drive to the shopping center where Belinda and I saw Lynn eating scones. In the parking lot he connects his left wrist to my right wrist and we struggle out the same door of the car, and then we walk, unnaturally joined, toward the Dean & Deluca.

"I'm starving," Gerry says and he pulls back the wax on a puck of Gouda so that we can eat it as we shop. It feels like we're doing something very bad, very outlaw, although he carries the price sticker to the cashier when we check out and says, "This too." We have bought too much, like people who will never eat again. Two small meatloafs, a piece of grilled salmon, a carton of four-pepper salad, and another of stir-fried pea pods. A baguette, a jar of olives, an oversized cream cheese brownie, a large bottled water, a split of champagne, and a banana. Food designed to be eaten with one hand.

Gerry and I take the bag outside to the fountain across from the store and begin to spread it out along a table. I must remember this for the next time I try to lose weight, that if I eat with my left hand it slows everything down and I find that I am not nearly as hungry as I first thought myself to be. I find that I can make do with a little less, that it does not vex me when a bite of salmon or a triangle of red pepper slides through my fork. He feeds me at some point, and I imagine a woman across the courtyard watching us, watching him lift his fork to my mouth. It is clumsy, not like a movie. His tine jabs the corner of my lip, the rim of his plastic champagne flute clicks against my teeth. Beneath the table he runs his hand inside my thigh, dragging my hand along with it. The logistics of collectively unpeeling the banana almost undo us. We are giggling, enjoying the latest in our silly, giddy secrets.

I am so preoccupied that for a moment I don't see the homeless woman who is approaching us.

"Do you want some candy?" she says. She is selling candy.

Gerry seems similarly confused. "No," he says, "no, thank you, we're fine," as if she were a waitress. There are so many cartons and bags on our table. The woman keeps standing there. She is wearing a trenchcoat and she looks as if she's pregnant. The tie of the coat is stretched across her hard belly, but she is much too old to be pregnant. I put my free hand on Gerry's arm.

But he is already reaching for the money in his back pocket. Gerry carries his bills with a rubber band wrapped around them and the woman notices this and says, "Do you want a wallet?" Evidently she sells wallets too. Wallets and candy. With my right hand and his left, we peel the rubber band off the wad of money and it pops open before us like a flower. Ones surrounded by twenties, twenties surrounded by fifties. He hesitates. If the homeless lady thinks it is odd that a man and woman are handcuffed together outside of a Dean & Deluca she makes no comment. The events of her life have evidently taught her a great tolerance.

I reach into the side pocket of my purse and pull out the little filigreed key.

"I'll do it," Gerry says, but I have already released him.

He fishes two fifties out of the pile of money. "I don't need a wallet, ma'am," he says. "But take this and thank you very much."

The woman shuffles away. She does not stop to talk to any of the other people at the other tables, who've been watching the whole scene with casual alarm. You don't see many homeless people in this part of town.

"You're a sweet man," I say.

He flushes. He doesn't want me to think he's sweet.

"No, really," I say. "You've got a pure heart."

He shakes the cuff off and it falls to the ground. Neither of us picks it up. Gerry begins to collect the bills from the tabletop. "Blessed are the pure of heart," he says, and his voice isn't quite steady. "For theirs . . . theirs is what? What do the pure of heart get?"

They get the kingdom of heaven, I tell him. They get it three or four times a day.

Chapter Forty-one

On the morning of the cookout Phil takes Tory over an hour early so they can help set up the yard sale. I stay home and make cupcakes, seventy-two of them, all individually wrapped and priced, and then I load them into the car and drive to the church.

The parking lot is already packed and the lawn is full of people. I have to ease my car in behind the Dumpster. I'm heading toward the kitchen door to get someone to help me with the boxes when I see Belinda walking down the sidewalk toward me. Walking fast.

"You've got to get out of here," she says. "He knows, he knows everything."

"What do you mean? He knows what?"

"Don't go inside. It's not safe."

"What the hell are you talking about? Where's Tory?"

"She's fine, she's fine, but don't go in there, Elyse. He's really upset. Just get in the car."

"I'm not going anywhere without Tory."

I start toward the front door and Belinda lunges forward and catches my arm. "I'll get her," she says. "I'll take her to Kelly's house. You go there too, go right now. Nancy said she felt like she had to tell him. You know how she is. She felt like she had to tell him, but he's very upset, Elyse, and you just need to get in the car and go." I am on the first step leading up to the sanctuary when the door flies open and Phil walks out.

His hands are full of letters, and I can see at a glance they're Kelly's, the ones I told her I would burn. He is walking down the steps, the letters in his hands, and behind him I can see Nancy at the church door holding a bright pink bag. It all comes to me. She went into my closet, just as I told her to, to get the clothes for the yard sale. She grabbed all the bags, including a bright pink one from Frederica's holding a camisole and pull-up hose and high heels that I bought months ago in a botched effort to seduce my own husband. Why would she think I was donating lingerie to the church? But of course she didn't—she realized her mistake the minute she opened the bag, but then she saw the letters inside. Nancy's human. She read them. Those letters, those careful letters with no names and no dates. Of course she assumed they were written to me. And then—you know how she is—she felt she had to tell my husband. How could any of this have ended any differently? I look at her and the expression on her face is one of raw envy, the same expression that doubtless was on my face the first time I read those letters, the same expression that comes to any woman's face when she witnesses—or thinks she has witnessed—the love story of another. She read the letters and then she gave them to the man who is coming toward me now, the man who failed to recognize the camisole and hose I was wearing on that pivotal night when he smirked and asked me just what I was trying to be. His face is ashen and he is taking the steps two at a time, almost running. The evidence against me is in his hands, another woman's love letters and a pile of tangled underwear I've worn only once. I look at the three of them, Belinda with her arm still extended between us as if she can somehow hold Phil back, Nancy, clutching the pink bag, her face ablaze with triumph, and Phil, who thinks he has lost something that he never had, and then I hear myself do the worst thing I could possibly do. I hear myself begin to laugh.

The letters flutter from Phil's hands.

I say, "I can explain," and Phil pulls back his fist and hits me.

Here is what I understand. This is the day I will pay for what I've done. Not for the silly stuff like the handcuffs, but for the big stuff, like trying to be happy. Phil pulls back his fist and Belinda's husband is on my right, tossing a Nerf football to the kids, the kind that makes a siren sound when you release it, and I think Tory might be with them. I say, "I can explain," and Phil says, "Not this time." He opens his palm, shakes his hand as if he has lost circulation, and then he reforms the fist and pulls it back and he hits me, so hard that I am spinning.

I hover on the edge of the church steps. I have never been struck before, never been in a fight. Two days from now Kelly will take pictures of my face, three of them to send to my lawyer and put in my file. She will be crying as she looks through the lens of the camera, she will tell me over and over that she can't believe this has happened and I will end up fixing her a drink. She will stand in the middle of her guest bedroom and whisper that the bruises look so much worse in person than they do in the picture and maybe we should use makeup. A bit of dark eyeshadow to bring out the color and it wouldn't be lying, not lying at all. She will lean toward me and ask why didn't I burn those letters, why didn't I, why? As soon as I get on my feet I must call Kelly. I must call Kelly, she will come and get Tory. Where is Tory? Is she over with the kids chasing the football or is she inside? Please God let her be inside.

Someone is screaming. I see Nancy's face frozen as I spin past her and I know what went through her mind when she found the letters, because I've felt it too. She thought, just for a minute, "Why her and not me?" And I know how it feels to give yourself up to this envy, to hold in your hands the evidence that another woman has been loved in a way that you have not. Is this all we want in the end? Are we really so shallow and stupid that our need to be loved overrides everything else, that it can make our work and our homes and our god and even our children just seem like ways to kill time? Nancy's face is very pale and she puts her hands to her jaw and leans back slightly, almost as if she is the one who has been punched. She felt like she had to tell him, that's what she felt, because you know how she is, and I am almost righted. I almost catch my balance. I stand for a moment wavering, and then Phil's form comes closer, falling over me like a shadow, and he hits me again.

Here, on the lowest step of the church I have attended for eight years, I give my body up to the air like a diver. In the moment of impact, in this moment where his fist meets my cheek, I know exactly what to do. I am not willing to fall flat and risk hurting my back so I turn, stretching my arms out in front to brace myself, and in the moment of the turn I look into Phil's eyes and I know this is the worst thing I have ever done to him, striking his hand with my face like I have. Later he will run into the wooded area behind the fellowship hall, crying, because he was not raised to hit a woman any more than I was raised to be hit. I should have burned the letters. How cruel of me to keep them, how cruel of me to fall and pull him down with me, to take a man who never wanted to be anything but ordinary and turn him into a man who beats his wife. Tomorrow, from Kelly's guest bedroom, I will call a lawyer, and I will tell this lawyer that I want to take the high road. I will tell this lawyer that there's no need to be vindictive, and I turn just enough, because I was a cheerleader once—on the bottom, yes, but still a cheerleader—and I know how to correct a position in motion. I know how to flex my knees and tuck, tuck just enough so that when I hit the ground I will roll onto my shoulder, protecting my face but landing just hard enough to make the bruise I must have. I will fall hard enough to do what I have to do but not hard enough to render myself seriously hurt. Because this is what I have come to understand, that I do not intend to be seriously hurt. Years from now Phil and I will sit side by side at graduations and weddings and the baptisms of our grandchildren and it will be okay in that way that things that are over always are okay, so I throw out my arms and reach forward to whatever future lies on the other side of this ground.

There are three reasons a woman can leave a man. He must hit her or drink or run around, and Phil does not drink or run around so my head snaps back as his fist meets my jaw, makes the sharp pop of a starting pistol, the familiar sound of something breaking, and the only horror is that Tory is seeing it all. Because she is there, yes, standing beside Belinda's husband. She is frowning, as if over a hard math problem, her mind furiously working, trying to make it all right. She thinks she does not see what she's seeing. She is already rewriting it in her mind. She does not want to stand witness to the sight of her father hitting her mother and even before I reach the ground she will have decided that she must have seen something else. And Belinda has moved beside her, she is pulling Tory back, and in her other hand she already has her phone. In three years, maybe four, it will be okay. Phil will be remarried and I will have a lover—someone undoubtedly black or female or younger or older or married or Muslim or somehow wildly inappropriate, for that is my karma, and they will all shrug and say, "Well, you know how Elyse is. Can't be settled, never could." In two years, maybe three, it will be okay, and that is why I stretch toward the future as if it were like the surface of water and I must enter it with the smallest splash possible. I am sorry Tory is here but Belinda seems to be handling it. She seems calm. She seems, in fact, the calmest I have ever seen her. She is pulling Tory back, turning her head away from us. I should have burned the letters, I should have gotten in the car and left, but here I am, falling, and the ground is rushing toward me, rising up to meet me like an old friend. Somewhere someone is screaming, or perhaps it is just the football.

And Jeff. Jeff is here, moving across the lawn. Once he and I had an argument about whether or not women belong in military school. Once we had an argument about whether a clue was acceptable in Charades. Jeff and I have often quarreled but today he will be the first one to reach me. He is already starting to run. He will yank me to my feet with one swift movement, a gesture more violent and surprising than the one that knocked me down in the first place. That will be the pain I feel first tomorrow morning. When I roll over in the bed in Kelly's guest room, this is what will make me wince, this arm he nearly dislocates in his eagerness to get me back on my feet. There is a certain irony when the man who comes to save you hurts you more than the man he was saving you from, but I will not contemplate this for weeks or months or years. Not until I am a much older woman, living out west with my best friend. Jeff will pull me up in one strong gesture as if by getting me upright he can erase everything that has just happened, as if he can make all these witnesses forget what they've seen, and then he will reach toward Phil, to pull him away. This last will be a somewhat empty gesture, for Phil is turning even as I am, he is getting ready to run into the woods. It is Jeff who will go into the kitchen for ice. He will wrap it in a paper towel and hold it to my face. It is Jeff who will say, repeatedly, that he is sorry.

Belinda is calling Kelly and Kelly will come fast. She will take Tory and put her in the car and she will want to take me too but I will say no, that I can drive, that I don't want to leave my car here. In my almost comical numbness I will insist on unloading the cupcakes before I go. I will tell everyone that I have made seventy-two of them and Belinda will finally take the cupcakes just to shut me up. She will carry them up the steps while I stand, alone for a minute in the emptying churchyard, looking all around me. I will fight the urge to run into the woods and make sure Phil is okay. His new wife will be nice. I will like her, Tory will like her. In two years, maybe three, she will come by some Friday to pick up Tory for the weekend and mention that she's going to run by Domino's and get pizza and I will say there's half a pizza in my fridge, that she can just take it. She will say, "I hate to think that I took your husband and your pizza too," and I will say, "Please, I was finished with both of them." And we will laugh, because she is a nice woman and her presence makes my life easier. We will pretend not to notice how much alike we are and we will be a kind of friends. Above me I see a single high band of blue, like a child's drawing of the sky. Music is coming from a parked car. I can smell the charcoal of the barbecue and the ground is rushing toward me and I exhale, just enough that there is a slight scream at the moment of impact. I can take this. It's not so bad. It hurts a little, but it's nothing I can't take. It's surprising, definitely surprising, to find myself here in mid air, and yes, it's a shame that this had to happen here and now, at the cookout, on the eve of Easter, but it had to happen, right? I could not have been allowed to get away with it. I think we're all in agreement on that. Jeff is saying he's sorry, he's so sorry, and he is pulling me up, pulling me roughly. I am now officially pitiful and a woman who has been struck (much less on the steps of the church) is certainly entitled to leave. Even the Christians admit that much, so I turn toward the ground and for a moment it feels as if my seams are splitting open and pieces of me are exploding out like beans from a rag doll. I will have to find so much more work. I will have to call every gallery owner I've ever known, I will have to figure out a way to get health insurance. Who is in that car? Why are they playing the radio and what is that song? I think it is Miles Davis, but then I think everything is Miles Davis.

Phil is a big man but Jeff is not and yet he pulls me to my feet effortlessly and I remember again how easily men can move women's bodies through space. This is why our bodies exist, to be moved through space by their bodies, so why pretend any differently? I think of Gerry bent over me on the bed, how he slides one arm underneath me and moves me, moves me all in one unit, carefully, as if I have been hurt in a crash. His face changes when he sees me, on the other side of a hotel door or in an airport, and, even though he knows I will be in this hotel or this airport, he always seems a little surprised. A little relieved. I will know Gerry all my life. He is the one goodbye I will not have to face. We will be lovers, then friends, and then lovers again, and years from now when I am what, sixty or perhaps even seventy, I will gaze down from my bedroom window with a white ceramic coffee cup in my hand, watching as he parks his car and walks toward my door.

I will rap the glass of the window and he will look up. His eyes are older and his body is thicker but when he lifts his chin and sees me there above him in the window, he will still have his airport face. We will find each other over and over, in airports and hotels all around the world, yet this is the part I must do alone, and that can't be him I see in the crowd, because he isn't here and who are all these people watching me? They have come so fast, from the grill, from inside the church and from the tables stacked high with clothes we have all outgrown. Who are these people, where have they come from, and why does the bad luck of our friends excite us so much? They are standing in a semicircle watching me and I think I can already hear them mumbling, talking among themselves. So that was it, that's what was wrong all along. He's a hitter. Who'd have guessed? These letters that have fallen out of Phil's hands and scattered on the lawn are not my letters, were never my letters, they are Kelly's letters and she will tell everyone that and then they will feel even more sorry for me. Poor Elyse who always was so unhappy but none of us knew quite why. These are Kelly's letters, not mine, and yet I hear the whoosh as the grass rises around my head, sweet with the sap of spring. You always forget this part, that life regenerates itself underground through the winter, that happiness comes back. You forget that your body has the capacity for joy, that it craves it like water. You forget that one thing can end and another can begin. There is always a way out, out through the broken places, although you don't know this at first—of course not, how could you? Pay attention, Tory. This is why things have edges.

I look down and see the ground beneath me, bright and green and scattered with love letters and I know it's not really the ground but a door, the door I've been looking for all my life, and I know the trick is to tuck and roll and I don't know why I'm the one who will be set free on a technicality. I don't why I'm the one who will get this second chance, but I am, and the noise that it makes when he hits me is like a champagne cork popping, like a pistol going off or prison doors sliding apart, like a well-read pitch that lifts a softball into the summer air. The grass rises around my ears and muffles the sounds of someone screaming, the fading jazz from the car. I close my eyes and breathe. The grass is thick and cool. It smells clean. It smells like grace.

Back when Kelly and I were cheerleaders I was always on the bottom of the pyramid because I was strong and able to lift. I used to look up at Kelly and envy her the guts it took to jump. She had something that I didn't have, a faith in those below. "The hard part is thinking about it," she would say, and I'm sure that I will understand all this later, when I'm old, when I'm safe, when I'm dead. Once upon a time there was born a baby girl and in the hot afternoons when we used to meet at the school track to learn the new routines, Kelly would sometimes say, "But don't you even want to try the top? There's only one life, Elyse." There's only one life, only one life . . . I have only one life, but it's huge.

One time I asked Kelly, isn't it scary, the moment when you let go and fall? And she said no, that when it finally happens it's not what you'd expect. She said you see everything clearly and you have all the time in the world. She was right.

Chapter Forty-two

After two weeks in Kelly's guest wing, Tory and I move into the apartment. Not the one I reserved on the day Pascal was killed, but another one that has the advantage of being ready right now, probably because it has a hideous bright turquoise carpet.

I go to Target. You can love one man and leave another and love a man and still leave him and leave a man without ever loving him, you can fuck everybody you meet or live like a nun and in the end you still wind up at Target. I get a toaster and TV and can opener and microwave and pots and pans and a muffin tin, three towels, three washcloths, a bathmat, two sets of sheets, a scale, that cheap knockoff Tupperware stuff, a colander, two wineglasses, and a vacuum cleaner. I buy socks and underwear and jeans for Tory, replicating everything but her shoes and coat so we don't have to carry so much stuff between the two houses, so it will be easier. I'm pushing one cart and pulling another and there are mops and brooms sticking out, whapping everything I pass. People get out of my way. It comes to over seven hundred dollars and I put it on my Visa, the new one in my maiden name. It takes the whole afternoon to get the kitchen set up and the appliances unpacked and working. The vacuum cleaner lies on its side as if it's been shot. Earlier today Kelly came over to help me but we bolted it together before we realized we had the roller in wrong and we had to undo the left side and start again. She brought a bottle of wine but I'd forgotten to buy a corkscrew. She went out to get one and came back with bags of groceries—ketchup and salt and Cascade and diet Coke and toilet paper, all the things you need when you're setting up a new house. I'm afraid to ask how much I owe her.

This is the first night since we left that Tory will be sleeping at her father's and Kelly has offered to pick her up from school and then stay with her until Phil gets home from work. The truth is that Kelly has gone by my old house every afternoon for the last two weeks, to turn on the lights. When I first asked her to do this, she agreed—just as everyone agrees to everything I'm asking of them right now—but I could tell she found it a strange request. "Just turn on the floodlights and a couple inside," I told her. "Maybe the TV." The one thought I can't face is Phil parking in the empty driveway, Phil walking up the dark and silent steps, Phil being denied even the briefest illusion that someone is in that house waiting for him.

If I am surprised at the tenderness I feel for my estranged husband, it's nothing compared to how much my compassion has shocked other people. The bruises on my face are gone now but when I showed the big honking uptown lawyer the pictures that Kelly took, he practically salivated. He said, "We'll go after the bastard hard," and when I said, "But I don't want to go after him hard," he looked at me curiously, as if I was one of those broken women who believe they deserve to be hit. My divorce lawyer has pudgy fingers, heavy-lidded eyes, an incongruous black ponytail, curled across his shoulder like a question mark. He looks foolish, like the last of the good old boys, but everyone has assured me he's the best in town and that even if I don't like him, I had get to him before Phil did. This is the sort of man who could get me half of Phil's boat, if Phil had a boat. "So what's your story, darlin'?" he asked me and for a moment I considered telling him, but he bills at four hundred an hour and at those prices I cannot afford to be completely understood by anybody. I started to say, "You know,

I really was cheating, he just got the particulars wrong," but even that opens up the heavy door of memory—another thing I cannot afford. At least not right now.

"I only want to be fair," I said, and he nodded slowly, as if it certainly was a novel experience to have Mother Teresa as a client. But there's no penalty for taking the high road. My husband hit me three times in the face on the steps of the church in front of about a hundred witnesses on the day before Easter. I am going to get a very generous settlement.

While Kelly is gone I rumble through the Target bags until I find a wineglass. I pull the price sticker off of it, grab a can of diet Coke, and go into the bedroom to make the bed. The mattress is an old one, borrowed from the guest bedroom in my mother's condo, and dots of my adolescent menstrual blood are scattered across its surface, like a map of the Caribbean. I forgot to get a mattress pad at Target too. I'll have to go back tomorrow. I need to start a list.

The act of unfolding the new sheets and yanking them over the mattress exhausts me and just for a moment I lie down and shut my eyes. This day will go on, and the next one, and the next. There will be many details and I will take care of them. The next few weeks and months are going to be tough and I wish I could fast-forward through them for us all. I think of the small brave smile Tory gave me when I taped the Disney prints to her wall. "They're nice," she said, "as nice as—"

She started to say "home," but then she quickly corrected and said, "Daddy's house," and my heart broke, just for a minute, and I said, "Yeah, Daddy's house." I told her that she's like the city mouse and country mouse in the story we used to read, and when she's with me she's the city mouse and when she's with her dad, she'll be the country mouse. She nodded vigorously, as if this were all some sort of grand adventure. Of course she wants to be in her old bedroom. The apartment is so empty it echoes. There is a price Tory will pay for what she has witnessed. There is a day of reckoning that will come for her, and for me, but I can't stop and consider all that now. The creases from the sheets are still intact, and when I lie on them they smell heavily of dye. I should have washed them before I put them on. I don't seem to be thinking clearly anymore. Garcia jumps up to the window frame.

"What do you see?" I ask her. "Do you see birds?" My apartment is on the third floor. I've climbed the steps a dozen times today, carrying full boxes up and empty boxes down. But it's worth it. I like it up here. I am as tall as the tops of trees and the breeze coming through the open windows is fresh and sweet. Garcia bats at the screen and makes a low rumbling sound in her throat. She doesn't yet realize that her hunting days are gone.

"You see them, don't you?" I ask her. "I'll have to take your word for it because I'm half-blind, you know." Great. First day on my own and I'm already talking to the cat.

I pat the bed but she does not jump over to lie beside me. "I think," I tell her, "that pretty soon you and me are going to start feeling some real peace."

She looks at me skeptically, tilting her head like Kelly.

"No, I mean it," I say. "Everybody thinks this is the hard part but you and I both know the worst is behind us."

The doorbell rings. It's the first time I've ever heard it.

Jeff is there, leaning against the frame with his thumbs through the belt loops of his jeans. "I only have a minute," he says. "But I wanted to run by and make sure you're all right."

"I have an interview at the community college on Monday. They might need a ceramics teacher."

"That isn't what I mean," he says. "I understand Tory's staying with Phil this weekend." His eyes are troubled. "Are you sure that's a good idea?"

"He'd never hurt Tory. I told you the truth. That was the first and only time Phil has ever hit me. He's a good man."

"I'm sorry," he says again. That's all anyone has said to me for two weeks. "Nancy thought she'd noticed bruises and I should have listened to her."

"It's more complicated than that. Someday when you and I are both really old, we'll sit down together and I'll pour you a cup of coffee and tell you a story."

I smile as I say this but he is not consoled. "You never really know people, do you?" he says, looking past me into the empty apartment. "You never really know what's going on inside a marriage."

I can tell this confession pains him. He's a minister, after all, a counselor. He was our friend. It was his job to know what was going on within our marriage. For a minute I think he is reaching out to touch me, but he stops short of my arm and instead grabs the doorframe as if he has momentarily lost his balance. "It isn't what you think," I say. "He'll be a good dad to Tory."

"But if you ever—"

"What? Need a job at the church?"

He has the grace to smile. "Nancy will be over in a day or two," he says. "She can't come quite yet. She feels bad about what happened."

"Jeff, there's a lot more to the story."

"She thinks I should have stopped it."

"How? Tell her I'm not mad at anybody. I thought I could handle it. I thought I had it all under control. But then—I don't know, things were happening so fast there at the end nobody could have stopped them. It started the morning the cat died."

"Today . . . What are you going to do today?"

"Finish unpacking. And then Kelly's going to take me out to eat. It's going to be okay, it really is."

Over Jeff's shoulder I can see Belinda coming up the stairs. She is carrying a rectangular casserole dish in her hands. It is covered with tinfoil and for the first time in two weeks my eyes fill with tears.

"It's not from a dead woman," she says, panting slightly as she takes the last flight of steps. "I made it myself. But it's the real thing. Chicken and noodles and Campbell's cream of mushroom soup."

"Oh my God," I say. "Thank you. I'll put it in my freezer."

She looks into my living room with the single canvas folding chair that I usually keep in my car and take to Tory's softball games, with the lamp on the floor and the vacuum cleaner on its side and the hideous turquoise carpet, and she says, "I like what you've done with the place."

"Thanks," I say. "I'm going minimalist."

Then it suddenly occurs to me they're both standing out on the landing and I say, "Would you two like to come in? We can all sit on the bed."

Is it just me or is everyone in this place beautiful?"

Kelly looks around. "It's just you."

We have walked three blocks to a Spanish restaurant. One of the advantages of being a city mouse is that there are a dozen restaurants within a ten-minute walk from my apartment. When Kelly came in from waiting with Tory she found me in my ridiculously clean white bathroom trying to pin a hairpiece to the back of my head. I didn't even know I had a hairpiece but one of the days Kelly had run by to cut on the lights she'd also grabbed a Hefty bag and thrown some of my stuff in it. I dumped the bag in the middle of the bed and the hairpiece had fallen out, along with a bunch of other things I'd forgotten I owned, like a lilac tunic and some jeans that used to be too tight.

"Look at you in Levi's with your hair all long," Kelly said. "You look sixteen. Where you'd get that stuff?"

"It's what you brought me in the Hefty bag."

"It is? Damn, I wasn't even sure what I took, I was in such a rush. Being in that house without you, Elyse, it's pretty weird."

"How'd she do?"

"Great. She ran to him. They looked like nothing had happened."

"Thank God."

"The whole afternoon, she seemed . . ."

"Happy to be home? You can say it."

Kelly picked up a tube of lipstick, pulled off the cap, and twisted it out. A shiny red cylinder, slowly rotating and elongating, blunted at the end with the shape of my mouth. "It looks obscene, doesn't it?" she asked. "The day you came home from New York with this all over your face I knew nothing was ever going to be the same."

"Do you want to wear it?"

She shook her head. "Not my color."

But she had helped me pin my hair and then, because I was wearing the Levi's and she had on a dress and we didn't quite match, we had rummaged back through the bag until we found jeans and a shirt for her. And then we walked the three blocks to this restaurant where, because they have a band on Friday nights, we were given a choice between an hour's wait and eating in the bar. Kelly said she didn't like eating in bars and started to take a buzzer but I persuaded her to give it back. Eating in bars will set you free.

Especially this bar, where it seems to me that everyone is beautiful.

"No they're not," says Kelly. "You're beautiful. Look at you." She points to the mirror behind the liquor bottles and I pause for a moment to study myself. The long hair is a shock, as is the lilac color of the tunic. I usually wear brown or black. I look different, true, but I am not the pretty one.

This is a rather self-consciously rustic restaurant and they have brought us wine in a jug. A white sangria, as clear as water, but there is plenty of it, and when Kelly decides to refill me, the jug is so heavy that she partially misses the glass and splashes it across the tile-covered bar. "Do you know what Phil tried to do when he saw me sitting there on your couch?" she asks. "You're not going to believe this, but he tried to talk to me."

"Really."

"He picks up Tory and he twirls her around and he has, you know, chicken in a bucket with him so I let myself out and he follows me into the driveway and starts trying to talk to me. You two were married for about a million years, during which time he and I never had a single conversation that I can recall, and now all of a sudden he wants one. He says to tell you that you can still come there during the day to use your studio if you want to, like that's some sort of great thing . . ."

"It is a great thing."

". . . and he says that it's good you have me. He says, 'I'm glad Elyse has you, Kelly, she's going to need you now.'"

"What's wrong with that?"

"Why did he say 'now'? Like, you know, when you were married to great big wonderful him you didn't need me at all. I mean, I don't want to offend you or anything or sound like I'm being critical, but sometimes your husband can be a little insensitive."

This from the girl who made a photo album of my bruises. "Baby," I say, "are you drunk?"

"What if I am? It's not like we're driving."

"Phil's full of shit. When I was married to him, that's when I needed you most."

"That's what scares me," she said, tossing her head, flipping her hair so hard that it strikes the shoulder of the man on the next barstool. "Now that you're not married to him, maybe you won't need me at all."

Funny that she'd say the same thing Gerry said. Funny that the two people who know me best would read this part so wrong. "Right, Kelly," I say, "I've lived with you for two weeks and you've loaned me money and called me a lawyer and picked up my kid every day and packed all my shit and moved it and paid for my ketchup and found me this hairpiece I didn't even know I had and stuck it to the back of my head. Yeah. I don't need you at all."

The bartender sets a plate down between us. Tuna and Marcona almonds and olives and curled strips of lemon rind, carefully laid out across a long thin white platter. "Look at this," I say to Kelly. "It's perfect." I take a slow deep breath.

"You're going to go off somewhere," says Kelly. "And have this big life."

The bar swims. I flex my back, shift my weight on the stool. My energy, so tenuous in these last days and weeks, seems to be failing me again. "Stop for a moment," I say, "and just look at this plate. It's so beautiful. It's like a painting."

Kelly looks down obediently. The tuna is bright pink and the olives are shiny black and the lemon rind, when I pinch it, sends a mist of citrus into the air. I pick up my fork, plunge it into the food. It won't last. Not the tuna, not this evening, not this sudden rush of joy. It's all temporary. The price for enjoying anything is using it up. Every pleasure eventually slips through our hands, and perhaps that is the greatest pleasure of all, the feeling of something slipping through your hands.

"Give me your lipstick," Kelly says.

I get it out of my purse and hand it to her. Kelly leans toward the bar mirror and begins to color her mouth.

"I can stay at your place tonight, right?" she says, the lipstick skidding off her mouth as she talks, leaving a smudge that extends nearly as high as her nose. I have put her in a series of impossible situations over the past few months. I have frightened her and exhausted her, just as, in the course of our long friendship, she has sometimes frightened and exhausted me.

"Look at us," I say.

"I thought I was supposed to be looking at the tuna."

"We're through looking at the tuna. Now I want you to look in the mirror at us." She puts down the lipstick and squints at the bar. We have always been photo negatives of each other, her so light and me so dark, but tonight, for the first time in years, we look a little bit alike. "Now see these women sitting before us," I say. "They're beautiful and strong and young. They are very significant people. Things are getting ready to happen to them. Both of them."

"Are you drunk?"

I reach over with my napkin to fix her lipstick. "Not at all."

"It's okay if I spend the night, right?"

"Of course. But Kelly—"

"I know. I know. We're significant. Shit's gonna to happen to us. We're the heroes of our own lives."

She makes a grand gesture as she speaks, a sweep of her arm that narrowly avoids striking the tuna, the earthenware jug, the shoulder of the man beside us. Instead she hits my lipstick, sending it rolling across the terra-cotta counter, a bright silver tube that goes spinning over the edge. Before I can move or even speak, Kelly does something that surprises me. She catches it in mid air.

Reading Group Guide

Discussion Questions

1. What do you think the title means? Obviously, Elyse meets Gerry on an airplane, but in what other ways does she remain "in mid air" during the course of the novel? At what point, if any, would you say she finally lands?

2. Although the novel is told from Elyse's point of view, the voices of the other women are a major part of the story and they represent varying, and at times contradictory, perspectives on love and marriage. Are all the viewpoints equally valid? Did you identify primarily with one character or did you find yourself siding with different women at different points in the novel?

3. What makes Gerry so irresistible to Elyse? Is it merely the fact that he isn't Phil, or are there other qualities in his personality and/or the way the two met that make it believable that Elyse would be easily seduced?

4. Is an affair ever forgivable? Do you find Elyse's situation sympathetic or do you see her as impulsive and selfish? Does the fact that she has a child make the situation worse? Do you agree with Kelly that society's double standard makes an affair more acceptable for a man than for a woman?

5. While watching a movie starring Elizabeth Taylor, Elyse says she can't bear to see other women unhappy and this is why she moved to a place "where the women hide their pain so well." Is this accurate? Is there evidence that other women in the group are also hurting or is the statement simply a projection of Elyse's own state of mind? Is discontent among women really contagious? What signs are there at the end of the book that Elyse's decisions have had an impact on how the other women view their own lives?

6. The book is full of symbols—broken pottery, falling, myopia, vintage movies, the cat, the casseroles, the handcuffs, the old love letters Kelly gives to Elyse, even the fact the women walk in circles for exercise. What do you think these symbols mean to Elyse and how does their significance change through the course of the story?

7. Would things have worked out differently if Elyse and Phil had kept the original marriage counseling session they'd scheduled instead of choosing counseling with Jeff? Did the fact that he was their pastor and friend hamper Jeff's ability to understand what was really going on in their marriage?

8. Lynn is an enigmatic character throughout the book, but especially at the end when, after saying that "Jesus and Elvis and wild horses couldn't drag me back" she abruptly reconciles with her ex-husband. Elyse imagines why Lynn might return to her marriage. Do you find Elyse's fantasy plausible or do you think Lynn could have other reasons for going back? Why do you think Elyse's postcard from Belize was the last to arrive? Why do you think she opts not to read it?

9. Elyse is upset that Tory is present during the scene on the church steps and wonders what stories she will tell herself later about what she's witnessed. How do you think these events—the affair, seeing her father strike her mother, the ultimate divorce—will affect Tory's future life?

10. Also in the scene on the church steps, Elyse literally "takes the fall" for something Kelly had done years earlier. Do you consider it ironic that it is her decision to keep Kelly's letters, and not the affair, that pushes the novel to its climax? Although Phil's actions are surprising and violent, Elyse believes she's been "set free on a technicality." Why do you think she compares being struck to a kind of religious grace? Did the reactions of any of the other characters who witness the event surprise you?

11. Elyse recalls at one point that her grandmother told her, "When you marry the man, you marry the life," and she concludes the inverse is also true; if she leaves Phil she will have to leave her comfortable life—i.e., economic security, the church, her close group of friends, and perhaps even her child. Is this what's happening at the end of the book? Or are there signs that the transition might not be as wrenching as she predicted?

12. Would you say that *Love in Mid Air* has a happy ending?

Bonus reading group questions can be found on the author's website: www.loveinmidair.com and on www.hbgusa.com.